P9-DNV-812

Also by Megan Goldin

The Escape Room

The Night Swim

Stay Awake

DARK CORNERS

DARK CORNERS

MEGAN GOLDIN

ST. MARTIN'S PRESS
NEW YORK

This is a work of fiction. All of the characters, organizations, and events portrayed in this novel are either products of the author's imagination or are used fictitiously.

First published in the United States by St. Martin's Press,
an imprint of St. Martin's Publishing Group

Printed in the United States of America. For information, address
St. Martin's Publishing Group, 120 Broadway, New York, NY 10271.

ISBN 9781250280688

To my parents

What a subtle torture it would be to destroy all the mirrors in the world: where then could we look for reassurance of our identities?

—TRUMAN CAPOTE

Chapter 1

Have you ever had a day when absolutely everything goes haywire and nothing goes as planned? I have. More times than I care to remember. Like the time my kitchen pipe burst just as I was heading off on a date with my old college crush who was in town on business.

Instead of rekindling the unrequited spark from college, I spent the evening frantically mopping the flood of water on my kitchen floor while waiting for the emergency plumber to turn up. My next-door neighbor Chloe kindly went down to the bar across the road to keep my date company while I dealt with the plumbing crisis.

By the time I joined them, they were hitting it off. Sparks flew like fireworks that night. Just not with me. Incidentally, they've been married for three years. One baby. Another on the way. Cutest couple ever.

It's unlikely they'd have met if my kitchen pipe hadn't blown. Was it fate, or destiny? Your guess is as good as mine.

It happened again this week. This time it was a telephone call that sent everything into a wild tailspin.

I'd planned to spend the day catching up on admin work and tidying my apartment. I'd hoped to squeeze in time to paint a mid-century dresser that I bought at a flea market and was in the midst of up-cycling. In the evening, I'd arranged to go to my producer's place with takeout sushi for a working dinner while we went over stuff that had piled up while I was out of town. It was supposed to be a hump day. A day to get stuff done.

That all fell by the wayside when the loud ring of my cell phone catapulted me out of a deep sleep some time before dawn. Within two hours, I was staring out an airplane window at an aerial view of the Eastern Seaboard, sipping ice-cold reconstituted orange juice as I winged my way to northern Florida.

By late morning, I was back on the ground. This time I was driving a rental car along the winding road of a state forest. Glimpses of the ominous guard towers and barbed-wire fences of a maximum-security prison peeked through sun-kissed foliage. The prison was incongruently located on the edge of the natural wilderness.

At that point, I still had no idea why I'd been asked to fly down. The FBI agent who woke me that morning had thrown in just enough information to pique my curiosity. I took the bait. No big surprise; curiosity and procrastination are my kryptonite. It didn't escape me that flying down to Florida without knowing why was the ultimate act of procrastination—proof that I'd do just about anything to avoid paperwork.

As I drove through the forest to the state prison, I passed a timber sign pointing to a rudimentary campground off the road. Crime scene tape cordoning off the campground entrance wasn't visible from my car.

It was only later that I found out what happened there. The campground, which I've since visited several times, is designed for hard-core campers. It has no amenities other than a shower-toilet block and the chance to camp under the stars.

That's what Bill Morrow and his family were doing on the night in question. Bill and his two sisters had come with their respective spouses and kids on what I guess you'd call a family pilgrimage. They wanted their kids to experience the simple back-to-nature camping trips of their childhood. Without phones or gaming consoles. Without every waking moment being documented on social media. Three days of uninterrupted family time. The way it used to be. #socialmediadetox #familyreunion #getmeoutofhere

They arrived in the afternoon in a convoy of three SUVs packed with camping gear and food. They remember noticing a camper van parked under a tree on the periphery of the otherwise deserted campground. The van's screen door was loose. It rattled annoyingly in the wind.

The campers paid it little mind. They were busy unloading equipment and erecting tents in a semi-circle around a rusted metal fire pit on the other side of the campground.

The campsite filled with the clang of tent pegs being hammered into the ground to a chorus of young kids hollering while playing tag, and teenagers whining about poor cell phone reception and the inconvenience of being dragged on a family camping trip they considered to be a refined form of torture.

Eventually, the exasperated parents tied a volleyball net between two trees and sent the teenagers off to play, which they did with the pained expressions of hard-core addicts going cold turkey. Their hard-done-by disgruntlement melted into genuine enjoyment when they won a kids versus parents volleyball tournament as the afternoon slid into dusk. By the time they were eating their dinner of barbecued hamburgers by the crackling campfire, everyone had shifted gears into vacation mode.

As evening moved into night, an easterly blew in, causing the camper van door to slam more frequently. It got on everyone's nerves. That's when the campers had the first inkling that something was wrong.

Ignoring their niggling disquiet, the parents sent the kids to bed. Once the kids were in their zipped-up tents, the adults pulled their canvas chairs around the campfire to unwind after the long drive and exhausting day setting up camp. They stretched their legs toward the flames and sipped beers, reminiscing about the camping trips of their childhood and how much simpler the world had been before gaming consoles and social media.

The nostalgic mood was ruined when a powerful gust violently slammed the camper van door shut with an explosive crack that ricocheted across the campground. Six-year-old Billy Jr. was woken by the noise.

"Daddy, I'm scared," he called out, holding his teddy bear under one arm and gripping his sleeping bag with the other as he stuck his head out of his tent.

His dad drained his beer bottle and rose from the canvas chair near the fire.

"I'm going to say something," Bill Sr. said. "Otherwise we can all forget about getting any sleep tonight."

He stormed toward the van. His brother-in-law followed him, holding out a large flashlight. The campground was close enough to a swamp called Rattlesnake Lake to make him want to see exactly where he was stepping.

"Anyone home?" Bill Sr. bellowed as they approached.

Bill's brother-in-law fixed the flashlight beam unsteadily on the van door while mosquitos tore into him. He scratched the bites until they bled. Bill Sr. started feeling uneasy as he pounded on the door.

"Even before I went inside, I could tell something was wrong. There were these eerie reverberations coming from inside the van."

When there was still no response, Bill opened the aluminum door. All he could see in the musty interior was a haze of gray. He stepped into the camper van. His brother-in-law heaved himself up as well. The van sagged under the cumulative weight of the two hefty men. Mosquitos and moths followed them in, attracted by the bright beam of the flashlight.

What happened inside that van is what this podcast is all about. It's consumed me ever since I came down here to look into this case. I've been looking for a predator. It turns out that a predator has also been looking for me.

Chapter 2

Rachel Krall pressed her foot on the gas as a view of barbed-wire fences and towering steel guard towers emerged from beyond the treetops. She drove until the road ended at a row of bright yellow boom gates under a sign as cheery as it was cynical.

"Welcome to the Central Florida Correctional Facility" it said in the childish bubble letters of a tourist billboard.

As Rachel waited for the gate to go up, she caught a glimpse of prisoners in orange jumpsuits exercising in a yard penned in by razor-wire fences. An officer at the top of a steel guard tower trained his high-powered rifle at the prisoners as they moved about the yard.

"Name and ID," a surly voice boomed out.

Rachel shifted her gaze from the prison yard to the driver's window, where a stocky guard with a down-turned rusty mustache glowered at her. He held a clipboard against his expansive belly.

Rachel lowered the window only to be assaulted by the blistering heat outside the cool air-conditioned interior of her car. She slapped her driver's license into the guard's outstretched hand.

"Pop the trunk," he barked.

The guard went around the back of the vehicle and lifted the trunk.

Inside was the mini carry-on suitcase that Rachel had packed in a mad hurry early that morning before rushing to the airport.

"This your first time here?" the guard asked when he returned to Rachel's half-open window. His forehead was covered in perspiration. Sweat marks were forming in the armpits of his uniform.

"It sure is." Rachel didn't answer his unasked question as to the purpose of her visit. The truth was that she had no idea.

"Boyfriend or husband?"

Rachel squinted as she looked up at him, perplexed.

He gestured toward her jeans and casual shirt. "You're obviously not law enforcement, or an attorney," he said snidely. "That means you're here on a personal visit. Which brings me back to my original question: boyfriend or husband?"

"Neither."

"Ma'am, I can't let you through until you tell me who you're here to visit." He had the officious tone of a petty bureaucrat on a power trip.

Through her side mirror, Rachel noticed that a line of cars was waiting behind her vehicle. Car engines idled impatiently. The guard chewed a wad of gum with the side of his mouth like he had all day.

"I have a meeting here."

The guard checked his clipboard again. "Your name isn't on our list, ma'am."

"It must be an oversight. I'll sort it out when I get in," Rachel said. "Are you going to let me in or not?" she added, when the guard showed no sign of budging. "Because if you're not letting me in, then you'll have to get all those cars behind me to move so I can back out. There's going to be an awful traffic jam. I'm *terrible* at reversing."

"I'll ask the warden's office what it wants to do with you." The guard droned Rachel's name and details into a radio mouthpiece fixed to his shirt.

"Send her through," a woman responded, her voice faint over the crackle of the radio.

The guard scowled at the decision. "Leave the car at the dirt parking lot and join the line outside the visitors' building. It's a long wait. At least an hour. In the sun. When you eventually get inside, tell them what you told me. Don't be surprised if they turn you back. Next time, remember, don't turn up without advance notice." He strode to the next car as the boom gate lifted up.

As Rachel drove into the visitors' parking area, she passed two men in dark suits and ties. Only a crazy person or a federal agent would wear a suit in the scorching Florida heat. Rachel parked the car and locked it with a remote-control key as she strode toward the men, studying them through the mirrored lenses of her sunglasses. Her copper-brown hair hung loose, the ends curling into untamed tendrils in the humidity. A jade heart on a leather band sat against the nape of her neck, just above the open collar of her oversized white linen shirt.

"I'm Special Agent Torreno. We spoke earlier." The sandy-haired man reached out to shake Rachel's hand once she'd joined them on the curb. "This is Special Agent Martinez."

Agent Torreno's deference was unmistakable as he gestured to his colleague. Agent Martinez had been watching Rachel with a panther-like intensity ever since she left her car. It had been obvious he was in charge from the moment Rachel first set eyes on him.

Agent Martinez's charcoal suit jacket was unbuttoned, showing a hint of a weapon in a black leather holster that matched the color of his neatly clipped hair. Rachel flipped off her sunglasses. Her green-flecked eyes met Agent Martinez's steady gaze as she stretched out her hand to shake his firm grip. She was annoyed at her uncharacteristic nervousness.

"I came here like you asked." She addressed Torreno. "What's this all about?"

Before Torreno could respond, Agent Martinez looked up at the blinding sun in the near-cloudless sky. "It's too hot to talk out here, and it's not very private. We'll talk inside."

They fell in step behind a mom carrying a toddler on her hip as she headed toward the visitors' building. There she joined the back of a long line of people waiting in the heat to go through security. The guard at the boom gate hadn't been kidding when he'd said there was a long wait. In Rachel's case, the FBI agents ushered her to a modern VIP building reserved for prison staff and law enforcement.

"Does the name Terence Bailey mean anything to you?" Torreno asked conversationally as they waited their turn while Martinez went through an airport-style metal detector machine at the entrance.

"Can't say I've heard of him before," said Rachel, putting her belongings onto the X-ray machine's conveyor belt.

"He sure knows you," said Torreno once they'd both gone through the metal detector and were collecting their things on the other side. "Bailey's a big fan of your podcast. I'm guessing getting that high school coach off the hook for murder has made you popular with super-max lifers," said Torreno.

"Could be," said Rachel noncommittally. She was somewhat embarrassed as to how she'd catapulted from a relatively obscure crime podcaster to a household name.

Rachel's podcast, *Guilty or Not Guilty*, had become a national sensation when the first season uncovered fresh evidence and a litany of mistakes in the trial of a high school coach convicted of murdering his wife on their second honeymoon.

Circumstantial evidence and the lack of a solid alibi had sealed Coach Murphy's fate. Among the most damning evidence were traces of cleaned-up blood splatter belonging to his wife, found by the forensic team during a chemical analysis of the carpet of his car. He'd claimed the blood was from a nosebleed, to which his wife had been prone, and that he'd bought a special carpet cleaner to get rid of it. The jury didn't buy it. They convicted him of all charges.

Thanks to crucial evidence that Rachel had dug up for the podcast, the coach received a new trial. The jury found him not guilty less than ninety minutes after it began deliberations. Outside the courthouse when he was released, he told TV cameras that he owed not just his freedom but his life to Rachel Krall and her podcast.

His words prompted inmates across the country to write to Rachel swearing they were innocent of the crimes for which they'd been convicted and imploring her to help them prove it. Rachel and her producer, Pete, were soon knee-deep in letters postmarked from a who's who of high-security prisons. After Season 2, when Rachel solved the cold-case murder of a hairdresser bludgeoned to death in her hair salon, the podcast was inundated with messages from relatives of crime victims begging Rachel to bring justice when law enforcement had failed.

Guilty or Not Guilty had inspired an industry of imitation podcasts catering to the public's insatiable appetite for true crime. One particularly generous newspaper reviewer said that all the podcasts that followed were but pale imitations of Rachel Krall's original:

"Krall's seductive voice and out-loud musings give her true-crime podcast the intimacy of pillow talk," he'd written. "I suspect Ms. Krall could record a podcast about paint drying and people would be hooked on her every intonation and the silky cadence of her bedroom voice."

Rachel had recently returned home after covering a contentious rape trial of a champion swimmer in the North Carolina coastal town of Neapolis. The case had been emotionally draining and Rachel had been looking forward to some much-needed downtime. That is, until Agent Torreno had sweet-talked her into flying to Florida that very morning.

That's how Rachel had gone from spending the day doing chores at home to filling out a three-page visitor's form at a Florida prison with two FBI agents in tow. Rachel handed the signed form to a prison clerk and was given a visitor's sticker with a barcode.

"You need to keep the sticker on your blouse at all times," the clerk instructed. "I'll need you to hand over all your belongings. Phone. Purse. Pens. Hair clips. Electronic items, including watches. Sunglasses," she added. "You can collect your things on your way out."

The FBI agents handed over their service weapons and holsters to the clerk, who locked them up in safety deposit boxes in a secure room behind the counter. The process took several minutes. Unlike Rachel, they were allowed to keep their cell phones and documents.

When they were all ready, they were directed to a "staff only" door that swung open automatically, leading them into a labyrinth of long soulless corridors. Eventually Rachel was ushered into a meeting room barely bigger than a janitor's closet. It had a square table with bucket chairs. An air conditioner blasted an icy chill. Agent Torreno turned to leave as Rachel sat down.

"You're not staying?" Rachel asked.

"Special Agent Martinez will fill you in, Ms. Krall."

"Special Agent Martinez? Don't FBI agents have first names like regular people?" Rachel remarked dryly when the door had closed. "I'm Rachel, by the way."

"Joseph." The FBI agent's dark eyes creased with a hint of amusement. "But as you pointed out, there's no need for formality. Call me Joe."

Martinez wasn't chatty like Torreno. He was a man who understood the power of silence. Rachel sensed that he noticed everything and said little enough that his every word counted.

"Thanks for flying down. We appreciate your help, Rachel."

"I never said I'd help," she clarified. "I only agreed to listen. Your partner was tight-lipped about the reason for bringing me down here."

"Torreno is not my partner. As for him being tight-lipped, that's because he was given strict orders to do whatever it took to bring you here."

"Whose orders?" Rachel asked.

"Mine," Martinez drawled. "Your name came up in an FBI investigation. I need to ask you a few questions."

Chapter 3

Thomas McCoy—Tommy to the handful of friends that he's ever had—taps his hand impatiently on the steering wheel. He's getting antsy. His passenger still hasn't appeared, despite two phone alerts telling her that he's arrived and she should immediately go to the pickup point.

Thomas gets bored easily. Nothing bores him quite like waiting. It's ironic because most of his days are spent waiting for one thing or another. Waiting for rides to pop up on his rideshare driver's app. Waiting for passengers to come down to his car. Waiting in traffic. Waiting for the right opportunities to present themselves. Sometimes he thinks the only reason he was put on the Earth was to wait.

Bees swarm around the bright pink flowers of a hibiscus bush next to his car. One of the bees hovers by his window. He leans his head against the glass and watches its translucent wings flap rapidly like a heartbeat as its plump body hovers in mid-air.

Thomas knows about bees. His father kept a hive in the citrus orchard when he was a boy. He knows a bee flaps its wings more than 200 times a minute to stay airborne. He also knows that bees remember faces. Every human face is like a different flower to a honeybee.

He feels a kinship with bees. He too is good with faces. He remembers each and every one of them.

He lowers the window. The bee darts inside, buzzing with excitement as it mistakes the cloying floral car deodorizer for real flowers.

Thomas slides the window shut. It doesn't take long for the bee to realize that it's been tricked. There are no flowers in the car. No pollen to collect. The bee buzzes angrily over the dashboard trying to get out. When that doesn't work, it darts around the vehicle, desperate to escape. There is no escape. The windows are all closed. It's just the bee, and Thomas.

Still tapping the steering wheel, he watches the bee's doomed bid for freedom with fascination as he dials his passenger's phone number to find out what's causing the holdup.

"Yeah?"

"This is your driver." He keeps his voice calm and professional even though he's seething. "I've arrived. I'm on the street outside your building."

He comes across as nice as pie, folksy even. It's amazing how friendly he can sound even when he is raging inside.

"Yeah. Yeah. I'm coming down now."

He restrains himself from giving her an earful. His time costs money. So does the gas he's wasted from idling the engine. The last time he lost it with a passenger for keeping him waiting, the guy gave him a one-star review. He learned two bitter lessons: the customer is king, and rideshare drivers need to not just lick their customers' boots, but to enjoy doing it.

That's why his car is spotless. That's why he keeps an extra-long phone charger for his passengers. That's why he regularly hands out bottles of cold water free of charge. That's why he's always friendly. Sickeningly friendly. It's for those five-star reviews. His business lives or dies by reviews.

The driver was polite. Check.

The car was clean. Check.

The driver was punctual. Check.

The driver knew where he was going. Check.

The bee shifts to the window next to him. It remembers that's how it got in and instinctively knows it can get out the same way. It buzzes loudly, tapping its wings against the glass as if begging Thomas to let it out.

Thomas opens the window a sliver. It's just enough to let the bee smell the fresh air. Just enough to give it hope. The bee buzzes in excitement. Freedom is within its grasp.

Instead of opening the window a fraction more so the bee can get out, Thomas presses the button and shuts it. He presses it again. The window opens. Just a sliver. He plays with the window button like a child, opening and closing it. Never wide enough to let the bee out. The bee buzzes frantically.

Outside, a gate clicks open and then clangs shut. The loud metallic reverberation makes Thomas look up into the rearview mirror, where he sees a woman approaching his car.

The bee hums by his window, like it's begging to go free. Thomas brushes the window switch with his thumb, contemplating whether to let the bee out. The bee's wings beat with excitement against the glass as it senses its impending freedom.

Instead of opening the window, Thomas makes a fist and pounds the bee against the glass. It stings him before it dies. The pain is intense enough to bring tears to his eyes. In a pleasant sort of a way.

The rear car door clicks open as he wipes his hand clean. He turns with a smile toward the passenger settling in the back seat. She's dressed in black and neon-pink workout gear and matching sneakers. She sips water from a translucent fitness club bottle before tightening the ponytail band securing her dark hair.

"How's your day been going?" he asks amenably, turning up the air con while she finally buckles in.

"Good," she says. It's obvious from her disinterested tone and pursed lips that she doesn't want to talk to some over-the-hill rideshare driver who's probably her dad's age.

Unsurprisingly, she doesn't ask about his day. Thomas finds himself almost wishing she did. What a hoot it would be to see her reaction if he told her exactly what he'd done that morning.

She retrieves headphones from her tote bag and puts in the earbuds. It's an obvious avoidance tactic. Just in case he doesn't get the hint, she pointedly looks out the passenger window as he drives her to her fitness club. He angrily tightens his grip on the steering wheel, steamed about how she acts like she's too good to waste her precious time talking to the "hired help."

That shouldn't be a surprise. She kept him waiting, wasted his gas, and made him lose out on other rides while she leisurely waltzed down in her own good time like an entitled princess.

He's no stranger to disrespect. It comes with the job. The previous passenger had snapped, "Just drive," when Thomas politely asked how his day had been. Thomas spent the rest of the ride silently contemplating suffocating the man with a plastic bag.

Chapter 4

Over the hum of the air conditioner, Rachel Krall took the measure of Joe Martinez as he sat across the narrow table from her. He was obviously in charge of a major operation. His phone buzzed constantly with incoming calls and messages, none of which he answered. He gave Rachel his undivided attention. Whatever Joe Martinez wanted from Rachel was important enough for him to step away from the fray to personally question her.

"I'm getting the feeling that Agent Torreno played fast and loose with the truth." Rachel made little effort to hide her annoyance at what was fast looking to be an FBI ruse to get her into an interrogation room.

"How do you mean?"

"I agreed to fly down here this morning because I was told that I was being given a front-row seat to an active FBI investigation," Rachel said. "You're now telling me that I'm the subject of that investigation. Which is it?"

"Can't both be true?" he asked. "Look, Rachel, your name has come up in an investigation, and I need to know why. If things check out, I'm willing to give you an exclusive story on this case. Once we're ready to go public."

Rachel had the uncomfortable realization that Joe Martinez had been pulling the strings all morning. It was he who had orchestrated what was clearly a finely calibrated FBI scheme designed to bring her to the windowless room where they now sat facing each other like combatants.

Martinez understood the powerful lure of curiosity. He'd used it to entice Rachel into flying to Florida at a moment's notice. Agent Torreno's pre-dawn telephone call was intentionally timed to catch Rachel when she was too woolly-headed to think rationally. She'd acted on instinct. The urgency of Agent Torreno's tone and the promise of exclusive access to an active FBI case was perfect bait for any journalist worth their salt.

Martinez hadn't left anything to chance. He'd anticipated that once Rachel was fully alert, she'd start doubting her decision. Indeed, Rachel had been having a change of heart when the doorbell rang as she hastily packed an overnight bag for the trip. Rachel looked through the peephole. A tall woman in a slim-fitting navy suit was on the threshold, holding up an FBI shield.

"I'm here to take you to the airport."

She'd waited for Rachel to finish getting ready and then quickly ushered her into a black government car parked outside her building. Like clockwork, an airport security official met the car as it pulled up at the departure terminal at Philadelphia International Airport.

"We need to hurry," he'd said, taking Rachel's carry-on bag and rushing her through VIP security in record time.

Rachel was the last passenger to board the flight. The plane door had shut just as she headed to her leather business-class seat in the second row. As the plane was taking off, Rachel overheard a conversation between the air stewards that revealed the flight had been delayed just for her.

When Rachel's flight landed two hours later in Daytona Beach, she was met at the arrivals gate by another airport attendant who'd handed her a large brown envelope. Inside was a note from Agent Torreno containing a car key, and details of her destination.

Nothing had been left to chance; every step had been carefully thought through. Rachel had been whisked away from her apartment by the FBI before she could get cold feet. Yet on arrival in Florida, Rachel was given the key to a rental car rather than being bundled into another government car by more federal agents and driven to an unknown destination.

Martinez rightly anticipated that Rachel would be well into regret mode by the time her flight landed. Booking her a car rental gave her a false sense of control. It ensured that she would continue to comply. And Rachel had complied. She'd complied all the way into this room deep inside a maximum-security prison where she was effectively at FBI Special Agent Joe Martinez's mercy.

There was no doubt that Martinez had played her. He was still playing her, Rachel realized as he tossed his jacket over a chair and rolled up his shirtsleeves like he was getting down to business.

Rachel studied Joe Martinez, mentally cataloging everything she knew about him as she looked for chinks in his formidable armor. He'd been in the Marines before he'd joined the FBI. She knew this because the words "Semper Fidelis" were visible at the bottom of a right bicep tattoo partly exposed by his rolled-up shirtsleeve. "Always Faithful." That was the translation of the Latin motto of the U.S. Marine Corps. There was an alertness about him that Rachel had seen before in combat veterans. Given his age, which Rachel guessed to be late thirties, that suggested Iraq, or Afghanistan. Maybe both.

On his wrist, he wore a platinum Audemars Piguet watch. He'd touched it reassuringly at one point in a way that suggested it was a cherished gift. Rachel guessed that it was from a lover, or a wife. His charcoal suit was tailored to his wiry physique. It wasn't off-the-rack and one size too big, like the suit that Torreno was wearing. What struck her most was his demeanor. Joe Martinez had the calmness and natural authority of a leader.

His phone pinged again with a series of messages. This time he glanced at the screen, his expression inscrutable other than a slight tightening of his jaw. Joe Martinez clearly had multiple irons in the fire. Rachel was just one of them.

The air-conditioning unit behind Rachel puffed out a stream of icy air against the back of her neck. It felt like another ploy to keep her off-balance.

"You don't mind, do you?" Rachel asked rhetorically, turning around and switching off the air con. "Maybe you can finally tell me what this is all about?" she said, when she'd turned back to face Martinez.

"Before I get into the details, I'll need you to sign a non-disclosure agreement." He took a form out of his folder. "It's a standard document in which you agree to keep everything we discuss confidential."

The FBI logo was on top of the legal document that Martinez pushed across the table to Rachel. The font was so small that it looked like a vision test at an optical exam. He clicked open a pen and handed it to Rachel.

She took a cursory glance at the form before discarding it and the pen on the table. "I don't sign NDAs. Not without my attorney present. It's unfortunate that Agent Torreno didn't tell me in advance that I'd have to sign a confidentiality form. I'd never have agreed to come down if I'd known there were strings attached."

"There are always strings, Rachel," Martinez said quietly. "The only question is what strings, and how are they attached."

"How are they attached, Joe?" Rachel asked, her furious eyes catching his steady gaze.

"Sign the forms and you'll find out."

Rachel was annoyed by his presumptuousness. He assumed that she'd go along with his latest demand just as she'd complied with everything else over the course of the morning. It was time to put a spoke in his wheel.

She pushed back her chair and stood up, heading for the door. "On second thought, I don't want exclusive access to your case. As for my name coming up in your investigation, we'll discuss it on the phone while I drive back to the airport. There's still time for me to make the next flight home."

"That wouldn't work." Joe Martinez leaned back in his chair, crossing his muscular arms as he watched her.

"Why not?" Rachel's hand was on the doorknob. She hadn't tried to open it yet. It was entirely possible that it was locked, in which case all her bluster would appear comical.

"Because I like to look a person in the eye when I ask them questions."

"In that case, cut to the chase. What do you want from me, Joe?" She swiveled around to confront him.

Martinez's dark eyes widened in admiration. Rachel knew she'd won this round. "Everything I tell you is confidential unless I tell you otherwise. I can't have anything leaking to the media."

"And if I don't agree?" Rachel kept her grip on the door handle.

"Then you're free to go," Martinez said. "You've got a flexible plane ticket. You have the rental car. You can head on back to the airport and take the next flight home. Of course, you may regret it."

"Why would I regret it?"

"I don't think you're the sort of person who walks away when lives are on the line."

"Are lives on the line, Joe?" Rachel asked.

"Very much so."

"Okay. I agree to your terms," Rachel said after a moment's thought. "Now tell me why you brought me here."

"Have you ever heard of Maddison Logan? You may know her on Instagram as @JustMaddie."

As Martinez spoke, he flipped open his folder and removed several photos. He held them in the air so that Rachel could get a good look.

Maddison Logan was in her early twenties. She had burnished gold hair that fell in waves below her shoulder. Her mouth was too wide for her narrow jaw. Her nose was slightly off-kilter. Yet it worked like a perfect harmony. Maddison's striking looks were enhanced by bronzer, a bold red matte lipstick, and thick fake eyelashes. A hint of smoky eyeshadow around her eyes made her look as mysterious as she was glamorous.

"Maddison's an influencer. Instagram, TikTok. YouTube. You name it. She has accounts on all of them. Last count, she had close to half a million followers on Instagram," he said. "Two days ago, Maddison came to see an inmate at this prison. His name is Terence Bailey. Ever heard of him?"

"Yes," said Rachel.

Surprise registered on Martinez's face. Rachel was pleased. She'd finally caught him off guard.

"Agent Torreno mentioned that name as we went through the metal detectors. He said that Terence Bailey is a big fan of my podcast," she explained.

"He did, did he?" Martinez said, clearly not happy that Torreno had revealed anything in advance.

"Who is Terence Bailey?" Rachel asked.

"That's a complicated question."

"I'm sure there's a simple answer," Rachel pressed.

"Depends on who you ask." Martinez shrugged. "Some say he's a petty thief. Others believe that he's a cold-blooded killer responsible for a string of abductions and murders of young women."

"So he's a serial killer?"

"He's never been convicted."

"What did a successful social media influencer want with a serial killer?" Rachel asked.

"That's where this gets interesting," he responded. "Maddison came here on false pretenses. She claimed to be with a restorative justice charity that sends in volunteers to meet inmates. Keep up their spirits. She specifically requested to meet Terence Bailey. Her request was granted because nobody visits Terence Bailey."

"You're telling me that he never gets visitors?"

"The only visitors Bailey's ever had were lawyers. Until Maddison Logan turned up."

"What did she want from him?"

"I was hoping you would tell me."

"How would I know?" Rachel asked, perplexed.

In answer, Martinez removed another sheet from his folder and held it in mid-air for Rachel to see. She drew in a sharp breath. Martinez nodded slowly as if to confirm her worst suspicions. Rachel let go of the door handle. She returned to her chair and sat back down. Agent Martinez had her full attention.

Chapter 5

Not far from the campground where the campers found that van, deep within the rugged terrain of the Delta Springs State Forest, is a ridge covered with a blanket of dense pine trees.

The hike up to the ridge is physically grueling and slightly perilous. Caution signs warn of rock falls and old mine shafts. It can be slippery too after it's rained, as the park ranger guiding me to the top reminds me intermittently.

"Watch your step over here, Rachel. . . . These rocks here are super slippery."

Ranger Owen Bragg's passion for the great outdoors is infectious. As we hike up the ridge, he stops to show me plants and insects, or chalky limestone rocks that tell the fascinating story of the geological history of this region.

Owen has a bushy beard and the placid temperament of a conservationist who's devoted his career to nature. His colleagues fondly call him "Doc" because he has a knack for reviving diseased and damaged trees.

Owen moved his young family here from Wyoming seven years ago when he took the ranger's job. The Delta Springs State Forest is Owen's "hood." He knows every square inch of it.

I'm embarrassed to admit that I am the person you can hear in the audio of this podcast breathing heavily in the background as we climb. My only excuse for sounding like I'm about to keel over clutching my chest is that the path is insanely steep in parts. It requires proper hiking boots rather than the flimsy fashion sneakers that I'm wearing as I follow Owen to the top.

There's no question the world looks more beautiful from above. Even the prison on the far edge of the forest has lost its stark grimness from this distance. Meandering channels of water, called oxbow lakes, surround the prison on three sides, giving it the deceptive air of a castle surrounded by a moat.

Looking through Owen's binoculars, I see inmates moving like bright orange ants around the prison grounds. The orange of the prisoners' uniforms sticks out against the patchwork of green stretching as far as the eye can see.

Occasionally a seemingly matchbox-sized car drives along the narrow road that traverses the forest and stops at the prison gates.

Locals tend to shun the forest as a hiking and picnic destination, despite its natural beauty. Bad things happen here; that's the state forest's reputation going all the way back to the seventies when for a time it was a known dumping ground for mob killings. The reputation has stuck.

The campers who found the van I mentioned earlier were unaware of the state forest's notoriety. They camped here because it was a convenient mid-point for their family reunion. Plus they liked the idea of camping in a wilderness that's near civilization.

By civilization, I mean the party town of Daytona Beach. That's where the campers fled after their horrifying discovery in the van. They bundled their sleeping kids into their cars and hotfooted it to the nearest five-star hotel.

While the park's reputation from the bad old days has deterred day-trippers, it has attracted illicit rave parties late at night. In fact, the worst problems that Owen Bragg has had to deal with over his tenure here are vandalism and zoned-out ravers who've lost their way.

There's one big exception. Six years ago, Owen Bragg stumbled onto something so disturbing that he's gone out of his way to avoid coming up to this ridge ever since. Until today, when he generously agreed to guide me up here. It was not an easy decision for him. You'll understand why shortly.

"My wife says I bottle things up and that's why I haven't been back here. To be truthful, I probably wouldn't have returned if you hadn't asked me to show you the way."

What Owen found that morning six years ago so disturbed him that, before he fled back to his truck, he carved a marker into the bark of the tree where it happened.

That's the reason why we've come up here. So he can show it to me. But first we have to find it. I'm following behind Owen. We're walking deep into the forest along a bed of fallen pine needles, as you can probably hear from the crackle of foliage under our feet as we step across.

"Look over there, Rachel." Owen points toward a small round clearing in the forest. "I'm pretty sure the tree we're looking for is in there."

Owen strides across the clearing. By the time I reach him, he is on his knees at the base of a good-sized pine tree running his fingers across the bark as he looks for markings. He calls me over when he finds it.

"It's faded. You'll have to get close if you want to see it."

The tree canopy is so dense in this part of the forest that it feels like dusk, even though it's the middle of the day. Owen takes out a flashlight. He shines the beam near the bottom of the tree trunk as he grimly describes the chilling events of that terrible morning.

Chapter 6

From the bird's-eye-view angle of the CCTV camera, filmed from above, the prison visitors' room looked like a life-sized game of tic-tac-toe. Nine round metal tables arranged in three rows of three. Some of the tables were empty. Others were occupied by prisoners in orange jumpsuits talking to jeans-clad visitors.

Joe Martinez pointed to a hulking prisoner in the surveillance camera footage that he was playing for Rachel on his iPad. The prisoner sat at the table in the dead center. He was slouched back in his seat, his chin lifted. His biceps bulged under the orange coverall fabric as he crossed his muscular arms. His body language screamed defiance.

"That's Maddison." Martinez tapped the screen, drawing Rachel's attention to a woman sitting opposite the prisoner in question. The young influencer had her back to the camera. All that was visible were thick tresses of dark blond-streaked hair falling well below her shoulders. Rachel could tell from their body language that they'd been arguing.

"Maddison and Terence Bailey talked for about fifteen minutes," Martinez told her.

"About what?"

"I wish we knew. The table had a hidden microphone." He paused when he saw Rachel's obvious surprise. "This is a prison. There's no expectation of privacy. The prisoners know their conversations may be recorded unless they're meeting an attorney. As it happens, when we listened back to the audio, all we heard was static. Turns out the microphone wasn't working."

Martinez sped up the video of Maddison's visit. Rachel watched it unfold in double time for a few minutes until he slowed the footage down again to let Rachel watch the tail end of the meeting in real time.

It appeared that Terence Bailey had removed a stub of a pencil from a pocket in his coveralls. He waited for a guard to stroll past him before he hastily scrawled something on the table while the guard's back was turned to him. None of the prisoners or their visitors at the surrounding tables appeared to have noticed.

Maddison immediately leaned forward to read what he'd written on the metal table before quickly rubbing it out with her fingers.

Rachel zoomed in on the security camera footage playing on the iPad so she could see what Bailey had written. She huffed with disappointment. The writing wasn't visible due to the security camera angle and the poor quality of the grainy video.

"A different CCTV camera got a shot of the message before Maddison erased it." Martinez produced the photo that he'd shown Rachel earlier to convince her to stay and hear him out.

"Bring Rachel Krall to me. Do whatever it takes to find her. It's time. . . ."

That was the message that Terence Bailey had scrawled on the metal table in lead pencil. He'd stopped writing mid-sentence when the guard turned back in his direction. Whatever he'd been trying to communicate to Maddison was so sensitive that he hadn't wanted to risk it being overheard or recorded by a prison listening device.

"Any idea why Terence Bailey wants to talk to you, Rachel?"

"I'm sorry to be the bearer of bad news, Joe, but I have no idea."

"Really?" Martinez pushed, his dark eyes fixed watchfully on Rachel's face. "Maddison Logan is the first visitor that Terence Bailey has had since he was locked up six years ago. You appear to be their main topic of conversation, and you have no idea why."

Rachel could tell that he was more interested in her reaction than her explanation. He wanted to know whether Rachel knew something that she wasn't telling him. That's why he hadn't told her any of this on the phone. He wanted to see her visceral response.

"If this is the reason you flew me down to Florida, then you really did waste my time. I've never met Maddison Logan or Terence Bailey. I've never even heard of them before," said Rachel. "As for what they wanted from me, it wouldn't be the first time that a felon reached out to me directly or indirectly because he thinks I can help him get out of prison. Maybe you should have done better research before bringing me down here."

"Maybe," Martinez agreed amiably as Rachel fumed.

"Why don't you ask Maddison?" Rachel suggested. "She'll be able to tell you what she discussed with Terence Bailey a heck of a lot better than I could possibly speculate."

"Unfortunately, that's where things get complicated," Martinez answered with unflappable calm.

Chapter 7

Thomas McCoy cruises along Main Street, listening to a shock jock talk shit on the radio. Two booking requests come up simultaneously in the rideshare app. He ignores them both. He's not in the mood to be nice to people. Besides, he hasn't had breakfast.

He pulls in at a Taco King and parks right outside the entrance, going inside to get his meal. Usually he prefers the anonymity of the drive-thru. Today he wants to sit at a table and stretch his legs instead of eating hunched over his steering wheel like a hobo. His body is cramped. He's been stuck in the car like a sardine all morning.

He gives his order of a burrito breakfast special to a slip of a girl wearing a red-and-green Taco King polo shirt. She takes his cash and slaps an order number onto the counter as she greets the next customer.

"Welcome to Taco King. What's your order today?"

Thomas brushes past a boy and his grandmother as he heads toward a huddle of customers waiting for their order numbers to flash on an overhead monitor. The boy twists around from the counter to watch Thomas go, wriggling as his grandmother holds his arm in a vise-like grip as she gives their order to the cashier. When they're done, she guides the boy to the collection point where patrons wait for their meals, their eyes glued to the monitor.

The kid slips out of his grandmother's grip and goes to a self-service counter, where he tears up sugar sachets, spilling crystals all over the counter. His grandmother pulls him away, dragging him to wait for their order near Thomas McCoy, who still hasn't received his burrito breakfast.

"You smell," the boy says to Thomas conversationally. He squeezes his nostrils together with his fingertips. "You smell real bad."

Grandma pounces. Her hand clamps around the kid's arms. "Shush," she tells him.

"But he does smell, Grandma," the kid shrieks. "He smells *terrible*."

Thomas edges away and disappears into the men's restroom. He trembles from the shame. It's the same humiliation that he felt as a schoolkid sitting alone at the back of the classroom. Kids would make choking sounds when the teacher forced them to sit near him in class. His face would burn and his eyes would well with tears but he never gave them the satisfaction of crying. Once again, a child has reduced him to a quivering mess.

He regrets not topping up his aftershave before leaving the car. The splashes of cologne that he dabs on regularly, and the heady fragrances of shampoos and soaps that he washes himself with two, three, sometimes even four times a day, usually overwhelm the sense of smell of most adults. He takes care to be so well groomed and neatly dressed that people naturally think they must be mistaken if they smell him. They assume the foul odor of rotting garbage is coming from somewhere else.

Kids are the worst. They are hyper-sensitive to unpleasant odors, and they have no qualms about airing their suspicions at the top of their lungs, as Thomas has found out yet again to his mortified embarrassment.

After he's taken a leak, he rolls up his shirtsleeves at the basin and rubs liquid soap from the dispenser onto his arms, neck, and face. He washes it all off and wipes himself dry with paper towels. His business shirt is stained with wet patches. He presses on the hand dryer and holds the fabric underneath it to allow the hot air to dry it off.

Thankfully, by the time he comes out of the restroom, the woman and her grandkid have gone. Thomas approaches the counter to collect his food.

"Enjoy your meal," the attendant says as she hands him his order in a Taco King paper bag.

He eats his lukewarm meal in the privacy of his car and listens to the latest news updates on the car radio while he devours the burrito and fries. The announcer talks about a fatal accident on the I-95 heading into town from Jacksonville. "Traffic is backed up almost two miles."

It's followed by the usual political bullshit and news of rumbling wars that don't interest him. There's nothing on the news about a missing woman. That should make him happy. Instead it makes him miserable. His accomplishments are always overshadowed by something else.

Ride requests flash on his phone screen. He ignores them. He's not in the mood for another passenger. He removes a Swiss Army knife from his pocket. It's a small knife with a hot-pink casing. It's a girlish souvenir that's designed for a woman's smaller hand and yet it is sharp enough to kill.

He opens the knife and runs his finger along the blade. He closes the blade and then opens it again, flicking it backward and forward.

Thomas thinks of the kid squeezing his nostrils after publicly humiliating him in the burrito place. He works the blade faster and faster with his thumb, clicking it in and out. He doesn't care about the cuts to his finger, or the thin trail of blood running down his hand. Anger builds inside of him. He's learned through trial and error that there's only one way to make his rage subside.

Chapter 8

The body-cam footage began rolling as the police officer pressed a "Play" button on the camera strapped to his uniform and stepped out of his patrol car. He slammed the door behind him.

The footage swayed with the movement of the cop's body as he walked. It captured everything that he saw. It wasn't much. Just a lone camper van parked in the dark under a tree along a dirt road.

"I can't believe this couldn't wait until morning," he complained to his partner as they walked toward the van. Twigs cracked under the tread of their boots as they approached. The van's white exterior was tinged violet from the whirling patrol car siren lights breaking up the pitch darkness.

The cop walked up the stairs and pushed open the squeaking screen door. Rachel winced when the policeman's flashlight swung around the interior of the van. The expletives that quickly ran through Rachel's mind were enunciated in far cruder sacrilegious detail by the police officer whose body-cam footage Rachel watched on Agent Martinez's iPad.

The van was infested with vermin. Rats desperately scampered across the kitchen counter and onto the floor. One rat ran hell-for-leather past the police officers to get out through the van door, which the officer was still holding open.

"Take a look at that," whispered one of the cops. Neither of them crossed the threshold as they stared at the chilling sight before them.

A snake soundlessly slid through a gap in a slightly ajar window set high up on the van wall. The reptile dropped onto the floor with a plop. It was followed by another snake. And another.

"The snakes must have come for the rats, which must have come for the food," the cop observed, pointing to plates arranged on the kitchen counter. It looked like a meal had been in progress, although the plates were licked clean.

One snake that had already fed on a rat was curled up on a sofa cushion, its stomach extended as it digested its meal. Another slithered through an open-toed stiletto shoe lying on the floor as it tried to corner a rodent. Yet another snake was wrapped around the legs of a video tripod that had toppled near the sofa.

"So this is what those campers ran from?" Rachel glanced up at Joe Martinez.

"The van was parked near a swamp known as Rattlesnake Lake. For good reason, as it turns out," Martinez said. As if to prove his point, the footage showed another snake sliding into the van through the open window.

Rachel's skin crawled as the tail of a snake rattled when the police officer's flashlight beam moved across the gloomy room and onto the kitchen stool where it lay curled up. "It's like a horror movie."

"Those campers took one look and got the hell out of there. Went to a luxury resort hotel at Daytona Beach instead," said Martinez, before explaining what happened next.

Once snake catchers removed the reptiles, the van was searched by police. The disarray inside was determined to be due to the rodent and snake infestation. The cops sent out a search party, assuming that the van's owners had fled in terror just like those campers did when they saw what was inside the vehicle.

"After an initial search of the campground indicated that nobody had run away, the local cops began to pay more attention to several crucial details they'd missed earlier. Things that were staring them in the face," Martinez recounted to Rachel.

"Like what?"

"There was no cell phone or wallet in the van. No credit cards. No driver's license. No cash. No car keys," he added. "They called me for advice. I told them the obvious."

"Which is?"

"Nobody in their right mind who's running out of a camper van into a forest due to a snake infestation would risk collecting their valuables before fleeing."

"You thought something bad had gone down in there *before* the wildlife invasion?" Rachel asked.

"I did," Martinez agreed. "Especially when they sent me photos that showed faint blood smudges near the front door and nail marks that looked as if they were made by someone holding on to that doorway for dear life. Whoever made those nail marks desperately wanted to stay."

"Because they didn't want to be dragged away."

"Exactly," said Martinez.

There were other anomalies that he'd noticed in the photos. The fridge was filled with food, all freshly bought. "A person doesn't usually go to the trouble of buying an assortment of delicious food and then disappear of their own volition without ever eating any of it," he told Rachel. "I didn't think that local law enforcement could chalk it up to an abandoned vehicle, which is where I'm guessing they were hoping to take it. It was obvious to me that something bad had happened in that van before the wildlife invaded."

Martinez had been giving a training course to law enforcement personnel in Miami when he was asked to provide his expertise on the case. He flew up with several of the agents he was training, figuring it was a good opportunity to get them some hands-on experience.

The cops were no closer to figuring out what had happened when Martinez and his team arrived.

"The local cops didn't know who owned the van when we arrived to help out," Martinez told Rachel.

The van was registered to a seventy-four-year-old Texan, but he'd claimed to have sold it to a dealer fourteen months earlier. That meant either the van was stolen or the transfer papers hadn't been filed properly.

"Either way, the cops couldn't identify the person who'd gone missing. All they knew was that someone had apparently disappeared from that van."

The first thing that Martinez did once he arrived in Daytona was visit the scene. He found things the local cops had missed. He retrieved three clothing buttons from under the sofa, cotton thread still caught in the buttonholes. It looked as if they'd been torn from a garment, supporting his theory that someone had been violently removed from the van against their will. He also noted that someone had been cooking, judging by fresh food scraps in the trash.

"It was all inexplicable," he told Rachel.

Then he examined a broken video camera, still connected to the tripod. It had not been accidentally knocked to the ground as the local cops had presumed when they'd recovered it during their search of the van. It had been repeatedly smashed so badly that the camera body had caved in and wires were hanging out.

"Someone wanted to be damn sure that video camera was broken beyond repair," Martinez said. "Fortunately, our lab techs were able to extract a video from the camcorder's damaged memory card. You're going to want to see it."

In a basket pushed under the van bed, Martinez had also found a pile of dirty clothes that hadn't been examined properly by the local cops. When he rummaged through the laundry, Martinez found a Central Florida Correctional Facility visitor's sticker with a barcode stuck to the front of a black top. He was able to cross-reference the barcode to the list of recent visitors at the prison.

"The visitor's sticker was issued to Maddison Logan," Martinez told Rachel.

"You think that Maddison Logan is the missing camper," said Rachel, cottoning on.

"It sure looks that way," said Martinez. "We believe she disappeared shortly after visiting Terence Bailey in prison."

Chapter 9

"Hiya," calls out a stunning young woman with long burnished gold hair. She talks directly to the camera like it's her best friend.

Rachel immediately recognizes Maddison as she watches the tightly shot video that Joe Martinez plays for her on his iPad. The FBI lab had apparently performed miracles retrieving it from the broken memory card of the smashed camcorder found in Maddison's camper van.

"You all are going to want to see what I've gotten up to today," Maddison tells the camera, sitting in the kitchen area of her van.

Her tone is over-animated in the fast-talking exaggerated style of a YouTuber. Her lipstick is a playful pink. She wears a denim miniskirt and a buttoned-down cropped top that displays a toned and very tanned belly.

"I'm on a raw foods health kick. You heard me, raw foods. I've never felt better. I've never been thinner. I've never eaten so much! That's why I'm sharing my secrets with you. Yes, you, my amazing followers. Take a look. . . ."

Maddison stands up and wiggles her sculpted butt in front of the camera with a few steps of samba before she perches back on the retro yellow stool alongside a Formica kitchen table in the camper van.

"I'm calling it Maddison's Mad Body Makeover. Yeah, yeah. I know what you're thinking," she says with a wink. "You're thinking this is another influencer pitching some crazy-ass fad diet that doesn't work. Well, this works. Trust me. You don't have to buy pills, or supplements. There's no protein shakes. You don't even have to buy a scale. All you have to do is follow these three simple rules. Best of all, it won't cost you a cent."

She holds up a finger close to the camera lens. "Rule number one: one serving of carbs a day." Then she adds a second finger. "Rule number two: water, water, and more water. I want you drinking so much water that you'll feel like you've swallowed a swimming pool." She rolls her eyes at her own lame joke. "Final rule: every meal is a big salad with a protein."

Maddison's holding three fingers in front of the camera. "So that's three rules. It can't get any easier than that. Just to prove this is something that every one of you can do, I made a few of the foods that I've been eating every day."

As she speaks, she picks up different plates of food that she's already prepared. There's a Greek salad in one bowl and a big green salad in another. A shallow bowl is filled with yogurt and berries sprinkled on top. She holds each colorful plate way too close to the camera lens as she runs through the ingredients at supersonic speed. When she's done showing off the food, she picks up an ice cream scooper and scoops a ball of ice cream that she places on a cut mango.

"I wanted a pick-me-up earlier, so I made dessert." She gives an exaggerated shocked expression to the camera. "No! I'm not cheating. Deserts are within the rules. I should know. I made the rules." She puts her hand naughtily over her mouth. "It's ice cream made from almond milk and real macadamias. The best part is that it's low in sugar and high in protein. I'll post the recipe on my blog."

She picks up a teaspoon and tastes the ice cream. "Oh my gosh, that is soooooo good," Maddison says with exaggerated delight.

The laughter on her face disappears very suddenly. Her gaze moves away from the camera filming her. Something has caught her attention. Rachel feels the gut-wrenching moment when Maddison's surprise at being interrupted filming her video in her camper van turns into wide-eyed fear.

"Hey! You can't come in. . . ." Maddison rises quickly out of frame. She's obviously confronting the intruder.

"What the hell are you doing. . . . Get your hands off me. Don't touch me!"

Buttons popping and fabric tearing are audible in the background, followed by muffled screams and the sound of a struggle. Something hits the ground. Hard. Then the camera itself topples, crashing to the floor. The shot spins and then goes black.

Rachel broke the thick silence that followed. "Maddison Logan filmed her own abduction."

Chapter 10

Six years ago, Owen Bragg was inspecting tree branches damaged in a storm not far from the camping area where the deserted van that I mentioned earlier was found. It was dawn. His favorite time of the day. Everything was still, and fresh, and glistening from rain overnight.

Owen noticed a narrow plume of smoke in the sky. It was coming from a remote mountain ridge that was particularly inaccessible to all but the most intrepid hikers. It was called Shepherd's Eye because the rocks at the top apparently look like a ram's head at sunset for those in a fanciful frame of mind.

Smoke billowing mysteriously from deep inside a forest is an emergency for park rangers. Upon catching sight of the smoke, Owen immediately jumped into his truck and sped across the park to the bottom of the ridge.

"I raced up the hill on foot with a fire extinguisher on my back and a shovel to put out the flames. I wasn't overly worried on account of the recent rainfall. I doubted the fire would get a foothold, but I needed to put it out before it became a problem."

When Owen got to the top, he pushed through the dense brush, checking the sky intermittently for signs of smoke as he tried to locate the fire.

"I smelled it before I saw it."

Owen followed the smoke trail until he found its source. It was coming from a small clearing in the middle of the pine forest. Sitting against a tree trunk was a teenage girl. Her chin lolled against her chest. It looked as if she were fast asleep. Smoke was billowing from a pile of pinecones alongside her. Owen assumed she'd made a crude campfire to keep herself warm.

"I thought she'd been at an illegal rave in the forest and gotten lost. It happens sometimes. I called out to ask if she was all right."

Owen's question went unanswered. He remembers hearing an ominous buzz of flies as he crossed the clearing and approached her. The significance of the flies didn't register until he reached the girl.

"Is everything okay?" he called out again.

The girl didn't move.

"I must have known then, but I checked her pulse anyway. It was pointless, of course, but I wasn't thinking straight by then."

The girl's body fell to the side like a dead weight. Her head landed on a pile of leaves, her eyes wide open. Unblinking. Her pupils fixed and dilated. An indication of death. Charred and partially burned rope bound the girl's wrists and ankles together.

"She looked like a trussed lamb at a slaughterhouse. I'd never seen anything like that before in my life. Lord help me, I hope I never will again."

Owen realized that the pinecones piled up like a pyre alongside the girl's body must have been put there by the killer to fuel the fire lit to burn her body. The fire must have fizzled out before it could do much damage to the body. Instead, the pinecones, damp from recent rains, smoldered, creating the plume of smoke that Owen had noticed earlier that morning from across the forest.

Owen's phone battery was dead. He returned to his truck to call for help on his short-wave radio. As he headed back down the slope, the heavens opened.

The ground turned muddy. Owen slipped, bruising his back from the fall. He got up and kept walking down, limping to the truck in pouring rain. He huddled in the truck cab and radioed the police. He was wet to the bone.

"I was shivering uncontrollably but not from the rain. I was in shock from finding the girl. Even when the cops eventually arrived, we all had to wait for the rain and thunder to subside. We sometimes get lightning strikes up there. We couldn't go up until the storm eased."

Once the rain stopped, Owen guided the cops up the same way he took me to the clearing. Despite his sore back, he insisted on staying to help out. He went up and down the treacherous slope countless times, helping the forensic team processing the scene as well as escorting down the workers carrying the girl's body to a morgue van parked at the bottom of the hill.

Owen gathered from overhearing the conversations of detectives and crime scene technicians that the storm had washed away whatever trace evidence had been left behind. Footprints. Tire tracks. Hairs and fibers. All gone. There was also no indication of the girl's identity.

As dusk fell and the last law enforcement vehicles drove away, Owen collected discarded crime scene tape and other forensic debris scattered on the mountainside. Before heading down to his truck, he picked a wildflower near the ram's head rock at the top of the ridge and returned to the clearing. Somberly, he knelt down and placed the flower stem at the spot where he'd found the body at the base of the tree trunk.

Since nobody knew the young victim's name, he flicked open his ranger's utility knife and carved into the bark of the tree the words "Unknown Girl."

Chapter 11

I'm heading out of here after nine days of desert dancing. I'm sunburned. I'm covered in sand. It's everywhere. And trust me, I do mean *everywhere.* I've barely slept."

Maddison steers a van down a bumpy desert road in New Mexico as she talks directly to a camera on her dashboard. Her voice is hoarse. Swirls of glitter decorate her sunburned cheeks.

"I would come here again. In a heartbeat. Burning Man was like . . ." Maddison closes her eyes briefly as she grapples for the right word. "It was spiritual. No, it was more than spiritual. It was like an out-of-body experience," she explains as she steers the van along the desert road.

The video was among a series posted on Maddison's social media feeds that documented her pilgrimage, as she called it, to the Burning Man festival the previous year. In one video, Maddison danced trance-like as "the man" burned behind her. In another, she lay on her back making snow angels in the desert sand, the sky lit up by the flames of the bonfire at night. In another, she ran barefoot through a stretch of desert blowing bubbles.

Rachel watched the video before quickly scrolling through Maddison's other Instagram posts on Joe Martinez's iPad. Rachel hoped the videos would help her get a read on the influencer who disappeared thirty-six hours ago. The upbeat vibe of Maddison's posts was echoed by her captions: #travelbloggerlife #lifestyleblogger #vanlife #dreamlife #yolo #vlogger

In one video, Maddison reclined on a beach chair outside her camper van. Her feet rested on another chair as she waited for the hot-pink nail polish she'd just applied to her toenails to dry. She lifted her arms into the air and danced while seated, eventually bursting into laughter.

"It looks like she's having the time of her life," Rachel commented when the video ended with Maddison poking her tongue out mischievously at the camera.

"It's carefully curated. That's the Maddison she presents to the world. The fun-loving, exuberant Maddison," Martinez responded.

"You don't think that Maddison really is bubbly and extroverted?" Rachel asked.

"Who knows what really goes on under the surface?" Martinez mused as Rachel clicked "Play" to watch another video.

In this video, Maddison sped her van past enormous cacti on an Arizona desert road. Her hair was arranged in a pyramid of aluminum highlighter foils. Maddison explained in a monologue to the camera as she drove that she'd run out of water while coloring her hair. She was rushing to the closest campground to find water to wash out the hair dye before it overdeveloped and damaged her follicles.

"If I don't get there in ten minutes then this will be a mega hair disaster," Maddison screeched dramatically. She gripped the steering wheel and stepped on the gas like a contestant on a reality TV show. It was typical of the videos that Maddison posted.

Her Instagram displayed a vivid array of outrageous photos and videos documenting Maddison's nomadic life zigzagging across the country. There were photos of Maddison snowboarding, and others of her emerging from the California surf in a wet suit zipped to her bare belly button, a longboard under her arm. Another photo at a whitewater river in Colorado showed Maddison laughing with open-mouthed excitement as she held an oar victoriously aloft in the air.

"Today I'm going to show you the best ever facial treatments," Maddison said in another video as she lay in a bubble bath. A vile green avocado facial mask was spread over her face. Perfectly sliced cross sections of orange rested over each eye.

Maddison stuck her tongue out to lick avocado off her chin. "I like to think of it as a meal for your skin. You really are what you eat!"

Rachel scrolled through photos of Maddison at restaurants, bars, and nightclubs where she took selfies with an array of people laughingly posing for photos. Tongues sticking out. Arms around each other. Fingers flashing V-for-victory signs. Wineglasses raised.

"Being an influencer is the twenty-first-century American dream," said Martinez. "It's a lifelong vacation funded by brands paying big dollars for influencers to promote products to their social media followers."

Going to college or getting a desk-bound job seemed lame when even better money could be earned by having a good time while roaming the world. It's what Rachel might have done a decade earlier when she'd been in her early twenties and hadn't been ready to join the grown-ups with a regular job and a mortgage.

"Someone in these photos must know something about Maddison's disappearance," said Rachel. "Maybe one of them abducted her."

"My people have been going through all Maddison's social media posts," said Martinez. "Locations. People. Likes. Comments. Everything. They're trying to figure out how much of Maddison's freewheeling wanderlust lifestyle is fact and how much is fiction."

"Fiction?" Rachel glanced up curiously from the iPad screen. It was the second time that Joe Martinez had intimated that there was more to Maddison than what met the eye.

"It would be a fatal mistake to think that Maddison Logan is anything more than a carefully cultivated persona," said Martinez. "All these photos are curated versions of her life. They tell us nothing about the real Maddison. Her disappointments. Her frustrations. Her fears."

As he spoke, Rachel scrolled through photos of Maddison sunning herself on her camper van roof. In another, she held up a barbecue fork skewering a sausage as she hugged a bunch of people in cutoff shorts, knitted beanies, and cropped tees.

#newfriends Maddison captioned the photo.

Ever since she started looking through Maddison's Instagram feed, Rachel had sensed there was something strange. After going through dozens of Maddison's photos and videos, Rachel realized what was bothering her. The people in Maddison's photos never appeared more than once or twice. There were no photos of anyone who could be construed as family. No pictures of Maddison with her mom, or dad. The photos were an endless parade of selfies of Maddison with an array of photogenic young people making fleeting appearances in Maddison's life like extras on a long-running TV series.

"Maddison rarely hangs with the same people more than once or twice," Rachel observed. "When was Maddison last in touch with her family?"

"We haven't been able to track down her family or friends. Everyone in the photos who we've contacted so far say they only met Maddison briefly while she was traveling. Their relationships with her were superficial, at best," Martinez said. "I'm fast coming to the conclusion that Maddison is not real."

Rachel glanced up at him. "What do you mean 'not real'?"

"Maddison is an invention. She created a persona of a free-spirited travel blogger flouting social conventions while having the time of her life crossing the country in a retro camper van."

"Even if it's true, does it really matter?" Rachel asked. "Maddison's missing. Find her. That's all you need to do."

"How much do you know about missing persons investigations, Rachel?" Martinez asked.

Rachel shrugged. "Not a lot."

"Our best chance of solving these cases is knowing everything we can about the person who's gone missing. Unfortunately, that's proving to be difficult in Maddison's case."

"Because you don't think that Maddison is who she says she is?" Rachel asked.

"We can't build a victim profile of Maddison because she doesn't exist outside of these social media posts."

"Surely you know something about her actual identity?" Rachel asked.

"We know her backstory from her own vlogging."

"Which is?"

"She claims to be a college dropout from Portland. As she tells it, she was in a sociology class in her junior year at Oregon State University. Her professor was on the podium droning on about Blau's social exchange theory when it suddenly hit her that she could learn more about sociology from meeting people than learning out of books. She bought a camper van and drove off the next day. Within weeks she was supporting herself by vlogging."

"Sounds like a heck of an inspiring story," Rachel said.

"It would be if it were true," Martinez responded. "Nobody by the name of Maddison Logan was registered at Oregon State during the period that Maddison claimed to have been a student."

Martinez opened a folder and removed the photo of Maddison that he'd shown Rachel earlier, with the smoky eyeshadow and glossy gold hair. He tossed it over so that Rachel could take a closer look at the stunning young influencer.

"I don't know her real name. I don't even know how much of her online persona is real. But I do know one thing," he said. "With each hour that passes, our chances of finding her alive are slipping away. I need your help, Rachel. You're the only lead we have right now."

Chapter 12

The high-pitched wail of a siren rang out through the prison complex. It was shatteringly loud. Rachel Krall and Joe Martinez stopped talking, unable to hear each other's voices over the deafening noise. Instead, they stared at each other with amused helplessness while an announcement blared over the loudspeakers. "All officers to your stations. Lockdown for Count in five minutes. I repeat. Lockdown for Count in five minutes."

"Don't tell me there's been a prison break?" Rachel said when the announcement ended and the siren wail had dialed down enough for her to be heard.

"Nobody's ever successfully escaped from this prison. It's surrounded by swamps for a reason," Martinez said pointedly. "The only guy who ever tried to break out was on a work crew outside the prison gates when he noticed that his shackles hadn't been locked properly. He dived into the water that surrounds this place and swam away."

"So he did escape?"

"His boots were found in the reeds the next day. With his feet still in them," Martinez added. "That's the prison lore, in any event."

"Is it true?"

"Maybe. There are alligator alert signs up by those swamps, although the head of the search and rescue team looking for Maddison tells me that alligators haven't been spotted for years."

"So if this isn't a prison break, then why are these damn sirens robbing me of my hearing?"

"It's for the after-lunch head count. Every prison counts inmates every couple of hours during the day to make sure all the prisoners are present and accounted for. It reduces the risk of a prison break," Martinez explained.

The head counts would also remind the prisoners of their place as they had to drop whatever they were doing and stand in line to be counted as if they were livestock, Rachel presumed.

"Rachel, are you certain that Terence Bailey has never contacted you?" Martinez broke into her thoughts. "I gather that you get flooded with letters from prisoners asking for your help. Maybe Bailey wrote to you, or maybe Maddison tried to reach out before she disappeared?"

"My producer, Pete, handles the podcast's correspondence."

When her podcast was first launched, Rachel tried to read every message sent to her. She felt obliged to, since people took the trouble of pouring out their hearts to her. Over time, reading the details of so many personal tragedies took a cumulative emotional toll on Rachel to the point where she considered quitting the podcast. After that, Pete vetted all the correspondence sent to her. It had been getting exponentially bigger as the show went from a cult hit to a mainstream sensation.

"Call your producer." Martinez handed Rachel his phone. "Don't tell him the reasons for your questions. We need to keep things on the down-low for now."

Pete answered on the second ring. Rachel quickly told him that she was in Florida. "It's a long story and I'm pressed for time," she said, glancing at Martinez, who was brazenly listening in on the conversation. "Pete, I need to know whether we've received messages from anyone by the name of Terence Bailey." Rachel spelled out his name. "Or Maddison Logan. Bailey is a guest of the Florida Department of Corrections," Rachel said. "As for Maddison Logan, she's—"

"An influencer," Pete interjected.

"You know her?"

"I've heard of her. She's a vlogger."

"She must be big."

"Not that big. But I do the podcast's social media. It's my business to know this stuff. Nothing rings a bell, although to be brutally honest, I'm still working my way through the backlog of messages that came through while I was in the hospital."

A few weeks earlier, Pete had been injured in a traffic accident. He was going stir-crazy as he recuperated at home.

"I'll go through the messages now. I'll get back to you as soon as I can, Rach."

"We have to get going," Martinez said when Rachel finished the call. He packed up his things and escorted her out of the room toward a double set of glass-windowed doors at the end of the hall. The doors contained reinforced wired glass panes that were de rigueur in prison so the guards could always see what lay ahead.

"There's an old rule of thumb in prisons," Martinez said as he rang an intercom buzzer for a guard to let them through. "Actually, it's more of a life lesson. Always know what you're walking into. Dark corners can be danger points."

Chapter 13

The mid-morning lull in the rideshare business is as predictable as the rise and set of the sun. It generally begins after ten in the morning. It ends about a quarter of an hour before midday, when the lunchtime rush hits with the full force of a hurricane.

Thomas McCoy uses the morning lull to drive to a warehouse-sized hardware store in a strip mall on the outskirts of town. A billboard above the store entrance has a giant photo of a family, all on ladders, building a white clapboard house. "Everything you'll ever need. And more."

Thomas has come to this particular hardware store because it offers the one thing that Thomas needs and definitely can't get at the family-run place in town: anonymity.

At this chain store, the young staff are more interested in clocking in and clocking out than remembering customers' names, or faces. Thomas doesn't want to be remembered. That's why he's brought cash. That's also why he slips on a baseball hat and switches his glasses to an ugly horn-rimmed pair from the nineties. He checks himself in the mirror before he leaves the car to confirm that he looks forgettable. He's another middle-aged man with a slight pot belly and a coarse bland face hidden behind dated glasses.

As he walks into the store, he avoids the security cameras by staring at a shopping list he prepared earlier while waiting for his previous passengers. He's been thinking about those passengers ever since he dropped them off at their destination.

They were a young couple, late twenties. Polite. They greeted him as they slid into the rear seat of his vehicle outside their hotel. That was more than he could say about many of his passengers.

The couple held hands throughout the ride. They referred to each other as "babe" and shared secretive smiles. They were obviously in the honeymoon phase.

It's all downhill from here, buddy. Thomas watched them surreptitiously through the rearview mirror.

The details of their relationship quickly became apparent from listening to their conversation as he drove through busy morning traffic toward the mall downtown.

They were shopping for rings. They'd wanted to choose the engagement ring together before he formally proposed. There was a lot of discussion about ring options. Cut. Carat. Price was a biggie.

She wanted him to buy the ring from a trusted jewelry store back home, owned by someone from her parents' church who she was certain would give them a discount. He wanted to buy the ring immediately even if it meant paying top dollar.

"That way I can propose in the hot-air balloon," he told her. "The ballooning company will livestream it so everyone back home can watch me getting on one knee. Plus we get a bottle of champagne and photos." He squeezed her hand. "What do you think, babe?"

"What about doing it at the beach at sunrise? The sunrises are super pretty here. We can hire someone to take photos."

"The beach is so clichéd, babe," he sulked. "None of our friends have done a hot-air balloon proposal. It'll be huge."

"Two thousand dollars for a proposal! There are plenty of things we could use that money for."

"Like what?"

"Like upsizing the ring."

McCoy groaned to himself when she mentioned a bigger ring. He knew all about engagement rings. He'd spent four months' salary on a diamond ring when he proposed to Audrey. That was three decades ago, when he was around their age. Audrey kept it when she broke off their engagement. She was still wearing his ring a few weeks later when he saw her at a restaurant with a new man. When he eventually swallowed his pride and asked for it back, she told him that she'd pawned it and used the money for a deposit on a flashy new car. Red. Audrey had a thing for red.

Thomas wondered whether to tell the couple about the pawnshop downtown where a diamond ring could be bought for a fraction of the price charged at the jewelry store. They'd be able to get their hot-air balloon proposal and a bling ring to impress everyone back home. It was a good deal, so long as you weren't superstitious about getting engaged with a ring that belonged to someone who'd fallen on hard times bad enough they'd had to hawk their jewelry. Some people were bothered by things like that.

"Where are you folks from?" he asked, thinking that he'd work his way to mentioning the pawnshop. The couple seemed nice enough and he wanted to help them out.

"Long Grove, Illinois," she responded in a singsong. "It's near Lake Michigan."

"I don't know it. Never been up north before," he said.

"You should go," they both responded in unison from the back seat. The conversation soon stalled into a silence so awkward that Thomas regretted saying anything at all.

The mall was a block away when he heard the sniff. It started off as a single uncertain sniff. The second sniff was curious, seeking confirmation. It was the third sniff that made his stomach drop like he was free-falling. That was when he knew they suspected. As if on cue, on the third sniff she whispered something to her fiancé.

"Hey, can you open a window back here?" he asked.

"Not sure if that's a good idea," Thomas responded matter-of-factly.

"There's a damaged sewage drain on this road. It can get a bit . . . er, unpleasant."

Thomas turned up the air conditioner to full blast so the pungent white-rose scent of the liquid air refresher capsule connected to the fan could circulate quickly. He hunched over the wheel, driving as fast as he could, hoping they wouldn't catch him out again before he dropped them off.

He had good days when his condition was under control, and bad days when he had to be hyper-vigilant. Today was a bad day judging by the fact that both the kid at the burrito place and now this couple had picked up on it. It must be his nerves. It always got worse when he was stressed. Right now he had plenty going on in his life. It would be over in a couple of days and then he hoped things would go back to normal. Normal wasn't good, but it was better than being caught out.

He'd been taunted about his "problem," as his mother had called it, since preschool. Kids look for weakness. It didn't take long for them to find his. They weren't imaginative with their insults either. "Trash boy." "Turd face." He'd regularly had trash thrown at him on the school bus. Eventually, he insisted on riding his bike to school. It was a six-mile trip but it was better than the alternative.

His mother didn't bother taking him to a doctor when his homeroom teacher called her into the school to find out if he had a hygiene problem. His mom told Thomas plainly that there was no cure. Her uncle had been afflicted with the same condition. So he learned to wash several times a day. He learned to slap on deodorants and cologne even when he was still in elementary school. The scents disguised the smell but only temporarily. There was always some fork-tongued kid around to remind him when it stopped working.

Thomas drove the lovestruck couple to the mall without any further upset, thanks to the heady fragrance of the car deodorizer, which he'd found over the years covered all manner of sins. After he'd dropped them off, he headed to the hardware store, which is where he is now, navigating through the aisles.

He's still thinking about the couple and how they almost caught him out, when a notification comes up on the rideshare app. It happens just as he's selecting a custom length of rope in aisle 12. He takes his phone from his pocket and checks the screen. The couple gave him five stars and a tip.

He selects a long length of rope and throws several bags of top soil and a few young lemon and orange trees onto his oversized metal cart. He adds a bag of gravel and a knife sharpener.

"I need advice on how to fix my back porch," he tells a sales assistant. "The brick pavers are in bad shape. Is there any way to freshen them up and get rid of the stains?"

"Only thing that works is this product." The attendant points to a two-gallon plastic container on a bottom shelf. "This stuff is mostly hydrochloric acid. It works great but there's no room for mistakes."

"Are you sure this will get rid of the stains?" Thomas asks, purposely dubious. He doesn't want the sales assistant to know that he has no intention of using the acid to remove paver stains.

"That's potent stuff right there. It'll work. I recommend you get yourself rubber boots and gloves as well. Thick ones. You don't want that acid dripping onto your skin. It'll burn right through. In fact, that stuff is strong enough to burn through human bones."

"Is that so?" Thomas says with mock surprise.

Chapter 14

Lunch service was over in the prison staff cafeteria. An aluminum grate was pulled down, shutting off the window opening where cafeteria staff dished up hot meals. Rachel could hear the clatter of pots being scrubbed as staff cleaned up behind the metal grate in the kitchen.

Several younger guards talked shop as they finished eating their lunch at a table near the door through which Joe Martinez and Rachel Krall walked in.

"Did you hear what happened in cellblock fourteen this morning?" said a big-bellied guard between bites of beef stew. "We were doing standing count at five A.M. The new guy refused to come to the entrance of his cell for the count. Said he was tired and that he wasn't a morning person." The guard used a baby voice to mimic the prisoner. The other guards laughed, not just at the joke but at the punchline they knew was coming.

"I bet you tucked him in. Gave him his teddy bear." Another guard mimicked the same baby voice.

"I went in there. Told him nice as pie: 'Would you like me to wake you in a couple of hours, son?' Hell, I even asked if he wanted me to bring him a breakfast tray."

"What did he say?" asked a younger guard, his shoulders shaking with laughter.

The guard telling the story couldn't speak for a moment, he was laughing so hard. "He said: 'Thanks, man. Eggs over easy. Toast and coffee would be nice too. Really appreciate it.' Then he rolled over and went back to sleep."

All the guards guffawed.

"Well, I stuck my ugly face right by his ear and yelled: 'No problem, son. Any time.' Then I hauled his ass out of his cell by the scruff of his scrawny neck. You should have seen his face. I thought he was going to piss . . ."

Rachel didn't hear the rest of the story over the chorus of laughter that followed. She trailed behind Martinez into an adjacent carpeted room that was clearly intended for staff events and conferences.

On the walls were oil paintings depicting prison life. Some were striking portraits of prisoners and guards. Others were landscapes, such as one of the vibrant green tops of pine trees visible through the bars of a prison cell in the foreground. Another painting showed the outline of birds flying into a clear blue sky as seen from a prison cell window. It was a melancholy painting that suggested a deep longing for freedom.

The most prominent painting was a portrait of a jowly man with wiry gray hair. From the way the man held himself with his shoulders square and chin up, he looked like an explorer who'd just planted a flag. It was in an ostentatious gilt frame and hung in pride of place in the middle of the wall. A brass plaque on the frame read "Fredrick Hughes: Warden."

"These paintings are really good," said Rachel. "Did they hire artists to paint them?"

"They used free prison labor," Martinez replied.

"Really? Inmates made these?"

"Most of the paintings, the good ones, anyway, were painted by Terence Bailey."

Rachel was impressed by Bailey's obvious talent. She examined a painting of prisoner gangs working under the watchful eyes of guards as they shoveled dirt in a field against a backdrop of barbed-wire fences and forests.

"He's prison taught," said Martinez. "From what I heard, he couldn't so much as do a stick figure drawing until he came here. He took a hobby art class run by a volunteer. Within a couple of years, Bailey surpassed his teacher and painted these."

Martinez told Rachel that the warden liked to show off Bailey's paintings to VIP guests as an example of the prison's rehabilitation programs. "Between you and me," he said, "that's pure PR bullshit. This is one of the toughest prisons in the country. There's no rehabilitation."

"You never told me what Bailey did to get in here," Rachel pointed out.

"Breaking and entering." Martinez led Rachel out of the room. "He was sentenced to two years. That was six years ago."

"Then why's he still in here?"

"Shortly before he was due to be released, he got into a fight with another prisoner. Claimed the guy jumped him. Bailey beat him to a pulp. Knocked out the guy's teeth. They were scattered like candies on the floor. He got another four years for assault."

"So he got six years all told. He must be due for release soon," said Rachel, doing the math.

"As a matter of fact, he gets out this week. In fact, he has forty-eight hours left of his sentence."

Rachel froze mid-step. It was all falling into place. Rachel had to give it to them; they'd reeled her in good and proper. Torreno providing her the scarcest of details when he woke her that morning. Martinez drip-feeding her information. It was deliberate.

"Terence Bailey has no reason to tell you anything about his meeting with Maddison Logan if he's about to get out of prison in two days' time," Rachel said. "You can't promise to knock a few weeks or months off his sentence if he cooperates, or to have him moved to a better cellblock. He's about to get out anyway. You have zero leverage over him."

"Zero leverage," Martinez agreed. "He has no reason to tell us anything. In fact, he has every reason to tell us nothing."

"That's why you brought me here. You want me to sweet-talk him into revealing whatever it is he knows about Maddison's disappearance before his sentence ends and he's let out of here."

"Sure," said Martinez without an ounce of shame. "It helps that he's a fan of your podcast. He'll be flattered that you came to see him. There's a good chance that he'll trip up and tell you something that helps move this investigation forward. I just have one request."

"What is it?"

"Don't let him know that Maddison is missing."

"You want me to lie to him?"

"Let him believe that Maddison contacted you just like he instructed her to when they met in prison. I'm hoping he'll spill the beans to you. I need to know why Bailey told Maddison to find you. There's a good chance it's connected to her disappearance."

"So you *do* want me to lie," Rachel confirmed, making no effort to hide her scorn.

"Do white lies count?" he asked.

"I won't lie for the FBI," Rachel said flatly.

"All you need to do is let Bailey think that Maddison asked you to come here and talk with him. If Bailey wants to spill his guts, then great. If he doesn't say anything, then he doesn't. Nobody is putting screws to the guy. There's no moral dilemma here, Rachel."

"There is for me," said Rachel. "I don't work for you, Joe. I'm not law enforcement. I'm a reporter. It's unethical for me to deliberately mislead someone to help the FBI with a case."

"I don't know about you, Rachel, but I tend to put ethics aside when me feeling good about my principles might cost someone her life."

"Don't guilt-trip me, Joe."

"It's not a guilt trip, Rachel. It's the truth. Maddison's survival may well depend on how successful you are at getting Terence Bailey to talk."

"I have a question for you, Joe," said Rachel sweetly.

"Go ahead."

"Has anyone ever accused you of being an asshole? I'm asking for a friend," she added, stepping aside as two prison guards passed by.

"I've been called a whole lot worse," he answered amiably.

"Why am I not surprised!" Rachel studied his grim expression. He wasn't messing with her. Maddison's life was in danger. Martinez really did need Rachel's help.

"Why would Terence Bailey know anything about Maddison's disappearance?" Rachel challenged him. "He's been stuck in prison for six years. It's probably a coincidence that Maddison visited him right before she went missing. After all, you said it yourself, she was staying at a remote campsite inside the state forest. She was probably taken by a stranger who stumbled onto her camper van."

"Do you believe in coincidences, Rachel?" Martinez asked.

"Not as a general rule."

"I don't believe that Maddison Logan's meeting with Terence Bailey hours before she disappeared is even remotely coincidental. It's connected. The question is how."

Martinez rubbed the back of his neck as he spoke. It was the first real indication that Rachel had seen of the immense stress he was under. "I believe that Terence Bailey either instigated Maddison's disappearance, or he knows who did," he said. "Right now, our only chance of finding Maddison alive is for you to get Bailey to tell us what he knows."

Chapter 15

Joe Martinez was relieved when Rachel Krall agreed to meet with Terence Bailey. It was the outcome that he'd hoped for. He'd bet big on Rachel. She was the only real lead that he had, which is why he'd pulled out all the stops to have her quickly flown down to Florida.

His team was working on many fronts. He had people reviewing traffic camera footage to retrace Maddison's movements in the days and hours before her disappearance. There were K9 teams in the field. He had people back in Quantico reconstructing Maddison's digital footprints based on her social media posts. Forensic teams were working through the physical evidence in the lab. There was no doubt that at least some of those lines of investigation would produce results. In time.

The problem was that Martinez was fast running out of it. Statistically, the first three days were the most crucial in abduction cases. After seventy-two hours, the chance of finding the subject alive plunged close to zero. Every hour that passed made it more likely that Maddison would be dead before they had a breakthrough in the case.

That's why Joe had invested so much in preparing Rachel. By briefing her on the intricacies of the case, Martinez hoped that Rachel would get too entangled to walk away. Martinez made sure to let Rachel go through

Maddison's Instagram feed so that Maddison wasn't just a name, but a face and even more importantly, a person, one whose life Rachel held in her hands.

"The guard will take you to the visitors' area at Bailey's cellblock." Martinez nodded toward a thick-necked prison guard with a buzz cut who was waiting a respectful distance away.

"You're not coming?" Rachel asked.

"Felons can sniff out a federal agent from a hundred yards. From my experience it has the unfortunate tendency of rendering them mute."

Martinez had played his own version of hardball with Rachel. He didn't feel bad about it. He'd done much worse. The stakes were high. Not just for Maddison, but for Rachel. Terence Bailey was getting out of prison in a couple of days. Even though Martinez reassured himself that Rachel wouldn't be in danger, he knew it wasn't that simple.

Joe Martinez had lied to Rachel by omission. He hadn't told Rachel the details of the murders that Terence Bailey was suspected of committing before he was locked up on unrelated charges. Local homicide detectives who'd investigated a string of abductions and murders of young women years earlier were convinced that Bailey was the killer.

"Terence Bailey is a cold-blooded serial killer who murders as instinctively as he breathes," a detective had told Martinez that morning. He said their working theory was that Bailey hadn't acted alone. There had been an accomplice.

The way Maddison was snatched from her van not long after meeting Bailey suggested there was something to that theory. It was entirely possible that Bailey had alerted his old accomplice via a cell phone. Despite the myriad of security measures at the prison, Martinez had it on good authority that burner phones circulated among the inmates along with other contraband.

"Get Bailey talking while telling him as little as possible," Martinez instructed Rachel. "Inmates are so starved for conversation that once they start talking, they don't shut up," he said. "You'll be seated at a table with a hidden microphone. It definitely works. Agent Torreno checked it. So don't worry if you don't remember all the details of the conversation. We'll be recording everything in case Bailey says something valuable."

"Should I say anything about Maddison?" Rachel asked.

"Throw in her name. See what reaction you get. But don't divulge details. We don't want him to know that she's disappeared. Got it?"

Rachel nodded toward the guard to let him know that she was ready. "Let's get this done."

"Remember, our goal is for Bailey to slip up and accidentally mention something that will help us find Maddison."

Rachel's eyes met Joe's. She swallowed hard. He held her gaze, nodding reassuringly. Sensing that it might not be enough, he reached out and gently squeezed her shoulders.

"You'll do great, Rachel. If you feel unsafe, or threatened in any way, just signal to the guard and get the hell out of there. Okay?"

"Sure," Rachel answered confidently.

"You're doing us a big favor, Rachel. After this is over, we should get together. Have a few drinks so I can thank you for being such a good sport," he added quickly, so the invitation wouldn't be misconstrued.

"You could thank me over the phone. Or by email." Rachel smiled through her nerves.

"I could," he agreed. "But it wouldn't be half as fun." He smiled back despite himself. It felt strange, like shoes that hadn't been worn for a long time.

Rachel Krall's name had first come up when the lab deciphered the message that Bailey wrote during his meeting with Maddison. Martinez immediately instructed one of his hotshot analysts to pull together background information on Rachel. There were plenty of news and magazine articles about her in the file he was given. Most were flattering. A few accused her of ghoulishly fueling a national obsession with true crime to build her brand as a podcaster.

The moment that Martinez met Rachel at the entrance to the prison, he'd seen that she was so much more than the sum of the media articles about her. As for the husky bedroom voice mentioned in one of the articles in the dossier, he had to admit that the reviewer had been scarily accurate with that observation. The only thing the reviewer had missed was that Rachel Krall's sexy voice had nothing on the rest of her.

"Goodbye, Joe. I'll see you on the other side," said Rachel, following the guard.

Martinez stood back, his hands in his pants pockets, watching Rachel and the guard disappear down a corridor. He did not believe that Terence Bailey would be a threat to her. Not with two days left of his sentence. Bailey was too smart to risk extending his stay in prison.

It was what would happen after Bailey got out that worried Martinez. He hoped that, along with finding Maddison, his team would find something that connected Bailey to her disappearance. Even a hint of evidence would be enough for Martinez to get a court order to keep Bailey in prison, mired in legal red tape until he was brought to trial on fresh charges. Rachel would never be in any danger.

The prison operations room was a long room with monitors of various sizes lining an entire wall. Prison officers sat at desks facing the screens, keeping a watchful eye on the movements of guards and inmates around the prison grounds. In reality, they often kept one eye on the surveillance monitors and the other on their phone screens.

Martinez headed to the main desk where Torreno was sitting at a high-backed desk chair, cradling a coffee mug. The footage from the cellblock visitors' area CCTV camera was displayed on one of two large monitors in front of him. They'd calibrated the angles of the cameras so they'd get a clear shot of both Rachel's face and Bailey's while they met. Martinez wanted to observe Bailey's tics when he met Rachel, and analyze the body language clues that he'd spent his whole career mastering.

The low-security prisoners, of which Bailey was one by virtue of the fact that he was about to be released, met their visitors in a converted holding cell on the ground floor of the low-security prisoner block. It looked like a giant lion's cage from the old days when zoos had barred enclosures. Inside the long rectangular space were round metal tables where the inmates met their visitors as a guard walked among them, making sure nothing untoward happened.

"Here she comes," Martinez said when Rachel came into view on the monitor.

Her pensive face filled the first screen as she sat at the small round metal table that had been set aside for her meeting with Bailey. She tugged at a piece of loose thread from her shirt as she waited. Martinez read it as a nervous gesture.

His cell phone rang in his pocket. He answered it, getting up and pacing the room while keeping an eye on the screens. Rachel's face was slightly upturned as if she was looking toward the camera for reassurance from him. The other screen showed footage of an empty chair. Bailey still hadn't arrived. He was being brought over from laundry duty at the other side of the prison compound.

"We're about to rock and roll," Torreno called out, gesturing to another CCTV monitor on the wall. It displayed grainy black-and-white footage of a prison guard escorting Terence Bailey to the table where Rachel sat waiting for him.

Martinez abruptly ended his call. He leaned across the desk so that he was close to the monitor screen. He wanted to see Bailey's reaction when he found out that he was meeting Rachel Krall, the famous podcaster who he'd told Maddison to contact before she disappeared.

Satisfaction flashed fleetingly on Bailey's face when Rachel introduced herself. It was the smug expression of a man who'd gotten exactly what he wanted. It came and went so quickly that most people wouldn't have noticed it. Martinez noticed. He'd given Bailey what he'd wanted. An audience with Rachel Krall. Now all Joe could do was hope that Bailey would spill his guts.

Martinez checked his watch. He'd told the caller that he'd leave immediately. He stood up abruptly and asked Torreno for the car key.

"You're bailing just as all the fun is starting?" Torreno glanced up from the screen.

"Call me with an update once it's over," Martinez instructed without providing any explanation for his sudden departure.

Torreno tossed him the key. Martinez snatched it in mid-air and then grabbed his jacket off the back of the seat. He took one last look at Rachel's face on the CCTV monitor as he let himself out.

Chapter 16

Over the years, the stench of male perspiration and stale urine had seeped into the walls and concrete floors of the low-security cellblock so that no amount of lye soap or bleach would remove the pungent odor. It was the smell of incarceration. The choking stench of prison.

Rachel noticed it immediately as she stepped into the building. Somewhere upstairs, a cell door crashed shut with a chilling clang. It was followed by a steady tap of footsteps. Rachel instinctively craned her neck and looked up at the metal walkways running along the internal atrium of the three-story concrete cellblock.

The guard led Rachel to a visiting area near the ground-floor entrance. It was in an enormous holding cell, with jail bars as walls. It had been repurposed as a visitors' area for the cellblock inmates.

Rachel took a seat at a small metal table. While she waited for Bailey, she glanced up at the security camera above her head. She could feel Joe Martinez watching her. She looked away self-consciously.

The rattle of metal shackles announced Bailey's arrival. Rachel squared her shoulders, bracing herself for the meeting. She stared ahead as the guard escorted him to the table. It took everything she had to show no outward sign of nerves as Bailey shuffled toward her, his movements impeded by his shackles.

His shadow loomed over the table as he arrived. He was an imposing man in height and build. He was so muscular that his orange prison coveralls were pulled tight over his thick arms and barrel chest. His hair was light brown. He had a beard the same color. It could have done with a trim. He looked older than his twenty-something years—cynical, and hard-bitten. His gaze was bitter and world-weary. Rachel supposed that prison aged a person's soul.

The guard roughly pushed him down by the shoulders onto the metal stool opposite Rachel. Once he was seated, Bailey's eyes looked directly into hers. They were pale blue. Ice-cold. Rachel swallowed her discomfort and stared at him for an unnerving moment before the guard reached out to lock Bailey's cuffs into metal rings screwed into the table.

"Is that necessary?" Rachel asked the guard.

"This is a low-security wing, so it's up to you, ma'am." The prison guard waited for her to decide.

"In that case, leave him as he is, please," Rachel said, against her better judgment. She had no doubt that Terence Bailey could lunge toward her and snap her neck with his powerful hands if the mood struck him.

Bailey's pupils narrowed into angry pinpoints. "Am I supposed to be grateful?"

"Not unless you want to be."

He glared at her. His pale eyes burned with resentment, and something else. Curiosity.

"Who are you?" he asked.

"My name is Rachel Krall."

A satisfied smile slowly spread across his face. "You don't look a bit like I thought."

"What did you expect?"

"A blonde. A hot blonde. You're better looking." He nodded to himself, his tone approving. "Heck, after six years in this joint, they could bring me an eighty-year-old woman with chin whiskers and I'd still think she was hot."

"Well, that's a backhanded compliment if I ever heard one," said Rachel lightly.

He flashed a cocky smile. It made him look surprisingly boyish. He rubbed his beard with his knuckles. "If I'd known that you were coming to see me, I'd have shaved. Maybe even ironed my clothes. That's what some of the other guys do when they get visitors," he said, smoothing the fabric of his lapel.

Orange wasn't Terence Bailey's color. It was loud and garish against his pasty skin, pale from a lack of regular sunlight. His sleeves were rolled to the elbow to expose a clever monochrome tattoo in blue ink on his left forearm. There was another tattoo on his neck. He must have done them himself with the ink of a ballpoint pen. Rachel couldn't imagine how he'd managed to work through the pain to tattoo himself.

Rachel sensed a rage simmering under the genial surface, disguised by the flash of a cheeky grin. She needed to be wary. She sensed his moods were like volatile weather patterns that could change at any time.

"I hear you're getting out soon?" Rachel grappled to get the conversation onto a safe footing. She looked down at his cuffed hands. A bandage wrapped around his left hand was getting loose.

"Two more days."

"Do you have plans to celebrate when you get out?"

"I'll get myself to a steak restaurant. Order the biggest T-bone they have on the menu. With a beer. Might even find myself a lady. No point eating alone." A spasm of anger ran across his face. "I shouldn't plan ahead. This place has a way of sucking you back in."

"Two days isn't long," Rachel pointed out. "What could possibly happen between now and then?"

"Have you ever been in prison?" Rachel shook her head. "I won't believe I'm free until I'm standing outside the prison gates. The parole board has rejected me every time. Always an excuse. I was a model prisoner. Didn't put a foot wrong. Except once, and that wasn't my fault."

He changed the subject abruptly. "You're the second proper visitor I've had since they locked me up in here. Never had visitors excepting for my cheating lawyer. And he charged by the hour. All these years and just as I'm leaving, two pretty ladies turn up. Suddenly I'm Mr. Popularity." He licked his chapped lips. "The good Lord does work in mysterious ways," he said sarcastically. His unblinking gaze made his attempts at humor chilling rather than cute.

Rachel presumed the other female visitor was Maddison. She decided not to ask. Yet.

"Every man here will be jealous as hell that you've come to see me. The famous Rachel Krall."

"I'm hardly a celebrity."

"You're better than a celebrity." He nodded to reinforce the truth of his statement. "When the wives and girlfriends stop writing and visiting, the men turn to praying to Jesus, and to you, Rachel."

"Why me?"

"Most of the men locked up here are lifers. The only chance they have left is if you cover their case for your podcast and get them a new trial. Like what you did for that coach." He shifted on the metal stool.

"He went free because he was innocent," said Rachel. "I'm betting you can't say that about most of the men here."

"Probably not," he admitted.

"What about you? Have you ever written to me?" Rachel asked.

"Once. I ripped it up. Never sent it."

"Why not?"

"Wasn't sure I could trust you." His eyes bored into Rachel.

He leaned forward intimidatingly. The prison guard pacing around the metal tables swung around in their direction when he heard Bailey's manacles rattle from the sudden movement.

"Can I trust you, Rachel?" Bailey's voice was as soft as a ghost in the night.

"That's up to you," Rachel said impassively, refusing to be intimidated.

"I don't think so," he said, leaning back again. "I've learned the hard way not to trust anyone. The few times I did . . ." He laughed to himself. "Let's say things didn't exactly work out."

"I'm sorry to hear that."

He scratched the bandage wrapped around his hand. The handcuffs rattled with each scratch. "Maybe I should tell you?" He paused. "Nah, you wouldn't believe me." This time his laugh was bitter.

"Try me."

"The prison brought in an art teacher to give classes to the inmates. Mr. Hendley."

Bailey told Rachel that he'd joined the class out of boredom. He'd never drawn in his life, and he'd had no real interest in learning. The classes were a diversion from the soul-crushing routine of prison. A chance to get out of work duties, or escape the four walls of his stark cell.

"I wasn't planning on enjoying it. But I did. I got good. Pretty damn good," he said. "It was around that time that I felt this need to tell someone. To get it off my chest. A man can only carry a burden like that for so long." He paused. "I wanted someone else to know. In case something happened to me. I decided to tell Mr. Hendley. He was the only one who treated me like I was worth something."

He was silent again, lost in his own thoughts.

"You confided in him?" Rachel prompted.

"In a manner of speaking. As it turned out, he wasn't around long enough to be much use." He scratched the bandage on his hand.

"What happened to him?"

"This big Russian guy, who I heard was a hitman for the mob way back when, got offended by Mr. Hendley's feedback on his watercolor painting. He tried to poke Mr. Hendley's eye out with the pointy end of a fine paintbrush. Mr. Hendley never came back. That was the end of art classes. No more rehabilitation." He pronounced each syllable so the word "rehabilitation" sounded like a curse.

"I saw your portrait of the warden and some of your other paintings on the way over here," Rachel said. "They're good. Very good, in fact."

He smiled. "There's a lot more to a painting than what meets the eye."

"What do you mean?" Rachel asked.

"You're a clever woman, Rachel." He smiled knowingly as he talked in circles.

Rachel suspected that he was trying to tell her something without coming out and saying it. Maybe he was being circumspect because he knew their conversation was being recorded by the prison.

"They give me a few boring colors and some canvases that I have to reuse. One painting over the next." His cuffs rattled as he scratched the back of his hand again. The loose bandage partly fell off, exposing a tattoo in black ink. At first glance, it looked like an infinity symbol. At second glance, Rachel realized the symbol was formed by a snake eating its own tail. It was intricate. Remarkable in its detail for a homemade prison tattoo.

Bailey noticed Rachel's eyes on the tattoo. He hastily pulled the bandage back in place like he was hiding something. "Why did you really come here, Rachel?"

"Maddison Logan," she responded succinctly. Joe Martinez had suggested that Rachel throw out Maddison's name and see what happened. That's exactly what she did.

Bailey's expression turned to ice at the mention of the missing influencer's name. "Maddison who?" His body was rigid. His tone hostile.

Rachel did a double take. This was not the reaction that she'd expected. "Two days ago, you instructed Maddison to contact me. Well, here I am."

He stared at Rachel.

"Why did you tell her to contact me?" Rachel pressed on, ignoring his pointed question. He looked like he was about to explode.

"Something stinks," he erupted. "If you'd really spoken to her, then you'd know everything. You wouldn't be here asking stupid questions."

Bailey raised his voice loudly enough that the guard spun around and warned him to keep it down. Bailey looked at Rachel derisively. "You bastards never give up. You'll do anything to keep me here. You'll even pretend to be a famous podcaster. You're not Rachel Krall. I'm betting you're an undercover cop."

"I'm not a cop," said Rachel.

"Prove it."

"I can't. Not right now. I had to check in my purse when I came to the prison." Rachel had no proof to offer him except her word that she was who she said she was.

"That's what I figured," he said skeptically. "Get me out of here," Bailey called out to the guard, pushing back against the table as he rose. "Get me the hell out of here." If the metal table hadn't been screwed into the concrete floor then he'd have tipped it over from sheer rage.

"Shut up or we'll take away your privileges," the guard threatened as he shackled Bailey.

"What privileges, man? I'm getting out of here in two days. Free and clear," Bailey said as the guard roughly pushed him toward the door. Bailey smugly shuffled away, his shackles rattling as he walked.

He halted for a fraction of a second near the doorway and called out something to Rachel. Whatever he said was muffled by the clatter of his shackles and the crash of an iron cell door slamming somewhere in the cellblock.

He went up the metal stairs and along a walkway on the floor above. The clang of Bailey's cell door closing somewhere upstairs reverberated as Rachel stepped out of the cellblock into blindingly bright sunshine.

"He said something to me before he left," Rachel told the guard as they walked back to the main building. "You were standing near him. Did you hear what he said?"

"Yes, ma'am, I did."

"Well? What was it?" Rachel pressed.

"I don't know if I should say."

"Why not?"

"Because it may give you nightmares."

Chapter 17

Special Agent Joe Martinez wasn't waiting to debrief Rachel when she arrived at the VIP visitors' building where she'd checked in earlier. Agent Mark Torreno was waiting for her instead. He was leaning casually against the counter, texting on his phone as the guard led Rachel inside.

Without saying a word to Rachel, Torreno raised his hand impatiently to signal to the prison clerk that they were ready to retrieve their belongings.

"Aren't you going to ask me how it went?" Rachel was surprised at Torreno's palpable disinterest, given how much had been riding on her meeting with Terence Bailey. Joe Martinez had emphasized that repeatedly.

"Sure. How did it go?" he parroted Rachel's question, still texting.

"Not well," Rachel answered. "But I guess you know. I assume you watched it all unfold on surveillance cameras?"

"I watched it. It's unfortunate that Bailey didn't say anything, but it was still worth a shot."

Torreno's low-key reaction surprised Rachel. What surprised her even more was that Joe Martinez wasn't there.

"Where's Joe?" Rachel asked as the clerk retrieved her belongings from a locker behind the counter.

"Special Agent Martinez has been called away," Torreno said. "He sends his apologies."

The clerk put Rachel's purse and other belongings down on the counter with a thud and then stepped over to assist Torreno.

"What's going on?" Rachel asked, scooping up her phone and purse.

Torreno didn't answer as he signed paperwork to reclaim his Glock.

"You said Joe was called away, but you never said where," Rachel said.

"It's not up to me to say," Torreno said. He collected his gun and strapped it into his shoulder holster. He looked like a man in a hurry.

As they headed out of the building, Rachel peeled the visitor's sticker from her shirt. She paused to put on her sunglasses before leaving the building with Torreno. He was once again too immersed in texting to talk.

Visiting hours had come and gone. The parking lot was empty. There were no family members waiting restlessly in line for a prison visit.

To hell with him, Rachel thought to herself. She wouldn't tell Torreno about the strange comment that Bailey had made as he'd stormed away.

They walked along the pathway to the parking area where Rachel's rental car was baking under the full heat of the afternoon sun, burning down relentlessly from a cloudless sky. Rachel was disappointed by her failure to extract any information from Bailey at all.

"We could try again tomorrow," Rachel offered. "I could meet Bailey again first thing in the morning. This time I'll tell him the truth about Maddison disappearing. He might be more willing to talk if he knows that I'm being honest with him."

"We appreciate the offer," said Torreno, choosing his words carefully. "We don't think that Bailey will come around. It's best that you head home and we take it from here."

Rachel glanced at him. She could tell when she was being sold a line. "So that's it then? I head on home like a good girl now that the FBI has decided to dispense with my services?"

"Agent Martinez asked me to thank you on his behalf for coming down today," Torreno responded robotically, like he was reading from a script. "He is sorry that he couldn't say goodbye himself. He asked me to let you know that he will definitely be in touch when this is all over."

"What about Maddison?" Rachel was surprised at how deflated she felt by Torreno's dismissiveness. "I thought Bailey was your only lead. How are you going to find Maddison now if you have no leads?"

Torreno once again became immersed in texting. His newfound reticence riled Rachel. All of a sudden she was being frozen out.

"You're booked on the 10:20 P.M. flight from Orlando," Torreno said, running through the logistics of her departure with the efficiency of a travel agent. "You're on a flexible ticket. You could head on over to the airport and fly home on standby now. I checked. There are several spare seats. Or you could stick with the original departure time. That gives you a few hours to sightsee or relax on a beach. Get yourself a nice meal. We're covering your expenses."

Rachel gritted her teeth. She hated being patronized. "Relaxing on a beach sounds wonderful. Maybe I'll get drunk on fruity cocktails with cute umbrellas stuck in morello cherries. I'm a sucker for fruity cocktails," she remarked. "And morello cherries."

If Torreno noticed her sarcasm, then he didn't show it. They said their goodbyes and Rachel headed to her car. Torreno went in the other direction, walking toward the prison boom gates. There was a parking area outside the prison compound that had been full when she'd arrived. Rachel assumed that was where he'd parked his car.

Before driving off, Rachel turned on the engine to cool the sweltering car. She took a notepad from her purse and jotted down her impressions of her meeting with Bailey. Rachel planned to write and record a special report for her podcast once the Maddison Logan case was resolved, hopefully with the happy outcome of Maddison being found safe and sound.

It was early days yet and Rachel had no idea what direction the podcast would take, so she jotted down everything she remembered from her visit to the prison. She always kept meticulous notes. It helped her keep track of small, easily forgettable details that might turn out to be important.

She drew the tattoo she'd glimpsed on Bailey's hand from memory. It wasn't a very good illustration but it would be enough to prompt her memory when she looked back at it.

Finally she wrote down Bailey's chilling warning, which had been drowned out by background noise of the cellblock. During their walk back to the visitors' area, Rachel had convinced the prison guard to reveal what Terence Bailey had called out as he was taken away.

"The scariest monster is the one that hides in plain sight."

Chapter 18

Identifying the young woman whose body Owen Bragg found propped up against a pine tree on the ridge in the state forest was not a simple task.

No phone or purse was found. There was no driver's license in her jeans pockets. She wore no jewelry.

Her palms were badly burned. The killer had poured lighter fluid on them to make sure her fingerprints were destroyed when he'd set fire to her body. The only reason her body wasn't burned beyond recognition was because it rained shortly after the fire was set, presumably while the killer headed down the ridge.

The forensic pathologist who conducted the autopsy did not think the victim was a runaway. Her body did not have the usual signs of someone who'd been living on the street. She was well-groomed. She had no needle marks or other signs of drug use. There were no old bruises or healed bone breakages indicating physical abuse. There were no obvious signs that she'd been sleeping in the rough. If anything, the pathologist's general impression was quite the opposite, as he told me when I met him at his office.

"She seemed to be well looked after. Well fed. Well cared for. I kept thinking that somewhere out there was a family that must have been worried sick about her. And for good reason."

All the police had was her basic physical description. She was a teenage girl, probably around seventeen to eighteen years of age. African-American. She was slim and of medium height, a fit and healthy young woman with a lifetime of living ahead of her until she'd been stabbed to death in a violent frenzy.

This teenager, who Owen had memorialized as "Unknown Girl" on the tree trunk where she'd been found, had suffered an unimaginably brutal death.

The forensic pathologist counted fourteen knife wounds, mostly to her abdomen. Some of the knife wounds chipped ribs. One knife wound was so deep that it partially severed her spinal cord. There was no indication of sexual assault.

Bruising around her neck suggested that she'd been choked for long enough to render her unconscious. The lack of any significant defensive wounds on her hands, palms, and forearms supported the theory that the killer had choked her until she was unconscious before launching the frenzied knife attack.

There were abrasions on her skin from the ropes binding her wrists and ankles. The bruising from the ropes indicated that she'd been tied up for some time before her death.

The murder weapon was likely a large serrated knife, possibly a hunting knife of the type commonly bought at outdoor adventure stores.

The victim might never have been found if Owen hadn't noticed the thin plume of smoke rising from a remote corner of the forest on that fateful early morning.

Instead, her body would have eventually been devoured by jackals and other scavengers. Maybe, one day in the distant future, a hiker heading up to the lookout point on the ridge would have found a human bone. It might have led to a search but it would never have recovered anything that would have told the authorities who she was, or what had happened to her.

Nature would have erased all trace of her. Her family left in a permanent limbo of grief, never knowing. Never having a grave to visit. Never being able to say goodbye.

It was fortunate that Owen Bragg found the body. It was luckier still when an attentive forensic technician found a tiny fragment of evidence with the potential to blow the case open.

Chapter 19

The boom gate rose up and Rachel drove out of the prison compound. She passed a bus stop where a man stood under a slither of shadow offered by the shelter. Rachel guessed the metal bus stop seat was too hot to sit on. It was only as Rachel drove past that she got a better look at the poor passenger waiting in the afternoon heat. It was Agent Torreno.

Rachel stopped the car with a sudden screech of brakes and reversed until the car was lined up with the bus stop. She lowered the car window.

"We really need to stop bumping into each other like this."

"Joe took the car," he explained ruefully. Sweat glistened on his face. The sun was scorching, and the paltry strip of shade was getting thinner by the second.

"Want a ride?" Rachel offered.

Torreno was visibly reluctant, looking down the road as if hoping a bus or taxi would miraculously appear. Sweat poured down his forehead. He brushed it away and loosened his tie as droplets dripped down his neck.

"Come on, jump in. I'll take you wherever you want to go," Rachel said. "My government minder tells me that I'm free for the rest of the day."

"All right," Torreno said grudgingly, the heat winning over his reluctance.

Following Torreno's directions, Rachel drove into the Delta Springs State Forest. The road twisted and turned for several miles until the car reached a fork. A tourist information sign on the right side of the fork pointed toward the campground where Maddison Logan had disappeared.

Torreno told Rachel to take the other road. It was narrow and poorly maintained. Loose asphalt crunched under the tires until the road turned into packed dirt.

A couple of miles down the bumpy potholed road they drove up an incline. At the top, they saw a plateau of wild fields running along an estuary to the banks of the oxbow lakes that separated the state forest from the prison. A K9 dog and handler came into view.

"Pull over," ordered Torreno when he saw the police dog. "I'll get out here. You can turn around and head on back."

He clearly didn't want Rachel going any farther down the road. That made her all the more determined to keep going. Rachel muttered that the road was too narrow for a U-turn and it would be easier to turn farther down the road where it widened at the bend. There wasn't anything Torreno could do to stop her.

As they drove past a thick crop of trees where the road curved, the view opened up. A white tarpaulin tent had been erected near the end of the field being searched by sniffer dogs. Several law enforcement vehicles were parked on the side of the road. A huddle of people stood around the tent.

"They found Maddison, didn't they?" Rachel asked in the quiet that followed once she cut the engine. Torreno unclipped his seat belt with a click and opened the car door.

"Thanks for coming down and for the ride," he said. He stepped out, shutting the door behind him.

Rachel rolled down her window. "You don't know me very well if you think you can leave me in the dark and send me on my merry way. That's not how this works."

"That's exactly how this works," he called out.

"I want to speak to Joe."

"Special Agent Martinez is too busy to talk right now. You'd better get going. Only authorized personnel are allowed in this area."

Torreno walked along an ad hoc pathway of crushed tall grass that had been stomped on by people going backward and forward toward the tarpaulin tent.

Rachel climbed out of her car. She closed the driver's door softly without locking it and followed a few yards behind Torreno, making sure to step in his tracks. The grind of a generator muffled the sound of her footsteps as she followed him toward the huddle of people working by the tarpaulin cover.

Agent Martinez was squatting on his haunches on the ground. He raised his head, turning to look in Torreno's direction as the younger agent approached.

It was Martinez who spotted Rachel first. Torreno was still unaware that Rachel hadn't driven off and that she was stomping through the grass behind him. Rachel was too far out of earshot to hear Martinez's exact words but she had a pretty good idea of what choice phrase he'd chosen. It was clear from his stormy expression that he was not happy to see her. He stood up abruptly and headed toward her.

"Didn't Agent Torreno tell you that you're free to go?"

"You found her?" Rachel asked, ignoring his question.

She stepped aside so she could get a better view of the scene by the tarpaulin. Forensic technicians worked around a muddy pit cordoned off with crime scene tape.

"We found *someone*," he responded.

"Is it Maddison?"

"We don't know yet. Most of the body is in thick mud. It will take the recovery team well into the night to get her out. That's why we're setting up spotlights and a generator."

"You said 'her.' So it is a woman?"

He nodded. "It's too early to say for sure whether it's Maddison. We're pretty sure it's a woman, probably on the young end of the spectrum, based on photos the cop who found her took before the body got pulled deeper into the mud. Her time of death is recent. Maybe within a day or two."

Logic would dictate that the body was indeed Maddison's. It was found only a few miles away from the campground where she'd disappeared.

"When will you know for sure?"

"It will take a while," he sighed. "The mud is acting like quicksand, which is causing us a lot of problems with the retrieval. The only identifying feature we have so far is a small snake tattoo on her hand. It's quite unique. We're hoping it will help us identify her." He looked over his shoulder at the team retrieving the body. "I should get back. We have a lot of work ahead of us."

"You said the victim had a snake tattoo," Rachel said. "Did the snake tattoo look anything like this?"

She scrambled in her handbag for her reporter's notebook and found the relevant page, holding it up so that Martinez could get a good look at the sketch of Terence Bailey's tattoo that she'd scribbled in the car. It was a snake coiled into an infinity symbol eating its own tail.

"Where did you get that from?" Martinez snatched Rachel's notebook and examined the drawing closely.

"Bailey had a bandage around his hand. He kept scratching it. Eventually the bandage slid down to reveal that tattoo. I drew the sketch of the tattoo afterward when I jotted down my impressions of the meeting."

"Wait here," he instructed.

Martinez took Rachel's notebook with him under the tarpaulin next to where a forensic crew was setting up a timber plank around the muddy pool where the body had been found.

Minutes passed. Rachel waited while Martinez conferred with his colleagues. He returned holding his iPad. When he reached Rachel, he zoomed into a close-up of a coin-sized tattoo on the victim's hand. He explained that the photo was taken by the K9 police handler shortly before the body sunk deep into the mud. He then held up Rachel's sketch of Terence Bailey's tattoo as a comparison.

"It's an exact match," he said.

Chapter 20

A dog barked in the distance. Rachel turned to see the sniffer dog team working in parallel lines, combing for evidence in the surrounding marshland.

Rachel studied Joe Martinez as he talked on the phone with his back to her. She detected an imperceptible change in his mood since they'd spoken at the prison. There, he'd done everything with an underlying urgency. He'd walked fast. Talked fast.

Now, he was contemplative and methodical. Checking and double-checking everything. Rachel guessed that it was the difference between running a missing persons investigation in which time was of the essence, and leading a murder investigation in which thoroughness was what counted.

In truth, Martinez had probably known all along that Maddison's fate had been sealed the moment she was snatched from her camper van.

"What's this sentence that you underlined in your notes? I can't read your shorthand properly," Martinez asked when he'd finished the call. He was holding out Rachel's reporter's notebook.

Rachel looked over his shoulder at the notebook. He pointed at her scribble above her sketch of Terence Bailey's infinity-shaped snake tattoo.

"It says, 'The scariest monster is the one that hides in plain sight,'" she said, deciphering her scrawl.

"Where the hell did you get that from?" Martinez asked.

"Terence Bailey said it just as he was taken back to his cell."

"It sounds like a threat."

"That's how I read it."

"It's time for you to head off, Rachel," Martinez said decisively. "This area is a crime scene. We can't have civilians here. I'm sure you understand."

"So it was okay to take me into the prison to see Terence Bailey. But now I'm too much of a civilian to be near your crime scene?" Rachel was annoyed at being summarily dismissed from the case.

"The investigation has moved into a new phase," said Martinez, without answering what he rightly took to be a rhetorical question. He walked alongside her down the pathway to her car. "We appreciate your time coming down here and all your help. We really do."

Like hell you do, Rachel thought to herself.

When they reached her car, Martinez gave her directions on the fastest way back to the main highway. "Have a safe flight home, Rachel."

He paused for a moment as if trying to decide whether to say something else. It was a strange, awkward hesitation that seemed uncharacteristic for a man so decisive. In the end, he opened the car door solicitously for Rachel. Once she'd climbed in, buckled up, and fired up the engine, he tapped the car roof twice before stepping away to let her drive off.

The gesture riled Rachel almost as much as being frozen out of the FBI's investigation. She turned off the engine, unbuckled her seat belt, and climbed out of the car.

"What's wrong now?" Martinez asked.

"Bailey didn't kill Maddison. He couldn't. He is in a maximum-security prison. Someone else did the killing and dumped her body here in this field. Bailey knows something. I could tell."

"What's your point?"

"I was establishing a decent rapport before Bailey caught me out in a lie about Maddison. Why don't I go back to the prison and talk to him again? This time I'll tell him the truth and bring my ID so he knows I am who I say I am."

"He stormed out. That seems to be a pretty conclusive sign that he won't play ball," said Martinez. "Besides, I don't like the idea of you seeing him again. Not after that threat about monsters he made when he left."

"Are you trying to protect me? Is that what this is all about?"

"Maybe," he conceded. "I took a risk bringing you down here. It didn't work. I don't want to put you in harm's way again."

"Harm's way?" Rachel scoffed. "The guy is in a maximum-security prison. You yourself told me that it's unescapable."

"He gets out in two days," Martinez reminded her grimly. "If Bailey's capable of even a fraction of the things that he's accused of doing, then you don't want to bump into him again once he's out on the street. Go home, Rachel."

"I don't work for the FBI. Where I choose to go and what I choose to do is entirely my own decision."

"Rachel," Martinez sighed. "This case has taken a tragic turn. I wish it had turned out differently. But it hasn't. As a result, we don't need any further assistance from you. Your ticket is flexible. You can get on an earlier flight. Head on home. I'll update you when there are any developments. Once we're ready to take this to the media, I will personally make sure you get an exclusive."

Rachel was offended that Joe Martinez thought all she cared about was getting an exclusive story. She'd watched Maddison's videos. She'd gone through reams of her photos. Maddison was an outgoing young woman who threw herself into life headfirst. She didn't deserve such a cruel death. Rachel looked toward the muddy pit where the forensic technicians were setting up winches to remove the body. She felt an overwhelming urge to find the bastard responsible for murdering Maddison.

"I guess that I'll see you when I see you, Joe," Rachel said, spinning around and returning to her car.

She drove away quickly with a screech of tires, passing Joe Martinez. He stood by the roadside watching her go with his hands in his pockets, still surprised by her sudden change of heart.

Rachel had no intention of taking an early flight. Once she'd driven out of the state forest, she turned toward Daytona Beach, the beach resort famous for its car racing and wild college spring break parties. It was also the place where Terence Bailey had been arrested for breaking and entering six years earlier.

Rachel had the rest of the afternoon and the evening to find out whatever she could about Maddison Logan and Terence Bailey. They knew each other. That much had been obvious from watching the CCTV footage of their meeting on the morning of Maddison's disappearance. How they knew each other would be Rachel's starting point.

As she drove, Rachel called Pete. She asked him to retrieve Bailey's indictment and any court records.

"Read me all the juicy bits," Rachel instructed when Pete called her back after pulling up the court records. Pete complied, quickly reading out choice excerpts. Rachel committed them to memory. When Pete was done, Rachel hung up and made a call to set up a meeting.

She was told to head to Café Hola near the Main Street Pier for a late lunch. Café Hola's candy-striped outdoor umbrellas were so eye-catching that they popped even against the neon swimwear of beachgoers, their bodies tanned and in some cases burned to a crisp as they walked along the boardwalk. Rollerbladers weaved among the crowds, handing out "happy hour" flyers.

A shirtless Rollerblader wearing oversized white headphones came around a sharp corner at full speed. He almost bumped into Rachel as she navigated around a crush of tourists bopping to Cuban music played by a trio of musicians near the Main Street Pier. The long rickety jetty was a well-known landmark and popular "selfie" backdrop.

"Watch it," he bellowed, like it was Rachel's fault, before speeding off.

Rachel chose a small table for two set away from the other tables outside the café with its prominent pink-striped sun shades. Rachel's phone rang as the waitress handed her a menu. It was Joe Martinez.

"Do you have an ID on the body?" Rachel presumed that was the reason for his call.

"Not yet," he said. "We're still working on it. I called to see whether you got on an earlier flight?"

"I'm still booked on my scheduled flight," Rachel answered.

"Good." He sounded relieved to hear that she was still intending to fly home.

Rachel wasn't sure whether to be flattered that he was checking up on her, or put out that he seemed so damn determined to get rid of her.

Chapter 21

Joe Martinez watched Rachel Krall's car drive off along the winding forest road before he returned to the crime scene, where the forensic team was hard at work. Getting the body out of the mud pool was turning into a highly technical and painstakingly slow operation.

Martinez had been at the burial site ever since he'd received the call from the K9 team commander just as Rachel's meeting with Terence Bailey began.

Since daybreak that morning, units of sniffer dogs and cadaver dogs had been moving in parallel lines across acres of fields lying between the campground and the prison. They were searching for Maddison or her belongings, particularly her phone, which, like all smartphones, contained critical geolocation data and other information that might help crack the case.

The K9 teams worked slowly and methodically. The terrain was more dangerous than it looked. The area was swampy and riddled with boreholes hidden amidst fields of waist-high grass. Almost half a day had passed before the loud barking of a cadaver dog rang out across a field.

The dog sat next to a small expanse of mud. When a handler approached the canine, he noticed the outline of a body floating just under the surface of the mud. A hand had caught in a nettle bush. It was the only part of the body that was floating above the surface of the mud.

The dog's handler lay on his stomach near the edge. He took photos before reaching to pull the body onto the bank. It turned out to be a mistake. Within seconds, the body was sucked into a vortex of mud. It disappeared into what the rescuers quickly realized was a treacherous pool of quicksand.

After receiving a call from the K9 team leader to tell him that a body had been found, Martinez drove down to the field, leaving Agent Torreno to observe Rachel Krall's meeting with Bailey at the prison. Martinez intended to watch the video recording of the meeting later. Upon his arrival at the crime scene, Martinez ordered an immediate recovery operation. By then, Torreno had called with the disappointing news that Rachel's meeting with Terence Bailey had been "a washout."

"What do you want me to do with her, Joe?"

"Cut her loose. We don't need her anymore." Martinez had known that wasn't true even as he gave the instructions to send Rachel home.

As it turned out, Rachel had come to the scene anyway after giving Torreno a ride there. She'd have stayed, too, if Martinez hadn't insisted that she leave.

As Joe Martinez watched Rachel's car disappear in the distance, he knew that he'd made a mistake letting her go. The FBI agent in him was fully aware that he should have taken up Rachel's offer to meet Terence Bailey again, especially since the case had most likely turned from a missing persons investigation into a homicide investigation. He'd have liked to have observed Bailey's reaction when Rachel informed him that Madison had disappeared and that a body had been found near the prison. Martinez was trained at reading emotions. He'd be able to tell if the news surprised Bailey or if it was expected.

It was rare that Joe Martinez allowed his personal feelings to override his professional judgment. Despite this, Martinez couldn't bring himself to send Rachel back to see Bailey. He'd already dangled her like bait in front of a suspected serial killer. He didn't want to do it a second time and risk the possibility that Bailey would fixate on Rachel when he was on the outside. The only other person who'd visited Bailey in prison was dead, Martinez thought as he looked toward the crime scene. He didn't want to put Rachel's life at risk as well.

Martinez told himself that he was protecting Rachel because she was a civilian. He knew that explanation was a lie, although he couldn't bring himself to delve into the real reasons why he was being overprotective of her.

"The scariest monster is the one that hides in plain sight," Bailey had called out to Rachel as he'd stormed away. It was obviously a warning. As far as Joe Martinez was concerned, it was another good reason to make sure that Rachel Krall was as far away from Terence Bailey as humanly possible.

Forensic technicians in white plastic coveralls lay on a scaffold of timber planks placed around the pit, removing quicksand with small trowels. A few team members were sifting for evidence in a pile of sludge that had already been removed. It was going be one heck of a long day.

"I want prints taken as soon as you reach the victim's hands. Send them straight to the lab for comparison to the prints we found in Maddison's camper van," Martinez instructed. He needed an ID on the body as quickly as possible so he could officially switch the missing persons operation to a homicide investigation.

"Joe," Torreno called out after taking a call from the prison warden's office. "The cellblock guards found something in Bailey's cell that might interest you."

Torreno showed Martinez a photo of a pencil sketch of a teenage girl that Bailey had drawn in his sketchbook. It was recovered during a cell search while he'd been at laundry duty. The teenage girl in his sketch had dark spiky hair cut extremely short. She wore thick kohl eyeliner and black lipstick. There were piercings in her ears and nose, as well as a safety pin piercing in her eyebrow. The goth style did nothing to soften her plain round features.

Around her neck was a dark ribbon. Hanging off it, pressed into the hollow of her throat, was a pendant. It was in the shape of a snake entwined with itself so that it formed the infinity symbol. It looked identical to Rachel's drawing of Terence Bailey's tattoo as well as the tattoo on the hand of the victim found in the swamp.

"Tell the team at Quantico to run the sketch through the missing persons database," Martinez instructed. "I want to know if anyone fitting this girl's description is listed as missing. If she is, then I want to know every detail about her disappearance. What, when, where, and the names of all possible suspects. Cross-check all of that against Bailey's known movements at the same time."

"What makes you think she's an actual person?" Torreno asked. "Maybe the girl in the sketch is a figment of Bailey's imagination."

"I doubt it," said Martinez. "This drawing is too specific to be conjured out of thin air. I think this girl is real. I also think there's a chance that she may be another of Bailey's victims. This could be a breakthrough."

"You think this sketch will help us find Maddison?" Torreno asked.

"No," said Martinez. "It won't help with the Maddison Logan investigation, but it might save other lives."

He explained that if they could show that the goth-looking girl in Bailey's sketch was a real person who'd gone missing before Bailey went to prison, and they could connect him to her disappearance, then they might be able to keep Bailey behind bars on fresh charges.

Martinez's jaw clenched as he remembered the chilling smile that had spread over Bailey's face when he sat in front of Rachel Krall at the prison.

"Terence Bailey won't stop until he satisfies his bloodlust. From my experience, a man like that is never satisfied," said Martinez. "Quite honestly, the thought of Terence Bailey being out on the streets scares the hell out of me."

Chapter 22

"Are you Rachel Krall?"

Adam Derwent didn't look a bit like a lawyer. He wore dark jeans and a black Led Zeppelin T-shirt. Rachel recognized his gravel baritone from their brief conversation over the car speakerphone while she drove to Daytona. He was older than she expected. Early sixties. His hair needed clipping as did his beard, which was turning gray.

From the court records that Pete had read to her during the drive over, Rachel knew that Derwent had represented Terence Bailey on the original burglary charges. He didn't represent Bailey for the assault charge when Bailey attacked an inmate shortly before the end of his initial two-year sentence. A public attorney had handled that matter.

"It was obviously self-defense. But the public attorney didn't put up a fight," Pete had observed when Rachel spoke with him in the car. "The lawyer took it on the chin."

"Not his chin, either," Rachel had observed. "He took it on Terence Bailey's chin. Bailey got another four years behind bars. Double his original two-year sentence."

After hanging up the call with her producer, Rachel had immediately called Adam Derwent, figuring that Terence Bailey's original defense lawyer would be able to tell her things about his client's case, and by extension his client, that never made it into the court records. Derwent invited her to join him for a late lunch at Café Hola on the Daytona boardwalk.

Without looking at the menu, Derwent ordered a burger and fries. Rachel ordered the same. She hadn't eaten since breakfast on the plane. From Derwent's conversation with the waitress, Rachel gathered the lawyer was a regular at the restaurant, a divorcé, and that he was semi-retired. He was also a terrible flirt.

Rachel took a notebook and a pen from her purse while Derwent bantered with the waitress. Once the waitress had moved on to the next table, Rachel asked Derwent if he minded if she took notes while they talked, as she was working on a podcast and liked to keep accurate records of all her conversations when she did research.

Since she'd promised Joe Martinez to keep information about Madison Logan's abduction and presumed murder strictly confidential, she kept things vague when Derwent asked her what the podcast was about.

"I'm looking at a few angles, and one concerns a former client of yours," she said.

"Which one?"

"Terence Bailey." Rachel threw the name into the air.

Derwent's forehead creased like he had no idea who Rachel was talking about.

"You represented him six years ago," Rachel prompted.

Derwent squinted as he searched the filing cabinet of his mind. "Terry?" he asked tentatively. "Terry Bailey?" he added with more certainty.

Rachel nodded. "That's the one."

"You lost me when you said 'Terence.' Sure, I remember Terry."

"What can you tell me about him?" Rachel asked.

Derwent paused as the waitress brought him a beer. "He was a mechanic and an aspiring race car driver. He had a crappy childhood. Moved here when he was eighteen to get into auto racing. He happened to work at the auto shop where I take my car. Kyle McFein is the owner. He's the guy who hired me to defend Terry."

Derwent took a long sip of his beer before he went on to tell Rachel about how Kyle McFein had been a successful NASCAR driver until he'd retired and opened an auto shop that specialized in vintage and racing cars.

"Kyle called Terry 'the car whisperer.' The kid had a natural knack at figuring out what was wrong with a car engine. When Terry was arrested, Kyle asked me to sort it out. Told me to send him the bill. He said that Terry was 'worth his weight in gold.'"

"Kyle must have thought highly of him if he was prepared to fund his legal defense," Rachel noted.

Derwent nodded. "Kyle has three daughters. No sons. Terry was like a son to Kyle. They raced together on weekends. Fixed cars at the shop during the week. Terry assured Kyle that the breaking-and-entering arrest was a misunderstanding. That's why Kyle posted Terry's bail and hired me to sort it out. He believed Terry. Of course, Kyle fired Terry when he found out that he'd let a fox into his henhouse, so to speak."

"He fired him?" repeated Rachel, surprised at the sudden turn of events. One minute, McFein was paying Terence Bailey's legal costs and treating him like the son he never had, and the next he was kicking him onto the street. "What changed?"

"Well, as I recall, a few days after I got involved, a homicide detective turned up at Kyle's house. Took him aside and told him confidentially that Bailey was a suspect in the abductions and murders of several young women. The detective said that he didn't want Kyle's daughters to be in harm's way. He warned Kyle not to be taken in by Terry. He said that Terry was a classic psychopath: smart and manipulative. He described him as 'extremely dangerous.'"

Rachel didn't scare easily but she had felt very uneasy after meeting Bailey, and that was before she found out about his veiled threat to her as he was taken away by the guard.

"Technically Terry's never been charged for murder. Not enough evidence," said Derwent. "And the cops had no right to pressure Kyle to cut the purse strings by sharing wild and unsubstantiated theories. Personally,

I call that sort of thing witness tampering. Except it's legal when the cops do it," he added.

"Maybe the cops really were worried about the safety of Kyle's daughters," Rachel observed. "Who was Bailey suspected of killing?"

"Working girls. Disappeared while turning tricks. Their bodies were found dumped a few days later."

The waitress arrived with their burgers and fries. They both said nothing for a few minutes while they dug into their food.

"What made the cops think that Bailey murdered those women?"

"The breaking and entering that he was arrested for," said Derwent. "He broke into the apartment of a prostitute. He was caught red-handed in her bedroom. His hands were literally in her lingerie drawer when the police burst in," he added after a sip of beer.

"Seems tenuous at best to me. The police must have had more than that if they were going to publicly accuse him of murder," said Rachel.

"It was all circumstantial," said Derwent. "The working girls who were murdered complained about having lingerie stolen in the days before they disappeared."

"So, that was the link," said Rachel.

"It's not much of a connection." Derwent didn't hide his scorn. "All my ex-wives kept cash and jewelry in their lingerie drawers. I bet you do, too. I never understood how the police were able to connect those dots to the point where Terry became a prime murder suspect, to tell you the truth."

Derwent couldn't remember the name of the woman whose apartment Bailey had broken into, but Rachel knew. Pete had read it out to her from the court records. Her name was Jessica Hewitt. She'd worked as a waitress at a popular strip joint in Daytona.

Hewitt's rap sheet went all the way back to when she was a troubled teen from a broken home. Her life was short and tragic. She was found dead from an overdose a few days before her thirty-ninth birthday. The needle was still in her vein when her body was found in an alley behind the club where she worked.

"Are you aware that Hewitt died not long after Bailey was locked up?" Rachel asked.

"I did not know that." Derwent took a sip of beer. "It's not a major shocker. If memory serves me correct, she was more than a little rough around the edges. Walking on the wild side does tend to get you in the end."

According to the documents that Pete had found, Hewitt left work at the strip club halfway through her shift after arguing with her manager because she said he was too cheap to hire proper muscle at the bar. There was only one bouncer that night. Not enough to stop a drunk customer from roughing her up. She'd taken a cab back home.

When she arrived at her building, she saw from the street that her apartment lights were turned on. She was always careful to turn off her lights when she went out so she wasn't stuck with blowout bills. Money was short. What little of it she had, she generally snorted up her nose or shot into her veins.

She had assumed that her former pimp was waiting for her in the apartment. He'd threatened to beat her up if she didn't pay him protection money. She'd called 911 and reported a possible break-in. That's how the cops had burst into the apartment and found Terence Bailey rifling through Hewitt's bedroom dresser.

"They found a screwdriver in his pocket," said Derwent, leaning forward. "They charged Terry with armed burglary on account of that screwdriver. That moved it from a third-degree breaking-and-entering charge to first-degree armed robbery. Terry was facing a potential life sentence."

"A life sentence for taking a screwdriver on a break-in?" Rachel said.

"You betcha. If the prosecution can prove deadly intent." He waved a French fry in the air to illustrate his point before scarfing it down. "The DA claimed Bailey brought the screwdriver to use as a weapon against Jessica Hewitt when she returned home from work with her cash tips."

"You don't think that's true?"

"He used the screwdriver to unlock a window bolt. That's how he got into the apartment. It wasn't a weapon. It was a tool. It was bogus of the cops to ratchet up the charges. Terry was a first-time offender. Normally he'd have been given community service."

"But that didn't happen because the police suspected Bailey was behind those murders as well," Rachel prompted.

Derwent nodded. "They wanted to lock him up and throw away the key but all they had was that breaking-and-entering charge, so they went to town with it," agreed Derwent. "Terry was out on bail for a while after he was charged. He'd been fired by Kyle by then. Found himself a job at a gas station out of town while I negotiated a plea bargain."

Derwent's voice became more confident as he remembered. He recounted the details of his old case from six years earlier at a galloping pace. Rachel found herself struggling to keep up as she scribbled notes for the podcast that she was researching.

"The cop's case was piss-poor. In the end, they agreed to vanilla breaking and entering. No suspended sentence," Derwent said. "Terry Bailey got two years. The cops were happy. It bought them time to put a case together against him for the murders of those prostitutes."

Derwent paused to eat the rest of his burger, wiping the grease off his hands onto a napkin when he was done.

"But Bailey has never been charged for those murders. I presume there still isn't enough evidence," Rachel said.

"You got it!" He paused before taking another sip of beer. "Hey, why aren't you talking to Terry? He can tell you all of this better than me. He's been out of the slammer for years."

"That's not exactly how things turned out," Rachel said. At Derwent's obvious surprise, she added: "He got into a fight a few weeks before he was due to be released. He was jumped. Beat the other guy to a pulp. Lost all of his parole time and got more years added to his sentence for assault. He gets out of prison in a couple of days."

"I guess I shouldn't be so shocked," said Derwent. "I heard from my sources with the Daytona PD that the DA's office did everything it could to get Terry's plea rescinded. But the judge had already signed off on it."

"The DA tried to rescind the plea deal?" Rachel said in surprise. "What prompted the turnaround?"

"The body of another victim, a teenage girl, turned up while he was on bail," said Derwent. "Something about the way the body was dumped suggested a connection to the prostitute killings. Don't ask me what," he added. "The police have kept this case very hush-hush. Since the police thought Terry was good for the prostitute killings, on account of the fact that he was arrested going through the panty drawer of the Hewitt woman, they naturally assumed that he'd killed the teen as well. That's why they wanted to rescind the plea bargain."

They both looked out at the boardwalk where a juggler on stilts dressed as The Cat in the Hat was juggling red and green apples, occasionally taking bites from them while he tossed them up into the air.

"So the bottom line is that Terence Bailey was a suspect in a string of murders, including the murder of a teen whose body was discovered after his plea deal was signed, but he was never charged for any of the murders."

"That's about right," said Derwent as he ate the last of his fries. "I'm not saying he didn't do it. All I'm saying is there's no evidence that says he did."

"You sound like a defense attorney," Rachel quipped.

Derwent drained the rest of his beer. "It's my turn to ask you a question. What's your interest in Terry Bailey?"

"I visited the prison today," Rachel said, careful not to reveal too much. "I happened to meet Bailey while I was there. He's an interesting character, and I wanted to know more about him."

She told Derwent about Bailey's paintings of the warden and prison life and how they showed intelligence and great emotional depth.

"Terry is smart," Derwent agreed. "Maybe not book smart, but street smart. He learned from the best school around, the school of hard knocks. The sorts of things he's been through toughen a man. It might even desensitize him to violence."

Rachel gave a shiver as she remembered the volcanic rage she'd sensed simmering under the surface. It was as if he was filled with barely contained anger. Bailey's intelligence was in some ways even more frightening. A violent streak combined with smarts was a lethal combination.

"Terence Bailey gets out of jail in a couple of days. The cops suspect he's a serial killer. You asked me what my interest is in Terence Bailey," Rachel said. "My interest is in making sure that he doesn't hurt anyone else."

Chapter 23

Down on the sand, shirtless muscle-bound beach attendants collected beach umbrellas and pulled recliners into a storage shed. Beachgoers packed up and headed back to their hotels to rub cream into their sunburn and relax before dinner and a night partying at the clubs along the strip.

For Rachel, it was definitely a wrap. She stifled an exhausted yawn. The day had turned out entirely different from what she'd anticipated when she'd gone to sleep the night before, intending to catch up after an extended absence while covering the trial in Neapolis for the podcast.

Now, Rachel was halfway across the country at a boardwalk café in the clammy heat of Daytona Beach talking to a lawyer about his former client, Terence Bailey, a man she'd never heard of before, even though he apparently knew her.

Rachel looked out into the distance. Somewhere in the Delta Springs State Forest, forensic technicians were removing Maddison's body from a muddy grave near the prison where Bailey was incarcerated.

As Rachel subtly grilled Derwent over the remnants of their meal, she thought to herself that it was too much of a coincidence that after visiting an inmate suspected of abducting and murdering young women, Maddison met the same fate herself hours later.

"Did the police ever bring in Bailey for questioning about the sex worker killings?" Rachel asked Derwent. She was eager to know more about the crimes that he was suspected of committing.

"They questioned him all right. I was there," he said. "Terry insisted that he didn't know anything. He was very calm about the whole thing. He didn't break into a sweat the entire time he was questioned. The homicide detective who spoke to him called him 'ice man.'"

"Suggesting that was a sign of his guilt?" Rachel asked.

"It's a little-known fact that an innocent man accused of a crime he did not commit always gets way more scared than a guilty man accused of a crime he did commit."

Rachel thought about Terence Bailey's demeanor when she'd met him that morning. Despite his young age, there was a toughness to him, a seething anger that she suspected would sustain him through even the toughest police interrogations. It had sustained him through almost six years in prison. Fear did not come easily to that man.

"I'd like to talk to his parents," Rachel said. She wondered if Bailey's family could shed light on how he knew Maddison. Maybe she was a childhood friend, or an ex-girlfriend.

"Terry didn't have parents."

"Everyone has parents," said Rachel.

"Not Terry." Derwent vehemently shook his head. "He was abandoned at birth. He went through the foster care system and was spat out the other end."

"What about foster parents? Do you have their contact details?"

"Which foster parents?" asked Derwent. "Terry had so many foster parents that he lost count. Nobody came forward once he was arrested. Definitely nobody who cared about him enough to cover his unpaid legal bills. I had to write them off," he said with a trace of bitterness.

Rachel checked the time. She needed to leave if she was going to make her flight. Derwent signaled for the bill.

"I always worked hard for my clients, Rachel. Even the guilty ones. I would have gotten the charges dropped to community service if I'd found a single chink in the DA's armor. Terry had no priors. I had a lot to work with to make sure he didn't serve prison time."

"But you didn't get him off," Rachel pointed out.

"Not my fault. The cops were determined to lock him up. It didn't help that Terry refused to explain why he broke into that woman's apartment."

"Why do you think he broke in?"

"Your guess is as good as mine," sighed Derwent. "You know, Rachel, I could write a book about all the crazy-ass stories I hear from clients trying to explain why they broke the law. I usually tell them to shut their mouths or they'll get deeper into trouble. Terry was different. He gave me nothing to work with. Nada. It was the rare instance when a client talking could have helped his case."

"In the end, he served six years for what was originally a two-year sentence," Rachel observed.

"Six years for what should have been a suspended sentence," Derwent corrected her. "That worked out very well for law enforcement. Not so much for Terry." Derwent shook his head in disbelief.

"Are you suggesting that the cops set it up? That they arranged for a prisoner to attack him so that Bailey would hit back and get slugged with an assault charge that extended his sentence?"

"It wouldn't be the first time that something like that happened," said Derwent. "They probably figured they were doing us all a favor, keeping a killer behind bars."

Chapter 24

Thomas McCoy guns the engine impatiently as he waits by a row of ragged palm trees near the entrance to a cheap apartment popular with vacationing college kids. He's been waiting for his ride to come down for at least five minutes. The wait is costing him money.

Booking requests ping on the rideshare app. There are better fares. Other rides he could be locking in, and yet he's stuck waiting while these spoiled college kids take their sweet time. He calls the phone number again.

"It's your driver. What's the holdup?"

"We're coming down."

The airhead forgets to hang up. Over the phone line, he hears a door closing and the click of a lock. There's an echo of laughter and girly voices talking over each other at a rising pitch. An elevator pings before Thomas hangs up.

While he waits, he looks up the website for the Central Florida Correctional Facility. There's a tab with information for relatives or friends collecting an inmate on the day of release. Thomas pays careful attention to the detailed instructions.

Bailey gets out of prison in a couple of days. He wonders if Bailey will recognize him. It's been a while.

Laughter rings out by the main condo doors, which are being opened.

Three girls emerge, dressed for a night dancing at the clubs. They tease their hair with their fingers and pull at skimpy skirts as if in the final stages of getting dressed. He locks his phone and stuffs the fanny pack back in the glove compartment.

To hurry his passengers, he inches the car forward so they'll worry that he's about to drive off. It works. They stop preening and teeter toward the car in perilously high heels.

He guesses by the unflinching glassiness of their kohl-outlined eyes that they are already halfway drunk. It's the same story with so many of the college students he drives to and from the Daytona nightclubs. They get drunk on cheap liquor before they leave and come home high as a kite with ketamine and who knows what else in their system.

"How you all doing tonight?" he asks as they get in.

The girls mutter something unintelligible and slide into the back seat in a cloud of perfume and liquor. Slinky handbags hang over their shoulders. They hold sparkly phone cases in beautifully manicured hands as they scroll on their phones.

He watches the passengers through his rearview mirror. Their skirts are hiked up so high that he can see their panties. His breath quickens as he releases the hand brake and presses the gas. He moves the car forward so quickly they all jolt back in their seats. He chuckles to himself as they glance up in surprise before returning their attention to their phones. They barely notice that he exists. They'd give a dog more attention than they give him.

The car is silent other than the burr of the engine as they head to Daze. He's there at least once or twice a night, driving college students in various stages of inebriation to or from Daze and the other bars and dance clubs alongside it.

One of the girls takes out a flask and shares it with her friends. The car fills with the smell of cheap rum as he drives in fits and bursts through heavy neon-lit nighttime traffic.

When he pulls into a spot outside the club, the passengers all scramble out, slamming the car door behind them without any thanks. They join the back of the line of revelers waiting to be let inside by bouncers. One of the girls looks in his direction as he watches them through his open car window. She whispers something to the others.

The loud eruption of laughter is the last thing he hears as he drives away. He has a pretty good idea of what was said. He's spent a lifetime being the butt of other people's jokes. What those drunk girls think means nothing. He is capable of doing things that regular people don't have the nerve to do.

He can feel the inclination rise up in him like a thirst that needs quenching. He forces himself to resist. It's too soon. He has to pace himself.

Chapter 25

Rachel's producer had tried to call her several times while she was in the noisy café talking with Bailey's former lawyer. She called Pete back as she walked to her car rental parked a few blocks away under a palm tree.

Pete picked up after the first ring like he'd been waiting for her call. "I went through the podcast's messages to see whether Maddison Logan tried to contact you."

"And?"

"There was nothing," Pete said. "Until I checked the office phone. It turns out that Maddison left a voicemail for you. Based on the date and time of her message, she must have called right after she met Terence Bailey. I'll play it for you."

Rachel listened intently as Pete played the audio file of the voicemail message down the phone line. She immediately recognized the voice from Maddison's Instagram videos.

"I, uhm, called to speak to Rachel Krall. Rachel, my name's Maddison. Maddison Logan . . . I need your help. My friend. She was murdered. A long time ago. I know who killed her. He knows that I know. I think he's going to come for me and I am really scared. Terrified, actually. I'll try you again. Or email you. I want to tell you about it so at least someone knows in case something happens to me. . . ."

Rachel and Pete said nothing as the dial tone beeped after Maddison had hung up.

"So Maddison did come to me for help." Rachel broke the silence.

"Rach, it's my bad. I should be checking the messages more regularly."

"It's not your fault. I'm just sorry that I didn't get to speak to her," said Rachel. "Are you sure she didn't send a follow-up email?"

"I'm certain. I even checked the junk mail."

"She was probably abducted before she got around to emailing me."

"What are you going to do, Rach? You have to be at the airport in a couple of hours to check in for your flight."

"I'm not taking my flight," said Rachel decisively. "I'm staying. I'm due for a vacation. Might as well have one here."

"At Daytona Beach?" Pete asked in disbelief.

"Why not! It's as good a place as any. Besides, it will be a working vacation."

"You're planning on doing a podcast series?" Pete asked.

"Not a series. I was thinking of doing a special report," said Rachel. "Besides, there are questions I want answered. Lots of them. I think I can shine light on what happened here. Law enforcement tends to be blinkered."

"You deserve a break, not more work, Rach. You had a tough few weeks at the Neapolis trial. Tell the FBI about Maddison's phone message and let them follow up. You can always fly back and do a podcast after."

"Pete, Maddison came to *me* for help. Not the FBI." An image of the muddy grave from which Maddison's body was being exhumed flashed through Rachel's mind. "You heard her message. Maddison was afraid for her life. If there's one thing you should know about me by now, Pete, it's that I don't turn and run."

"I am well aware of that," Pete agreed. "It's a blessing and a curse. Are you going to tell the FBI about Maddison's voicemail message?"

"Of course."

Rachel texted Martinez with a request to call her back before firing up the engine and pulling out of the parking spot. She did a U-turn and drove toward the busy downtown precinct. Pete offered to change her flight to the following week and find her a hotel while she returned the FBI's rental car.

"I can't find a decent room for you anywhere," Pete told Rachel when she called him back twenty minutes later after returning the car to the rental agency. "There are a bunch of medical, energy, and IT conferences in Daytona this week. Plus BuzzCon is in town."

"BuzzCon? Am I supposed to know what that is?"

"It's a conference for social media influencers. You're invited every year and you refuse every year." Pete's sigh of exasperation was his standard response whenever he discussed social media with Rachel. That was Pete's expertise. They had a clear division of labor.

Rachel snapped to attention at Pete's mention of influencers. "Maybe Maddison was at BuzzCon."

"There's no 'maybe' about it," said Pete. "I just got off the phone with a BuzzCon organizer. She told me that Maddison attended the conference on the opening day. That was three days ago."

"Nobody's noticed that she hasn't been around since?"

"It's being held at a glamorous beach resort. It's as much a luxury vacation to produce content to fill up their Instagram and TikTok feeds as it is a conference. The guests come and go, so they probably haven't noticed she's missing," Pete said. "The organizer told me there's a deluxe room available. She's offered to let you stay for free if you post about the conference on the *Guilty or Not Guilty* social media accounts."

"I don't feel comfortable accepting a 'freebie.' Find me somewhere else to stay. It doesn't need to be a luxury resort," said Rachel.

"If only it were that easy. Daytona's booked solid," said Pete. "It's impossible to find a room at any half-decent hotel in town. Frills or no frills."

"What about out of town?"

"Are you seriously telling me you'd like to stay at a Norman Bates–style motel where there's a plastic curtain across the shower?" Pete joked, describing the famous murder scene of the Hitchcock movie *Psycho*. Rachel had once told him she'd never watched the whole movie because the shower scene always freaked her out.

"I give up!" said Rachel. "Get me the room at the BuzzCon hotel. It's a good opportunity to talk to the influencers. Maybe someone there knows what prompted Maddison to contact me before she went missing. But tell the organizers that I insist on paying, and I don't want to attend under my name. I'd rather use an alias."

"It'll be tough getting people to confide in you if you don't use your real name," said Pete.

"I'm a reporter. I'm good at getting people to talk."

"You don't know the world of influencers, Rach. Nobody will give you the time of day unless you're relevant."

"Relevant?"

"You need to have lots of followers on social media to be taken seriously by other influencers. Luckily you *have* lots of followers," Pete pointed out. "All you have to do is tell them that you're Rachel Krall. They'll all want to talk to you. You'll have to beat them off with a stick."

"I'd rather not, Pete. I want to keep things low-key."

"But nobody will talk to you if you're not popular on social."

"Sounds like high school all over again," muttered Rachel.

"High school on steroids."

Rachel was firm. She didn't want to attend the conference under her own name. Pete knew that she wouldn't budge on that point.

Rachel went out of her way to keep a low profile. While she was the name and voice behind the podcast, she wasn't the face. She didn't want to be, either, even if that was the easiest way to get influencers to talk to her at BuzzCon. Rachel's reticence to leverage her name wasn't just because she valued her privacy; she'd received creepy letters and vile threats over the years. Ever since, she'd been careful to keep a line of separation between the podcast and herself.

"I have an idea," Rachel told Pete. "Maddison created an invented persona on social media. How about I do the same thing?"

"You want to set up a new Instagram account from scratch under a pseudonym? We don't have the time to build it up." Pete thought for a moment. "How about we use your old running Instagram account. What's it called?"

"@runninggirlRach," she said.

Pete looked it up. The @runninggirlRach account had just under 19,000 followers, and Rachel hadn't used it since she launched the podcast. It was an account that documented preparations for the triathlons Rachel had competed in before a combination of the podcast's busy schedule and a strained Achilles tendon had forced her to wind down on her endurance sports.

There was nothing that specifically identified the account as belonging to Rachel. She'd even removed photos of herself, focusing instead on her diet and training regimen as well as motivational messages. Pete suggested that he soup it up with fresh images and build out an active online persona so the account didn't look as if it had been abandoned for almost two years.

"If anyone at the conference asks, tell them that you're a micro-influencer," Pete suggested.

"A micro what?" Rachel said.

"A micro-influencer," said Pete patiently. He was used to Rachel's abject disinterest in social media. "They're influencers with a small but very specialized following. They can sometimes be more influential in their niche than influencers with more followers."

Rachel gave Pete the username and password so he could manage the account for her, and he made her promise to send updated photos so he could freshen up the account. He'd buy a batch of followers to make her numbers look more impressive. He'd heard of a guy in Bangladesh who sold a thousand real followers for just $150.

"I'll call the conference organizers now and tell them you're attending but you're using an alias. I'll promise them a plug on the podcast so it'll be worth their while. By the way, there's a conference dinner tonight." Pete said it hesitantly because Rachel was notorious for avoiding star-studded events.

"Great," said Rachel like she meant it. "It'll give me a chance to ask the other dinner guests about Maddison. I want to retrace her movements in the days before she went missing."

"You need to be careful, Rach," said Pete. "Terence Bailey might have orchestrated Maddison Logan's death, but somebody else killed her. It's entirely possible that Maddison's killer might be at BuzzCon."

Chapter 26

Joe Martinez swiped his key card and pushed open his hotel room door. He took out his service weapon and put it in the hotel safe before stripping off his clothes and getting into the hot shower. The bathroom quickly turned into a steam room.

He'd spent hours in the suffocating heat while the quicksand pit was painstakingly dredged so they could retrieve the victim's body. By the time he'd left, floodlights were lit up, turning night into day around the gravesite. The generator had groaned so loudly under the strain that the recovery team had to use hand gestures to communicate.

Martinez had returned to Daytona in the early evening to get updates from his team who'd been following a slew of possible leads. He was running the operation to recover the body in tandem with the Maddison Logan missing persons investigation. The missing persons investigation would only be called off once they had a confirmed ID. Until then, they had to keep looking for Maddison with the same single-minded determination they'd shown before they'd found a body near the site of her disappearance.

The body would be lifted out in a couple of hours. Once that happened, they'd begin the complicated process of identifying her.

Meanwhile, a team would return to the crime scene in the morning to sift through the rest of the dredged mud for personal effects and trace evidence. They were still looking for the victim's mobile phone and any other evidence that may have been discarded with the body. Things like ropes, a murder weapon, and bullet casings, if she'd been shot. They didn't know the cause of death, so it was hard to know exactly what they were looking for.

Martinez got out of the shower, a white hotel towel wrapped around his waist. The mirror was opaque with steam. He knew that if he looked into it he'd see red-rimmed eyes and dark stubble on his jaw.

His suit and the rest of his clothes lay in a puddle on the floor. He tossed it all into a laundry bag and hung it over the doorknob. He'd drop it off at the concierge's desk on his way out. It was his ritual to shower and wash his clothes when he came home from the scene of a homicide investigation. He'd done it ever since he was first married.

When they'd bought their first house in Stafford, Virginia, after their wedding, Stephanie had chosen a home with a bathroom just off the garage. She'd set it up with fresh towels and clean changes of clothes so that he could go straight in and wash up before entering the rest of the house. They'd even installed a washing machine so that any clothes could be washed separately from their household laundry.

The shower ritual helped compartmentalize his work from his home life. Over the years he'd seen colleagues burn out, lose their families, and destroy their health, all because their work had seeped into their private lives.

At first he'd been guilty of the same mistake. Early on in their marriage, Stephanie had stumbled across a folder of gruesome crime photos that Joe had carelessly left on the hall table. He'd consoled her as she sat curled up on the sofa. It was bad enough that those images would trouble his sleep until his dying day. He didn't want such horrors to haunt the woman he loved.

After that, he'd ensured that all the work he did at home was contained to the downstairs den. That's where he took the calls that inevitably came for him at all hours of the day or night. Weekends included. The door was always closed. Stephanie never stepped foot in there.

Sometimes when they had a live case underway, he'd sleep on the leather sofa in the den with a blanket thrown over him so that Stephanie could have a decent night's sleep. She was a corporate lawyer working at a top-ten firm and she needed to be alert at the office without her sleep disturbed by telephone calls all night.

Martinez slid open the closet and took out a pair of neatly folded jeans and a navy polo top to wear to the incident room at the local police headquarters. After he changed, he picked up his phone to check for messages. Nothing new had come through.

Stephanie's photo was on the home screen. She was wearing a cream cashmere cable-knit sweater that flattered her long blond hair and peaches-and-cream complexion. The photo had been taken at a ski lodge after a day on the slopes two winters ago. He dialed Steph's number. Her voicemail immediately picked up.

"This is Stephanie. I'm not available right now but leave a message. I'll get back to you. I promise." He hung up at the first beep.

This case was turning out to be far more complicated than expected. Maddison Logan was unlike any other missing person that Martinez had encountered in his years investigating such cases.

Maddison had gone to great efforts to hide her past. It was almost as if she was in a witness protection program of her own making. She'd gone off the grid, taking on a new identity. They hadn't been able to find any trace of her until she surfaced as a social media identity a couple of years earlier. Her social media feeds were so heavily curated that they were practically fictitious. So far all inquiries to find Maddison's friends or family had hit dead ends.

Maddison had done such a thorough job of hiding her true identity that Martinez's team still didn't have a handle on who she was, despite the FBI's extensive resources. Whoever she was, she'd gone to a lot of trouble and significant subterfuge to see Terence Bailey.

Based on what Martinez's investigators had found so far, Maddison Logan had signed up for the volunteer program of a local charity that visited inmates via an online registration portal. She'd immediately completed a virtual training module, which earned her a temporary electronic volunteer's card that she had presented at the prison reception desk the next day, falsely claiming the charity had arranged for her to meet Terence Bailey as part of its program.

The prison clerk, who had no record of such a visit, assumed the paperwork had been mislaid, as occasionally happened. She gave Maddison a new form to fill in while she arranged for Bailey to be escorted from his work duties at the prison laundry to the cellblock meeting room.

Martinez was certain that Maddison Logan and Terence Bailey had crossed paths before.

It was for that reason that Martinez had sent Agent Torreno back to the prison with a burner phone and instructions to liaise with the prison Intel team. The Intel team used electronic surveillance and a network of snitches to find out what was going on among the prisoners. Always being one step ahead helped the guards maintain control.

Martinez wanted the burner phone planted in Bailey's cellblock. There was a steady supply of burner phones surreptitiously moving among the prisoners, so it wouldn't have looked suspicious if another phone suddenly appeared.

Torreno had reported back to him earlier that prison Intel had given the phone to a longtime snitch in a cell on Bailey's floor, who brought the phone back to his cellblock after kitchen duty that evening. The story he was instructed to give the prisoners was that a lifer he washed dishes with had temporarily given him the phone because his hiding place had been compromised. The snitch was told to get word out that he'd rent the phone to the highest bidder each night until he had to return it to its original owner.

Of course, it was all rigged. The snitch was instructed to give the phone only to Terence Bailey if he asked for it. If anyone else asked, then he was told to demand a price higher than they'd be willing to pay.

Martinez called Torreno for an update while he sat on the edge of the bed to put on socks. "Does Bailey have the phone?" he asked without any preliminaries.

"You bet he has it. He bartered a mattress for it."

About the highest value currency in prison was a prisoner's mattress. They were changed every five years. By the time the five years was up, the mattresses were thin and lumpy. It was impossible to get a good night's sleep on them. Bailey had received his new mattress the previous year when he'd completed the fifth year of his sentence. The inmates in his cellblock would be jostling to get their hands on it once he got out.

"The cell phone is with Bailey in his cell. He hasn't used it yet. It's currently turned off. We hope he'll use it once everyone goes to sleep."

"Keep monitoring the phone signal. I want to know the second he uses it," said Martinez. "I assume we have an undercover cop at that influencers dinner tonight?"

"We do," Torreno answered. "He was at BuzzCon events earlier in the day as well. Came back with nothing. He says they're all off-the-charts arrogant, and very cliquey. They only talk to people they consider to be in the same orbit. He says the only way to get them to talk is to send in cops with badges to question everyone."

"That's not happening." Martinez was curt. "At least not yet. If the influencers find out that Maddison's missing, it will go viral on social media in two seconds flat. That will make it almost impossible to investigate this case," said Martinez. "Let's hold off for now. Once we get an ID on the body then it won't matter if we go public. I'm heading down to the station shortly for the evening briefing with the team. I'm guessing that nobody's eaten. Any special requests?"

"Pizza from Louis would go down well," said Torreno. "It's just across the road from your hotel."

"You got it," said Martinez.

Before leaving his room, he opened his laptop and quickly typed a couple of responses to work matters that couldn't wait. He was about to close the computer when he changed his mind and pulled up the dossier on Rachel Krall that his analyst had compiled when her name first came up in the investigation.

The cover page contained all of Rachel's biographical details. Age: Thiry-one. Status: Single. Rachel had been married for a couple of years. It appeared to have been an amicable breakup. She was a former triathlete. She'd competed seriously until two years earlier when she'd dramatically pulled out of a marathon with an injury. Since then, she had been focused on her hit podcast.

Rachel Krall had apparently gone to great lengths to keep a low profile. She'd hired a company to scrub as much of her private information as possible from the Internet, including photographs. Her phone numbers were unlisted. Even her apartment was rented under another name.

Martinez supposed it was the price a reporter paid for covering the crime beat. Rachel Krall had filed several police complaints over the years. Perhaps the most serious was when a blue velvet engagement ring box addressed to Rachel was delivered to the newspaper where she was working at the time. It contained a single spent bullet. "Next time you won't see it coming," read the accompanying note.

With those sorts of threats, it was no wonder that Rachel tried to avoid being photographed in public. She was so successful at keeping a low profile that his team had struggled to find recent photos of her. Eventually they'd pulled together a few old photos from college along with her driver's license photo.

Martinez zoomed in on that photo. Rachel's coppery hair was tied up loosely at the top of her head. She had greenish eyes and wide cheekbones that gave her the look of a Viking princess. The fierce intensity in her gaze suggested that life hadn't always been smooth sailing despite the tiniest hint of a smile on her full lips.

Martinez shut his laptop screen abruptly. He knew the Rachel Krall dossier almost from memory. He'd reviewed it closely before telling Torreno to bring Rachel down to Florida to see Terence Bailey. That had resulted in nothing other than potentially baiting a suspected predator who was about to get out of jail. It was not his finest moment.

Not for the first time, Joe Martinez decided that involving Rachel Krall in his case had been a complication that he could have done without.

Chapter 27

Five weeks before Owen Bragg's grisly discovery in the forest, a twenty-one-year-old man was arrested for breaking into an apartment at Daytona Beach.

The man's name was Terence Bailey. He was an auto mechanic with no previous criminal record. I've seen the mug shot that was taken when he was charged that night. It's a study of contrasts. His expression is surly, like he's too cool to care. Yet his eyes are wide, like a frightened animal caught in headlights.

Terence Bailey was charged with burglary and fingerprinted before being put into an overnight lockup.

Bailey used his one telephone call to ask his boss for help. Bailey was an exemplary employee. His boss trusted the young mechanic's assurance that the arrest was a misunderstanding that could be sorted out with the help of a good lawyer. The following morning, Bailey's boss posted bail and hired a local hotshot attorney to defend his young employee.

Terence Bailey resumed work servicing cars while he waited for his case to go to court. He'd probably have been given a suspended sentence as a first-time offender if not for a conversation that took place at the police station a few days after his arrest.

The patrol cop who'd arrested Terence Bailey happened to be shooting pool with a homicide detective in the police station basement late one night. They got talking, as cops often do. The homicide detective, Detective Castel, mentioned that he'd recently taken over the case of the abduction and murders of two sex workers. Both bodies were wrapped in trash bags and left in dumpsters in the same neighborhood on the edge of town.

When Detective Castel went back through the files, he found that four other sex workers had disappeared under similar circumstances. Their bodies were never recovered. However, all six sex workers were last seen heading into empty parking lots in the same part of town to take a ride with a "john" before they disappeared for good. Detective Castel suspected the cases might be linked.

Earlier that day Detective Castel had interviewed the friend of Belinda Roy, one of the murdered sex workers. He asked whether anything unusual had happened in the days before Belinda vanished.

The friend mentioned that a week or so before she disappeared, Belinda had been frantically searching for an expensive white lace bustier that had mysteriously disappeared from her bedroom closet.

Detective Castel's interest was piqued. He wondered if the killer stalked his victims, perhaps even creeping into their homes to steal intimate garments as trophies, before abducting and murdering them days later.

As they played pool in the police station basement, Detective Castel asked Terence Bailey's arresting officer, a seasoned beat cop, whether he had heard any talk about lingerie disappearing from washing lines or homes in the area of town where the victims had all lived.

Detective Castel remembers the discussion quite clearly. "The cop's eyes lit up like he'd had a light bulb moment."

The police officer told the detective that it just so happened that he'd recently arrested a young mechanic by the name of Terence Bailey for breaking into a known prostitute's apartment in the same dodgy part of town. The beat cop told Castel that Bailey was arrested red-handed, going through a lingerie dresser.

"Boy, did that get my attention. It felt like we'd hit the jackpot."

Certain they were onto something big, Detective Castel compared the handful of fingerprints taken from the trash bags that contained the bodies of the two sex workers found by the dumpsters to Terence Bailey's fingerprints, taken after his breaking-and-entering arrest.

The prints were not a match. Detective Castel had struck out. He had no evidence with which to connect Terence Bailey to the murders.

The setback did not deter Detective Castel. He was convinced that Bailey was somehow involved. He felt it in his gut. Here's what he told me when I met with him recently.

"There was no hard evidence. All we had was instinct, and instinct's not enough to get an indictment, let alone a conviction. We did what we could with what little we had."

There was no rap on the knuckles for Terence Bailey for the breaking-and-entering charge, even though it was his first offense. He wasn't offered community service in lieu of prison as is customary with first-time offenders. Prosecutors grudgingly offered a stiff two-year sentence for aggravated robbery. By then, Bailey's boss had fired him. He couldn't afford to go to trial, so he took the deal.

For Detective Castel, the victory was bittersweet. A clock was ticking. He had two years to find evidence to prove that Terence Bailey was behind the sex worker killings.

"He butchered those women. He absolutely butchered them. I've never seen anything like that before. A monster like that should be locked up for the rest of his life."

Around the time Terence Bailey's plea deal was being signed, park ranger Owen Bragg found the partly burned body of a teenage girl in the forest.

Most of the forensic evidence was destroyed or badly damaged by fire, smoke, and rain. Police didn't hold out much hope that any of the remaining evidence was salvageable.

As it happened, a young forensic technician at the lab who'd been trained in a new fingerprint technique succeeded at lifting a couple of partial prints on a section of rope that hadn't been damaged significantly by fire or smoke.

The homicide team investigating the case were excited by the breakthrough. Detective Castel remembers getting the call from the lab telling him the good news. A partial print from the rope matched Terence Bailey's fingerprints. Detective Castel felt vindicated. He finally had the evidence he needed to charge Bailey for murder.

"We had Bailey right where we wanted him. At least I thought we did."

Taking prints from a soft surface such as rope, especially a surface with curves and ridges, is tricky. To do it successfully, the technician used an experimental technique involving an algorithm that completed the likely pattern of the print to a high degree of certainty. It turned out to be a great technique for getting a lead on a suspect, but it couldn't be presented as evidence in a court of law. The fingerprint evidence was inadmissible.

For Detective Castel and the rest of the homicide team, it was a devastating blow.

I asked Detective Castel what went through his mind when he was told that Terence Bailey couldn't be charged for murder.

"To tell you the truth, I just felt incredibly sad for his next victim."

Chapter 28

Rachel Krall rolled her mini overnight suitcase along the corridor to her hotel room. She slid her key card into the door and entered a plush room filled with the scent of orange blossoms from an essential oils room fragrance. Orange and navy petals were scattered on the white quilt of a king bed. A spa bath was separated from the bedroom by a glass pane so that guests could decadently watch TV while soaking in the tub.

Rachel stepped onto the balcony where she looked out into a void of darkness interrupted by the occasional flicker of a ship's distant light.

The colorful flashing lights of the Daytona Beach Ferris wheel rotated at an amusement park farther down the beach. It was a perfect destination for her evening run. She ran or cycled most days. Occasionally she swam laps. It helped clear her mind and always left her feeling as if she'd at least achieved one worthwhile accomplishment for the day.

Rachel quickly changed into running shorts and a T-shirt before heading downstairs through the busy lobby and into the pool area where a gate led directly to the beach. Rachel had to pass the BuzzCon cocktail party being held on the grass near the pool to get to the gate. She was guiltily skipping the party so she could squeeze in her run.

Rachel zigzagged among people holding vividly colored daiquiris in frosted glasses as they posed for photos on a red carpet that had been rolled across the grass, leading to the French doors of the hotel ballroom where the conference dinner was being held.

"Are you all having fun?" A photographer dressed all in black encouraged a huddle of men in tuxes and women in shimmering evening dresses posing for a group shot. As he took their photos, the group turned their backs to him and took selfies of themselves being photographed by him while on the red carpet. Rachel quickly stepped out of the way so she wouldn't be in their shots in her distinctly unglamorous running gear.

She noticed the influencers pause to type captions and hashtags before posting their selfies onto their Instagram accounts. They moved into exaggerated poses for the next round of photos as notification beeps from "likes" and "shares" rose like a melody.

A waiter holding a tray of daiquiris moved among the guests. The bright sherbet colors of the cocktails hinted at their flavors: strawberry, pineapple, and kiwi.

Rachel stopped at a conference registration table set to the side, since she hadn't checked in yet. A young woman with oversized glasses that emphasized her large brown eyes looked askance at Rachel's running shorts and tank top.

"I'm registering for the conference." Rachel pointed to the @runninggirlRach Instagram handle handwritten at the bottom of the typed list of names she spotted on the table.

"You're the runner," the woman said, as if it hadn't been obvious from the running shorts and top that Rachel wore. She leaned forward to hand Rachel a gold-and-red lanyard and then lifted up a huge glittery bag.

"You'll love the giveaways," she enthused. The bag was crammed with freebies. "Our sponsors ask that when you post about the products in the bag, you don't mention that it's an ad. They want organic seeding of content. There are codes with each item so that you can get your ten percent referral fee for any purchases made by your followers."

"Thanks but it's not necessary. I'm about to go for a run." Rachel handed back the bag. "Why don't you keep it?"

"That's really nice of you but I'm not allowed," said the woman. "The gift bag is only for influencers. What room are you in? I'll get the hotel porter to leave the bag in your room so it's there when you get back."

Rachel reeled off her room number before heading toward the gate to the beach. As she did so, a smiling woman with dark braided hair called out her name.

"Rachel? I'm Kesha, one of the organizers. We're excited to have you at BuzzCon."

"Thanks for allowing me to sign up on such late notice."

"It's our pleasure. Don't worry, my lips are sealed," she whispered. "I won't let anyone know who you really are. You are joining us for the gala dinner tonight?" Kesha asked, racing ahead without letting Rachel get a word in edgewise. "I've arranged for you to sit with all the cool kids."

"Tell me the dinner isn't too dressy," said Rachel. "I only have an overnight bag with me. I definitely did not pack for a gala dinner."

"One of our marquee sponsors is the #FML fashion brand," said Kesha. "We have a rack of clothes they've given us to hand out. I'll have a few outfits sent to your room."

She asked for Rachel's dress and shoe sizes. "If you need anything else, please don't hesitate." Kesha looked up as a waiter beelined toward her. "Looks like there's another mini crisis. I'd better go and deal with it. I'll see you at dinner."

Rachel let herself out of the gate connecting the hotel pool area to the beach. She ran along the beach until she reached the Ferris wheel's flashing neon lights. Laughter and music drifted over from the amusement park as if beckoning Rachel to join the fun. Instead, she turned and sprinted back, aware that she'd been running longer than she'd intended.

Rachel took the elevator up to her room to shower and dress for the BuzzCon dinner. On her bed were the dresses and boxes of shoes that Kesha had promised to send up to her room, as well as the enormous glittery gift bag. Rachel was late for the dinner but curiosity got the better of her. She tipped the contents of the bag onto her bed.

Among the freebies were cosmetics, branded sunglasses, lingerie, and even a fitness watch. There were also T-shirts, yoga gear, a hot-pink Swiss Army pocketknife designed for women, and a key ring with pink self-defense equipment, including a mini stun gun disguised as a perfume bottle.

Instructions were taped to each product about what to say in social media posts to promote it. A note stapled to the bag itself asked Rachel to post a photo of the contents of the bag to her Instagram account along with the BuzzCon hashtag. Rachel dutifully took a picture of the give-aways piled on her bed before getting dressed.

She put on a midnight-blue cocktail dress that hugged her toned figure. She twisted her hair in a tight topknot and quickly applied makeup before leaving her room.

While in the elevator, Rachel photographed her feet in the slinky stilettos and typed out a caption: These feet were made for dancing. . . . Thrilled to be at @BuzzCon #BuzzCon #footpic

She sent the photos to Pete to post as she rushed to the ballroom.

"Keep it coming," Pete texted back.

Chapter 29

Thomas McCoy's next passenger is waiting for him at the pickup location outside a bar. He's young and good-looking, and doesn't he just know it as he stands restlessly at the curb when Thomas pulls up.

The rideshare app flashes the passenger's name: Jonny Macon. He wears jeans, ankle boots, and a tuxedo T-shirt that's so tight it shows off the cubes of his washboard stomach.

"You're going to the hotel where that big YouTube conference is being held, right?" Thomas says, merging into evening traffic.

"Yeah. BuzzCon." The passenger checks his phone as he talks. "It's for influencers, creators," he says. "Hey, do you know where I can get quality blow?" He looks up, making fleeting eye contact with Thomas in the rearview mirror.

There's a pregnant pause as Thomas decides how to respond. It's a question that he's often asked by tourists visiting the notorious party town. He's always circumspect with his answers in case it's a police sting. Thomas has no record. Not even a driving citation. The cops don't know him. He wants to keep it that way.

"I can give you a phone number," he answers carefully.

"I don't have time to get it myself," says the passenger. "I'm supposed to give a speech at this conference tonight. I'll make it worth your while if you pick it up and bring it to me."

The passenger takes a wad of cash from his wallet and waves it in the air. "Get me a couple of grams of premium blow and I'll give you twice as much in cash for the delivery. That's $600 just for bringing it to me. Easiest money you'll ever make."

Thomas is tempted. He has to work his ass off for that sort of cash. It's more than he earns from rides in a whole day. "I'll see what I can do."

"Good." The passenger writes his cell phone number on a piece of paper that he tosses along with a bundle of cash onto the front passenger seat. "Call me when you have it."

The passenger takes a call on his AirPods as they approach the hotel. He is obviously talking to an accountant, or a lawyer.

"How much money are you talking about?" he asks. "Are you kidding me?" he explodes. "This needs to be fixed. I'm in talks to launch a lifestyle show. It's with a big streaming service. . . . No, I can't say yet which one. This cannot come out. It will destroy my brand and kill the deal. Do what you have to do, okay?"

Thomas drops Jonny Macon outside the lobby door of the hotel. As he drives out of the circular hotel driveway, he calls a dealer he knows by reputation.

The Best Buy parking lot is deserted when Thomas gets to the drop-off location. He reverses into a parking spot at the back near a pile of empty cargo pallets. Three minutes later, the powerful headlights of an SUV enter the parking lot and drive toward him. The SUV pulls to a stop next to Thomas's car, the driver's-side windows facing each other. They roll down their windows in unison.

Thomas tosses over a bundle of cash. The dealer checks that it's legit and then throws back a tiny bag of white powder. It lands on the floor near the gas pedal. By the time Thomas has picked it up, the SUV has driven away.

Thomas opens his glove compartment. He takes out a first aid kit and opens it on his lap. He slips the bag of powder into a pouch. He transports anything dodgy in the first aid kit. Cops don't search medical kits emblazoned with a red cross. It's like they know it's sacrosanct. He opens up a second compartment in the first aid kit and pulls out a pile of bandages. Hidden inside are a serrated hunting knife and zip ties. He runs his finger along the blade. For the first time that day, he feels in control. He feels respected.

Chapter 30

Red-and-gold helium balloon centerpieces decorated round tables covered with white-and-gold tablecloths at the BuzzCon dinner. The color scheme matched the hypnotic shape-shifting ink blots on the screen behind the podium where an MC struggled to get laughs from a crowd more interested in their phones.

The event had an abundance of red-carpet pizzazz and souped-up glamour. The influencers wore outfits ranging from full-blown tuxedos and flashy evening dresses to jeans and faded T-shirts; scruffy being the new black.

Rachel looked around in bemusement as she found her seat at a table in the center of the room. Most of the guests were so engrossed in posing for selfies and uploading the photos to their feeds that they made no eye contact with their table companions.

Everyone seemed to be silently communicating with each other via their phones. Text messages bounced back and forth across the room while the MC trilled on. His F-bomb-laced standup routine was one of the least funny bits Rachel had ever heard. If scruffy was the new black, then profanity apparently was the new humor.

Waiters brought out square plates with appetizers that looked like edible artwork. Ravenous from her run, Rachel immediately dug into the grilled shrimp appetizer with coriander and mango salsa salad the moment the waiter put the dish in front of her. When she'd eaten almost everything on her plate, she slowly stopped chewing as she realized that she was one of the few people eating her meal. Everyone else was engrossed in photographing their food from every possible angle. Some even used lighting kits.

The beautifully plated gourmet meals were props for the influencers to produce content for their social channels.

Rachel texted Pete. "I appear to have eaten my content!"

A few people picked at their appetizer once they finished photographing it. Most summoned waiters to take the uneaten plates back to the kitchen to be thrown away. Nobody seemed to care about the inordinate waste of food.

Rachel chatted with Chad, a fair-headed man in a tux sitting next to her. He was the only other person at the table whose face wasn't buried in his phone. Chad was a brand manager at a cosmetics company that worked with influencers. Rachel gave him her potted @runninggirlRach bio. She told him that she was an aspiring influencer who'd been allowed to join the conference to learn from the best.

"Are you in a pod?" Chad asked. "If you're not, then you should join one."

"Pod?"

"Influencer pod," Chad explained. "It's when a group of influencers work together to boost their popularity by liking, commenting on, and sharing each other's content. It tricks the algorithm to surface their content and helps get them more followers. Also, it means they can sometimes take a short break from posting content without their followers plunging."

"Sounds like I do need a pod. I also need to get better at posting content more regularly," said Rachel.

"Think of your social media platforms as a chicken that lays golden eggs," said Chad. "You want eggs. You need to keep feeding the chicken. With content."

Rachel knew that the biggest influencers made millions by promoting brands through their social media feeds. Even less-successful influencers could bring in a cool six-figure income from their channels if they had a strong base of followers.

"Are you sure you want to get into this business, Rachel? It can be grueling, especially if you're doing it alone. Burnout is high in the world of influencers," Chad added.

Whatever else he said was drowned out by the MC returning to the microphone to introduce one of the keynote speakers of the night. The young man he introduced picked up the microphone to wild applause and screeches from a crowd of mostly young women standing behind a velvet cord on the side of the room. Their phones were all pointing toward the podium filming him as he put up his hands to thank everyone for their applause before he spoke.

"Is he famous?" Rachel asked Chad.

"He's not famous enough to attract groupies. The screaming girls are probably paid extras hired to add glamour to the night," Chad concluded.

"If the fans are fake, what part of this evening is real?" Rachel asked, bemused.

"Social media is all about perception," said Chad.

On the podium, the speaker began a somewhat incomprehensible speech, his words stirred with so much emotion that it sounded as if he was accepting a lifetime achievement award.

"You guys. You're all amazing, talented, incredible people. I'm so lucky to have you all in my corner. Every day I wake up and thank God for blessing me with such amazing friends. I love you. Each and every one of you. Without you, I'd be nothing."

"That's so true," said Chad, softly enough for only Rachel to hear, as resounding applause filled the ballroom.

The MC took the microphone long enough to make a couple of jokes that fell flat before calling up a new speaker dressed in jeans and a tuxedo T-shirt so tight that it displayed the grooves of his washboard stomach.

"That's Jonny Macon," Chad whispered to Rachel.

"We love you, Jonny!" someone screamed after the applause died down.

Jonny gave a short speech about how he'd gone from being a college dropout to becoming an influencer after his Instagram posts had taken off one rainy afternoon when he'd been playing around with his phone, trying to figure out what he wanted to do in life.

"My message to y'all is keep plugging away. Your dream will find you like it found me," he concluded. He flashed a peace sign and jumped off the stage. The groupies behind the velvet barrier mobbed him for autographs as he passed by.

"What does he do to get such adoration?" Rachel asked.

"He takes off his shirt," said Chad. He laughed at Rachel's surprise. "I mean it. He literally takes off his shirt. Here." He pulled up Jonny Macon's Instagram account on his phone. There were endless photos of Jonny working out with his shirt off.

"Jonny's a fitness influencer. He became famous doing shirtless push-ups and planks in unusual places. He did one yesterday on the roof of a 1969 Mustang. He planked for over eleven minutes. He promotes everything from sports drinks and vitamins to breakfast shakes. We're launching a new range of men's face cleansers. He's signed on as a sponsor."

"Who else is here that I should know about?" Rachel asked.

Chad looked around the room. "See that woman over there with the long dark hair? She's the one wearing the black cocktail dress." He pointed to a pretty young woman near the front who was rising from her seat to take the podium. "That's Reni. She's a wellness influencer. She's Jonny's girlfriend."

When the applause died down, Reni went up to the podium, where she spoke about her battle with Lyme disease. "I couldn't get out of bed. For days." She told the audience how doctors prescribed her medication after medication. Nothing worked. Eventually, in desperation, she created her own diet and supplement regimen. It energized her and changed her life.

"Now I'm going to help you change your life," she told the guests. "We can be our best selves together," she finished off to enthusiastic applause.

“And so a healthy living brand was launched,” Chad whispered to Rachel as Reni left the podium. “You can try her diet and coaching app for just $29.99 per month.”

Chad gave Rachel an equally cynical rundown of the bios of some of the other influencers in the ballroom. There were half a dozen fitness influencers.

He pointed out a striking blonde being photographed by a man with floppy bangs and horn-rimmed glasses. “Watch how Zoe brazenly follows Jonny Macon around with her eyes even while her ‘Instagram husband’ slash boyfriend photographs her,” he said. “Zoe is obsessed. I’m not sure if it’s because she’s in love with Jonny or she wants his success to rub off on her. Meanwhile, Zoe’s boyfriend thinks that if he takes enough photos of her, then she’ll stick with him. Trust me, I’ve been there. She won’t.”

“What can you tell me about Maddison Logan?” Rachel finally asked the question she’d been wanting to ask ever since she began chatting with Chad.

“She’s the up-and-coming #vanlife travel influencer, right?” Chad asked. “Why are you asking about her?”

“She’s a friend of a friend. I hoped we could meet up but I don’t see her anywhere,” said Rachel, thinking on her feet.

“I’m not surprised that she’s made herself scarce,” Chad remarked.

“Why?”

“I heard that she hooked up with Jonny Macon. It didn’t end well. Jonny and Reni are dating and Maddison was accused of trying to break them up to boost her own followers. Things got ugly.”

“How ugly?”

“Ugly enough that Maddison lost thousands of followers overnight. She must have gone somewhere to lick her wounds. Nobody’s seen her since.”

Chapter 31

It was getting close to eight in the evening when Joe Martinez came down the stairs into the police department basement carrying a pile of pizza boxes. He placed the boxes in a long row on a trestle table so that everyone could help themselves.

The taskforce had only been set up the previous day but it was already a well-oiled machine. He had twelve people working in the taskforce with analysts supporting their efforts at Quantico and the Miami bureau.

Martinez had chosen the basement of the city's police headquarters for his incident room. Desks and whiteboards were arranged across the cavernous space. A printer had been brought downstairs and set up in the corner. A steaming hot-water urn was on a table along with mugs and sachets of instant coffee and sweetener.

He'd been offered use of a much smaller, well-furnished room upstairs. It would have been more comfortable. He'd opted for the basement partly because it was more spacious, but mostly because it enabled the taskforce to work separately from the rest of the police department. Martinez preferred it that way. There was less risk of leaks to the media and less chance the politicians in the police department would interfere in the investigation.

What it offered in terms of space and privacy, it lost in comfort. The air conditioner rattled and whined as it struggled to keep the temperature and humidity to a comfortable level. The walls were covered with faded police recruitment posters going back decades. A pool table and a dartboard on a wall covered with tiny holes were indicative of how the room had been used before Martinez commandeered it for the Maddison Logan investigation.

Martinez took a piece of pizza for himself and headed over to his desk near the pool table. He dialed the forensic team supervisor at the crime scene while he ate.

"What's the latest?" he asked.

"We're about to winch up the body," the team lead shouted over the roar of the generator. "Once she's up, it'll take us an hour or so to photograph and fingerprint her. After that we'll send her to the morgue and shut up shop here for the night."

Martinez was relieved the operation to extract the body from the pool of mud was finally wrapping up. He hoped they'd soon know whether the victim's fingerprints and blood type matched the prints and blood type of the smudges of blood taken from Maddison's van.

Conclusive DNA results would take a few days longer. Usually in such cases they'd take DNA from the victim's relatives and compare it to the body to get a confirmed identification. In this case, they had no way of contacting Maddison's relatives, since they didn't know her real identity.

They'd have to compare the victim's DNA to DNA found in Maddison's van to determine whether the body found in the mud was definitely Maddison. That alone would slow the process as the forensic team looked for viable DNA that could tie to Maddison among her belongings. They'd failed to find DNA on her toothbrush. She'd apparently washed it thoroughly after brushing her teeth when she'd last used it. They had to look at other options.

Martinez called everyone over to his desk once they'd finished the pizza. He held up a copy of the pencil drawing of a goth-looking teenager from Terence Bailey's sketchbook that had been photographed by the prison guards during their search of his cell earlier in the day.

"Any updates on her identity?" Martinez asked, tapping the drawing of the goth teen with short dark hair and an infinity symbol on a ribbon choker around her neck.

"So far nothing," said the agent who'd been assigned to cross-check the sketch against missing persons photos. "It's tricky running a pencil sketch through our missing persons photo database."

Martinez had suspected that might be a problem. The sketch was an artist's interpretation rather than an accurate drawing of the girl in question. Also, because the sketch was in pencil, they didn't know her eye or skin color, or approximate weight and height. That information would narrow the database search considerably.

"Talk to the local cops upstairs. See if anyone remembers a girl who dressed as a goth disappearing."

"Maybe she's one of Bailey's foster sisters," said another agent. "Terence Bailey moved through the system a lot."

"Compile a list of all Bailey's foster parents. Contact each of them and ask if they recognize the girl in the drawing. Show them a photo of Maddison as well. Maybe they'll recognize her."

"Why's the sketch so important?"

"If we can show that Terence Bailey drew a portrait of a missing person, that could be deemed an admission that he was involved in her disappearance, especially if there are things in his drawing of the victim that were never released to the public, such as the piercings. It may help us to convince a judge to delay his release from prison, or at least give us a warrant to put him under tight surveillance once he gets out. Now, do we have any more information on Maddison Logan's real identity?"

Information was coming in at a slow trickle. The undercover cop at the conference had found out a few scraps of information, including that Maddison might have stayed at a hippie beach camping area north of town rather than at the BuzzCon hotel. A visit to that campground by another agent came up with nothing. Nobody he spoke with there had known Maddison.

Martinez dismissed the team after the evening briefing. A few left to get some sleep. Several stayed behind with Martinez and Torreno, who was on a phone call at a nearby desk.

"Joe," said Torreno, joining Martinez by the coffee urn after he finished the call. "That was the prison Intel team. Terence Bailey used the contraband phone we planted."

"Who did he call?" Martinez poured boiling water from the urn into a mug to make himself instant coffee.

"It wasn't a call. He texted someone. The message is being sent to me now."

Torreno's phone pinged a moment later. He took one look and wordlessly handed his phone to Martinez to read himself.

"Rachel Krall was here. Nice! Our meeting was cut short but that's okay. We'll finish this for good when I get out."

Chapter 32

Agent Joe Martinez scattered the colored pool balls across the green felt table near his desk before picking up a pool cue. He lined up his target and in a single motion sank a yellow ball into a corner pocket. He moved around the table, bending down to examine angles as he chose the next ball to strike. All while mulling over the files he'd just read.

It was almost midnight. He was alone in the situation room with Mark Torreno and two junior agents knee-deep in traffic camera footage from across the city. They were trying to track the movements of Maddison Logan's van so they could figure out where she'd gone and what she'd done in the days before her disappearance.

It appeared that she had left her van at the beach camping area and taken rides into town. That made sense. The camper van was too big to park in town.

Torreno leaned back in his chair, his feet on the desk, flicking through photos from the national missing persons database displayed on his oversized computer screen. He was looking for anyone who vaguely resembled the goth girl that the prison guards had found in Terence Bailey's sketchbook.

Keyboard clicks were the only sounds in the otherwise empty room.

Someone had turned off the air conditioner earlier. It made the room stuffy, but it meant they weren't subjected to the annoying metal grind of the air con's motor.

Martinez settled on a red ball across the pool table. He bent down to line it up in his sights and squinted as he held the cue in place. Then he released, shooting the ball with a click straight into a side pocket.

"I need a break. How about we play a round?" Torreno rose from his desk. He picked the ball out of the pocket and tossed it in the air.

"You're on." Martinez tossed a pool cue to Torreno, who caught it in mid-air. Martinez set up the balls in a triangular ring and stood aside to let Torreno do the honors.

Torreno took the break shot, sending the balls scattering all over the table. They took turns, sometimes sinking them, often not, until all the balls were in the pockets around the table. Martinez picked out the balls when they were done, showing as little emotion in his victory as he'd shown every time he'd expertly sunk a ball.

"That has to be the quietest game of pool I've ever played," said Torreno. "You didn't say a single word the whole time."

"It's meditative," said Martinez. "It gives me a chance to think."

"Think about what?"

"The women that Terence Bailey was suspected of abducting and murdering before he went to prison on that burglary charge."

Martinez tossed the pool cue onto the table and returned to his desk, where he swept a pile of photocopies into his hand. He walked over to a whiteboard and snapped a magnet over a color photocopy of a photograph of a young woman.

"Victim 1. Belinda Roy."

The photo of Belinda Roy was pulled from a posting on a call girl website. It showed a pretty brunette with a pouting smile sitting in a provocative pose on the edge of a bed. She was dressed in a powder-blue satin teddy with a garter belt. According to the post, she went by the name "Belle" and promised a "girlfriend experience that will keep you coming back for more."

"She's a college dropout from Miami," said Martinez. "Moved here. Worked as a high-priced call girl for a while before getting into meth. She was last seen alive heading out for a night working the streets."

Martinez put up a photo of Belinda Roy's body wrapped in black trash bags. It had been thrown into a dumpster the night before collection day. It just so happened the garbage driver on that route was new to the job and had forgotten to empty the dumpsters down that particular alley. A forklift driver working in an adjacent factory noticed a smell a couple of days later.

Martinez wrote out her vital stats on the whiteboard. Belinda Roy was five foot four, brown hair. Caucasian. She was twenty-nine years old when she died. Cause of death: strangulation, before her throat was cut with what was believed to be a jagged hunting knife. She was bound and gagged when she was cut up.

"Victim 2." Martinez slapped up a photo of another woman with brown hair and big almond-shaped eyes. "Minnie Love. Real name Marissa Hubert."

Her biography was relatively similar. Minnie Love was twenty-seven when she died. She'd been studying to be a hairdresser when her boyfriend had gotten her hooked on drugs and pimped her out. She left him and came over to Daytona, where she ended up working on the street as well. Her body was left in a dumpster a block from where Belinda Roy's body had been found fourteen months earlier. She too had been strangled and her throat cut.

"Both were wrapped in trash bags," Martinez told Torreno. "When questioned, their friends mentioned they'd both expressed concerns that they were being watched before they disappeared. They'd also both mentioned items of intimate apparel mysteriously going missing from their apartments before they disappeared."

"The cops were looking for a lingerie thief and Terence Bailey was arrested rifling through a lingerie drawer. He fell in their lap," Torreno said. "What about the third victim? Was it the same story with her?"

"Well, that's the strange part. Victim 3 doesn't fit the pattern at all."

Chapter 33

There are a lot of folks in law enforcement who've worked the murder cases that Terence Bailey is suspected of committing who will openly say that it's a very good thing that he's been kept off the street all these years. Ask them and they'll unabashedly tell you that he is a monster.

For years, Bailey has been the lead suspect in the serial killings of six sex workers. Only two bodies have been found. Four victims are still officially missing, although all signs point to the likelihood they too were murdered. The names of the two known victims are Belinda Roy and Minnie Love.

Both women have been given various labels such as prostitutes, street walkers, and hookers by the media and the detectives who've investigated their murders.

They were more than the sum of their tragic lives. They were also sisters, daughters, and friends. Neither woman imagined dying before they hit thirty. Their bodies cut up and dumped like trash.

Belinda was a romantic. She wanted to travel the world and fall in love.

In the end, she never traveled outside her home state. She was unlucky in love. The boyfriends she fell in love with were not worthy of her affection.

Minnie Love, or Marissa, as she was known by her family, was a sweet, trusting young woman who worked as a hairdresser. She dreamed of owning her own salon.

Life, fate, and a string of abusive relationships led these women to drug addiction and prostitution.

Many of the details of the police investigation that led to Terence Bailey being a prime suspect in the sex worker killings have been cloaked in secrecy.

We know that the bodies of Belinda Roy and Minnie Love were dumped near the auto shop where Bailey worked. It's a notable coincidence but hardly incriminating.

Bailey only came onto the police's radar when he was arrested breaking into the apartment of another sex worker and allegedly attempting to steal her lingerie. Before that his name hadn't come up as a possible suspect.

When police found out about Bailey's troubled childhood, they decided that he could well fit the profile they'd pulled together of a possible serial killer.

The only discrepancy was his age. Bailey would have been in his late teens when the sex workers disappeared. He would have been just twenty when Victim 3, the murdered teen, was found in the forest by ranger Owen Bragg. It's unusual but not unprecedented for serial killers to ramp up so quickly and at such a young age.

That's why the homicide detective investigating the murders of Belinda Roy and Minnie Love initially had doubts about whether Bailey could have done it. That changed when the murdered body of the teenager was found.

As we discussed earlier, Bailey's fingerprint was found on the partially burned rope binding the girl's ankles and wrists. Even though this forensic evidence was not admissible in court, forensic experts are certain their technique is accurate. They have no doubt that Terence Bailey definitely handled the rope. Bailey constantly refused to explain how his prints got there. The only possible explanation is that he murdered her.

But it turns out that it wasn't just Terence Bailey's prints on the rope. Someone else's prints were on that rope, too. Someone whose profile doesn't appear on the FBI's extensive database of tens of millions of fingerprints.

It's for this reason that homicide detectives came up with what they called the "two killer theory."

The theory explains why there are two people's fingerprints on the ropes. It also explains how Bailey, who was still in his late teens at the time, might have become a serial killer at such a young age. Usually, a killer will first test out their bloodlust with a series of violent crimes until they escalate to murder.

It's rare for a man to kill so many people at such a young age. But it is known to happen when a younger killer pairs up with an older one as a sort of apprentice.

Another perplexing question for detectives had been the profile of the murdered teen who Owen Bragg called "Unknown Girl." Her profile is vastly different from that of Belinda Roy and Minnie Love. It again raises the possibility there were two killers working together with different preferences in victims.

When she was eventually identified, police discovered that the third victim had no connection whatsoever to the murky world of drugs and prostitution.

Her name was Aysh Philips. She'd recently graduated from a local high school where she was a model student who played volleyball and sang in the school choir. Her friends describe her as a quiet girl who was kind to everyone, almost to a fault. Aysh was planning to study nursing in the fall. She was younger than the other victims by almost a decade. She was also the only victim who was Black.

The way that Aysh was killed as well as the manner in which the killer set fire to her body was different from the MO used in the sex worker murders. Police also believe that it would have been very difficult for one person to have carried her body to the top of the forest ridge where she was dumped.

It is for these reasons that homicide detectives have long believed that Terence Bailey did not act alone. They suspected that someone else helped him with his killing spree.

Police never found out the identity of his accomplice. Throughout his time in prison, Bailey did not receive visitors, calls, or even letters from anyone other than lawyers.

That changed a few days before his release when he was summoned from laundry duty to talk to a young woman who'd come to see him under false pretenses. She'd claimed she was a volunteer with a charity that visited prisoners. She wasn't.

Hours after her meeting with Bailey, she disappeared only a few miles from the ridge where the body of the Unknown Girl was found. This time it was one coincidence too many.

Chapter 34

Strobe lighting and a bubble machine turned the lawn by the hotel pool into a nightclub when the afterparty began immediately after the BuzzCon dinner. The dance floor quickly filled up; the pulsating music was loud enough to drown out the crash of waves on the beach beyond the hotel grounds.

Some influencers videoed themselves as they danced. A few of the bigger names that Chad had pointed out to Rachel earlier were being filmed by their own photographers as they danced and mingled by the pool.

"There are almost as many photographers as there are influencers," Rachel noted to Chad.

"More," said Chad, who'd joined her to watch the influencers party hard on the dance floor. "Some aspiring photographers build their portfolios by offering their services for free or at a cut price to influencers with clout. A few of the photographers you see here are in a relationship with the influencer they're photographing."

"That's convenient."

"It's a full-time job filming and posting content, so it helps when they're a couple," Chad explained.

"It sounds like you're talking from experience." Rachel noticed the bitterness in his tone.

"My ex was a lifestyle blogger. It felt as if every moment of our relationship was spent photographing her life. I'd roll out of bed seven days a week while it was still dark to shoot her doing yoga poses at dawn when the light was soft. Face cream in the morning shots. Shampoo in the shower shots. We never had a proper vacation. Every vacation was work. Shoot, caption, post. Repeat. We couldn't go to a restaurant without photographing each course," he lamented. "I honestly don't think I ate a hot meal the entire time I dated her."

"So you broke up with her?"

"She broke up with me," said Chad. "I adored her. Still do. I'd still be with her, even though I knew deep down in my heart that Aliza didn't want a boyfriend; she wanted a mirror."

"It's a narcissistic world they operate in, isn't it?" observed Rachel as they watched the influencers posing for selfies as they danced.

"You don't know the half of it," said Chad. "Speaking of narcissistic," he added, gesturing to the dance floor where Jonny Macon, stripped to the waist, was break dancing. His muscles rippled as he moved. The dancers all shifted to the side and were clapping to encourage him.

"A year ago, Jonny was a scrawny teenager lifting weights in a gym and studying accounting. He's now a full-time influencer and he's making a fortune. He has an app with nutrition advice and a 'How to get ripped in eight weeks' exercise program."

When Jonny fell into a plank for a few minutes, straining to stay in position, Zoe, the blond fitness influencer Chad had pointed out earlier, joined him on the dance floor. She lowered herself to the ground, put a cocktail glass on Jonny's back, and did her own plank while sipping the drink through a straw. Her boyfriend with the floppy bangs and eyeglasses lay on the ground, clumsily filming her.

"That was not cool," Jonny told her when he was back on his feet. Someone handed him a gym towel to wipe off the sweat on his pecs and sculpted six-pack belly before he headed over to sign an autograph directly on the bare midriff of an ecstatic fan. When he'd signed his fill of autographs, he headed toward the bar, where the bartender handed him a tall glass of ice water.

Rachel sidled up to the bar, placing herself next to Jonny, who was drinking the glass of water while the bartender fixed him a drink.

"I bet it took a lot of hours at the gym to be able to plank for so long," Rachel observed.

"More than you can imagine. Lucky I love my job," Jonny said, taking a vodka on the rocks from the bartender and slugging it down. "What's your handle?"

"I'm @runninggirlRach."

He looked up her Instagram handle on his phone and immediately saw the dismal number of followers, despite Pete's huge efforts over the past few hours to boost the numbers. "I didn't know they let micro-influencers into this conference." His tone was disparaging.

"I've come here to learn the ropes from the experts," said Rachel.

"You want to learn the ropes? Lesson one, don't be so obvious." He gestured toward Zoe, who was watching him with doe-eyes while drinking a cocktail with her boyfriend. "Lesson two, why be micro when you can be the real deal?"

Before Rachel could respond, he took out his phone and took a selfie of the two of them leaning back against the bar, holding their drinks.

"@runninggirlRach is lonely. Make friends with her . . ." he typed before pressing Post.

He tossed down the rest of his drink, then called the waiter and ordered two microbrews. The bartender expertly flipped the lids off two beer bottles and handed the beers to Jonny. He passed one to Rachel. They clinked the bottles together before each taking a sip.

"How did you get into this business?" Rachel asked.

"It's a long story," he said, half shouting to be heard over music blasting on the dance floor. "Actually, let's get out of here. It's too loud to talk." He grabbed Rachel's hand and led her through the rear hotel gate to the beach.

Rachel had a split second to decide whether to go along or disentangle herself from his firm grip. Chad had told her earlier that Jonny Macon had hooked up with Maddison before her disappearance. Rachel definitely wanted to talk to him. She was less keen about doing so on an empty beach in the dead of night.

In the end, she decided to go with the flow. She paused to take off her heels, holding them by the straps as she followed Jonny Macon across the beach toward the edge of the ocean. They both paused to watch the lights of a container ship twinkling against a midnight-blue sky as it sailed near the horizon.

"So how did you get into the content creation business?" Rachel asked again. Chad had warned her earlier that influencers preferred to be called content creators.

"I was studying business at college," he said, lifting up his beer bottle and downing half of it in a single gulp. He swayed slightly when he was done. Rachel realized that he was well on the way to getting drunk. "Don't laugh. I was planning to be an accountant."

"What happened?"

"In the summer between my sophomore and junior years, I started working out. After a couple months, some guy asked me how I went from being puny to getting muscles. I told him about the diet and exercises that I'd been doing. He suggested I start an Instagram account and post updates on my training regimen and diet. So I did. I set it up right there in front of him. He was my first follower."

Jonny showed Rachel an Instagram post of himself before he started working out. He looked like a geeky undernourished teenager with acne and biceps the size of a golf ball. "In high school, I was voted most likely to get a boring desk job."

"You certainly defied those predictions, didn't you?" said Rachel. Jonny Macon was far from geeky. He was insanely good-looking, sexy, and clearly very successful. He was anything but a boring wannabe accountant. "Your Instagram account must have really taken off."

"I went from having eight followers in my first week to over 60,000 within six months. Brands were hounding me with offers to promote their products. It seemed dumb to keep studying to get a degree so I could get a job when I already had one. I owned a successful fitness and healthy living content business."

"What did your family think about you dropping out of college?"

"They were not happy." He chugged down more beer. "I dropped out anyway," he slurred. "I've been doing this full-time ever since. I just bought myself a Porsche and a condo. This is the beginning. The sky's the limit. The Kardashians should watch out. I have big plans for the future. New apps. New sponsorships. New products."

"I heard your girlfriend, Reni, also has a successful wellness app," said Rachel, edging the conversation toward Maddison.

"Reni's in talks with a big streaming company to launch a show. In fact, the producers want us to do it together instead of separate shows but . . . These things can get complicated." His eyes were glazed. "Why are you really here?" He spun around, unsteady on his feet as if all the alcohol had just caught up with him.

"I told you already, I'm here to learn about the influencer business."

"I've been watching you tonight." He slurred his words, gesturing toward her with the beer bottle. "You're not here to party or to network. Are you, Rachel? Why are you really here?"

"I work at a podcast," said Rachel, avoiding the question. "That's why I was invited. A friend of a friend told me to look out for Maddison Logan. Do you know her?" Rachel didn't let on that, at least according to the rumor mill, he and Maddison had recently had a fling.

"Yeah. So?"

"I haven't seen her around. Any idea why?" Rachel asked.

"It's a typical Maddison move to bolt when things don't play out her way."

"What way is that?"

Jonny turned and walked away, teetering as if he was about to lose his balance. In the space of a minute, he'd gone from being warm and playfully friendly to suspicious and distant.

"You'd better go back to the party," he called out.

"Why is Maddison such a touchy subject?" Rachel pressed.

"Because Maddison does what suits Maddison. She probably took a time-out. That's why you haven't seen her around."

"Why would she take a time-out?"

He let out a loud hiss of frustration. "This is all glamorous and lots of fun." He waved his arm drunkenly toward the hotel where the afterparty was still raging by the poolside deck. "What people don't realize is that being an influencer is like feeding a monster. An insatiable monster. Nothing is ever enough. No matter how much you give, there's always someone giving more. Eventually you have to give your soul. Even that's not enough. People self-destruct all the time."

"You think that's what happened to Maddison."

"Maddison broke one of the cardinal rules of The Infinity Project."

"The—what?"

"Never betray your friends," he shouted.

He took a swig of beer before moving along the beach away from Rachel, holding the beer bottle tightly by the neck. He swung it drunkenly as he walked. "Never betray your friends," he slurred, poking his finger into the air as he enunciated each syllable for emphasis. "Ne-ver be-tray your fri-ends."

"The Infinity Project?" Rachel called out. "What is that?"

He didn't turn around. Her voice was swallowed by the wind. Rachel ran after him. When she reached him, she grabbed his upper arm to get his attention. He whirled around to face her.

"You want to know about The Infinity Project? It's that," he said through clenched teeth, pointing toward the afterparty. "Making money. Making more money than you could hope to spend in a lifetime. And fame. Instant recognition."

"Is that what all this is about? Money and fame?"

"What else is there?" he said, like Rachel was stupid. "Once you're famous, you can do anything. It doesn't matter how you became famous. Marrying a prince. A sex tape. Planking for YouTube videos. It's all about name recognition. That's a license to print enough money to last you for eternity." He stumbled off.

It was too dark for her to see more than his silhouette walking in drunken zigzags toward the ocean, where the tide was coming in with a ferocious persistence.

"Being an influencer is the game of life, Rachel. Until someone finds out you're a fraud. Then everything falls apart," he shouted out. "Then you crash and burn." He raised his beer bottle into the air in a silent salute before stumbling away, enveloped by darkness.

Chapter 35

Rachel picked at a plate of cut fruit with her fork. She was sitting at a table on the outdoor terrace of the hotel café, eating breakfast while looking out at the ocean. The sky was threaded with the delicate apricot of dawn. She loved being awake early when the morning still held the tantalizing possibility of new beginnings.

Rachel had disappeared from the afterparty just before one A.M., a modern-day Cinderella rushing up to her hotel room before her carriage turned into a pumpkin. She'd been too exhausted to do much more than brush her teeth and undress before collapsing in bed. She'd been vaguely aware of a chorus of laughter mixed with throbbing music drifting from the poolside afterparty through the open balcony door of her room as she slept.

Sunlight shining into her east-facing room woke Rachel just after dawn. She'd forgotten to close the drapes before she'd gone to sleep.

She'd risen from bed and changed into her running clothes before heading down to the beach. She passed a sound engineer packing up his equipment and hotel workers collecting dirty glasses left around the pool area as she headed to the hotel gate leading to the beach. The staff worked slowly. Their bone-tired weariness indicated the party had only recently wrapped up.

On the beach, Rachel had run in the direction of the amusement park. The Ferris wheel and other rides sat idle like discarded toys. Deflated by the haunted stillness, she turned around halfway there and ran back to the hotel. She had a hot shower to revive herself and changed into the jeans she'd worn the previous day paired with a figure-hugging black boatneck top that exposed the breadth of her collarbone and the hollow of her throat.

The hotel restaurant had a full breakfast buffet set up with a chef at an omelet station. Another chef stood behind a pyramid of fruit and vegetables to make fresh juice blends for guests. Only Rachel and two other guests had appeared for breakfast. Everyone else was apparently still asleep. Rachel helped herself to a bowl of granola and a plate of fresh fruit. She gave a barista her coffee order before heading back to her table on the balcony with its sweeping views of the pool and the beach beyond.

As Rachel ate, she glanced at the couple at a table farther down the terrace.

She recognized the woman as the fitness influencer, Zoe, who'd spent the afterparty trying to be filmed with star-power influencers like Jonny Macon. Zoe wore workout leggings and a bright blue halter-neck top. She had long, straight bleached hair that she wore in a high ponytail.

With her was her boyfriend, sporting floppy bangs and Clark Kent–style glasses. He was filming everything that Zoe did with the professionalism of a director shooting a Hollywood blockbuster. He filmed multiple takes, stopping to show Zoe the footage and then conferring with her on whether the angle was right or a reshoot was needed.

"Eric, come in closer," Zoe directed her boyfriend as she sucked down on a translucent straw stuck into a bright purple fruit shake.

Rachel watched Eric move in for a close-up of Zoe sipping through the straw and then smacking her lips when she was done. Zoe then proceeded to go into a monologue detailing the nutrients in the shake and all the ways they improved health.

"Check out my blog for more revitalizing shake recipes," she said, mentioning her preferred blender with a special blade that brought out the intensity of the fresh ingredients.

Rachel presumed that Zoe was getting a referral fee. That's what Chad, the marketing guy, had told Rachel was standard practice for many influencers. It's how they turned their platforms into lucrative marketing businesses.

Eric filmed two separate angles of Zoe sipping a bright green shake made from kale and sour apple. Zoe's initial dubious expression after sipping the drink turned into delight.

"Oh my gosh. I never thought that drinking kale would taste so good," she enthused. "It has a peppery sweet combination from the kale and the arugula. The sour apple and ginger give it one heck of a kick."

"The angle wasn't good when you lifted up the glass," Eric cut in after she finished talking. "We need to shoot it again."

"You can't be serious!" she snapped.

Eric signaled for the waiter to bring a new shake. When it arrived, they filmed the sequence all over again. Rachel marveled at Zoe's ability to drink what must have been a gallon of vegetable juice by the time they were done filming the segment to her satisfaction.

When they finished shooting her drinking health shakes, Rachel assumed they'd both get down to the business of eating breakfast. Instead, Zoe put an organic cotton T-shirt over her halter top, applied fresh lipstick in a different shade, and moved to another table with a sea view behind it to film a new segment.

While Zoe waited for her boyfriend to get the camera angle right, she took down her hair and brushed it out so that it hung loose, giving her a relaxed, beachy vibe.

"Okay. Let's go," Eric called out.

Zoe leaned back on her chair with her hands behind her head and began a chirpy monologue about how burned out she'd been feeling until she made a few simple lifestyle changes. "You need to be in charge of your sustenance. Remember, sustenance is more than what you eat or drink. It's what you do. It's loving yourself. Don't be afraid to fall in love with you."

The impromptu photo shoot going on at Zoe's table reminded Rachel that Pete had asked her to send fresh content in the morning for the @runninggirlRach account. Once again, she'd forgotten.

Rachel took a close-up shot of a big slice of watermelon on her plate as well as her glass of water with a lemon slice floating on top. Rachel was astonished when she checked her Insta feed after posting the photos. @runninggirlRach had risen to 41,000 followers. She'd doubled her followers virtually overnight. It must have been the photo that Jonny Macon posted with Rachel at the afterparty. Rachel tapped over to his profile and saw some of his followers had asked whether he was dating @runninggirlRach.

"Just having a good time with a great gal!" he'd responded.

Rachel winced at the false implication before putting away her phone when the waiter arrived with a copy of the local newspaper that she'd requested. She flipped the pages. There was nothing about a body being discovered in the state forest the previous day. There was also nothing about Maddison Logan's disappearance. Joe Martinez hadn't been kidding when he'd told her he was keeping the investigation out of the media for now.

Rachel had spent most of the afterparty the previous night trying to find out more about Maddison. Mostly the influencers would shrug when she asked, before disappearing into a crush of people on the dance floor. Rachel suspected that it wasn't personal. The influencers spent so much time on their phones that they almost flinched and ran for cover at the "threat" of direct human contact.

Still, Rachel had learned that Jonny Macon was in the same influencer pod as Maddison, as well as @SerendipityZoe and a few of the others she'd seen at the conference.

The term "influencer pod" evoked images of dolphins swimming together. From the way that Chad had described it the previous night over dinner, it was more like a school of sharks. The influencer business was cutthroat.

One of the guests at the afterparty had mentioned to Rachel that some of the travel influencers were staying at a beach campsite north of the town. Rachel had asked why they weren't staying at the conference venue. It was, after all, a luxury resort hotel on the beach with a lagoon pool.

"Can't pretend to despise consumerism and then stay at a five-star hotel," he'd answered. "They have to be authentic to their brands. Otherwise they'll get slaughtered online."

Rachel thought about that remark as she looked across the terrace at the restaurant table where Zoe's "Instagram husband" was filming her monologue about why everyone should "step out of the rat race and take time to connect with their inner self and loved ones."

"Can we take a break?" Eric asked Zoe after the dozenth take. "I've got to eat. I'm starving." Without waiting for an answer, he headed to the buffet to get his breakfast as Zoe glared at him.

Rachel rose from her table. She waited behind Eric at the omelet station as the chef broke fresh eggs and whipped them up, pouring them into a copper fry pan.

"You two are working hard," Rachel remarked.

"If it was up to me, we'd still be sleeping," he said, checking his fitness watch. He stifled a yawn. "Zoe insists on fresh content every morning. She's a workaholic and hyper-competitive, especially with so much at stake."

"What's at stake?"

"Winning the Influencer Awards."

"What are the Influencer Awards, and how do you win?" Rachel asked.

Eric stared at Rachel as if she'd fallen from outer space. "You really don't know?"

"I really don't."

"Whoever adds the most followers and gets the most engagement during BuzzCon will win a place at the Influencer Awards finals in New York."

"What's the big deal about that?" Rachel asked.

"The winner in New York gets a five-million-dollar contract and a content deal with a big streaming company. Is that a big enough deal?"

"That's a lot of money," Rachel agreed.

"It's more than the money. Whoever wins will be well on their way to becoming a mega influencer. We're talking about making tens of millions of dollars a year."

"I wish I'd known earlier. I'd have put more effort into photographing my breakfast," Rachel said dryly.

"Zoe may have a chance to edge out her main competition. @JustMaddie is sulking because everyone turned on her when they found out about her cheating with Jonny Macon. She hasn't posted in days. Now I'm hearing that Jonny Macon's girlfriend, Reni, is in trouble. If that's true, then Zoe becomes a front-runner," Eric said as the chef flipped his omelet.

"How is Reni in trouble?"

Eric looked slightly mortified, like he'd slipped up. "There are rumors that she funneled capital she raised from investors for her wellness app into private bank accounts. If it gets out, she may lose the deal she's negotiated to produce a web series. It's a seven-figure deal."

He stopped talking when the chef handed him a plate with a mushroom omelet neatly folded. Swiss cheese oozed out of the sides. "I'll see you around." Eric headed back to his table, where Zoe was visibly fuming.

"What did she want?" Rachel overheard Zoe hiss as he sat down.

Rachel left the restaurant and wandered along the beach. It was too early for her to chase down any other leads. She decided to follow Zoe's advice and "connect with her inner self," at least until people started waking up and she could get back to work.

After just twelve hours at BuzzCon, Rachel had already learned there were plenty of people who benefited from Maddison's disappearance. Zoe, Eric's girlfriend, would have a better chance of winning if the competition was less stiff and Maddison wasn't around. Jonny Macon was bitter. He'd accused Maddison of betraying him.

Rachel couldn't even imagine what his girlfriend, Reni, who had apparently masterminded some sort of financial fraud, might do to punish Maddison for sleeping with her boyfriend. Rachel had no doubt that she'd find others too.

The influencer world was hyper-competitive. Everyone seemed to be "frenemies." They hugged and kissed each other's cheeks in person. They all gushed about each other online. But Rachel suspected that they'd happily stick a knife in each other's back if they thought they could get ahead by doing it.

Chapter 36

The orderlies who worked at the city morgue called it "the stairway to hell." It was a staircase that spiraled down to the business end of the morgue on the lower floor, where bodies were stored in refrigerators and autopsies were conducted.

At the bottom of the staircase was a glass window with a curtain. When relatives came to identify loved ones, the curtain would be opened to reveal a body on a gurney. That was why the orderlies called it "the stairway to hell." No relative ever went back up those stairs the same way.

The curtain was drawn when Joe Martinez came down the spiral staircase to the bottom floor. Nobody was around. It was just after six in the morning. Martinez headed down a long corridor to a door marked "morgue." An orderly was playing Candy Crush on her phone when Martinez entered. The room was lined with floor-to-ceiling stainless steel refrigerators.

"A woman was brought in last night from the state forest," Martinez said.

"Marsh Girl? She's in there." The orderly pointed toward a set of swinging doors. "The autopsy is about to begin. Dr. Padres came in early. He is not in a good mood. But then, what else is new."

Martinez headed toward the autopsy room.

"You can't just go in there," the orderly called out. "Dr. Padres is very particular. FBI or no FBI, you have to suit up."

She tossed Martinez goggles, a gown, a cap, and gloves. Once he put them on, she held out a vial of camphor rub to stop the smell. He rubbed it under his nostrils and then headed inside.

The body of a woman covered in mud was laid out on a slab in the white tiled room. Dr. Padres was looking into a microscope, fiddling with a slide.

"You're the FBI agent who got me out of bed to rush this autopsy?" The pathologist didn't look up from the microscope when Martinez entered.

"Guilty as charged," said Martinez. "We're dealing with a missing persons case and we need to know if she's our missing person or whether we need to keep looking."

"Is your missing person blood type AB?" the pathologist asked, his eyes still pressed to the microscope.

"We think her blood type is O positive," Martinez answered. "That's based on blood smudges found at the entrance to her camper van."

"If it's O, then she isn't your missing person. The blood types don't match."

"Unless the blood smudges at the crime scene belong to someone else," Martinez wondered out loud.

The pathologist took out a slide and inserted a new one. He twisted the microscope lens to focus on the specimen.

"This is interesting. Take a look."

"What am I looking at?" Martinez asked, looking into the microscope.

"It's mud. It was taken from the victim's mouth," said Dr. Padres. "She sure swallowed a heck of a lot of mud before she died. I'll know more once I open her up."

His assistant, a bearded giant of a man dressed in an enormous plastic apron tied over scrubs, entered from a back room pushing a creaky metal cart with autopsy equipment taken from a sterilizing autoclave machine.

"You can stay and watch if you like," said Dr. Padres.

Putting on magnified glasses, he examined every square inch of the body with ultraviolet light. Using tweezers, he removed a few bits of trace material from the dead woman's skin, which he put into clear plastic bags. He typed notes on a nearby computer terminal as his assistant turned on the hose and washed the body.

Martinez stood to the side, watching the mud soften and melt as the body was washed. Martinez noticed the coin-sized coiled snake tattoo on the back of her hand. It was the only tattoo on her body. Her long blond hair, washed clean of mud, was around the same shade as Maddison's hair. He put her age at early to mid twenties, which approximated Maddison's age. She was of average height for a woman, as was Maddison. Despite these similarities, it was impossible to conclude whether "Marsh Girl" was Maddison based purely on a visual inspection. They'd need more.

The fingerprints taken when the body was exhumed last night would be compared that morning to prints lifted from Maddison's camper van. Martinez hoped that would give them a preliminary ID while they waited for DNA confirmation.

The pathologist checked her again after her body was washed. "There's no obvious sign of external wounds," he said, glancing up at Martinez. "No ligature marks or bruising either. It will be interesting to see what we find when we open her up."

Martinez left before the formal autopsy began. As he took the stairs up to the main entrance of the morgue, he checked his phone. He paused to look at Stephanie's photo on the home screen before scrolling through his messages.

Among them was a text message from Rachel Krall. It had come through the previous evening when Martinez had been driving back to town from the crime scene. He hadn't had a chance to call her back. He'd do it later. He had the morning team briefing to attend to first.

Mark Torreno was sipping coffee like it was a lifeline when Martinez came down the stairs into the basement at police headquarters fifteen minutes later.

"I thought I was going to do the morning briefing and you'd do the later shift," said Torreno. That's what they'd both agreed to when they'd left well after midnight.

"I had to get up early anyway," said Martinez. "I've just come from the morgue. The autopsy is underway. Do we have any fresh leads from overnight?"

"Nothing," said Torreno. "Bailey didn't use the contraband phone again. As an added complication, the phone number he texted is also a burner phone. Purchased in Canada."

Martinez groaned to himself at that news. A burner from another country created a whole lot of jurisdictional hoops to jump through to get a trace. It would slow things down.

"If we still have no major lead on Maddison by tomorrow morning, then I'm calling a news conference. I'll take it to the media."

"It will be a circus," Torreno responded.

"It'll be a shitshow, not a circus," corrected Martinez, looking up as his team came down the stairs in single file. "But if we can't find out anything by then, we really do need the help of the public."

Martinez called everyone together for the team briefing, where he handed out fresh investigative assignments for the morning. As the meeting wrapped up, Torreno received a call. He stepped away to his desk to take it.

"Joe," Torreno called out after he got off the phone. He looked troubled.

"What's going on?"

"The guards tossed Bailey's cell this morning when he was at breakfast. He was sketching again last night. There's a new drawing in his sketchpad. They've just emailed it to me."

"What's he drawn this time?"

Torreno pulled up a photo on the large computer monitor on his desk. It was a portrait of Rachel Krall drawn in black ink. Using minimal lines and shadows, Terence Bailey had drawn a remarkably accurate portrait of Rachel, capturing her delicate beauty and her determination.

On the border of the paper, under the sketch, Bailey had drawn the same symbol that he'd tattooed on his hand and which they'd found on the hand of the victim they'd dubbed "Marsh Girl." It also matched the necklace charm drawn on the picture of the mysterious goth girl that the guards had found in Bailey's sketchbook the previous day.

It was a drawing of a snake eating its tail. Underneath the snake insignia were the words "Memento mori" written in a whirl of flowing calligraphy.

"Remember, your death awaits you," Martinez said, translating the Latin.

"It sounds like a threat," said Torreno.

Martinez nodded grimly. It was his fault. He'd brought Rachel Krall to Terence Bailey's attention. He'd roused the devil, and the devil was about to become a free man.

Chapter 37

Flipping open the ironing board, Thomas McCoy lays out his freshly laundered pants while he waits for the iron to heat up until it's steaming hot. It burns his finger when he tests it by pressing his fingertip against the hot plate.

He keeps it there until the pain becomes intolerable, and he rips it away. Sucking his burned finger, he runs the iron down his pants legs, pressing hard against the ironing board to create knife-like creases just the way his mom taught him.

He neatly hangs the pressed pants over the back of a chair and then picks up a newly laundered light gray business shirt. He slides the iron backward and forward over the fabric before working the iron through the trickier front panels and the lapel.

It's early but he's already had a busy morning. He fed the chickens and filled Millie's food and water bowls before tethering her to a front porch rail with a stretch of rope. He's seen the carcasses of run-over dogs often enough to know better than to let his girl roam free, even though the roads surrounding the house rarely get traffic.

Millie's a Doberman-mongrel bitch. Seven years old. He found her when she was a puppy dumped on the edge of the Delta Springs forest. She'd run into the road to chase his car as he took a corner. Luckily, he saw her in time and swerved out of the way. She'd snarled at him when he scooped her up. He took her home anyway. She's guarded his house ever since.

After feeding Millie, he used the garden hose to water the roses lining the path to the front porch. They were his mother's prize-winning roses. He promised he'd take care of them when she was no longer around. The roses might not win prizes anymore but at least they were still alive. That was more than he could say for his mother.

He'd buried her in a garden bed and planted azaleas on top. The flowers remind him of his mother: beautiful and yet toxic. He sprays them with the garden hose.

The property isn't the thriving farm it was in his father's day, but it's still well-kept. Thomas is an orderly man. That was his beef with Stacey. She became a slob once she started drinking again.

Thomas looks out toward the lime tree in the citrus orchard to the side of the house. It's all that's left of the expansive orchards his father farmed until the government requisitioned his fields for highway work.

Underneath the lime tree is a rock. Thomas put it there to mark Stacey's final resting place. It's been six months now. Ever since he buried Stacey, he's felt an insatiable urge to do it again.

Before changing into his neatly ironed clothes, he sprays on a thick cloud of deodorant and splashes on cologne. He wears designer colognes when he's working. It smells classy and it lasts longer than the cheaper scents.

He dresses fancy when he drives. He always wears a business shirt and pants. Neatly ironed. Sometimes he even wears a jacket and tie. Good first impressions make all the difference. Like it or not, people judge by appearance. He puts on his pants. The fabric is still warm from the iron. He buttons up his shirt and flips a tie into a knot around his neck.

When he's finished dressing, he fixes his damp red-brown hair, threaded with gray, in the hall mirror and tidies up his beard. He glances at the closed basement door. He hasn't heard a peep out of her since last night when he brought her a sandwich and water.

When he dropped down the food, she was lying listlessly with her eyes open, staring into the darkness. He was troubled by her submissiveness. It's too soon for her to give up. He needs her alive for another day. Until tomorrow. Because tomorrow is "get out of jail" day for Terence Bailey, and Thomas has big plans to celebrate his freedom.

He tosses a few crackers along with a couple of apples and a bottle of cold water into a supermarket bag. Then he carefully unlocks the basement door and steps into the dark, musty interior. It's filled with old boxes of unsold sporting memorabilia, accumulated when he ran the online business with Stacey, before he closed it down and took up work as a rideshare driver.

He'd imported fake products like players' jerseys and sports bags from China and sold them online with a decent markup. Stacey had suggested they fake autographs on baseballs and jerseys so he could sell them at an even steeper markup. Stacey was pretty good at writing out fake autographs. It worked well until one of his clients took a signed Red Sox baseball he'd sold him for $100 to be valued. The collector told him it was worth two dollars. Less than the cost of a new ball. The autograph was fake.

He'd received an angry complaint from the customer and threats to take the issue to the police. He immediately refunded the guy's money with a heartfelt apology and a bullshit claim that he too had been deceived by a dealer. He'd waited a week and then shut down his e-store. He couldn't take the risk of getting caught over something as stupid as passing fakes as signed memorabilia. Not when he had so many more important things to hide.

"Are you awake?" he calls out when he's halfway down the stairs.

"Yes," she rasps.

Her voice is hoarse from screaming. He did warn her not to bother. There are no neighbors nearby. The closest sign of civilization is the highway ramp a quarter of a mile away. It's just him, and her. And Millie, of course. His loyal guard dog.

"I brought you breakfast," he announces, standing halfway down the stairs.

"Please let me go," she pleads in response. "I promise I'll never say a word to anyone."

"You should have thought of that before you poked around in other people's business," he says.

"I didn't poke around."

"Don't lie," he screams. She cowers as his violent fury bounces off the basement walls.

She's tethered with rope to one of the timber pillars supporting the staircase. The rope is just long enough for her to reach the basement toilet and sink area. He holds the bag with the food over the banister for a second before letting go. It lands with a thump on the basement floor.

"There's soap by the sink. Wash yourself before you eat," he orders, before mounting the stairs back to the top.

He slams the basement door behind him and locks it with the key and a bolt. Before he leaves the house, he turns on the radio on the hall table. It will block out her screams and cries for help in the unlikely instance that someone comes to the house while he's out. He takes every precaution. He keeps the driveway gate locked, and he has Millie. Still, a man can't be too careful.

He bites into a green apple with a loud crunch as he leaves the house and heads toward his car. His first ride for the day flashes on the rideshare app.

Chapter 38

Rachel watched the zigzags of her shoe tread press into the sand as she walked along the beach, listening to Maddison Logan's voicemail message.

"My friend. She was murdered. A long time ago. I know who killed her. He knows that I know. I think he's going to come for me. . . ."

Rachel couldn't understand why Maddison hadn't contacted the cops. Instead, in the hours before she'd disappeared, Maddison had turned to Rachel for help. Why Rachel, and not the police? Rachel was determined to find out.

The high-pitched screams of a toddler broke into Rachel's train of thought. Rachel looked up to see a child running into a broken wave, screeching in delight.

In the distance, people were gathering hurriedly on the beach near the rickety pier. Something was wrong. The commotion was palpable even from where Rachel stood, hundreds of yards up the beach. Siren lights of emergency response vehicles flashed as they pulled up on the boardwalk.

Rachel moved into a jog. By the time she reached the area, a knot of onlookers was watching first responders work in a huddle under the pillars of the jetty. Police set up an accordion-style screen to block prying eyes while other officers ordered the crowd to move away. An ashen man sat on the sand, staring into space.

Rachel mounted the stairs to the boardwalk, where she paused at the higher vantage point to get a better view of the chaotic scene below.

"So you decided to stay after all." The voice came from behind Rachel. "Why am I not surprised?"

Rachel swung around to face Joe Martinez.

"I thought you flew home last night," he said. He looked troubled to see her but inexplicably pleased at the same time.

"I'm a sucker for sunshine and the ocean. I couldn't bring myself to leave," said Rachel, trying not to sound defensive. "What happened over there?" She gestured toward the first responders crowded around the underbelly of the pier.

"I was on my way to get breakfast when I saw the siren lights. I gather there was some sort of an accident. Looks like the paramedics and the cops have everything under control." He glanced at his watch. "Would you like to join me for a quick breakfast?"

They walked down to another café not far from the one where Rachel had eaten burgers with Terence Bailey's former attorney the previous day. Martinez ordered coffee and two eggs over easy. Rachel, who'd already eaten breakfast, ordered an iced coffee.

Martinez kept things light, deliberately avoiding any discussion of Terence Bailey as he cut up his food and ate with methodical thoroughness.

In between mouthfuls, he asked Rachel how she'd become involved in the podcasting business. She explained that she'd gone through a career crisis after she was laid off from the newspaper where she'd worked as a crime reporter due to editorial cutbacks. It was around that time that Pete contacted her out of the blue to ask her to work with him on a podcast series.

Pete had seen an award-winning article Rachel had written about an up-and-coming jazz musician who'd been raped and murdered on her way home from the bar where she'd worked as a waitress and occasional performer. He'd liked the way Rachel brought humanity to an unspeakable crime, focusing on the grief and the quest for justice more than on the gory details. He sensed that she'd bring the same compassion to a true-crime podcast. Rachel agreed to work on the podcast, thinking it would be a sideline. She'd never imagined it would catapult her into a new career.

"I'd never done broadcast journalism before, or podcasts. I figured that I'd give it a shot. I never expected to enjoy it so much or that it would take on a life of its own," she told Martinez.

"I've listened to all three seasons of your podcast, including the rape trial you covered in Neapolis," Martinez said. "They're very good. Astonishing investigative work. I'd say there's a cop inside of you trying to get out."

"Not a cop. Never a cop," said Rachel. "I'm a reporter through and through."

After Rachel finished giving Martinez a quick overview of how she came to make podcasts, she asked him whether there were any updates on the body they'd found the previous day.

"It's early days yet," he said cryptically, biting into a piece of buttered toast.

"What does that mean?" Rachel asked, refusing to allow him to change the subject. "Is the dead girl Maddison or not?"

Martinez continued eating. If he was aware that Rachel had stopped drinking her coffee and was glaring at him, then he didn't show it. The moment he finished his mouthful of food, Rachel asked him the question again.

"We can't conclude anything for sure until we get the results of DNA tests," he answered.

"I'm hearing a 'but'?"

"*But,*" he said, emphasizing the word in acknowledgment that Rachel guessed right, "the fingerprints of the girl in the marsh don't match any of the prints collected in Maddison's van. Also, her blood type is AB positive. The blood we found in Maddison's van is O."

"The blood types don't match. The fingerprints don't match. So it's not Maddison?"

"The simple truth is that we don't know yet," Martinez said. "We're waiting for results on DNA taken from items found in Maddison's camper van. We're looking for a DNA match to the woman found in the mud. Until then we are treating the Maddison Logan missing persons case as open."

"That reminds me, did you get the text I sent yesterday asking you to call me?" Rachel asked.

"I was going to get back to you this morning. What did you need?"

"My producer found a voice message that Maddison left on the podcast office voicemail before she disappeared. I thought you might want to hear it."

She played the voicemail message for Martinez. He listened to it intently before asking her to send him a copy of the audio file.

"Are you sure that Maddison didn't contact you again or send you emails with more information?"

"Pete triple-checked. Maddison left this one phone message. It sounds as if she stumbled across something, or someone, from her past. I think that's why Maddison went to see Bailey. I'm willing to meet him again and ask him straight out what he knows," Rachel offered.

Martinez pursed his lips thoughtfully as if seriously considering Rachel's offer. "Bailey didn't scare you off with what he told you yesterday? 'The scariest monster is the one that hides in plain sight,'" he said, repeating Bailey's comment to Rachel. He watched her reaction over the rim of his coffee mug.

"He doesn't frighten me, if that's what you mean," said Rachel.

"Well, he should," said Martinez, putting down the mug abruptly like he'd made a decision. "It's best that you don't see Bailey again. If he really is a predator, then the last thing we want is for him to fixate on you."

At Rachel's arched eyebrow, he added decisively: "I am keeping you out of it from now on, Rachel." Martinez's flinty gaze matched his firm tone. It was obvious that he wouldn't budge.

"You don't know me very well if you expect me to do as I'm told, Joe," Rachel said quietly.

"It's not that straightforward." Martinez pushed his plate away. "This morning while Bailey was down at breakfast, the guards searched his cell. They photographed something that you should see."

He showed Rachel the photo on his phone. It was a cleverly drawn portrait of her. Under the portrait was the symbol of the snake eating its tail that Bailey had tattooed on his hand. A Latin phrase was written at the bottom in a swirl of calligraphy.

"Memento mori." Rachel read the Latin words out loud. She flicked her eyes up uncertainly.

"It roughly translates as 'Remember, death awaits you.' I take it as a threat. That's why I'm keeping you out of this, Rachel. In fact, if I had my way, you'd already be at home, which is exactly where I thought you were until I bumped into you this morning," he added pointedly.

"I don't work for you, Joe. I decide where I go and what I do."

"I am well aware." Martinez's eyes locked with Rachel's gaze. "I can't change your mind?"

"Not likely." Rachel took a sip of her iced coffee before changing the subject. "Terence Bailey sure likes that snake symbol. He tattooed it on his hand. He's now drawn it on a portrait of me. It must mean something?"

"I had a symbology expert give me a rundown earlier," said Martinez. "That intertwined snake is called an Ouroboros. It's one of the oldest and most universal symbols in the world. It's sometimes rendered in the shape of a circle. Other times it's in a sideways figure eight like this one. It's similar to the mathematic symbol representing—"

"Infinity," said Rachel.

Martinez nodded. "Some believe the infinity symbol used in math derived from the natural phenomenon when snakes eat their own tails."

"Snakes really eat their own tails?"

"They mistake their tails for prey," said Martinez. "They get so carried away eating themselves that it becomes a frenzy. They don't stop. In the end, they kill themselves."

"What's the origin of the symbol?" Rachel asked.

"I've been told that it's almost as old as time itself," said Martinez. "The Ancient Greeks gave it the name 'Ouroboros.' It means 'tail eating.' It appears in medieval alchemy books and even in Norse mythology. It generally means the same thing across cultures."

"A symbol of infinity?"

"It's more than that. It means infinite renewal. The life cycle. Ashes to ashes. Dust to dust. Endless continuity until the end of time. It's also used in the occult. It's a powerful symbol in black magic."

"What does it mean in the occult?"

"It's a sign of death, Rachel."

"Are you telling me that Terence Bailey has marked me for execution? That he's coming for me when he gets out of prison?"

Chapter 39

By the time Rachel and Joe came out of the café, the beach around the pier and nearby boardwalk had been cordoned off with police tape. Police officers were pushing back spectators down the beach until the onlookers were huddled near a row of beach recliners, where people tanned, oblivious to the drama unfolding nearby.

"Excuse me while I find out what's going on." Martinez quickly took the stairs down to the sand, where he showed his FBI badge to a young police officer.

Rachel stood on the boardwalk watching Martinez bend under the police tape and disappear behind privacy screens put up to shield the scene from onlookers filming with their phones.

While she waited for him to return, Rachel read up on the Ouroboros. It was a natural phenomenon. Snakes sometimes killed themselves by eating their own tails until they died from toxic shock. Self-cannibalization. Just the thought of it gave Rachel the creeps.

Before they left the restaurant, Martinez had reiterated his earlier warning to Rachel. He'd sounded very concerned.

"You really think that Terence Bailey wants to kill me?" Rachel had asked.

"He was the prime suspect in the abduction and murder of a string of women before he was locked up on an aggravated burglary charge. That's why I really hope you will take note and head home. It won't be safe for you here when Bailey is released tomorrow."

"I told you already. I'm on vacation. R&R."

"R&R at Daytona Beach?"

"What's that supposed to mean?"

"It's a party town, Rachel. If you're looking for a relaxing vacation, head over to the Caribbean. Try the Bahamas. If you must stay in Florida, then go down to the Keys."

"I didn't realize that FBI agents moonlighted as travel consultants. I must remember to check in with you next time I plan a vacation."

"Rachel, it was my mistake bringing you here. Go home. Forget about all of this. It's not your problem."

"You flew me down to talk to a suspected serial killer and now you're losing your nerve? We haven't known each other long, Joe. But the one thing you should already have figured out is that it takes a heck of a lot more than Terence Bailey getting out of jail to rattle me."

Rachel privately found Joe Martinez's concern unexpectedly charming. It was rare for anyone to worry about her. Even her mom, a renowned worrier, rarely spared a thought for her eldest daughter. No matter what life threw at her, Rachel always picked herself up and dusted herself off. Even when her marriage had crumbled, she'd wiped away the hidden tears and marched on.

Rachel scanned the beach for Joe, who was still behind police lines looking at the crime scene. She was about to head off when Martinez emerged. He grimly wound his way back through the police barriers up the stairs to the boardwalk where Rachel waited.

"What happened?" Rachel asked when he'd joined her.

"They fished a body out of the water. It was found floating under the pier."

"The water looks so placid. How terrible to think that someone drowned here not too long ago."

"I'm told that it's not unusual. There are riptides in this area, especially around the pier," Martinez said. "Still, there's something about the body that strikes me as strange. . . ."

Martinez took out his phone and flicked through photos before stopping at one particular image. He zoomed in and out, his face pursed in concentration. He flicked to another photo, forgetting that Rachel could see his phone screen.

On Martinez's screen was a photo of a man lying faceup on the sand by the pier where he'd obviously been dragged out of the water. His eyes were open. They were as lifeless as his skin was drained of color.

Rachel gasped.

"What's wrong?" Martinez looked up at Rachel.

"It's the photo," she said shakily.

"I'm sorry, I should have been more discreet." He noticed Rachel's shock. "I'm so used to seeing photos of dead bodies that I forget how upsetting they can be."

"I've seen photos of bodies before. They don't usually get to me," said Rachel. "It's just that . . . I think I know the victim."

Chapter 40

A relaxed repose hung over the beachside camping area. Campers scraped cutlery against picnic dishes while silently eating breakfast by their tents as if reluctant to interrupt the quiet of the natural setting. Birds chirped in the trees scattered around the campground. Across the way, the constant beat of the tide added to the laid-back vibe.

It was into this tranquil atmosphere that a blue car drove into the campground. It dropped off a passenger and drove away, dust billowing around its tires.

Rachel had taken a rideshare to the camping area right after leaving Joe Martinez by the pier. His case had become a whole lot more complicated once Rachel told him the name of the drowning victim whose photo she'd seen on his phone.

"That's Jonny Macon," Rachel had burst out in shock.

"How do you know him?" Martinez had pulled her aside on the boardwalk so they could talk without being overheard.

"I met Jonny last night. At the BuzzCon afterparty. He's an up-and-coming fitness influencer. One of the big-name guests at BuzzCon. We talked for a while. It's hard to believe that someone I was talking to only a few hours ago is dead."

Rachel had shuddered as she remembered how she'd watched Jonny disappear into the darkness in the direction of the pier where his body was found this morning.

"It adds to my conviction that you should go home, Rachel."

"That's ridiculous. Why would it have anything to do with me?"

In response, Martinez had scrolled through the photos he'd taken of the body. He showed Rachel a photo of Jonny Macon's ankle. The skin was pale, drained of all color other than a small tattoo. Rachel whipped up her eyes in shock. Martinez nodded.

"It's another Ouroboros," she whispered.

"Two bodies found in two days. Both with Ouroboros symbols," said Martinez. "The exact same symbol that Terence Bailey tattooed on his hand."

"He's locked up in prison. How could he possibly have known the symbol would turn up on dead bodies?"

"Unless he's involved. Unless he knows the killer," said Martinez. "Either way, the Ouroboros is the link between all these cases: Maddison, the girl in the mud, Jonny Macon. And . . ."

"And what?" Rachel asked.

"And you, Rachel."

"Actually, Joe, there's another link between Maddison and Jonny Macon besides the Ouroboros. They had a brief relationship."

"How brief?" he asked tersely. It was obviously news to him.

"I heard they hooked up a few days ago. Much to the disgust of Jonny's girlfriend."

"Who's his girlfriend?"

"Her name is Reni. I don't know her last name. She's a well-being influencer."

"What the hell is a well-being influencer?" Martinez asked.

"She makes social media content about how to stay healthy. She founded a healthy lifestyle philosophy and healthy living plan after battling a serious health condition that she says almost ruined her life."

Rachel hadn't mentioned what Eric had told her at breakfast about Reni being accused of fraud. Rachel had taken it with something of a grain of salt, since Eric's girlfriend, Zoe, was one of Reni's main rivals. Rachel suspected that Zoe would do just about anything to undermine her competition.

"I have people who've been discreetly asking questions at BuzzCon but all this is new," said Martinez, visibly frustrated that he had to hear this information from Rachel and not his team.

"I'm attending the conference as an influencer, under an alias. It gives me an 'in' with the influencers," said Rachel. "I could ask around for you. The place is a cesspool of gossip. Somebody will know more about Maddison and Jonny's brief entanglement."

"Okay." From Martinez's grudging tone, it was obvious that he was reluctant to involve Rachel further. "Let me know if you hear anything. It's been tough getting information out of that lot without going in with our badges. But please be discreet, Rachel. The last thing we need is for the influencers to speculate on social media. And I'd still like you to fly home before Bailey's released tomorrow."

"I'll think about it, Joe. No promises."

Before they'd parted on the boardwalk, Martinez had asked Rachel to keep the information on Jonny Macon's death to herself while his family was notified. He'd also promised to update her on the case once he knew more. Rachel wasn't exactly holding her breath. She was perfectly aware that she was a means to an end for Joe Martinez. He'd only update her if he thought it would help his investigation.

As Jonny Macon's body was carried across the beach in a body bag, Rachel decided not to mention to Martinez that she was heading over to the beach campground where she'd heard that Maddison had stayed in the days before her disappearance. Rachel had her own cards up her sleeve. Like Joe Martinez, she wasn't quite ready to show them.

Less than an hour later, as Rachel walked through the sleepy campground, she thought about how Jonny Macon had been the life of the party just hours earlier. His eyes had gleamed when he was mobbed by admirers. His fans had been a mixture of fawning marketing executives desperate to ingratiate themselves with him so he'd promote their products, as well as less successful influencers hoping his success would rub off on them.

Rachel sensed the real Jonny Macon had been far more insecure than the swaggering rising star persona that he projected. He'd been belligerent when they'd gone to the beach during the afterparty. Rachel thought the liquor was mostly to blame, because before he got drunk, he'd struck her as genuinely decent. Without being asked, he'd helped @runninggirlRach by encouraging his social media fans to follow her. In the world in which he'd operated, that was generous to a fault. Rachel had sensed that deep inside Jonny's egotistical exterior was a good man struggling to get out.

Jonny's callout to his followers to follow @runninggirlRach had exploded her decoy Instagram account. They were genuine followers. They weren't bought from Craigslist or via the guy in Bangladesh who Pete had planned to contact.

These followers were the real deal. Incredibly, Jonny Macon had catapulted @runninggirlRach to Instagram fame with a single drunken post asking his followers to make friends with her. And now he was dead.

Rachel walked among tents pitched under trees on the campground. Across a dirt road was a simple rustic beach that felt like a world away from the rowdy boardwalk and noisy beach parties at Daytona.

Last night at BuzzCon, Chad had told Rachel that travel influencers were divided into two distinct groups. There were travel influencers who stayed at luxury hotels and resorts and boasted about their jet-setting lifestyles. They were all staying at the BuzzCon hotel.

Rachel had seen some of their posts on Instagram. One had uploaded a photo of herself drinking an iced daiquiri while lying in a bubble bath, watching television in her hotel room. Another had photographed himself sipping a whiskey in a snifter glass as he floated in the lagoon-sized hotel pool.

Then there were #vanlifers like Maddison. They lived a wanderlust existence in which they eschewed luxury vacations and embraced adventurous life experiences.

At the afterparty, Rachel had talked with the boyfriend of a well-known travel vlogger who embraced a similar nomadic stress-free life traveling around the country. "All you need is a tent on your back and some attitude," she boasted in a caption accompanying a photo of herself standing on the side of a road with her thumb out, hitchhiking.

The boyfriend had confided to Rachel that his girlfriend had secretly moved into a suite at the hotel for the duration of BuzzCon.

"Don't let her followers know," he whispered, his face flushed from the liquor that had loosened his tongue. "They'll accuse her of selling out. Like a vegan sneaking a beef burger. It will kill her brand."

As Rachel stopped to chat with campers sitting on canvas chairs eating breakfast outside their tents, she thought to herself that the people staying there were luckier than those at the hotel. The languid pace gave them time to savor every moment. The changing light of the day. The crash of the surf. Even music, Rachel thought, hearing the strum of a guitar coming from the beach.

On a whim, Rachel followed the music, crossing the dirt path separating the campground from the beach. When she came out through the brush onto the sand, Rachel saw a gray-haired man with a full beard in a T-shirt and torn jeans sitting on a driftwood log strumming a battered guitar.

Rachel quietly sat cross-legged on the sand, looking out to sea while he played the guitar and sang the final chorus of a Vietnam-era folk song, his voice at times swallowed by the wind.

"You look lost," said the man when he finished the song.

"Aren't we all." Rachel smiled. "I'm looking for an old friend. I was told that she was staying here."

"What's her name?" the man asked as he tightened the strings of his guitar.

"Maddison," said Rachel. "Maddison Logan."

He put down the guitar.

"You know Maddison?" Rachel asked.

"Can't say I do. She seems to be popular. Someone else came here asking about her."

"Who?" Rachel asked.

He ignored the question as he strummed the first chords of a Bob Dylan tune on his guitar. "Never gave me his name." He spoke in tune to the music. "Had a reddish-brown beard and wore sunglasses. Pretended to be friendly. He was not friendly."

"What do you mean?"

"I have a sixth sense about people, and I had a *bad* feeling about that fella."

"Did you tell him anything about Maddison?"

"Not a word."

"Did he speak with anyone else besides you?" Rachel asked.

"He was sniffing around at the campground, that's for sure. I think he might have knocked on Shaz's door. That's her van over there." He pointed toward a small classic caravan painted navy blue that was parked across the dirt road from the beach.

Chapter 41

I'm getting dressed. I'll be out in a second," the singsong response of a woman called out as Rachel knocked on the door of the refurbished vintage caravan. It was parked under the branches of a live oak tree on the edge of the campground overlooking the ocean.

When the woman eventually flung open the aluminum door, the late-morning sunlight was bright enough that she had to shield her eyes using the side of her hand like a lazy salute. Her welcoming expression turned to wariness once her eyes adjusted to the sunlight and she saw Rachel, a stranger, and not the fellow camper she'd obviously expected when she'd heard a knock on her door.

"Who are you?" she asked suspiciously.

"I'm Rachel. Are you Shaz?"

"Why are you asking?"

Shaz's wariness of Rachel seemed at odds with her free-spirit persona. She wore a blue-green tie-dyed sundress with a long, beaded necklace wound twice around her neck. Her hair was dyed bright burgundy. Silver bracelets around her ankles jangled as she came down the caravan stairs in her bare feet.

"I'm looking for Maddison," Rachel said. "I was told you know her."

"I know lots of people."

Shaz jumped down onto the grass and unpegged clothes from a string line she'd tied from a tree branch to her caravan. Ignoring Rachel, she dropped each item of clothing into a wicker laundry basket lying on the grass by her bare feet.

Rachel walked around the laundry line so that she was facing Shaz, who was doing her best to ignore her as she unpegged her clothes and tossed them into the basket.

"I heard a man was here asking questions about Maddison a few days ago," said Rachel.

Shaz glared at Rachel, refusing to answer. "Where did you hear that from?" She rolled up a beach towel and tossed it angrily into the basket.

"The guy over there with the guitar saw him talking to you." Rachel pointed toward the beach where the man with the guitar was strumming chords while drawling the lyrics of "Tangled Up in Blue."

"Gary should mind his own business."

"What did that man want with Maddison?" Rachel asked.

"I'm not sure that I trust you any more than I trusted that creep, sniffing around like a fox looking for dinner." Shaz picked up the laundry basket and turned to take it into her caravan. "What's it to you anyway?"

"Maddison came to me for help," Rachel said.

Shaz froze just before mounting the step of the caravan. "Why would Maddison need your help?"

"I'm a reporter. Maddison left me a voicemail. Now she's not responding to messages on social media or taking calls. She wasn't at the influencers' conference last night either."

Rachel was careful with her explanation. She'd promised Martinez that she wouldn't reveal information about Maddison's disappearance and likely murder until the FBI was ready to make it public. "I have a bad feeling that Maddison's in trouble." That was the closest Rachel could get to the truth without breaking that promise.

"What makes you think she's in trouble?" Shaz looked visibly concerned.

"Maddison sounded scared in the message she left me."

Shaz glared at Rachel like she was weighing her up. "It wasn't just that man who's been snooping around. There was a plainclothes cop in a suit here yesterday asking questions. Stuck out like a sore thumb. I don't like cops. I don't talk to them. And I sure as hell don't trust 'em."

"Good, because neither do I," said Rachel. "I'm here to help Maddison. That's all."

Shaz's hostile tone softened at the sincerity in Rachel's voice. She sat on the caravan step and began folding her laundry on her lap. "What do you want to know?"

"Let's start with anything you can tell me about the man who was here asking questions."

"He came three days ago. Maddison was downtown. I heard afterward that he took an interest in Maddison's van. Asked some backpackers who the van belonged to. They're the ones who told him her name. Later he knocked on my door, chatted with me to soften me up, and then asked me where he could find Maddison."

"What did you tell him?"

"That I didn't know her," Shaz said. "I didn't like him one bit. I wasn't going to help him out."

"What did he look like? This man."

"He wore a baseball cap and he had a rusty-colored beard. Sunglasses. Between all of that I couldn't really get a sense of what his face looked like. His clothes were smart and nicely pressed. I remember that. But there was something rank about him."

"You mean in his manner?"

"I mean his smell," said Shaz. "He had the weirdest body odor. It was like rotting garbage but worse. He tried to cover it with too much aftershave but I have a good nose. I could smell it even through all that cologne. Do you know who he is?"

"No," said Rachel. "Maddison isn't contactable, so I don't know the details of why she came to me for help."

"I wouldn't worry too much. Maddison can be like that."

"Like what?"

"Flighty. Unpredictable. We bump into each other frequently on the #vanlife trail, so I know her pretty well. I'm sure she'll connect with you as soon as she's ready," Shaz said as she folded jeans. "Why did Maddison come to you for help if you don't really know each other?"

Rachel removed a *Guilty or Not Guilty* business card from her purse and handed it to Shaz. "She knows me from my podcast."

"Yeah, I've heard of it," said Shaz. She slipped the card in her jeans pocket and then continued folding the rest of her clothes as she told Rachel about the last time she'd seen Maddison.

They'd taken a rideshare to Daytona with another camper. They'd had brunch together, after which they split up to go about their separate business. But Maddison hadn't turned up at the meeting point. She didn't answer her phone either. In the end, the two passengers had returned to camp without her.

Maddison showed up hours later without an apology or an explanation about why she'd ditched them.

"I was pissed. We had words. I don't like being messed around with and I'm one of those people who speaks their mind," said Shaz. "Maddison apologized. Then I finally got around to mentioning that a man had been here asking questions not long before. Maddison asked me to describe him. I told her pretty much what I told you."

"Did she say whether she knew him?" Rachel asked.

"Her reaction told me all I needed to know."

"What do you mean?"

"When I mentioned that he had a rank smell, Maddison turned white as a sheet and swayed like she was going to pass out. She sat on this step and sort of spaced out. Then she thanked me for letting her know and rushed back to her camper van. Next thing I knew she was driving out of here like she was being chased by a ghost."

"Maddison left immediately after you told her about the man?"

"Twenty minutes later, I kid you not. I've never seen anyone pack up and leave so fast. I waved to her to stop when she was driving out. She rolled down the window and told me that if anyone asked I should say that I didn't know who she was. She said it was for my protection. Then she hit the gas and sped off."

"Any idea where she might have gone?"

"Your guess is as good as mine."

"What is your guess?" Rachel pressed.

"That she went to stay with someone down in Daytona."

"Any idea who?"

"I got the impression that she grew up around here. I figured she must still have people here."

"What gave you that impression?"

Shaz told her that Maddison always seemed to know the best places to eat. The best beaches. The best stores. "Local knowledge," said Shaz. "You can't beat it. I could be wrong but the impression I got was that Daytona Beach was Maddison's hometown. She knew the place like she belonged. But by the same token, I don't think she has much love for this place."

"Did she ever say why?"

"Nope. Maddison's not like that," said Shaz, putting aside the neatly folded laundry. "She's a very private person. I told you that already."

"I know. It surprises me," said Rachel.

"Why?"

"I would have thought someone who spends so much time documenting their life for their social media channels wouldn't care too much about their privacy."

"It's make-believe, Rachel. The whole influencer thing. I've seen travel bloggers and #vanlife influencers come and go." Shaz tossed Rachel a bedsheet and asked her to take one end so she could fold it more easily. "They think it's an awesome idea, traveling while making money. The problem is that most of them don't make all that much money."

"I thought being an influencer is a lucrative business," said Rachel as they folded the sheet together. "That's how they make it sound at Buzz-Con."

"Maybe some make money. But from what I've seen, everyone else works real hard. Every aspect of their life becomes a commodity. Every sunset. Every meal. Everything they buy is about how their audience will react. Everything they order at a restaurant is about how many likes they'll get on Instagram," said Shaz. "They become a slave to their social media presence. I've seen it happen time and time again. Living the influencer dream can turn into a nightmare."

"I'm starting to get that impression," said Rachel.

"Take Maddison. She's constantly online. Her moods rising and falling depending on whether she gets enough likes and shares for her posts. Her happiness is a function of how she'd performed on Instagram that day. Or TikTok. Or whatever."

"Which shows that it's very unusual for her to have stayed off social media for days," Rachel pointed out.

"Not really," said Shaz. "Maddison sometimes does what she calls a digital detox. She claims it keeps her sane. She's probably detoxing right now. Wait a few more days. She'll get in touch. When she's ready." Shaz sounded confident.

Rachel was less sure. She thought of the video that Maddison had been filming when she was taken. Her fear was visceral. Rachel wondered if the man who'd been snooping around at the camping area had found her. Maddison had obviously been afraid of him. Just hearing that he'd been asking questions about her had prompted Maddison to flee the beach campsite and presumably move to the remote campground in the state forest from where she was snatched.

"Did Maddison ever tell you anything that might help me locate her family?"

Shaz folded the last laundry item and rose from the caravan step, the basket of clothes tucked under her arm. "When we first came here, we both got a ride into town with one of the campers who's since left. Maddison asked him to drop her at a run-down condo on the edge of town. Before we drove off, I heard her stop someone walking out the gate to ask directions. She wanted to know where she could find apartment 4D."

"4D?" Rachel repeated.

"I'm pretty sure that's what I heard her say," said Shaz, opening the caravan door with her free hand.

"Did Maddison say why she wanted to go there?" Rachel called out.

"Not a word." Shaz stepped into her van. She turned around to face Rachel, holding the screen door half-open. "And I didn't ask. The way I see it, everyone is entitled to their secrets."

Chapter 42

A single palm tree that had lost most of its fronds stood forlornly at the entrance of a Spanish Mission–style apartment building that had seen better days. The external walls of the building were marked with graffiti tags.

Rachel only realized the full extent of the neglect once she was dropped off by her driver. She entered on foot through a rusty gate. Flower beds on each side of the footpath were overgrown with weeds. Many of the shrubs were flat-out dead.

Rachel had gone straight to the apartment in a rideshare after she'd finished talking with Shaz, as well as a German couple staying in a two-person tent. They had borrowed a hammer from Maddison to set up their tents when they'd arrived at the beach camp three days earlier. Maddison had disappeared before they could return it.

As Rachel finished talking to the German couple, Shaz came after her to say that she'd remembered the name of the condo where Maddison had gone looking for someone who lived in apartment 4D. It was called the Santa Rosa Villas.

The condo was a block away from a discount shopping strip and as far from the beach as it was possible to be while still being within the city limits.

Rachel paused near a fountain drained of water and littered with cigarette butts to check a wall sign with a map of the complex. Apartment 4D was in the opposite wing of the U-shaped building. It faced a kidney-shaped pool filled with water so murky that it was hard to imagine anyone brave enough to swim in it. Beyond the pool was the entrance to a stairwell where a sign indicated that apartments 1D to 4D were located.

Rachel gripped the rickety banister as she walked up the poorly lit staircase. A television in an apartment somewhere was blaring a classic Hollywood Western movie, judging by the old-fashioned dialogue and a musical score that conjured up images of horses riding on a prairie.

Rachel took the last flight of stairs to the top floor. Halfway up the stairs, gunshots blasted in quick succession. Rachel instinctively gripped the handrail until she realized with some amusement that the shots were coming from a shootout scene on the TV.

Nobody answered when Rachel knocked on the door of apartment 4D. Someone was in there though. Rachel heard a rustle of movement inside. She kept knocking, this time on a pane of yellow glass next to the front door. The front door swung open to reveal a woman so thin that Rachel could see the distinct shape of her shoulder bones poking out of her pale flesh. She wore a sleeveless T-shirt and cutoff jeans. Her face was drawn and bony. Her eye sockets were prominent. She must have been in her forties but she looked decades older.

The woman drew deeply on a cigarette, stopping only when a racking cough made it impossible to keep smoking.

"What do you want?" the woman asked when she was able to talk again.

"I'm a reporter looking into the disappearance of a young woman."

"Disappearance? Who's disappeared now?" The woman opened the door to let Rachel in.

The apartment was furnished in battered furniture. Worn sofas. Mismatched chairs. The place was spotlessly neat. The woman obviously did the best with what she had. She didn't have very much.

"I'm looking for a young woman in her early twenties who goes by the name Maddison Logan," Rachel said once she was seated on a tattered sofa. "Do you know her?"

"No." The woman looked perplexed. "Is she the one who's gone missing?"

"I was told that she visited your apartment a few days ago," Rachel said, without answering the question.

"I live alone. Nobody's been here."

On the shelf near where Rachel stood was a framed photo of a woman hugging a young girl with chestnut pigtails and a gap-toothed smile. The girl was clutching the ribbon of a red helium balloon that hovered over her head. The mom was young and curvaceous but the resemblance with the skeletal woman who'd answered the door was still uncanny.

"Is that your daughter?" Rachel asked.

The woman picked up an envelope stuffed with cash that was sitting on the shelf. She shoved it into her pocket before drawing hard on her cigarette. "Hailey." She nodded. "She was six when those photos were taken. That's almost twenty years ago now."

"I bet she's grown into a beautiful woman."

"I wouldn't know," said the woman, puffing nervously on her cigarette.

"Are you ready to order?"

Rachel looked up at the waitress from behind a laminated menu.

"What would you like, Grace?" Rachel asked the emaciated woman sitting opposite her in the booth, whose name she'd learned was Grace Milroy.

Grace appeared to be lost in thought; her eyes were glazed as she looked around the diner. She looked up with a start when Rachel repeated the question. "Hailey used to love the fried chicken here."

"Good, then let's get you some of that." Rachel ordered Grace the largest serving of fried chicken in a basket with fries and slaw as well as fresh orange juice and the dessert special. She figured that whatever food was left could get wrapped up and taken home by Grace.

"Tell me about Hailey," Rachel said once the waitress had taken their orders.

"Hailey was my princess. But things got crazy when she got into high school. She became impossible. I couldn't handle her. Jed, that was my boyfriend at the time, he had a temper. Pushed me around." Grace squinted with the effort of trying to remember. She stared at Rachel in dawning horror. "You're not one of those do-gooders? Bringing me here for a meal and then making me come to church every week to save my immortal soul? Because I don't take charity. I don't need it. And I don't want it. As for my soul, I'm sure that it's beyond saving."

"I'm not here to save anyone's soul. I just want to talk to you and I figure we might as well do it over a hot meal."

The older woman had become light-headed back at the apartment. Assuming it was due to low blood sugar, Rachel had gone into the kitchen to fix her something to eat only to discover there was almost no food in the apartment. That's when she'd suggested they continue their conversation over lunch at a local restaurant.

It didn't take long until the waitress brought their meal on a big tray. Rachel let Grace eat in silence as she ate the corned beef sandwich that she'd ordered along with a soup. She bided her time until they'd finished eating and the waitress was taking away the leftovers to wrap up for Grace to take home.

"I haven't been here since Hailey went missing," Grace said, looking around the diner as she ate a slice of apple pie for dessert.

"When did Hailey go missing?" Rachel asked.

"Six years ago. July."

Rachel did a quick mental calculation. That would have been before Terence Bailey was locked up on the breaking-and-entering charge. Rachel wondered if Hailey Milroy might be another of Terence Bailey's victims. She asked Grace whether she'd ever heard Hailey mention Terence Bailey. Grace said that she hadn't, but that didn't mean much because Hailey hadn't been living at home when she was last seen.

"It was a difficult time. For the both of us," Grace said. "Then it became even harder when she went away."

"Have the police been helping to look for her?" Rachel asked.

"The cops haven't done shit. All they ever do is give me forms to fill. I asked them why they weren't out on the streets looking for my baby. They said she'd probably run away from me because I was a junkie." Tears filled Grace's eyes.

"Can you run me through what you know about Hailey's disappearance?"

"Hailey came to visit on her way to work. She'd just bought herself a car and she wanted to show it off. She saw a big bruise on my thigh. Jed and I, well, we'd had a big fight the night before. Hailey told me to leave him. Offered to pay for a program. I said to her, 'How you going to pay for a program, baby doll? You can't even pay your rent. What are you going to do, work on your back?'" Grace paused. "She stormed out. Told me that she never wanted to set eyes on me again. Said a few choice words about Jed, too. Jed went after her. That man always had a short fuse."

Grace described how she had stood by her bedroom window watching her daughter and her boyfriend screaming at each other on the sidewalk until a neighbor yelled that she'd call the cops if they didn't break it up. Hailey threw the key to her mother's apartment onto the ground by Jed's feet before climbing into the old car that she'd bought and speeding off.

"That was the last time I ever saw or heard from my daughter."

Chapter 43

Grace Milroy has been waiting for her daughter to come home for a long time. Six years ago, Grace and her then nineteen-year-old daughter, Hailey, had a terrible argument that ended with Hailey threatening to break off all contact with her mother. Grace hasn't seen her daughter since.

Grace is the first to admit that she was a mess at the time. She struggled with addiction. She had a succession of men in her life who were violent and abusive. She freely admits that she'd been a neglectful and self-absorbed mother who hadn't done right by her daughter for some time before that argument.

In the intervening years, Grace has cleaned herself up after years of substance abuse that began after she was abandoned by her then boyfriend, Hailey's dad.

Today, Grace lives in a modest apartment inherited from an aunt. She doesn't have much. Among her most prized possessions are a few well-thumbed photos of Hailey as a pigtailed little girl.

All of Grace's other photos of Hailey are being held as collateral by her ex. He refuses to return the rest of her belongings until she pays him money he claims she owes for rent when they lived together before their acrimonious breakup. It is money that Grace simply doesn't have right now. She really has lost everything.

"All I have left of Hailey are memories."

The day after their terrible argument, Grace tried to contact Hailey to apologize. When she couldn't get hold of Hailey by phone, she went to look for her to apologize in person.

She went to the vet clinic where Hailey worked as an assistant. The staff told Grace that Hailey hadn't turned up for her shift that morning. It was uncharacteristic of Hailey not to turn up to work, especially since she'd worked the previous night and had told her supervisor that she'd be back bright and early in the morning to feed the animal patients that were hospitalized overnight.

"I thought Hailey was ignoring my calls because of the argument. So I asked the woman at the vet clinic to call her. They called her on speaker-phone while I waited. It went straight through to voicemail."

Worried about her daughter, Grace drove to the rambling share house where Hailey rented a room with various other young people her age, many of them also from broken homes. Hailey's bedroom was near the entrance on the ground floor. It appeared that someone had rummaged through her dresser drawers and closet.

"Everything was a mess. Hailey's clothes were thrown all over the place. Drawers were left open. I had a really bad feeling."

Grace went to the local police station to report Hailey as missing. It wasn't an unexpected surprise when the police officer on duty made light of Grace's concerns for her daughter's welfare.

He pointed out that Hailey had a history of running away. She'd run away a few times while in high school. It was not Grace's first trip to the police station to report her daughter as missing. In the past, Hailey had always turned up after spending a night or two on a friend's sofa.

The duty officer reassured Grace that it was a positive sign that Hailey's car was also missing. He said it indicated that she might have gone on a road trip to cool down.

"He told me to come back the following day if Hailey still hadn't surfaced." Grace's recollections of that time are vivid.

When Grace returned the next morning to say that Hailey still hadn't turned up, the police reluctantly opened a missing persons file for her daughter.

"They said they were doing it because it was protocol, but they were sure that Hailey would be back in a few days." Grace says that the police were reluctant to do anything other than give her forms to fill out.

Grace did what she could to find her daughter in the days that followed. She designed and printed "Missing" posters that she put up on streetlight poles and supermarket noticeboards in Hailey's neighborhood. She stood on street corners to hand them out in other parts of town. She door-knocked and she spoke to all of Hailey's roommates to find out if they'd seen or heard anything.

Every day, Grace turned up at the police station to ask for an update and share any information that she'd collected. Every day, the police assured her that Hailey was a legal adult who'd probably skipped town for a while to escape her troubled family life.

Due to her daily visits and constant calls, Grace effectively busted the ass of the local police's missing persons officer, who eventually relented and sent detectives to ask questions at the share house where Hailey had lived before she disappeared.

The police also finally agreed to track Hailey's phone, which had been going straight to voicemail since Hailey disappeared. They were able to determine that the last time the phone had been on, Hailey had been in the vicinity of the veterinary clinic. It would have been the night she was last seen. The night she worked the late shift at the animal clinic.

I obtained the missing persons reports for Aysh Philips and Hailey Milroy. They are both flimsy reports, brief and lacking in detail.

It's obvious that the police only went through the motions in the search for these two young women. It was only when Aysh's body turned up in the state forest that the police pulled out all the stops. After all, they were now investigating a murder.

It's been six years since Aysh's body was found and the cops are still no closer to solving the case.

As for Hailey, there is still no trace of her after all these years. The police have no idea what happened to her. It didn't have to be that way. They only really started looking once the trail went cold.

Not knowing has left Grace in an emotional limbo that she says has taken her into dark places over the years.

Over lunch at a local diner, Grace tearily tells me about her enduring torment. "There's no closure when your daughter is still missing. No grave. No way to say goodbye. Each night I hear Hailey screaming for help. But I can't help her if I don't know where she is."

The one thing that Grace is proud of is that she's finally cleaned up her life.

"I did it for Hailey because wherever she is, I know it would make her happy."

Chapter 44

Kittens Gentleman's Club stunk of stale beer when Joe Martinez entered through the swinging doors of the loading bay entrance to the rear of the strip club. He brushed past a burly man in a black T-shirt carrying a crate of beer. The beer bottles rattled as the man put the crate on the bar counter before returning to his truck for another crate.

On the empty half-circle stage, a cleaner sprayed and wiped the chrome dance poles until they shone. Another bent on her haunches to clean the mirrored panels behind the poles so that patrons would see the girls at every angle as they danced when the bar opened later that day.

At the far end of the bar, a balding man with a goatee checked a pile of invoices with a blue pen. Martinez sat down at a stool across from him.

"We're closed! Come back in a couple of hours," said the manager, his eyes fixed on a packing list invoice that he was checking.

"Now is good," Martinez said.

"I told you, we're closed." The man ticked off items on the invoice without glancing at Martinez.

"Not for me, you're not." Martinez's tone was steely.

The man slowly raised his murky eyes from the invoices. They paused when they reached Martinez's chest. A tightened jaw indicated that he had registered the discreet outline of a weapon under Martinez's jacket.

He lifted his gaze higher, to the FBI shield that Martinez held in the air. The man dropped the pile of invoices on the counter.

"What do you want?"

"Let's start with cold water. It's hot as hell out there."

"Jessica Hewitt," Martinez said after he'd drunk a glass of water. "Ever heard of her?"

"She worked here for a while. Started as a dancer but moved onto bar work eventually. She's dead. Died years ago."

"Six years ago," Martinez clarified.

He tossed Terence Bailey's mug shot from his breaking-and-entering arrest onto the counter. "Have you seen him around before?"

The man picked up the photo. "Yeah, I remember him," he said after a quick glance. "Don't know his name but I know the face. In this business, you have to remember faces to stop the troublemakers getting in."

"He was a troublemaker?"

"Hung out here for a while. He'd come and talk to Jessie while she worked."

"Was he harassing her? Scaring her?"

"Annoying her more like it with stupid questions."

"What sorts of stupid questions?"

"It was six years ago, man. I don't remember what questions he asked. I just remember they were the types of questions you don't ask a girl who's making ends meet by working in a place where she serves beers in a G-string." He signed off the last invoice and handed it to the bearded man in the black T-shirt.

"That kid would buy one beer for the whole night and sit around staring at Jessie like a lovesick teenager. She found it uncomfortable. Eventually she told the bouncers not to let him in. That's why I remember him."

"Did Jessie ever say what he wanted? Was she frightened of him?"

"I doubt it. She wasn't afraid of much other than being sober," he said. "She overdosed right here behind the club. It was a real shame. I liked

Jessie. We all did. But hey, all that's ancient history, man," he said. "Why the trip down memory lane?"

Martinez took a business card out of his wallet and flicked it across the counter. "Here's my card. If you think of anything else or know anyone who remembers the kid in the photo, give me a call."

He left the bar the same way that he came, jumping down from the loading bay and heading to his car. His phone rang as he was driving off.

"The autopsy's done." It was Dr. Padres. "Thought you'd like to know that her cause of death is drowning."

"Are you telling me that her body was moved from wherever she drowned to the mud pit where we found her?"

"Her body wasn't moved, Agent Martinez," the pathologist interrupted. "She drowned in the mud that she was found in. Her lungs were filled with that gunk. I'm putting 'Death by Drowning' on the death certificate."

"Were there signs of a struggle? Maybe her head was forcibly held under the surface?"

"No signs of a struggle," Dr. Padres said. "No abrasions. She wasn't tied up or beaten. Her nails are intact. No defense wounds. She drowned, plain and simple."

"You've surprised me, Doctor," said Martinez.

"Life is full of surprises. In fact, I have another one for you, if you think your heart is strong enough to take two surprises in one day."

"I'll risk it," Martinez said.

"They brought in the body of the guy found floating under the pier. Jonny Macon."

"Yeah, I happened to be there when his body was found. The local cops say it was an accidental drowning."

"They're wrong," said Dr. Padres. "There was no water in his lungs. He didn't drown."

"Then how did he die?"

"He had a heart attack. I just finished his autopsy now. However, I believe he was electrocuted moments before his death."

"What makes you think that?"

"There were classic burn marks on his chest that indicate electrocution, as well as burst blood vessels in his eyes and eyelids. I also found traces of cocaine in his nostrils. That didn't help with his heart health."

"How could he have been electrocuted in the ocean? Was there lightning last night? Or electrical cords under the pier?"

"None of the above," said the pathologist. "No lightning. We checked the weather. No power cords in the vicinity either."

"Well, it didn't happen by itself."

"From the burn marks, my guess is that he was hit by a Taser gun. The electrical charge caused him to have a heart attack. That's what killed him."

Chapter 45

The farmhouse sits alone on a field about a quarter mile away from an on-ramp to the I-95. It had been built decades earlier when the area was a rural heartland. Today the farm is a quaint rustic throwback to the past.

It's a single-story white clapboard. Modest in size and without any adornment. It was built by Thomas's grandfather after the war, when returned servicemen were given swampy tracts of cheap land in what was then rural Florida. The outside walls need painting. The paint cans sit in the corrugated shed where Thomas McCoy parks his car overnight. He'll get to it when he has time.

The house has a large porch in the front. An even bigger one in the back. There's a rickety old metal water windmill in the yard from the days before plumbing. His granddad used it to pump water from an underground well. Thomas keeps it there, alongside a vintage tractor that's all rusted through. They're relics of the old days. They're all he has left of his family other than the house itself.

On the boundary line farthest from the house are the remnants of his father's once expansive citrus orchard and Stacey's final resting place. The location of her grave next to an enormous Tahitian lime tree is particularly apt. Stacey picked limes from that tree for her favorite drink. Vodka and a twist of lime. She'd joke that the lime juice was her daily shot of vitamins. Except it wasn't daily. It was more like hourly toward the end. He considered it a mercy killing.

Millie is asleep on the porch when his car approaches the property. She barks manically until she recognizes the familiar burr of the engine as he turns into the driveway, pausing to open the gate before he drives inside.

"Daddy's home," he says when he climbs up the front porch stairs after he's parked by the house. He pauses to pat the dog before letting himself into the house.

He hears her screams for help as he enters through the front door. They're muffled by music on the radio he left on and the sturdy construction of the brick basement. For once his father's meticulousness has paid off.

"Keep screaming, honey," he calls out, tossing the car keys on the hall table. "Nobody can hear you," he taunts through the basement door keyhole before heading to the kitchen.

He takes out a loaf of bread and various fixings. He stands at the kitchen counter looking out into the front garden as he butters the bread and layers it with sliced ham and cheese with a touch of Tabasco sauce. He likes his food hot.

Sitting at the table by the kitchen window he eats the sandwich, chewing slowly. He works in neat rows from one side of the sandwich to the other. When he's done, he makes another sandwich and takes out a small bottle of water. It's the same bottled water he sometimes gives passengers when he's in an amenable frame of mind and he needs good ratings.

Thomas unlocks the basement door, leaving it wide open so the natural light of the front hall comes into the top of the stairs. He knows the layout well enough that he can navigate his way in the dark.

She looks up passively as he comes down the stairs. She's becoming less feisty as the days pass. When he first brought her home, she screamed and railed at him. One time she charged toward him until she was snapped back by the rope that's just long enough to give her access to the toilet and the sink.

"I brought you lunch."

He tosses a sandwich wrapped in cling wrap and the bottle of cold water from the top of the stairs in her general direction. It lands near her outstretched legs. She doesn't pick it up. She still has enough life in her not to give him the satisfaction of seeing how hungry she is.

"Throw your old clothes to me," he orders. He gave her a fresh change of clothes last night and told her to wash and change into them.

She bundles her discarded clothes into a ball and tosses them up as far as she can throw them. They fall on the edge of a stair near where he stands. He picks up the ball of clothes and leaves the basement, locking up behind him.

He takes it all to the back garden, where he throws her sweaty shirt into an oil drum. As he prepares to toss in her pants, he hears a rustle in a pocket. Inside is a piece of folded paper. He opens it up. On it, she's scribbled a phone number and a name.

He throws the pants into the oil drum and squirts gasoline on everything. Then he lights it up with a match, standing back to watch it burn. As the fire licks her clothes into ash, he heads back into the house and storms down the basement stairs. This time he goes all the way to the bottom, where he picks her up from the floor by her shoulders and brutally shoves her against the wall so hard they can both hear the crack of her skull hitting brick.

"Who's Rachel Krall?" he demands.

Chapter 46

By the time Rachel returned to the hotel after taking Grace Milroy to lunch, the influencers had emerged from their hotel rooms having recovered from hangovers after partying all night. They were making up for lost time by filming fresh content at the hotel's lagoon pool deck and its lush tropical gardens.

Several influencers were lying on recliners in string bikinis, their bodies glistening from fake-tan and coconut oil as their personal photographers snapped them from various angles.

One woman with a skinny bikini body and long straight hair executed a perfect dive into the water. She swam back to the side of the pool and climbed up a chrome pool ladder, giving a sultry stare into her boyfriend's camera and flicking her wet hair behind her shoulders as she stepped out.

"You look gorgeous," he called out. "Let's do it again. This time I'll shoot from a different angle."

Zoe, the influencer Rachel had seen at breakfast, sat in a lotus position on a timber yoga deck near the pool emitting a dramatic "Om." Her eyes were gently closed. Eric filmed her while lying uncomfortably on his belly to incorporate ferns and a clay Buddha behind her into the shot.

"You're too close." Zoe interrupted her meditation to check on his progress. She rolled her eyes before resuming her serene "Om" while he wiggled backward to get a wider shot.

On the other side of the pool, hotel staff were setting up round banquet tables for the conference's outdoor seafood barbecue dinner that night, which would be followed by a nighttime pool party.

Given that it appeared to be business as usual at BuzzCon, Rachel assumed that Jonny Macon's death was still under wraps while the police told his next of kin.

She headed to the lobby to go up to her room, passing two men talking with a hotel manager to the side of the reception desk. Rachel recognized the men as the detectives she'd seen at the beach that morning when Jonny Macon's body had been found.

As Rachel headed toward the elevator, the hotel reception manager said something to the detectives that prompted them to look in Rachel's direction. Rachel was waiting for the elevator to come down when she felt a tap on her shoulder.

"Rachel Krall?"

"Yes, that's me." She turned to face the two detectives.

"We're from the Daytona PD. We have some questions for you," the shaved-headed detective said. "Would you come with us?"

"Why?" Rachel asked.

"This isn't really the place to explain. A lot of people are watching," the detective said. "It will be more discreet if we talk at the local police station. It's a short drive away. We'll give you a ride back when we're done."

"Give me the address. I'll get cleaned up, and then meet you there in, say, thirty minutes?"

"We have a car outside. It's no problem to take you there and bring you back."

"I really wouldn't want to put you to any trouble," said Rachel sweetly. It was quite clear that she wasn't being given a choice in the matter.

"It's no trouble at all," said the detective. "Please." He gestured with his arm that Rachel should walk ahead of him.

Rachel headed out the main lobby doors flanked by the two detectives. A Ford SUV was parked next to a police car in the hotel driveway. Instead of opening the door for the unmarked vehicle, one of the uniformed cops waiting by the patrol car opened the back door for Rachel to go in.

"We'll take you from here."

She was being taken to the police station in a patrol car. Rachel bit back the sudden desire to ask whether they were planning on reading her Miranda rights as well. She restrained herself. This would go a lot easier if she kept things on a polite footing.

The police station was a ten-minute drive away. She was escorted to the third floor, where the patrol cop led her through the detectives' offices to a small broom-closet-sized room. It had a single venetian-blind window set high up on the wall.

"Take a seat," said the cop who'd brought her in. "Detective Orvis will join shortly."

Rachel sat down. Minutes passed. The door remained firmly closed. Detective Orvis was nowhere to be seen. Rachel found the whole scenario tiresome. She knew when she was being left to stew before an interrogation. This was not how she'd intended to spend her afternoon. Instead of going for a refreshing swim, she was locked in a police interrogation room cooling her heels.

Not locked, Rachel reminded herself. She'd come voluntarily. That meant that she was free to go. She picked up her purse and headed out the door. As she'd predicted, it was unlocked.

"You can't leave," said a cop waiting outside the door.

"Really?" Rachel swung her purse over her shoulder. "Watch me!"

A row of detectives' desks was all that stood between her and the exit. The detectives had all pulled chairs over to one of the desks to watch a basketball game on the computer screen, judging by their heated discussion about a disputed referee's call.

One of the detectives looked up in surprise when he realized that Rachel was walking out. He hurriedly headed over with his hand outstretched to shake hers.

“I’m Detective Orvis,” he said, dropping his hand when Rachel kept hers by her side and made no effort to comply with his handshake. “Thanks for coming down, Ms. Krall. We have a few questions to ask you.”

“So I heard,” said Rachel. “The problem is that I ran out of time while you were”—she glanced at the computer—“watching that Orlando game.”

“I don’t have many questions. It won’t take long.”

Rachel glanced at a clock on the wall. “I can give you five minutes. We’ll sit at your desk.”

Rachel pulled over a chair to Detective Orvis’s desk. Her arrival sent the other detectives scurrying to their desks.

“What’s this about?” she asked.

“Jonny Macon. What can you tell me about Jonny Macon?”

Rachel wondered if she should disclose that she knew Jonny Macon had drowned under the pier. She decided not to say anything. She wanted to find out what was going on.

“Jonny Macon is an influencer at the BuzzCon conference, which I’m attending. I’m @runninggirlRach on Insta. He took a photo with me yesterday at the afterparty and put it on his social media feed. It was a nice gesture. He has a huge social media following. He posted the photo with a suggestion that we’re dating. As a result, my follower count tripled.”

“Hang on, let’s back up here,” said Detective Orvis. “*Are* the two of you dating?”

“No!” said Rachel. “We’re not dating. I met him for the first time last night. I had a ten-minute conversation with him at the bar, during which time he took that photo and uploaded it with a caption that suggested we’re an item. Trust me, Detective. We are not an item. Shortly after he took the photo, we went out onto the beach, where we talked briefly.”

“What time was this?”

“Around midnight,” said Rachel. “He went for a walk on the beach. I turned back and returned to the hotel. And that is the sum total of my relationship with Jonny Macon.”

“What did you talk about?” the detective asked.

"Honestly, I don't remember exactly," said Rachel, loath to get into the issue of Maddison Logan. "We talked mostly about the conference. The life of an influencer. How it's more challenging than most people realize."

"I see."

"You really don't, Detective," Rachel interrupted. "The hotel has CCTV cameras everywhere, including on the gate overlooking the beach. If you look at the footage you'll see me walking out with Jonny at around midnight and then returning ten, maybe fifteen minutes later. I am not responsible for Jonny's death, if that's what you're thinking."

Interest flickered on the detective's pug face. "How do you know that Jonny Macon is dead?" He leaned forward. "We've kept his identity quiet until his next of kin is notified."

"I was at the beach this morning, shortly after a body was found under the pier," sighed Rachel.

"There's no way that you could know the identity of the body. We haven't released his name."

"I happened to have breakfast with Special Agent Joe Martinez, from the FBI, near the pier this morning. When we were done he went down to the scene to take a look. He'd taken a photo of the victim on his phone. I happened to glance at it and I recognized him. I told him that it was Jonny Macon."

"So that's how the FBI knew," said the detective, almost to himself.

"I had nothing to do with Jonny Macon's tragic and premature death. Now, if you'll excuse me. I have a busy afternoon ahead." Rachel rose from the table.

"We may have more questions for you, Ms. Krall. This is a homicide investigation. You might want to hire yourself a criminal attorney. You being the last person to see him alive makes you a person of interest in this case."

"Bite me," Rachel muttered under her breath as she walked out.

She checked her phone as she went down the stairs. She'd received a missed call and a voicemail message that must have come through while she was talking with the detective. She listened to it while she waved down a passing cab.

"Rachel, this is Shaz. We met at the beach earlier. You helped me fold my laundry. I got talking to a backpacker from Sweden who's staying here. She told me something that freaked me out. Not in a good way. Can you come back to the campsite? You're going to want to hear what she has to say."

Chapter 47

The beach campground was eerily quiet when the cab dropped Rachel off at the entrance. The only movement was tents flapping in the afternoon breeze. Rachel knocked on the door of Shaz's camper van. There was no answer.

From the top step of the van, Rachel noticed people scattered across the beach. That's where all the campers had gone. She walked down a sandy path to the beach where backpackers were kicking a ball in a barefoot match of beach soccer. The goals were demarcated on the sand with seaweed.

The chill vibe was so different from the bustling tourist beaches in town. Here there were no sun loungers in long parallel lines. No loud beat of trance music. No dance parties on the sand. No jet skis whining in the water or noisy promotional beach volleyball matches commentated over loudspeakers. The only sound was from waves lapping and retreating.

People lay on towels listening to music via headphones, or sleeping in the sun. Surfers waited patiently on their boards in the water for the next round of waves to roll in. A couple of backpackers arranged driftwood in the shape of a bonfire to be lit at nightfall.

Rachel looked around the beach for Shaz's bright red mop of hair.

She eventually found her suntanning on her stomach on a large tie-dyed sarong alongside a few other people.

"I got your message. What's going on?" Rachel said.

In answer, Shaz leaned over and tapped the shoulder of a woman in denim shorts and a lime halter top lying on her stomach on a towel. "I told you she'd come."

The woman sat up abruptly and turned around to greet Rachel. She was young, early twenties at the most, with long wispy light brown hair. She introduced herself as Elsa.

"Let's go for a walk," said Shaz, reluctant for their conversation to be overheard by any of the people sunbathing nearby even though most of them wore headphones.

Shaz lifted up the sarong she'd been lying on and wrapped it around her like a towel as she rose to her feet. The three women walked along the beach in an untidy row.

"Elsa's on her way to Mexico to study Spanish," Shaz told Rachel.

"I'm not so sure I'll go now," Elsa interjected. "I am thinking to fly back to Stockholm early."

"Why?" Rachel asked.

"Because of what happened. Can we sit?" Elsa asked haltingly. "I don't feel good when I talk about it."

"Of course."

They found a quiet stretch of sand without driftwood and seaweed, where they sat in a semi-circle facing the water. Elsa took several deep breaths, gathering her courage to speak. She told Rachel that she'd been backpacking down the East Coast to Miami for a few weeks, after which she was due to fly to Mexico to do an intensive Spanish course.

"A few days ago, I was camping in Jacksonville. I went to the bus stop to take a bus south to start the last part of my trip in southern Florida. The bus came early. It sped straight past without stopping before I could get to the stop. The next bus wasn't for another hour. I was upset. I was hot and I had the start of a headache. I didn't think I could sit in the heat for an hour until the next bus. While I was trying to decide what to do, a car pulled up. The driver wound down the window. He'd seen the bus drive off and told me I should complain to the bus company. He offered me a ride."

"And you took it?" Rachel asked.

"I wouldn't usually but he seemed nice. Friendly. He was dressed well. Spoke politely. His car was very clean."

Elsa told Rachel the driver suggested that she sit in the back, where there was more leg space. He couldn't have been more gracious. He told her to help herself to the cell phone charger next to her seat. Her phone was already charged, so she declined. He offered her a bottle of water. She said that she already had her own.

He did most of the talking, asking her about herself and her trip. She told him about her plans to study Spanish in Mexico. Elsa swallowed hard to compose herself before continuing her story.

"Then what happened?" Rachel prompted.

"He kept suggesting that I use the phone charger so that my phone battery wouldn't die. And telling me how great the mineral water was, and that I should try some 'American mineral water.' It was weird how pushy he was getting. I noticed a coil of rope sticking out from the compartment in the driver's door. He kept touching it nervously and looking at me through the rearview mirror. He'd been so nice at first, but I suddenly felt uncomfortable being in the car with him. He began to scare me."

Rachel waited without comment for Elsa to finish her story. She could hear the fear and panic in the backpacker's voice as she recalled what happened.

"There was a weird smell as well. It was horrible. I wanted to get out of there."

"What smell?" Rachel jumped on that comment. Shaz had mentioned the man who'd come looking for Maddison also had a distinct odor.

"The car had a strong smell of deodorizer and men's cologne but I slowly smelled this terrible smell masked by all that. It smelled like rotting garbage. Between that and the rope in the door, I was really scared."

Elsa's heart was racing. They were driving on a busy road. Cars were driving fast in both directions. She noticed that the driver had moved the rope from the door compartment to his lap.

"I knew that I had to do something drastic or it would be too late."

"What did you do?" Rachel asked.

"I asked him to pull over. I told him I was carsick and I was going to throw up." Her shoulders heaved with sobs.

"He stopped?" Rachel prompted.

"Yes," she said, taking a deep breath to pull herself together. "He skidded to a stop on the side of the road. He definitely did not want me vomiting in his nice clean car. I opened the car door and I ran like I've never run before in my life. I ran onto the road into incoming traffic. A car driving toward me braked just in time. I was hysterical by then. Crying. Shaking. She let me get into her car." By then the driver had gone.

"A lucky escape," observed Rachel.

"Sometimes I think it was a lucky escape. Other times I think that I was paranoid and I was the one acting crazy. Maybe he was a regular guy and he didn't intend to hurt me."

"You have to trust your instincts in these situations," said Rachel.

Elsa shrugged. She said that she still wasn't sure if she'd made a fool of herself, or she'd escaped a deranged killer. She rose to her feet and the trio started walking back to the main part of the beach where the campers were suntanning.

"Did you report what happened to the police?" Rachel asked.

"No! I didn't remember anything about the car. The only thing I remembered was the smell. I'll remember that smell for the rest of my life."

Chapter 48

There was always a moment in every investigation when Joe Martinez received an inevitable call summoning him upstairs to talk to the local brass. As a federal agency with sweeping powers, the FBI had an unfortunate tendency to step on toes. It came with the badge.

It was therefore no great surprise when Martinez received a call from Chief Alvin Rice's secretary not long after he'd returned to police headquarters from Kittens nightclub. She politely asked him to come up to talk with the chief. Martinez took the stairs to the fifth floor, curious to find out whether Chief Rice's beef was to protect his turf, or cover his ass.

"He's at a late lunch but he should be back any minute," his secretary said when Martinez arrived at her desk.

"Maybe we should do this another time," said Martinez, thinking to himself that it must have been one heck of a long working lunch given that it was mid-afternoon.

"He won't be long. Can I get you a coffee in the meantime?" She rose anxiously from her seat. She was obviously under orders to keep him there until the chief arrived.

Martinez accepted even though he'd just drunk a coffee downstairs. Once she'd disappeared into a kitchenette, he walked through the open doorway into the chief's office. It had big windows overlooking the city and a large desk with all the trappings: flags, shields, awards and accolades. On the walls were the usual collection of framed photos. Martinez studied them as he waited for the secretary to return with his coffee.

The photos were all identical in one peculiar way. They all showed the balding police chief vigorously shaking hands with dignitaries ranging from political leaders to celebrities and famous sports stars. The chief's jaw stuck out proudly like a bulldog as he beamed in each photo. There were no photos of the chief posing with his own cops.

There were also no family photos other than a single photo of the police chief with his arm around the shoulders of a young man in a graduation gown whose discomfort was evident by his clenched jaw, a near identical version of the chief's.

Based on the photos alone, Martinez determined the police chief was a vain name-dropper who craved recognition and enjoyed throwing his weight around. Martinez also guessed that he was a divorcé who had a cool, possibly even acrimonious, relationship with his grown son. The way his son flinched away from his father's embrace in the graduation photo suggested the father bullied people behind closed doors.

From Martinez's experience there were two kinds of police commanders: those who rolled up their sleeves, and those who took the bows. He bet the Daytona police chief was in the second category. That was also why he'd had his secretary summon Martinez to his office well in advance of his arrival. It was a power move. He wanted to make sure that Martinez knew his place. Martinez was more than a little pissed off at the disruption to his own work.

"What's this I'm hearing about you federal boys stickybeaking into cases that have nothing to do with you," the police chief barked as he strode into his office. His secretary followed behind, holding a coffee mug that she handed to Martinez with a glare of admonishment for letting himself into her boss's office.

The chief took off his jacket and heaved himself down onto his desk chair. Prominent corpuscles on the chief's ruddy cheeks and nose suggested to Martinez that he'd been drinking over lunch. Not one drink either, Martinez noted, noticing the chief's unsteady hand as he tidied up the papers on his desk blotter.

"I hear you threw our investigation under the bus," the chief said, putting on reading glasses that fell to the bottom of his nose and opening a file.

"Which investigation and what bus?" Martinez asked.

"The victim down by the pier, Jonny Macon. I heard you shared confidential details with the last person to see him alive, who happens to be our number one suspect," said the police chief in a blistering tone.

"And who might that be?" Martinez asked, genuinely confused.

"Rachel Krall."

"Rachel Krall is a suspect?" Martinez sat up straight.

"Very much so."

It was clear to Martinez that the chief was there for a fight. Following the advice of George Bernard Shaw to avoid pig wrestling, Martinez explained how Rachel had come to see a photo of the pier victim on his phone.

"I very much doubt that Rachel Krall was involved in Jonny Macon's murder. I was with her when she found out that he was killed and her surprise and shock were real."

"Might I suggest, Special Agent Martinez, that you focus your attention on the Maddison Logan case, which is the reason you are here. Incidentally, I thought you feds were going to crack the case wide open within twenty-four hours."

The police chief made little effort to hide his pleasure at the lack of progress. "Maybe it's time for my people to take over. I'm sure you have more important cases waiting for you back in Virginia."

"That's very kind of you to offer," Martinez said. "I think we'll be all right for a few more days. After that, if there's no break in the case, then we can certainly talk." Martinez rose. "Well, if that'll be all, then I'll head on downstairs to get on with my work." He was halfway out of the office when he swung around, remembering something.

"By the way, I'd appreciate the chance to talk with the detective who investigated the Aysh Philips murder and the serial killings of those working girls."

"Didn't we give you the files to go through?" the chief asked.

"I have a few questions for Detective Castel. He's been difficult to pin down." That was an understatement. Martinez had left half a dozen messages for the detective. Castel still hadn't returned his calls.

The chief called over his secretary. "Tell Castel to assist Agent Martinez with all of his inquiries. Make sure he knows the request is coming from me."

Castel was at his desk when Martinez stopped by. He was a barrel-chested, fair-haired cop in his mid-thirties whose first case as a detective had been the Belinda Roy case, one of the two prostitutes who'd gone missing and turned up dead. It was obvious that Castel had received a heads-up from the chief's secretary telling him to be cooperative. His tight lips and crossed arms suggested that he wasn't happy about it.

"What is it that you want?" Castel snapped.

"You've been hot on Terence Bailey from the get-go. Why?"

"I sure have," Castel said. "I've had Bailey in my sights ever since he was arrested going through the Hewitt woman's underwear drawer. Finding his partial fingerprint on the ropes binding Aysh Philips's hands and ankles just reinforced my view."

"How do you explain the different victim profiles?" Martinez asked the question that had been bugging him ever since he'd gone through the case files.

It was unusual for a killer to have such varied victims: in this case, prostitutes and a high school honors student. And there were different MOs. Aysh Philips was stabbed in a frenzy. Martinez had looked at the photos of her body. It seemed to him the killer had been frustrated and angry when he'd killed Aysh. The other victims were strangled and then slashed across the throat with a clinical thoroughness that contrasted sharply with the profile of the Aysh Philips murderer.

The victims were disposed of in distinctly different ways as well. The bodies of two of the sex workers had been wrapped in trash bags and thrown in dumpsters on the outskirts of town. Aysh's body was dumped in a forest and set on fire. Meanwhile, the bodies of the four other sex workers who'd disappeared under similar circumstances had never been found at all.

"This killer is all over the shop," Martinez continued. "Don't get me wrong. I've seen it before. But what's driving it? What's motivating him? And why are his kills so different?"

"Bailey likes variety," said the detective tersely through a set mouth, his arms still crossed. "He tests his skills on prostitutes. Prostitutes are easy targets because they voluntarily get into a car. Aysh Philips was a crime of opportunity."

"You think Bailey chose prostitutes because it was easy to get them into his car?" Martinez asked. Detective Castel nodded. "Except I read in the files that Bailey had a motorcycle. No car," Martinez added. "How do you explain that?"

"Bailey was a mechanic. He had access to cars. Then there's the theory he had an accomplice."

"Because a second fingerprint was on the rope."

"Exactly. Also, it would be a struggle for one person to carry Aysh Philips's body up that steep ridge at night."

"How do you think he, or they, snatched her?"

"Standard roadside abduction scenario," Castel answered. "The accomplice's car is parked on the side of the road. One guy is at the wheel. The other is in the back seat. The guy in the back opens the rear door and gets out just as she's walking past. He wraps his arms around her, slaps his hands over her mouth, and pulls her into the vehicle. They drive off. The whole thing takes under five seconds."

Martinez nodded. That was as good an explanation as any. "There's one other thing," said Martinez. "Jessica Hewitt?"

"The woman whose panties Bailey was stealing when he was arrested," said Castel.

"That's her," said Martinez. "I can't find her DNA in the system."

"Bailey's crime was breaking and entering her apartment. No DNA needed to prove that. He was caught red-handed. Anyway, you won't be able to get hold of her DNA now. She died from a drug overdose years ago."

"So I hear," said Martinez. "I'd still like her DNA."

"That's impossible. Unless you get a court order to exhume her."

"You wouldn't know whether the working girls in this city happen to go to a particular clinic for their contraception and STD care?"

"There's a health center downtown where they go." Detective Castel wrote a name on a piece of paper and handed it to Martinez.

"Nice doing business with you, Detective," said Martinez, flicking the note in his hand as he walked away.

Chapter 49

The mechanic's legs stuck out slightly from under the pale green 1959 Buick Electra as Rachel walked across the oil-stained concrete floor of the auto shop.

"Hello?" Rachel called out. All she could see of him were his black boots.

When he continued tinkering without responding, Rachel raised her voice. "Anyone here?" she asked, as if she hadn't noticed that he was under the car.

A screwdriver dropped with a clang onto the oil-stained concrete. The coaster wheels of a creeper board clattered as the mechanic rolled out from under the car.

"How can I help you?" He lay on the board staring up at Rachel. He had a bushy mustache and a thick crop of matching wiry gray hair that fell over his forehead.

"I'm looking for Kyle."

"You've found him." He wiped his hands on a grease-smeared oil rag and clambered to his feet. "What do you need?"

Rachel introduced herself briefly as a reporter. "I have some questions for you about Terence Bailey."

Kyle stared at her like he didn't know what she was talking about.

"He worked for you about six, seven years ago," Rachel added to jog his memory.

"I know who Terence Bailey is. Why are you asking about him?" Suspicion crept into his clipped voice.

"He gets out of prison soon. Did you know that?"

"I did not. Now that I know, I'll keep my shotgun loaded and be on the lookout."

"Why would he come after you?"

"Who knows what grudges he holds," he said. "If that's all you wanted, then you'll have to excuse me. I need to finish this car by the end of the day."

Ignoring Rachel, he leaned through the open driver's window of the Buick and fired up the engine. He then lifted the hood and stood over the engine while it idled, watching and listening. Realizing Rachel was still there, he looked up. "I already answered your questions."

"Not all of them," Rachel said. "Do you know whether Terence Bailey had a girlfriend by the name of Maddison Logan?"

"I don't remember him bringing friends here." He closed the car hood with a thud. "I told the same thing to the cops when they came asking questions for their murder investigation. They thought he had partnered up with someone to kill those girls. I told them that Terry was a loner. He didn't like people very much. Only cars."

"Do you think he killed those girls?" Rachel asked.

"Like my ex-wife used to say before she finally caught me in bed with another woman: 'Where there's smoke, there's fire,'" Kyle said. "Law enforcement doesn't go around making accusations like that without evidence. That's what I told my daughter Emily. She told me she didn't believe any of it. She's a sweetheart. Emily sees good in everyone."

"I'd like to talk to Emily," said Rachel.

"She's working under the car over there." He pointed to a tomato-red vintage MG convertible in the far corner of the shop. "Don't tell Em that Bailey is getting out of the slammer. I don't want her to know."

"Sure," said Rachel.

He nodded slowly as if to confirm that Rachel had agreed to his terms. Then he lowered himself to the board and rolled back under the car again.

Emily was on a creeper board under the MG. Rachel called out her name.

"She can't hear you," Kyle shouted to Rachel from under the vehicle he was repairing. "She's listening to music."

Rachel bent down to look under the car. Emily noticed her and immediately rolled out from under the vehicle. In a single movement she jumped to her feet.

Despite being dressed in grease-smeared mechanic's coveralls, Emily was more naturally striking than any of the influencers Rachel had met at BuzzCon. She wore a light pink T-shirt under her coveralls. A baseball hat turned backward covered a spray of light brown curly hair. She had several gold earrings in her ears and a gold butterfly necklace around her neck.

"Nice car," said Rachel as Emily wiped her hands on a rag and rubbed in hand moisturizer.

"It's a 1974 MG M. She's mine. She's going to drive like a dream when I'm done." Emily went through a container of screwdrivers on a stand, looking for a particular size as Rachel introduced herself.

"Terence Bailey. What can you tell me about him?" Rachel asked.

"He worked here before he went to prison." Emily picked out several screwdrivers, checking them and throwing them back until she found a couple that she set aside.

"Your dad said that you trusted Bailey. Doesn't sound like your dad agrees with you on that score."

"I didn't believe any of the terrible things they said about Terry, if that's what you mean." As Emily spoke, she slipped the tools she'd chosen into the compartments on a leather utility belt that hung low on her waist like a gunfighter's holster.

"You've never visited him in prison."

Emily looked up. "How do you know I've never visited Terry?"

"I was at the prison yesterday," said Rachel. "They told me that nobody has ever visited him. In all the years that he's been there."

"I tried to visit. Early on," Emily clarified. "He refused to see me. A week later I received a letter from him telling me not to contact him. He said he didn't want to have anything to do with me and that I should get on with my life," she said. "That was years ago now."

"How well did you know him when he worked for your dad?" Rachel asked.

"I was going on seventeen. He was nineteen or twenty. One weekend I came down to the shop. I'd left a school book behind in Dad's office. Between you and me, I did it on purpose in the hopes I'd bump into Terry when I came to get it. He was working on a 1956 Chevy, reconstructing the engine using original engine parts that he'd scrimped and saved for. Every weekend, he'd work on it. I started coming down, too, to help him. I loved it. I realized that was my passion."

"So you became a mechanic?"

"After Terry was locked up, I went to college, like Dad wanted. I hated it. After one semester I dropped out and found a job up in Jacksonville apprenticing with a mechanic. Dad was furious. Eventually he forgave me. I've been working with him for the past couple of years. The plan is that I'll take over when he retires."

Emily selected a couple of wrenches and put them in her utility belt as well. "You haven't said why you're asking about Terry."

"Do you know whether he knew a girl called Maddison Logan?" Rachel asked.

"He never brought girls around when I was here. It's a good thing he didn't. I'd have eaten them alive." Emily lowered herself down to the creeper board and put in her headphones.

"One last question before you get back to work," said Rachel. "What did Terry do for money after your dad fired him?"

"He worked at a gas station near Doreen. They have a big towing business. Why are you asking all these questions about him, anyway?"

"Just looking into the case," said Rachel.

"He didn't do it," said Emily before sliding back under the car. "Terry is not a killer."

Chapter 50

The place where Terence Bailey worked after Kyle fired him was a run-down old repair shop and gas station on a country road near Doreen, about eight miles northwest of Daytona. In the front were four gas pumps, all idle. An old tow truck was parked near the back.

A sign on a metal roadside diner near the main building said "Open" next to a faded menu taped to the glass. Rachel peered into a window. The place was empty other than a pile of boxes and a stepladder. The windows were nearly opaque from dust and cobwebs. Some were boarded up. The diner had obviously shut down years earlier, probably around the time a new highway extension bypassed the town.

Rachel asked the cab driver who'd driven her there to keep the meter running while she went into the gas station. She'd arranged for him to drive her back to her hotel when she was done.

The gas station store was a tiny office with a cash register and a cigarette rack behind it. There was a display with candy and chips in front of the counter. An old-fashioned fridge with sodas and other drinks for sale was in the corner by a shelf of dusty bottles of engine oil. Rachel took a couple of sodas out of a fridge and pressed a metal bell on the counter to call for service, as instructed by a small handwritten sign.

A shrunken man with a wispy white beard emerged from a side door leading to the auto shop, engine grease smeared on his coveralls. He wiped his blackened hands clean on a cloth hanging out of his pocket as he slid behind the cash register counter to serve Rachel.

"Is that all you need?" he asked as Rachel handed him cash for her purchase.

"Well, I was hoping you could help me with something else," said Rachel. "You employed a young man here a few years back. Terence Bailey."

"Yes, I did." He squinted inquiringly at Rachel, although he wasn't curious enough to ask her why she wanted this information. "Terry was on bail but I took a chance with him. I was that desperate for workers at the time. How is he?"

"Still in prison," said Rachel. "He assaulted another prisoner and his sentence was extended."

"I'm sorry to hear it." He sounded sincere.

"What was he like?" Rachel asked.

"Always struck me as a decent fella. To tell you the truth, I kind of liked him. Maybe it's because of the way he helped that girl. Not too many young people stick their necks out these days."

"What girl?"

"Well, that's kind of a long story," he said, looking out the window at the cab waiting for Rachel near the tire air pressure machine.

"It's okay. I have plenty of time," Rachel reassured him.

"When Terry worked for me, he slept at the gas station at night because he had nowhere else to live," he began. "He camped out behind the cash register, where I'm standing now. Kept a camping mattress and a sleeping bag in the back room that he'd bring out at night. Occasionally, we'd get a towing call after hours. I paid him extra for the overnight jobs," he paused, realizing that he was rambling.

"Go on," Rachel encouraged.

"Well, yes, so, one night a car pulls in. It's well past midnight. The man puts in gas. When he comes to pay, he asks if his sister can use the restroom. Terry gives him the restroom key. Tells him to leave it in the restroom door because he's locking up and going back to sleep. Next morning, Terry wakes at dawn to the sound of thumping. It's coming from the restroom. Except the door is locked. Someone is banging on the door. He jimmies it open and lets out a teenage girl who's been locked inside the restroom for most of the night."

"Were you here when she was rescued, or did Bailey tell you the story afterward?" Rachel asked.

"Terry told me when I came in later that morning. I was furious with him. Almost fired him until he told me what happened."

"Why did you want to fire him?"

"Because when I arrived at work, the place was shut. The tow truck was gone. I thought he'd robbed me. He apologized and told me that he'd driven the girl he'd found in the restroom back home. Never did say how the girl had gotten locked up in there. A couple of days later, he quit. Out of the blue. I paid him what I owed him in cash. Found a replacement the following week."

"You never found out what happened with that girl?" Rachel asked.

"I never did. But that's not the end of the story," he said. "I was hosing down the restrooms later on the day he found the girl when I noticed something lying on the floor in the corner."

"What was it?"

"I'll show you. I still have it. Nobody ever came to claim it." He removed an object from a hook by the cash register. "I keep it as a good luck charm." He hung it over the edge of his finger so that it swung like a pendulum in front of Rachel. Hanging from a dusty black ribbon was a silver charm. It was in the shape of a snake wrapped around itself. "It's an Ouroboros," said Rachel.

When Rachel finished asking him the last of her questions and taking photos of the necklace, she thanked him and took the soda cans she'd bought back to the cab. She handed the cab driver a soda and then opened hers and took a sip.

"There's something else that you should know," the gas station owner called out suddenly as he came out of the shop.

"Terry was scared of something," he said when he reached Rachel. "I think that's why he quit."

"What was he afraid of?"

"He never said. Terry told me that if a man ever came asking about him, then I should say that he moved up north."

"And did a man ever come?" Rachel asked.

"About two weeks later, a man turned up. He said he owed Terry money and he wanted to send him a check. He asked for his address. I told him what Terry told me to say, about him going up north. The man said he was sorry to hear it and then he left."

"Do you remember what this man looked like, or the type of car he drove?" Rachel asked.

"Nope," said the gas station owner. He hesitated. "Except for one thing." He seemed embarrassed. "This probably doesn't sound very charitable."

Rachel nodded to encourage him to go on.

"That man smelled something awful. It was like . . ." He searched for an apt description.

"Like rotting garbage?" Rachel asked.

"Yes! How did you know?"

"Just a lucky guess."

Chapter 51

As Rachel walked into the hotel, someone walking in the opposite direction accidentally slammed into her hard enough to send her reeling a few steps backward.

"Ouch," she said, rubbing her shoulder.

"Are you okay?" It was Eric, @SerendipityZoe's boyfriend who Rachel had seen filming content for Zoe's social media channels earlier that day. "I didn't see you. Are you sure that you're okay?"

"I'm fine," Rachel said, even though her shoulder burned from the collision. Eric didn't look fine at all. He looked extremely agitated. "Is everything okay?"

"No. Not really," he said. "She's so goddamn demanding."

"Who is?" Rachel felt obliged to ask even though she had a pretty good idea of the answer.

"Zoe," he said. "We spent the afternoon filming by the pool. Yoga poses. Swimming shots. Strolling on the beach. You name it. She hated every shot." He exhaled a puff of air in frustration. "I'm a terrible photographer. That's what she told me. More like screamed at me. She said that if she'd known how shitty I am at camerawork she'd have brought a professional to this conference. Do you have any idea how insulting that is?" he asked Rachel rhetorically. "I am done. Done." He made a cutting gesture with his hands to emphasize the finality of his statement.

"Sounds like your day has been worse than mine," said Rachel, who was still bristling over being hauled into the police station.

"You don't know the half of it," he said, noticing Rachel was still rubbing her shoulder from their collision. "How about you join me for a drink at the lobby bar so I can apologize for barging into you?"

"It wasn't your fault," said Rachel. "I wasn't looking where I was going either."

"You got the brunt of it. Come on. One drink. To say sorry."

"Okay. Just one." Rachel relented even though she'd have much preferred to swim in the hotel pool than listen to Eric gripe about his girlfriend.

Rachel followed Eric to a low table with two plush armchairs on the far side of the bar. The dim light of the bar area and the length of the long mahogany bar itself shielded them from hotel guests moving from the pool area across the lobby to the elevators. Their table was next to a glass window overlooking a fernery. Rachel had the impression that Eric had deliberately chosen one of the more discreet tables so that Zoe wouldn't see them there if she happened to pass by.

"Zoe's been on the warpath all day. I've never seen her so angry," Eric said. His face was flushed and sweaty from filming outdoors all day. His damp bangs hung limply over his forehead.

The waitress arrived with their drinks and a few miniature tapas bowls containing spicy roasted peanuts, crushed marinated olives, and a pesto dip with a plate of mini-breadsticks.

"Why is Zoe in such a bad mood?" Rachel asked curiously once the waitress had left the table.

"She gets like this when she's stressed," he answered. "She collapsed on the bed in tears because she says she doesn't have any decent content to put up on her channels today. I couldn't take being screamed at anymore."

"She takes it very seriously," said Rachel, remembering how Zoe and Eric had been filming at the crack of dawn at the breakfast buffet.

"She's desperate to get chosen for the Influencer Awards," he said. "She thinks that if she doesn't win, then her career as an influencer will wither and die. I think she's afraid that she'll end up marrying me instead! Apparently, I'm the consolation prize," he said bitterly, pausing to take a sip from his organic microbrew.

"How long have you known each other?"

"We met in college. We fell head over heels in love with each other. But ever since her influencer career took off, things have gone downhill. There are days when she acts like she can't stand the sight of me."

"In what way?"

"The more successful Zoe gets, the worse things are between us," he said. "Some days, I don't think she even notices that I exist other than as her personal photographer. She's fallen in love with the lifestyle. She loves being around famous 'grammers."

"Like Jonny Macon," Rachel said.

"Him, and others," he mumbled, staring into his beer glass morosely. "I'm overthinking things," he chided himself. "It's actually a good thing that she's spending time with the other influencers. That's why she's here. This is a networking event."

"I'm sure it's fun for everyone to get together in person instead of virtually."

"Oh, sure. It's fun. To a degree. It's also stressful and the stakes are high," he said. "They're friends but they're also rivals. Bitter rivals."

"Bitter in what way?"

"They might be in the same influencer pod but they still compete with each other for the awards, the sponsorship deals, the followers. Each and every one of them is determined to win."

Rachel finished her drink. She was trying to find a delicate way to wrap up their little tète-â-tète without hurting Eric's feelings. He was obviously feeling low, but Rachel was not in the mood to play therapist.

"It is more competitive than you can imagine," Eric continued. "Take that travel vlogger Maddison Logan."

"What about her?" Rachel kept her tone even and disinterested.

"Nobody has seen her in days. Zoe is convinced that she deliberately left the conference. She thinks that she's working on a stunt to push herself to the front for the awards."

"What sort of stunt?"

"Who knows! You can't imagine what people will do to get noticed. There's one girl who takes 'extreme selfies.' A few weeks ago, Zoe showed me a selfie this chick posted of herself dancing on the ledge of an apartment building. She sent it to Zoe with a message begging her to let her join her pod. Take it from me, some people will do just about anything to go viral."

Rachel wondered if Maddison's disappearance was just a stunt. Perhaps she hadn't gone missing at all. Maybe Maddison hoped the cops would take her disappearance to the media and it would become a major news story. By extension she'd become a household name. That would certainly help her win the Influencer Awards.

"Is Zoe's theory about Maddison just a theory or does she have a reason to think that's what happened?" Rachel asked.

"Zoe's suspicious of everyone," Eric went on. "Even you. She says there's something weird about the @runninggirlRach account. She says it was dormant until recently and now it's taken off. She thinks you're a spy. Get this, she even suggested that you might be that famous podcaster."

"Who?" Rachel asked without missing a beat. She was grateful for the drama classes she'd taken at college.

"Rachel something. Krall, I think," he added. "She's the reporter who covered that rape trial in North Carolina."

"I'm sure she has much better things to do than attend an influencer conference in Daytona."

"Yeah, that's what I told Zoe," he said. "Like I said, Zoe's suspicious of everyone. She wants to win that damn award. God help anyone who gets in her way. Even the members of her own pod."

"How do these pods work? Can anyone join?"

"It's like a private club. They're very picky about who they let in. All the influencers in the pod have to vote in favor," he said. "Zoe's pod has a name, an insignia. The works."

"What's the name of her pod?"

"It's called 'The Infinity Project,'" he said. "They chose it because everyone in the pod wants to be famous forever."

Chapter 52

Thomas McCoy sits on his front porch, patting Millie as he searches the name "Rachel Krall" on his phone. That's the name written on the note he found in the pants that are still burning in the oil drum at the back of the house.

A lot of information comes up. Too much. Thomas McCoy reads the first paragraphs of a newspaper article. It describes Rachel Krall as a journalist and a podcaster. The article includes a link to the first season of her podcast about a high school coach convicted of killing his wife on their second honeymoon. Thomas clicks the link and listens to Rachel Krall's silky voice. It feels as if she's talking just to him.

"The invitation for the wedding ceremony said 'no shoes' and 'no gifts.' It was a barefoot ceremony on a beach, less than a mile away from the cove where the bride's body would wash up in the tide a few days later on what was supposed to have been their second honeymoon."

He listens to the podcast as he tries to find out more information on Rachel Krall. Among the Rachel Krall search results that come up is a post on Instagram from someone called @SerendipityZoe. She's put up a photograph of an influencers' conference at a luxury Daytona hotel. It's the accompanying caption that grabs his attention.

"My spidey senses told me there was something off about @runninggirlRach, who's at #BuzzCon with me. So I poked around and I'm pretty sure that she's the famous podcaster Rachel Krall. Earlier today, she was talking to cops at the hotel lobby and then she left in a cop car. Weird, right?"

The post is followed by speculation in the comments by people noting that it's odd the @runninggirlRach Instagram account was inactive for a long time. Eventually someone puts up an old photo of Rachel Krall on the thread. There's a long discussion comparing the Rachel Krall photo to a hazy nighttime selfie of @runninggirlRach and Jonny Macon by a bar at BuzzCon. In the photo, @runninggirlRach's face is partly obscured by a beer bottle she holds up but there's enough of her face visible to lead to a lengthy debate by posters on the possibility that @runninggirlRach and Rachel Krall are one and the same person.

Thomas goes through more posts on Zoe's Instagram account, all of which are geotagged. He knows the hotel. He's been dropping and picking up people from that conference for days. It's where he dropped off that Jonny character the previous night and then later brought him the cocaine that he'd asked him to courier over. He dials the hotel.

"How can I direct your call?" an operator says.

"I'd like to speak with Rachel Krall," Thomas says. "She left me a voicemail with the room number but her voice is muffled. I think she said room 328?"

"It's room 541."

"My bad."

"I'll transfer you now."

He waits on the line as the call is transferred and then he hangs up.

Chapter 53

In Joe Martinez's experience, breakthroughs in missing persons cases often came when they were least expected and from the most unlikely source. The other lesson he'd learned over the years was that even a small breakthrough could change the trajectory of a case.

That's what happened with the Maddison Logan investigation. Security camera footage at a strip mall had captured Maddison's camper van entering the parking lot on the day she went missing.

Maddison went into a supermarket, dressed in the same skinny jeans and top she'd worn to see Terence Bailey in prison. She'd forgotten to take off her visitor's sticker. It was still stuck to her blouse.

Twenty minutes after entering the supermarket, Maddison left carrying two grocery bags. She'd returned to her van and driven out of the parking lot, turning in the direction of the Delta Springs State Forest. These were among the last images of Maddison before her disappearance other than the video of the abduction itself, which specialist audio technicians were working their magic on back in Quantico.

Human voices were as unique as fingerprints, and if the technicians were able to extract the voice of the intruder who'd barged into Maddison's van from the video, then it might lead directly to a suspect. That was one of the key investigative lines of inquiry that Martinez's team was chasing.

The CCTV footage from the supermarket could be equally useful, as it might reveal whether anyone had been following Maddison as she bought her groceries.

The footage showed Maddison pushing a shopping cart around the store, selecting produce and other groceries and paying in cash at the checkout. An initial analysis of the video by Martinez's team concluded there was no indication that anyone had been following Maddison at the supermarket. The footage helped provide a timeline of Maddison's movements on the day she disappeared. It did nothing to explain what had happened to her.

But when Martinez reviewed the footage, he saw something that nobody else on the taskforce had noticed.

"Take a look at the car there." Martinez pointed to a black Ford sedan with tinted windows. It was six car lengths behind Maddison's van in a line of cars waiting to turn out of the parking lot.

It was the only car that turned in the same direction as Maddison. All the other cars went the opposite way, toward Daytona Beach and the I-95.

Martinez checked the map. The road taken by Maddison and the black Ford went straight back to the Delta Springs State Forest. He rewound the footage to rewatch Maddison's arrival forty minutes earlier. He wasn't surprised to see the same black Ford had entered the parking lot shortly after Maddison drove in. Once again several vehicles had separated the suspicious car in question from Maddison's van.

"The driver went to a lot of effort to make sure that Maddison wouldn't notice that she was being followed," Martinez said.

Martinez ran the plates of the black Ford in the national car registration database. The vehicle was registered to Dwain Aubrey, aged sixty-two. Martinez telephoned the number in the listing.

"Is this Dwain Aubrey?" Martinez asked when the call was answered.

"It sure is," a man responded jovially. "At least it was the last time I looked in the mirror," he joked.

"I'm calling from AIM car insurance. Are you the owner of a black Ford?" Martinez read out the plate number.

"That's my car." Dwain Aubrey's tone turned serious. "What seems to be the problem, sir?"

"Your vehicle dented another vehicle while parking earlier this week at a supermarket."

"Which supermarket?" Aubrey asked.

"Just outside Daytona Beach." Martinez reeled off the name of a big Florida supermarket chain.

"Did you say that it happened at Daytona Beach?"

"Yes, sir," Martinez said.

"Well, that's the proof right there that I didn't do it. I'm in Little Rock, Arkansas. And so's my car. My eldest daughter just gave birth to our first grandchild. A seven-pound boy. We've been here for almost two weeks, helping with the baby. There's obviously a mistake."

"It sure sounds that way," Martinez apologized. Based on what Dwain Aubrey had revealed, the car's plate number was forged.

Martinez called over Agent Torreno. "Mark, find out the exact model of this vehicle in the CCTV footage. Then pull together a list of owners of this make of vehicle, the model, and the year. I want details of every car that fits the bill within a 100-mile radius of Daytona."

He turned to the rest of the team. "Let's talk about plans for tomorrow. Terence Bailey is scheduled to get out at around eleven in the morning. He'll be staying downtown at a halfway house for released prisoners. We can't get a court order to carry out electronic surveillance, so we'll have to do it the old-fashioned way."

Plainclothes cops in an unmarked car would follow Bailey when he left prison. Another car would wait outside the halfway house. Two cops would keep watch on foot. The taskforce had enough reinforcements to keep Bailey under twenty-four-hour surveillance for seventy-two hours.

It was a given that Terence Bailey hadn't personally abducted Maddison, since he was in a maximum-security prison at the time that she disappeared. However, Martinez believed that Bailey may have instructed his accomplice to carry out the abduction by communicating via a contraband prison phone.

Martinez believed there was a real possibility that Maddison was being kept alive for Bailey's release. It was this possibility that prompted him to push his taskforce hard, cracking the whip and keeping them working in shifts virtually around the clock.

"Once he's out, all bets are off. That's why we need stringent surveillance on Bailey from the second he steps foot out of prison," he instructed his team. "We need to know where Bailey goes and who he meets with. I don't want him taking a dump without me knowing."

Martinez moved on to set assignments for the rest of the team. He gave a junior agent the note with the name of the STD clinic that Detective Castel had given him.

"Ask if Jessica Hewitt was a patient there. If she was, then I need the pathology lab to release her pap smear slides or any swabs they've kept of hers."

"Why do we need the slides?" the agent asked.

"Because they'll contain her DNA," said Martinez.

He put on his jacket and drove to a hotel on the Daytona Beach strip. The mom of Terence Bailey's suspected third victim, Aysh Philips, worked there. Her name was Mary Philips. Martinez had read Mary's statements in her daughter's file, but he wanted to talk to her himself in case the local cops had missed something when they'd interviewed her. Perhaps she unwittingly knew of a connection that would help him figure out the identity of Bailey's accomplice. Martinez had called her just before he briefed his team. She'd said that she was happy to answer his questions so long as he didn't mind doing it while she cleaned.

When he arrived at the hotel, Martinez spotted her cleaning cart in a carpeted corridor around the corner from the executive lounge on a high floor with expansive views of the beach.

Mary Philips came to her housekeeping cart to collect a pile of fresh white towels just as Martinez was about to poke his head into the hotel room to look for her. She was a petite woman, around fifty, with stoic eyes.

"You're that FBI agent who called me earlier?" she said as she picked up a pile of laundered white towels.

"That's me." Martinez showed his badge. "I have a few questions about your daughter, Aysh."

"What is it you want to ask me?" She headed into the bathroom with the towels. Martinez followed behind her.

"Did Aysh know a man called Terence Bailey? Some people called him Terry?"

"I don't recall hearing her mention that name before," Mary said, hanging several towels over metal rails in neat rows. "Did you come all this way to ask me that? If you did, then you should know the police asked me the same question at the time."

She returned to the cleaning cart, where she scooped up a handful of toiletries and soaps, which she artfully arranged on the bathroom counter near the taps.

"Have you ever heard the name Maddison Logan before?"

"No. Why do you ask?"

"I was wondering if Aysh had a friend by that name?"

"I don't believe so," she said. "Is that all you wanted to talk to me about, Detective?" She seemed nervous.

"It is for now," said Martinez. "What did you think I wanted to talk to you about?"

"I thought you were here about the money." She sounded relieved, like an enormous weight had been lifted.

"What money?"

"The other night I came back from my weekly bridge game down the street. There was a woman standing on my stoop. She shoved an envelope in my hand and ran off. It was full of money. Thousands of dollars in cash."

"Did you see what she looked like?"

"I wasn't wearing my eyeglasses. I'm blind without them. My son, Brian, is studying law at Emory. He said I should give the money to the police in case it's stolen. Is that why you're here, Agent Martinez? Did I do something wrong?"

"You've done nothing wrong," Martinez reassured her, his interest piqued. He filed the information away for later. Right now, he needed to find out everything she knew about her daughter's disappearance. "Can you tell me what happened the night Aysh disappeared?"

Mary gave him a shorthand account of how her daughter had gone into work on the night she'd disappeared because they'd had a staffing problem. Aysh could have said no when her supervisor called and asked her to come to work that evening after a staff member went home sick.

"Aysh didn't like to let people down, so she finished eating her dinner and quickly dressed for work even though we'd planned an evening watching television together. She rode over on her bicycle."

As she spoke, she stripped the king bed and remade it with fresh sheets that she flapped into the air to remove the creases before expertly smoothing them down across the enormous mattress.

"I'm sorry to be opening up old wounds," said Martinez.

"Opening up?" Mary said wearily as she tucked in a bottom sheet and smoothed it out. "How can you open up a wound that's never closed?"

She leaned across the bed, tugging at the bottom sheet to remove any creases before changing the pillow covers. As she worked, she told Martinez the little she knew about her daughter's movements on the day when she was last seen alive.

"I didn't realize that Aysh was missing until the following night. I'd left early the next morning to go to work. Her bedroom door was closed. I didn't want to wake her. It was only when I came home from work that Brian and I compared notes. We realized that neither of us had seen or heard from Aysh in almost twenty-four hours. We checked her room. Her bed hadn't been slept in. We immediately went to the police."

"What did they do?"

"Nothing. They said it was too soon to file a missing persons case."

"So nobody started looking for her once you reported her missing?" Martinez asked.

"No, sir. They did not," Mary said. "They told us to come back the next day if she hadn't turned up. Aysh ran away once when she was younger during a difficult high school freshman year. It must have still been in the police files because they said she might have done it again and I should wait a bit longer for her to come home before reporting it. We returned the next day, sick with worry. She still hadn't come home. The police officer at the desk took the details. Even then nobody snapped into action," she said. "The day after that it didn't matter anymore because it turned out they'd found my baby's body out in that forest."

Mary Philips's anguished voice reverberated through his head, leaving Martinez feeling ashamed as he left the hotel. It wasn't the first time he'd heard about missing persons cases that had been shunted aside by local cops unwilling to commit resources until there was more definitive proof. As a result of these delays, police lost the trail while it was still fresh.

The missing white woman's syndrome was a real thing. When a young middle-class or upper-class white female went missing, it was front-page news. That wasn't the case when the missing woman was a person of color, or poor. It also wasn't the same for missing boys and men. These missing people didn't capture the imagination of the public or the media in the way that a missing blond-haired white girl from an affluent family did.

Martinez called Torreno as he headed toward his car. He wanted a full review of the Aysh Philips case. From what Aysh's mom had told him, it sounded as if the investigation had been haphazard. "I want fresh eyes on the files," said Martinez.

"Is there anything particular they should keep an eye out for?" Torreno asked.

"They'll know it when they see it," Martinez said. "By the way, someone gave Aysh's mom an envelope full of cash the other day. Her mom still has the envelope. Send an officer to her house tonight so we can dust it for prints."

"I'll get someone on it," said Torreno. "In the meantime, I have an update for you."

"Go ahead," said Martinez.

"They found a cell phone in the mud excavated from the quicksand pool where we found that girl's body," Torreno said. "There's no way to know whether the data is salvageable. It was submerged for several days. The lab is working through it now."

"Good," said Martinez, pressing his car key fob to open the vehicle. "Any updates on when the Canadians will give us the name of the owner of the phone number that Bailey's been texting to from his prison cell?" Martinez asked as he slid into the driver's seat.

The phone that Bailey had messaged from prison was registered in Canada. Jurisdictional issues and red tape were slowing down accessing a simple and yet vital piece of information that might reveal the identity of Bailey's accomplice.

"We're still waiting," said Torreno.

"Ask the bureau liaison to pressure the Canadians. Tell them we may have a killer getting out of prison and we can't wait any longer. Have there been any new messages?"

"I was just getting to that. Bailey sent a text message from his cell after lunch today."

"What did it say?" Martinez paused for the answer before firing up the car engine.

"I'll read it to you," said Torreno. "'*I get out tomorrow. Bring me Rachel Krall. It's time to end this.*'"

Chapter 54

The BuzzCon cocktail party was in full swing by the hotel pool when Rachel came down from her room for an evening swim and run on the beach. The exuberant party atmosphere and incessant selfie-taking were an indication that Maddison Logan's disappearance and Jonny Macon's death were still not public knowledge. Otherwise, Rachel presumed, the evening's festivities would have been canceled.

Rachel went around the perimeter of the poolside patio where the cocktail party was underway. The only person who seemed to notice her was Eric. Visibly uncomfortable after spilling his guts to her earlier, he gave an embarrassed half nod in Rachel's direction as he knelt on one knee photographing Zoe.

"You look amazing, Zoe," he called out. Zoe held up a champagne glass in the air like a trophy while sticking a tanned leg outside the thigh slit of her floor-length white gown.

It was getting close to twilight when Rachel reached the beach. She stripped to her swimsuit, leaving her beach towel and clothes on the sand before diving into the waves. When she was done swimming, she jogged in her wet swimsuit and bare feet toward the pulsating neon lights of the beachside amusement park in the distance. Without intending to do so, she sped into a fast sprint for the final stretch.

"Rachel! Rachel!" The frantic call of her name broke through her single-minded concentration. "Rachel, this is fun, but how about we take a breather for a second. I'm getting flashbacks to my first weeks of basic training."

Rachel stopped and turned to see Joe Martinez running behind her. He'd been gaining on her when she stopped.

"Why are you chasing me?" Rachel asked, her hands on her hips as she caught her breath.

"You wouldn't stop when I called your name."

"I'm sorry. I didn't hear you calling me."

"Don't be sorry. It's the first proper exercise that I've had all day."

"You're hardly dressed for running." Rachel pointed out.

"I always run in a suit and tie," said Martinez, loosening his tie and his top shirt buttons. He slipped off his suit jacket, swinging it over his shoulder as they walked alongside each other toward the amusement park in the distance.

"I was looking for you at the cocktail party," he said.

"Yeah, I'm skipping it. I don't think I can take another BuzzCon event," Rachel said. "They're all so . . ." She grappled for an appropriate word.

"Vacuous? Narcissistic? Self-indulgent?" he suggested.

"The world could be burning down and all they'd care about would be whether they should airbrush their selfie. Even now, nobody seems to care that Maddison hasn't been online for days. I think they're secretly relieved she hasn't been at the conference or posting to her followers."

"Why would they be relieved?" Martinez asked.

"They're competing for some prestigious Influencer Award that could get them millions in sponsorship deals. Maddison not being around means one less person to compete with," said Rachel as they turned around and walked back toward the hotel. "What's so important that you had to chase me across a beach?"

"Jonny Macon."

"Don't tell me that you also think that I killed him."

"I heard the local PD hauled you in." Martinez paused to slip off his shoes. He shook out the sand that had collected in them as he'd run, removed his socks, and continued walking alongside Rachel in his bare feet.

"I think the local PD hoped to get a confession out of me," said Rachel. "I told them I couldn't have done it. For one thing the timelines don't match up. I told them to check the hotel grounds' CCTV footage."

"They checked it. You went to the beach with Macon and came back inside eleven minutes later."

"So they do believe me?"

"Let's just say they're coming around. The detective in charge of the case wants to make sure you didn't leave the hotel through another exit later in the night. They're checking other CCTV cameras at the hotel as we speak."

"It's ridiculous. Why would I want to knock off Jonny Macon? I met the guy for the first time an hour before he died. What's my motive?"

"They're too busy chasing their tails right now to think logically," Martinez sighed. "You're the last person who saw Macon. That makes you an obvious suspect in their eyes. I told them they're wasting their time with you. They need to start looking at other suspects."

"Like Jonny's girlfriend, Reni. I hear she can be vindictive. She was not happy to find out that Jonny had cheated on her with Maddison a few days ago. I bet Maddison wasn't the first either," said Rachel, thinking about how Jonny had flirted with her at the bar.

"You're very good, Rachel," Martinez said. "None of the agents that I've sent to sniff around at BuzzCon know a fraction of what you've found out in less than twenty-four hours."

"No big surprise there. Influencers talk to influencers," said Rachel. She paused to pick up her swimming towel and the long T-shirt that she'd left on the sand after her swim.

"Isn't it interesting that two people in that love triangle are out of the picture?" Martinez mused as Rachel slipped on her T-shirt and stepped into her shorts. "Jonny Macon is dead and Maddison, the influencer he hooked up with, has gone missing. I think the influencers at BuzzCon know more than they're saying."

"Undoubtedly," said Rachel. "I'll see what I can find out."

"Actually, I'd prefer that you didn't," he said. "I'd feel a lot more at ease if you'd head home first thing tomorrow morning."

"So that I'm not around when Bailey gets out tomorrow," concluded Rachel. "I thought you'd realized by now that I'm here for the long haul, Joe. I'm also more useful here than at home. I've cultivated sources at BuzzCon who I can milk for information."

"Why do you care enough to put yourself on the line, Rachel?" Martinez asked.

"You heard Maddison's voicemail message. She turned to me for help. I feel responsible for finding her," said Rachel. "I know it's technically your jobjob—"

"Technically?" he interrupted in amusement.

"Okay, yes, it is your job," Rachel agreed. "But I've had some success finding out things that your people haven't figured out. They haven't even come close to cracking the influencers at BuzzCon the way that I have."

"It would be helpful to know what else you've found out," said Martinez. "I've commandeered the basement of police headquarters, where my taskforce is working. How about we get takeout and work there?"

"I was already at police headquarters earlier today. Once was more than enough," said Rachel. "Let's meet up somewhere else."

Rachel ran through places in her mind where they could meet. The hotel lobby bar was the most obvious place, but it was often noisy and it was hardly private. The same with a restaurant. Her hotel room had a big balcony where they could have a working dinner. She suggested they work there.

"Sure. I'll pick up food while you get ready."

As they approached the hotel, a colorful glow of bright lights hovered over the pool. Laughter and music rang out from the cocktail party.

"It's so weird that everyone at BuzzCon is still partying like there's no tomorrow despite the fact that Maddison has disappeared and Jonny Macon is dead," said Rachel.

"They'll find out about Jonny in the morning. A team of local detectives is going to turn up to ask questions," he said. "I expect that will put a damper on the conference."

"Don't count on it," said Rachel. "The influencers will lap it up if it brings media attention and notoriety. Believe me, the news will be all over their social channels as soon as they hear about Jonny's death. There'll be a hashtag and memorial tributes in minutes."

Chapter 55

Just a minute," Rachel called out.

The knock on the hotel room door was barely loud enough to hear over the crash of water hitting the marble shower tiles under Rachel's bare feet.

Rachel turned off the shower tap and threw a fluffy white hotel bathrobe over her wet body, pausing to tie it tightly around her waist. She dried her wet hair with a white hand towel as she left the bathroom and swung open the hotel room door. Joe Martinez was waiting on the other side holding two large pizza boxes and a brown paper bag along with a bottle of red wine.

"Sorry," said Rachel. "I'm not quite ready yet." She felt strangely vulnerable and disheveled standing in a robe. This was not how she wanted Joe Martinez to see her.

"I'm the one who's sorry," said Martinez. "I should have given you more time to get ready. I'll come back in a few minutes." He turned toward the door.

"It's fine. Really. Stay, Joe." Rachel led him to the sliding doors of the balcony, where there was a small outdoor table and two chairs. Before her shower, she'd set the table with wineglasses and soda cans from the bar fridge. "I thought we'd eat outside."

"Nice view," said Martinez as he stepped onto the balcony, where they could see flashing neon lights across the boardwalk.

Rachel stood next to him on the balcony, her hand almost touching his on the chrome rail. "It's even better during the daytime. You can see the different colors of the ocean. It's breathtaking."

Martinez abruptly pulled away to pour them each a glass of the wine. They took a sip, catching each other's eyes when they were done. This was supposed to be a professional debrief. Instead, it felt like a date.

"Excuse me for a moment while I get dressed." Rachel broke the awkward silence. "I feel like I'm dressed for one of those health spas where everyone wanders around in bathrobes."

"I once spent a weekend at one of those places. It was the longest weekend of my life," he said.

"You don't strike me as a health spa sort of guy."

"It was a birthday present from my wife. It was the year we got married, so that's twelve years ago now. I kept sneaking off to play racquetball with one of the other husbands. Steph was not happy."

"I bet." Rachel kept her tone upbeat, even though she felt a pang of disappointment that he was married. She hadn't seen a ring on his finger, although she had noticed the way he'd fondly touched his watch when she'd first seen him. It had given her the impression that he was taken.

Rachel was annoyed with herself for caring about Joe Martinez's relationship status. She told herself that she had no romantic interest whatsoever in the FBI agent, even though in truth, he'd intrigued her from the moment they'd first met.

"I really should get changed," she said again after another sip of wine.

"It can wait until after we've eaten. Cold pizza is the worst. Besides, you look perfectly fine the way you are." He flipped open the pizza boxes. He'd bought pepperoni and vegetarian, since he'd forgotten to ask her food preferences.

Rachel helped herself to a piece of vegetarian pizza. Martinez rummaged in the bag and removed plastic cutlery as well as a container of antipasto and a big leafy salad in a clear plastic container. Finally, he took out two shot glasses containing a decadent chocolate mousse.

"I thought dinner would be a pizza slice out of a box," said Rachel. "This is turning into a three-course meal. All that's missing is the candlelight."

Martinez looked up at the bright stars in the midnight-blue sky. "There's your candlelight," he said with a smile. "As for the three-course meal, I haven't eaten since breakfast. I'm starving. I often don't get time to eat when I'm away for work, so when I do, I try to do it properly."

"Your wife must hate you being away so often," said Rachel.

"Steph understood. Her job was demanding, too. We often only saw each other on weekends."

"You're divorced?" Rachel asked, confused about why he'd switched to talking about his wife in past tense. A spasm of pain fleetingly shifted across Joe's face like a storm cloud on a summer day. Rachel immediately regretted asking the question.

"Steph died last year," he said.

"That's terrible. I'm so sorry," said Rachel.

"Steph was a lawyer. Very driven. Very successful. That's how our marriage survived my career. Eventually we decided to have kids. When we couldn't conceive, the doctors ran tests. They found a tumor on her left ovary. Cancer. It had already spread by the time they found it. She died five weeks later."

"Sounds like you've had a hell of a time."

"A hell of a time would be an understatement," he said quietly, examining the contents of his wineglass. "So what did you get up to today?" he asked, trying to change the mood. "I'm betting that you didn't spend it on the beach. You don't strike me as being in vacation mode at all."

"I'm not," said Rachel truthfully. "Maddison's disappearance got me curious."

"How curious?"

"Curious enough," she said, toying with the green salad leaves on her plate. "Besides, I see a potential podcast once this is all over. I've been talking to people. I can share all the gory details if you're interested."

"I'm interested."

"Well, I found out that aside from having a fling with Jonny Macon, Maddison visited a run-down condo building on the edge of town a few days before she disappeared."

"Do you know why she went there?"

"That part I haven't nailed down yet," Rachel admitted. "I think she went to apartment 4D, which belongs to a woman called Grace Milroy. But Grace has never met Maddison, so there's always a chance that we got the apartment number wrong."

"Who is Grace and why would Maddison go looking for her?"

"Grace's daughter, Hailey, went missing a few years back. It would have been around the time that Terence Bailey went to prison," said Rachel. "As for why Maddison went looking for Grace, your guess is as good as mine, although I suspect that it may have had something to do with Terence Bailey. Has the name Hailey Milroy come up in your investigation?"

He shook his head after a moment's thought. "It hasn't. I'll get my team to get hold of the case files." He paused to text someone those instructions.

"I've been thinking about Grace all afternoon," said Rachel. "Grace's life has been in perpetual limbo since her daughter went missing. To this day, she doesn't know if Hailey ran away or if she was taken."

"Another teenager, Aysh Philips, was abducted and murdered at around that time, as well," Martinez said. "I wonder if they knew each other?"

Martinez briefly told Rachel about Aysh's murder as well as his meeting with Aysh's mom, Mary, earlier that day. "She lives with the constant heartache of knowing that her daughter's last moments in this world were brutal and terrifying."

"After talking to Grace, I don't know if it's better to know what happened and somehow come to terms with it, or to never know at all," Rachel mused.

“Honestly, Rachel, I don’t know the answer to that question,” Martinez said. “I’ve handled missing persons cases that have turned into homicides so gruesome that it might have been kinder if the families never knew. By the same token, I’ve seen families destroyed by the psychological torture of never knowing.”

“Either way, it must be a living hell,” said Rachel.

Chapter 56

The jarring buzz of Joe Martinez's phone heralded the arrival of the Hailey Milroy missing persons file in his email inbox. He paused to read the summary page. When he was done, he put his phone away.

"According to the police report, a neighbor told police that he saw Hailey leave in a tow truck on the day she was last seen. It appears that she left of her own volition. She was a legal adult. That's why the police were reluctant to investigate further. You seem surprised," he added, looking at Rachel.

"Terence Bailey worked as a tow truck driver before he went to prison," Rachel said. "In fact, his old boss said he disappeared one morning with the gas station's tow truck. When he returned, he told his boss a convoluted story about finding a teenaged girl locked in the restroom a few hours after a man filled up on gasoline in the middle of the night."

"Sounds like a 'dog ate my homework' sort of story," said Martinez. "Bailey was probably trying to cover up for arriving late for work."

"I think it really happened," said Rachel. "The gas station owner found a silver Ouroboros pendant on a black ribbon in the restroom later that day. He thinks it belonged to the girl who Bailey found locked in there."

"He found a necklace with a black ribbon in the gas station restroom?" Martinez asked with sudden interest.

"He still has it. Keeps it for good luck." Rachel showed him the photo of the pendant that she'd taken earlier.

His eyes widened.

"What's wrong, Joe?"

"Terence Bailey drew a sketch of a teenage girl wearing a similar necklace just the other day. It was the same pendant on a black ribbon just like the one in the sketch. What are the chances?"

"If Terence Bailey was the tow truck driver who picked up Hailey Milroy from her shared house, then he was the last person to see Hailey alive. Hailey could be another of his victims," said Rachel. "None of this is relevant to the Maddison Logan investigation, though."

"It could be very relevant," said Martinez. "Terence Bailey has been communicating with someone using a contraband cell phone in the prison. We believe the person he's communicating with is his accomplice; the person who helped him kill Aysh and perhaps those other women as well. Maybe Hailey, too."

"Is this the accomplice who you think might have abducted Maddison as well?" asked Rachel. She remembered Martinez mentioning this at the prison when she'd pointed out that Bailey couldn't have taken Maddison, since he was behind bars in a maximum-security jail.

"Yes, the same one," he conceded.

"Any idea who that accomplice might be?"

"There are a lot of candidates. Bailey was a foster kid. It's a long story but he was shunted around for years. Broken homes. Rejection. Possible abuse. No chance to bond with a maternal figure. It's the sort of background we sometimes see with psychopaths," he said. "Anyway, to cut a long story short, we're taking a close look at his foster families and foster siblings. It's possible one of them is his accomplice."

"When you're making a short list of accomplices, look for people with body odor problems," said Rachel.

"That's weirdly specific," said Martinez, looking up at her curiously.

Rachel ran through Shaz's story about how Maddison had high-footed it out of the beach camp the moment she heard that a man with a foul body odor was asking about her. She also told him the story of the Swedish backpacker, as well as the anecdote from Bailey's former boss at the gas station about a man with a foul odor coming to look for Bailey after the girl was found locked in the restroom.

"Has anyone described this guy?"

"It appears that he is well-groomed. He wears suits and splashes himself with expensive colognes, presumably to hide his body odor problems. The Swedish backpacker said his car was spotlessly tidy and he was super polite. That's why she didn't feel afraid getting into his car."

"You're thinking that he smells because he has a health condition?" Martinez asked.

"The thought did cross my mind," said Rachel, taking a sip of wine. "Everyone I've spoken with describes the smell in the same way: like rotting garbage."

"I'll text a doctor friend," said Martinez.

When he was done texting the message, he pushed aside his plate and watched Rachel drink her wine. His expression was veiled. Rachel felt heat rise inside of her as he watched her, and not just from the wine.

She caught something flickering in his intense gaze for a second until he broke the connection by abruptly standing and looking out into the ocean from the balcony rail. It was too dark to see anything except the pulsating lights of a ship in the dark expanse of ocean. He seemed tormented by something.

"Is something wrong?" Rachel asked.

"Nothing." He shook his head like he was trying to break a spell. "I've been working this case too hard. Not enough sleep."

Chapter 57

Joe Martinez waited on the balcony while Rachel changed in her bathroom into a navy dress. It was one of the items sent to her by the conference organizers when she'd arrived. She paused to brush her damp copper hair in the bathroom mirror, twisting it into a French knot that she pinned to the top of her head. As an afterthought, she applied lip gloss and a touch of mascara on her lashes. As another afterthought, she dabbed perfume on her pulse points.

Rachel stared at herself in the mirror, embarrassed at her sudden regression into a giddy teenager. She was tempted to wash it all off. Joe noticed everything. She wondered what he'd think when he saw that she'd put on makeup for what was supposed to be a professional catch-up, comparing notes on the Maddison Logan investigation. Then again, he'd brought wine.

Martinez turned his head toward her as she came out of the bathroom in the skintight dress. His expression was unguarded. Rachel thought she saw a flash of raw desire before it disappeared under his usual inscrutable expression.

"I spoke with Dave," he said. "He's an old friend who works in diagnostic medicine at Stanford. You were right, Rachel. The man with the odor you mentioned probably has a health condition. Dave thinks it might be trimethylaminuria."

"That's a tongue twister," she said. "What is it?"

"It's a metabolic condition in which the body can't break down certain compounds from food. It leaves a noxious smell like rotting garbage."

"Is there a treatment?" Rachel asked. "A specific medication? Maybe we can check with drugstores in the area and find out which pharmacies have sold the medication recently."

"There's no medication. People cut certain food from their diet. Some get vitamin B_{12} infusions. Many have anxiety and depression," he said. "Of course, due to medical confidentiality, it would be difficult to get information from local shrinks and other medical professionals. But it's given me an idea as to how we can catch him."

"How?" Rachel asked as she tidied up the remnants of their dinner.

"I'll arrange for an ad to be placed on social media. It will be geolocated so it only hits the social media feeds of people in this part of Florida. We'll ask for volunteers interested in getting free samples of a new experimental product that gets rid of severe body odor. If our man has this condition, then there's a chance he's looking for a cure and he'll respond to the ad."

"So you're hoping to bring him to us!"

"Well, that's the plan," he said. "I'll make a call and get the ball rolling."

Rachel sat with her legs curled up under her on the bed, scrolling through Instagram on her phone while Martinez spoke to a colleague about getting ads put up on various social media platforms offering a possible treatment for trimethylaminuria, targeting people who'd previously looked for information on the condition during web searches. People interested in getting the product would be directed to a sign-up form to fill in their personal details.

"Let's hope he takes the bait," said Martinez.

As Rachel scrolled, she noticed that Zoe had put up the photos of herself doing yoga near the pool after all, despite throwing a temper tantrum earlier saying they were substandard. Rachel didn't think they were terrible at all. If anything, they were flattering. A photo of Zoe in a lotus position caught Rachel's eye. She zoomed in on a tattoo on Zoe's bare midriff. It was not just any tattoo either. Zoe had a monochrome tattoo of a snake eating its tail.

"Look at this." Rachel held up her phone screen so that Martinez could see the close-up of Zoe's tattoo.

"It's the Ouroboros tattoo design. There must be a reason why this symbol keeps coming up."

Rachel scrambled off the bed and retrieved the bag of goodies that she'd received when she'd registered for the conference. In the bag was a BuzzCon promotion booklet. Rachel went through the pages until she found what she was looking for.

She handed the brochure to Martinez and sat on the arm of his chair so she could point it out to him. The page in question contained fifteen swirly computer-generated images that were identical to the images that had flashed on the screen at the BuzzCon banquet dinner the previous night. Among the images was an abstract version of the Ouroboros symbol. Rachel thought she knew why the symbol kept coming up.

"The influencers are arranged in pods," explained Rachel. At Joe's confused expression, she added, "Think of them as prestigious clubs. The influencers get invited or apply to join a pod with other influencers. They help each other get popular by sharing and 'liking' each other's content," she said. "Like many select clubs, they each have their own name, and their own symbol."

"The Ouroboros is the symbol of Maddison's influencer pod," said Martinez, realizing where she was heading.

"Yes! Jonny Macon was in that pod as well. Zoe too. They both have tattoos of that symbol."

"The dead girl from the swamp must have been in the pod as well. That's why she had the same tattoo," said Martinez.

"Have the BuzzCon organizers mentioned whether anyone else is missing?" Rachel asked.

"No. They haven't," said Martinez. "My people have spoken with them. More than once."

"I don't know how effective they are at keeping tabs on the influencers," said Rachel. "People are coming and going all the time." Rachel thought for a moment about how they could verify whether someone else was missing. "Ask the hotel management. The hotel has a record of all check-ins and check-outs."

"They also track every time a person enters or leaves their room," said Martinez. The only problem with the theory was that a handful of influencers weren't staying at the hotel, but Martinez could deal with that later.

He picked up Rachel's room phone and asked the switchboard operator to transfer him to the night manager. Rachel listened to Martinez's side of the conversation as he identified himself and asked whether any BuzzCon guests had not accessed their hotel rooms over the past few days.

While they waited for the night manager to get back to them, Rachel direct-messaged Eric via his Instagram to ask whether all the members of Zoe's pod were at the poolside dinner going on downstairs. "Everyone's here except Maddison. And Jonny Macon. Nobody's seen him since yesterday," he wrote back.

"Are you sure nobody else is missing from the pod?" Rachel texted back.

"Everyone's here," he responded. "What gives?"

The hotel room phone rang before Rachel could message a reply. Martinez reached out to answer it.

"I see," said Martinez, grabbing the notepad and pen that Rachel had left on the bed to take notes. "You're absolutely sure?"

Even before Martinez hung up the call, he was dialing someone on his cell phone. "See what you can find on Dee Dee Rivers. She booked a room at the BuzzCon hotel but she hasn't used it in three days, according to the hotel's key card records."

Rachel perched on the edge of Martinez's armchair as she looked up Dee Dee's account on Instagram. She was an emerging influencer who'd boasted about being offered a free ticket to attend BuzzCon after winning a competition through an influencer modeling agency. Dee Dee put up a post to thank her followers for the support. "I won't let you down. Florida, here I come!!!"

"Her last post was four days ago." Rachel showed Martinez the photo of Dee Dee standing on one leg on the side rails of the Main Street Pier while taking a selfie. "She must be the influencer who does extreme selfies."

Rachel told Joe that Eric had mentioned an aspiring influencer had bombarded Zoe with texts begging her to let her join The Infinity Project pod. Rachel imagined that someone that eager might even get a tattoo of the pod symbol as a show of her commitment.

Martinez pulled out photos from the crime scene. At the banks of the swamp a dozen or so yards from the mud pool where the body had been found was a rusty sign that said "Danger: Alligators."

"Maybe she was posing for a selfie with the sign behind her when she became trapped in the mud," Rachel suggested.

"It's entirely possible," Martinez agreed.

He made another call and quickly reeled off a long list of instructions to determine whether the body in the morgue was Dee Dee Rivers. He then called a local detective who over the speakerphone sounded decidedly unhappy to have his evening disturbed by the FBI.

"Belinda Roy and Minnie Love's pimps," said Martinez. "Ask them whether either woman complained about a client smelling bad. Maybe they didn't want to see him again." Martinez listened while the detective spoke. "I know it was six years ago but it's the sort of thing that people remember. And there may have been more recent complaints by other girls."

While he talked, Rachel prepared them both decaffeinated coffee from the mini capsule coffee machine in the room. Rachel drank her coffee as she listened to Martinez talk on the phone while he paced up and down the hotel room. Eventually, she lay flat on the king bed, looking up at the ceiling lights as he spoke.

Rachel thought that she could listen to his mellow voice forever. She had felt an electric rush ever since they'd first met. It hadn't lessened. It only became more intense each time she saw him. In retrospect, it had been a truly dumb idea to invite Joe to her room given what Rachel finally admitted to herself was her attraction to him.

Being together in private, even if it was to work, created an intimacy that made it hard to rein in her most primal desires. Rachel opened her eyes when she heard Martinez finish the call. She wasn't sure if she wanted to rein things in.

"We've made good progress tonight," he said. "I'm sure glad I ran into you on the beach, Rachel." He put his hands in his pockets as he stood over the bed looking down at her.

"Ran into me, or chased me down the beach?" Rachel sat up. Her hair had come undone and it tumbled over her shoulders.

"You make it sound as if I was pursuing you." His voice was husky.

"You weren't pursuing me?" Rachel joked. She melted inside as her eyes locked with his.

"I would certainly like to pursue you, Rachel," he said softly. "I'm not so sure that now is the right time."

"Is there ever a right time?" Rachel stood up and stepped so close to him that she was certain he could feel her pulse racing.

He reached out and brushed a tendril of her hair out of her eyes. "You're lovely," he said. "I haven't been able to stop thinking about you since we met." It was the first time he'd touched her since they'd shaken hands the previous morning at the prison. Rachel's skin burned.

"So what happens now?" They both knew Rachel wasn't talking about the case.

He sighed. "I know what should happen. I should go back to my hotel to get some sleep."

"You don't strike me as the sort of man who needs a lot of sleep." Rachel ran her hands up his chest until they interlinked behind his head.

"After this case is over, I'd very much like to get to know you, Rachel. In and out of bed." He ran his thumb across her bottom lip.

"There's something important you should know about me, Joe," said Rachel, her mouth so close to his that they were almost kissing.

"What's that?"

"I'm a firm believer in living for the moment."

"Are you sure?"

"Absolutely certain."

He put his hands on her lower back and pulled her to him as he lowered his mouth to hers. Their kiss was deep and hungry. By the time he'd pulled his mouth away from hers, their bodies were pressed together and they were both breathing heavily. Rachel's fingers frantically unbuttoned his shirt, tugging them free of his pants.

"Your coffee is getting cold," Rachel whispered as he ran his mouth down her neck before lowering the zipper of her dress.

"I like cold coffee."

Chapter 58

Thomas McCoy wakes in the small back room where he's slept since he was a boy. Still in his button-down pajamas, he goes to the living room and opens the chintzy floral drapes, tying them back with the decorative pink ropes on each side of the window. He looks out at the flower bed of azaleas in the front garden.

"Good morning, Mommy," he says out loud, stretching his back as he yawns.

Even though his mother has been dead for almost eight years, he has never considered replacing the drapes with something less fussy. Just as he hasn't gotten rid of the matching frilly cushions or the floral sofa where his mother sewed the bleak tapestries that still line the hallway walls.

His parents' bedroom is exactly the way they left it. His mother's bedtime novel is next to her bed, a bookmark tucked between the last pages she read. Their clothes hang in their closet. Their toothbrushes are just as they left them, each one inside a plastic cup in their bathroom.

Nobody has ever shown interest in their sudden disappearance. His parents weren't social people. They hadn't even been churchgoing. The few friends they'd had died or moved away to retirement villages years before. Occasionally Christmas or birthday cards arrived in the mail from far-flung relatives. Eventually the cards stopped coming. People tend to stop writing when they never hear back.

It had been a hot blue-skied summer afternoon when he killed his father. They'd been hoeing and planting a vegetable garden out back. That vegetable garden was about the only thing his father ever cared about. That and his beehives.

Thomas had stripped off his T-shirt as he worked. It hadn't helped. The more he sweated, the worse he smelled, until his father squirted him with water from the garden hose.

"No wonder you can't find yourself a woman." His father roared with laughter. "Just the smell of you sends 'em running for cover."

Thomas had stewed over the comment while they'd finished planting. His father had teased him about his problem his whole life. The worst part was that Thomas knew it was true. Every woman he'd ever dated had eventually rejected him, especially since his problem became worse when he was stressed. It got so bad that he couldn't even pay working girls to screw him without them ridiculing him while they did it. "Might want to take a shower first next time, hon," one had told him before he'd choked her slender whorish neck.

Thomas recoiled as his father dropped a pile of timber posts with a crash by his feet. Then his father threw a serrated hunting knife into the ground.

"Pick it up," his father had ordered. "Cut the ends of those sticks into stakes for the tomatoes."

Thomas had picked up the knife and whittled the first stick into a sharp stake.

"This sharp enough, Dad?"

His father was leaning on a rusty shovel wiping the sweat off his face with the sleeve of his work shirt. He'd been more surprised than his son when he'd looked down to see the newly sharpened stake sticking out of his chest.

"Your mother will flay you for this," his dad had said before he collapsed.

"Not if I flay her first," Thomas had answered.

For once his father hadn't gotten the last word. He was already dead.

His mother had arrived home with groceries while he was still burying his father near the vegetable garden. "Tell your father to come and help me," she'd called out from the back porch shortly before he put the second stake through her abdomen.

In truth, he hadn't had anything against his mother other than that it was her genes that had made him this way. Her stories about her old uncle Reg, who had the same condition as he did, had always terrified him. After a lifetime of humiliation, his uncle had died a hermit in a shack by a river in southern Louisiana where her family was from. Only a handful of relatives turned up at his funeral.

"Everyone had Kleenex in their hands. Not because they had genuine tears but to block the stench." His father always guffawed when he'd told that part of the story. "I wonder if anyone will come to yours, Thomas."

After his parents, there had been a string of others. Prostitutes. Runaways. Then he'd met Stacey two years after his parents had gone. Things had been good until she started drinking again. Alcohol loosened her tongue.

"I can't stand the sight or smell of you one minute longer," she'd said when he'd tried to take her liquor bottle from her as she'd slumped over the kitchen table. His mother's kitchen table. He'd strangled her from behind.

Thomas puffs up the cushions on his mother's floral sofa and makes sure that everything is tidy. He likes spending time in the living room. He'd been banished from it when his parents were alive.

"What if we get company?" his mother once complained when she caught him sitting on the sofa. She was always afraid he'd infest the room with his terrible body odor. Of course, there was never company. Thomas couldn't remember anyone stepping across their threshold.

Thomas goes to the bathroom, where he turns on the cold water and steps into the shower. He only ever has cold showers. It helps control the smell. He's found through trial and error that hot water makes his condition worse. Sometimes he can't bear the smell or sight of himself any longer. He is a freak.

Last night he shaved off his beard with the straight razor that belonged to his father. He'd been thinking of doing it for a while. It was the Swedish backpacker running away that pushed him over the edge. He was afraid that she'd give a description to the cops. After he shaved clean his neck area, he pressed the razor blade close to his carotid artery. If he'd pressed it any harder, he'd have cut it open and bled out. Instead there's the tiniest nick in his skin.

He rubs his smooth jaw. He likes being clean-shaven. Stacey used to tell him that he was good-looking. From a distance. "So long as nobody ever gets near you," she'd once told him.

After his cold shower, he changes into a white cotton shirt and the dark funeral suit that he ironed the night before. He'd worn the suit when he'd buried his mother. Not the actual burial. He'd worn old working pants and boots for that, since he'd had to do all the digging. But for the ceremony he'd held afterward in which he'd read out a few words about his mother, he'd worn the dark suit for that. His mother's funeral was even smaller than the one held for Uncle Reg. It was just him in attendance.

His parents had fought like cats and dogs in life. Thomas thought it a kindness that his mother is buried in the front garden while his father is buried in the back.

When Thomas is dressed in the somber but smart outfit, reminiscent of a limousine driver's livery, he goes into the kitchen to eat breakfast. Once he's done, he neatly spreads peanut butter and jelly onto two pieces of white bread. He cuts the sandwich into triangles before wrapping it up in plastic wrap. He takes a bottle of cold water from the fridge.

He knows she's awake because he sees her move as he comes down the basement stairs. He drops the sandwich and the bottle of water so that it's within reach of the leash tethering her to a pillar.

"You'd better wash up," he calls. "You're getting a visitor today. An old friend. You'll want to look your best. I know you will."

He locks the basement door behind him, dropping the key into the single drawer of the hall table and turning on the radio. He hums to himself as he unbolts the front door and goes outside. He throws feed to the chickens and puts kibble in the dog's bowl.

In a cluttered metal cabinet in the corrugated iron shed where he parks his car overnight is a toolbox. Under that is a set of license plates, authentically dented. He rubbed dirt into them the other day so they'd be harder to read. He removes his existing license plates with a special screwdriver and then screws in the new ones on both ends of the car.

He pops open the trunk and removes a small sports bag that he takes to the front seat. In the bag is a piece of laminated cardboard that he had professionally printed a while back. It says "Private Driver" in a fancy font. Underneath is a logo of the silhouette of a chauffeur's hat above the name "Daytona Limousines."

On the slate, he writes "Rachel Krall" in bold capital letters. He stuffs the other items into the compartment of his door. He'll need them later.

He pauses to spray cologne on himself before he gets into the car and backs it out of the shed, down the driveway, and into the road. He has a stop to make before his rendezvous with Rachel Krall. He turns toward the Delta Springs State Forest and drives through the forest until he sees the sign for the Central Florida Correctional Facility. It is almost time to pick up his passenger.

Chapter 59

It was staring them in the face. That's what I thought when I walked the route that Aysh Philips had taken to work the night that she went missing.

Two teenagers, both around the same age, go missing within a day of each other, based on the dates of the missing persons reports. It doesn't occur to the police that it's more than just a coincidence.

To be fair, the cops did ask Aysh and Hailey's moms if their daughters had been friends or acquaintances. They had not. The girls had gone to different high schools and had grown up in different neighborhoods. They'd lived parallel lives that never seemed to cross over at any point.

The cops treated the cases as unrelated, since they'd found no link between the missing girls. Except the cops were wrong. There was a connection.

It was a connection so obvious that I picked up on it immediately as I retraced Aysh's movements that fateful night when I walked the two miles or so that she'd biked from her home to the supermarket where she worked at the deli counter.

While we can't be sure which way Aysh rode to work that night, the route that I walked would have been the most logical way for her to go.

As I turned the corner a block away from the supermarket, I passed a veterinary clinic. Outside was a giant noticeboard with a printed sign that said "Kittens for Sale. Inquire within."

This wasn't any neighborhood veterinary clinic. It was the 24/7 veterinary clinic where Hailey Milroy had worked.

So I went into that animal clinic and here's what I've found out.

Eleven days before she went missing Aysh Philips was riding her bike to work when she noticed a big sign on a noticeboard outside the emergency veterinarian clinic.

"Kittens for Sale."

Aysh had wanted to get her mom, Mary, something special for her birthday, which would be taking place in a couple of weeks while Aysh was away working as a summer camp counselor. She felt guilty about leaving home for college, and she was worried that her mom would be lonely. It had only ever been the three of them: her mom, Aysh, and her younger brother, Brian.

When she saw the kittens sign, she pulled over and went inside the clinic to find out more. I know this because when I went into the clinic and asked some questions, they eventually found a carbon copy of a receipt in an archived receipt book that showed that Aysh had put down a twenty-dollar deposit for a kitten. The receipt had been signed by Hailey Milroy eleven days before both girls went missing. So, you see, there was a link after all.

Presumably Hailey showed Aysh the litter of kittens that were for sale. They were being kept in a small enclosure in a back room. The setup was the same when I went into the vet clinic. In the back was a litter of kittens in a special enclosure suckling from their mom.

Aysh picked out a velvet-gray female kitten with white socks on her paws. Those are the details written on the receipt.

There's a note at the bottom that stipulates the kittens will be given away after being weaned. From what I've pieced together so far, Aysh would sometimes stop by to check up on the kitten's progress on her way to work. She and Hailey struck up a friendship during those visits.

On that last night when Aysh disappeared, she stopped in again to check on the kitten. Hailey told her the kitten was now weaned and suggested that Aysh take the kitten home that night. However, Aysh had taken her bicycle to work. She couldn't ride home in the dark juggling a box with a kitten balanced on her handlebars.

Hailey, who'd just bought a car with her savings, offered to drive Aysh and the kitten home after they both finished work that night.

They probably arranged for Hailey to pick up Aysh on the main road at the bottom of the supermarket parking lot just after eleven P.M. when they were both due to finish work. That was the same road where Hailey's veterinary clinic was located about a mile down the road.

From what I've pieced together, instead of going straight home, they went to a local restaurant strip to get food. Presumably both girls were hungry after working busy shifts. Maybe Aysh wanted advice from Hailey on how to care for the kitten.

Since parking is always bad around there, Hailey parked a block away in the parking lot of a discount store. We know this because when her mom, Grace, asked around for information after her daughter went missing, one of Hailey's friends said she saw Hailey's car turning into that parking lot on that fateful night.

As the two girls walked away from the car toward the neon lights of the restaurant strip, they had no idea they were being watched by a driver slouched behind the wheel of a car parked deep inside that dark lot.

While they were gone, a trap was set for them. One they didn't see coming.

Chapter 60

The hotel lobby was empty when Joe Martinez left before dawn. His departure was watched by a sleepy reception clerk and a bellboy slumped on a chair behind a bell cart near the lobby door.

Martinez stopped off at his own hotel for a quick shower and a fresh change of clothes before heading to the incident room at police headquarters. He rubbed his jaw self-consciously as he headed to his car. There hadn't been time to shave. He was running late to the taskforce briefing that he'd set up last night with a reminder to everyone to be punctual.

Less than forty minutes earlier, Martinez had climbed out of Rachel Krall's bed. He'd picked up his clothes, which he'd found lying in the strangest places across her room, and changed in her bathroom so as not to wake her. He wrote a quick note on hotel stationery and left it next to the cup of coffee he'd never gotten around to drinking.

Before they'd fallen asleep in each other's arms only a few hours earlier, he'd tried again to convince Rachel to fly out in the morning. He'd offered to arrange for a car and driver to take her straight to the airport. He'd said he was worried that Terence Bailey might come for her to make his "Memento mori" message, and his veiled threats about monsters, a reality.

Rachel had snuggled up to him while sleepily reiterating that she was staying. Joe Martinez hadn't known Rachel Krall for very long but he'd quickly learned that she didn't intimidate easily.

He'd dated a couple of women since Steph died but he hadn't felt anything close to the roller-coaster dip in his stomach that he'd felt the moment he first set eyes on Rachel walking across the parking lot at the prison, her expression hidden by her aviator sunglasses.

That intense attraction had only intensified each time he'd been with her until thoughts of her intruded into his mind disconcertingly at the most inopportune times. He'd intended to arrange to meet up with her after the case was over on the pretext of taking her out to dinner to thank her for her help. He'd wanted to see if his reaction to her was more than momentary lust, and to test whether the attraction was mutual. As it turned out, that hadn't been necessary. It was definitely mutual. They'd fallen into each other's arms last night.

While Martinez didn't for a second regret spending the night with Rachel, he wondered if he should have found the willpower to resist, if for no other reason than for the good of the case. God help him but as he walked down the stairs to the police headquarters basement, he couldn't think about anything except for Rachel.

Everyone was standing around drinking coffee and eating Danish when he stepped off the last stair, ducked his head under the low doorway, and entered the incident room. They all seemed mildly surprised that he was late. Twelve minutes late, to be exact. In the short span of time they'd worked together, everyone in his taskforce had learned that Joe Martinez was early to everything.

Martinez poured himself an instant black coffee. Cradling the mug in his hands, he called everyone to gather around the whiteboard by the pool table to run through the game plan for the day.

He'd scrambled a plainclothes team from the local police force to help carry out surveillance on Bailey for his first couple of days out of prison. If the operation went beyond three days, then they'd need reinforcements.

"I want to know where Bailey is and what he's doing every second of the day," he emphasized. "I especially want to know who he meets. Based on the texts that he sent from prison, we think that Bailey will meet up with his accomplice as soon as he gets out."

The warden's office had told Martinez that Bailey's release would take place sometime between ten and eleven in the morning, after he signed all the paperwork and retrieved his personal items. Since no friends or family were meeting him at prison, Bailey would have to take the public bus into town. The bus stopped outside the prison gates at a quarter after every hour.

An undercover team of local cops would wait in an unmarked car outside the prison gates until Bailey walked out as a free man.

"Follow the bus into town, keeping your distance. We don't want him spooked. If he suspects he's under surveillance, then he'll keep a wide berth from his accomplice," Martinez warned.

It was the FBI's working theory that Bailey's accomplice had taken Maddison, and that their best hope of finding her was to let Bailey lead them to his accomplice's hideout, where they believed Maddison was being held.

To this end, Martinez assigned a second team of FBI agents from the Miami office to watch the halfway house where Bailey was booked to stay while he got on his feet.

Martinez passed around a pile of information sheets on Bailey. On one side was a colored full-page copy of Bailey's mug shot from six years earlier as well as his basic description. On the other side was a recent, hazy photo of Bailey in his prison coveralls taken from a prison CCTV camera. He'd lost the youthful callowness evident in the mug shot taken before he went to prison. He was now a fully grown man in his mid-twenties. His body was muscular and covered in tattoos. His face bore the scars of his time behind bars. His nose had been broken several times during prison fights. A scar from a switchblade marked his forehead.

"He looks like one mean son of a bitch," said one of the local cops.

"And don't you forget it," said Martinez.

When the team had dispersed, Martinez's phone rang. It was Detective Castel. "I had the vice team ask a couple of local pimps about a client with a terrible smell."

"What did they say?"

"Apparently there's a guy who occasionally cruises around. The girls charge him triple. Even then they say it's not enough."

"Any name or other details?"

"No, except that he's an older guy, fifties, maybe sixties. He was last seen driving a dark Ford."

When Martinez finished the call, he called Torreno over. "Have you pulled together the short list of black Fords of the same make and model as the one that was following Maddison's van?"

"I just finished printing it out." Torreno handed Martinez a thick file of papers. There were 701 cars on the list of that exact make and model registered within 100 miles of Daytona. Ninety-two of those cars were black. Torreno had pulled the names, dates of birth, and addresses of each owner.

Martinez flipped through the papers in the folder as he leaned against the pool table. He went through the pages with a red pen, crossing out all females and anyone under forty or over seventy. He'd reduced the list of black cars to just thirty-nine.

"Follow them all up," he said, handing the list back to Torreno before going across the road to get a coffee and a sandwich. His phone rang as he left the coffee shop with his order.

"Joe?" The rustle of bedsheets told him that Rachel was still in bed. His stomach tightened as he pictured her naked under the sheets.

"How are you this morning?" he asked.

"Feeling decadent. I don't know when I last slept this late."

"You're tired. We didn't get much sleep last night."

"No, we didn't. You left early, Joe. You must really be exhausted."

"It's nothing a grande Americano can't fix," he said, sipping his coffee. "Bailey gets out of prison today. Things are going to get busy. We might not be able to talk for a while."

"I know," said Rachel. "I'm sorry for disturbing you. I wondered if you could send me Terence Bailey's sketch of the girl with the necklace that you told me about last night. I want to show it to a few people. See if they recognize her."

"I'll forward it to you," he said. "You can show it but don't say where it comes from."

"I won't. I promise." Rachel stifled a yawn. "I'd better get up. I want to run on the beach before it gets too hot."

"There's a state-of-the-art fitness center at the hotel. You could hit the treadmill," he suggested gently. He was not at all keen on the idea of Rachel leaving the confines of the hotel while Terence Bailey was about to be let out of prison.

"Sure." Rachel relented at the obvious concern in his voice. "I'll take it easy today. Swim in the hotel pool and a run on the treadmill like you suggested. Just until you have the Bailey situation in hand."

"Thanks, Rachel. That eases my mind. A lot."

Martinez crossed the road and returned to the police station. He knew something was wrong the moment he stepped inside. There was almost complete silence. Every head turned in his direction as he entered.

"What's going on?"

"Our plainclothes surveillance team arrived at the prison forty minutes before Bailey's release."

"Good. So what's the problem?"

"The prison received a busload of new inmates from the county jail early this morning. They needed the space. There was a mix-up. Terence Bailey was let out over an hour ago."

"Are you kidding me?" he said. "We gave specific instructions that he wasn't to be let out until at least ten."

"Someone forgot to tell the morning shift. Either way, Bailey is out. He should be on the bus heading into town. We estimate that he'll arrive at the halfway house within the next fifteen minutes."

As he returned to his desk, Martinez resisted the urge to warn Rachel that Bailey was on the loose. He didn't want to suffocate her by harping on and on about his concerns for her safety, and he really did need to focus on the case.

"I just got off the phone with the bus company," said Torreno. "The bus has already finished its drop-offs in town. The bus driver said there were three released prisoners on the bus this morning. All of them old guys. None of them come close to matching Terence Bailey's description."

"So Bailey wasn't on the bus?" Martinez asked.

"Doesn't look that way. He hasn't arrived at the halfway house either."

"Then where the hell is he?"

It was a rhetorical question. He already knew that nobody had the faintest idea. Martinez grabbed his jacket and car keys.

"I'm heading to the prison."

Chapter 61

Rachel was swimming laps in the hotel lagoon pool when she heard her phone beep all the way from the sun recliner where she'd left it lying on a swimming towel. Rachel completed the lap and swam over to the recliner, pulling herself half out of the pool to check the message as she dripped water everywhere.

The message was from Joe. As Rachel had requested, he'd sent her Terence Bailey's sketch of the goth girl. The girl had short spiky black hair and matching heavy makeup that gave her wide face a ghoulish appearance. Around her neck was an infinity pendant on a dark ribbon. It looked exactly like the pendant that Rachel had seen at the gas station.

Rachel called Grace Milroy. When Grace answered, Rachel asked her if she could have a look at a drawing that she was sending to her phone. Rachel stayed on the line while she texted the photo of the sketch to Grace.

"You should have it now," Rachel said.

"Where did you get this drawing of Hailey?" Grace asked.

"Hailey?" Rachel said in shock. She'd noticed no resemblance between the teen in the sketch and the cute pigtailed girl in the family photographs that Rachel had seen at Grace's apartment. "Are you sure it's Hailey?" Rachel asked.

"I think I know what my own daughter looks like," said Grace. "Hailey was obsessed with the color black and piercings. Plus she's wearing the necklace that I gave her when she turned sixteen. It's real silver. She insisted on wearing it on a black satin ribbon even though I'd given it to her on an expensive silver chain." Grace was in tears. "Where did you get this drawing from?"

Rachel felt bad that she couldn't tell Grace more at that point. "I'll get you more information as soon as I can, that's a promise. I have one other question for you, Grace."

"What's the question?" Grace sounded weary.

"Do you recall whether Hailey had a friend called Aysh Philips?"

"Aysh Philips? Isn't that the girl whose body was found in the forest? You don't think that Hailey . . ." Grace's voice dropped off.

Rachel tried to reassure Grace that she didn't have any information suggesting that Hailey was with Aysh on the day that she died. Still, the timing of both girls' disappearances before Bailey went to prison struck Rachel as too coincidental.

Rachel called Joe to let him know that Grace Milroy had identified Hailey as the girl in Terence Bailey's sketch. The phone call went straight to voicemail. He must have been on the phone. Rachel hung up. She'd tell him later. He'd warned her that he might be swamped for the rest of the day because Bailey was getting out of prison.

She left her phone on her towel and returned to her swim, slicing through the cool water with a perfect freestyle stroke. As she swam, her mind kept drifting to Joe and the night they'd shared together.

Their chemistry was combustible. Rachel reminded herself that it was just that, a physical attraction. She couldn't allow herself to get entangled emotionally. Joe Martinez didn't wear his wedding ring anymore but she'd seen the photo of his beautiful late wife on his phone screen. It told her everything she needed to know about the chance of turning last night into anything more than a brief, pleasurable interlude.

Rachel pulled herself out of the pool a few laps later. She lay on her lounger with her eyes closed, allowing the sun to dry her off.

"How are you enjoying the conference? I didn't see you at the poolside dinner last night."

She opened her eyes to see Chad standing over her. He was the marketing guy she'd sat next to at the BuzzCon dinner that first night.

"I skipped it," Rachel said, covering her eyes with her hand to block the glare of the sun.

"I'm guessing you've had an overdose of 'OMG I'm so iconic' influencer navel-gazing," Chad said.

"Something like that."

"Well, if it's any consolation, there were a few people missing last night. Even Jonny Macon wasn't there," he said. "His absence was notable."

"Why?"

"He's been very involved in raising funds for the development of his girlfriend's wellness app. I heard there have been some financial irregularities. When I didn't see him last night, I figured that maybe he's keeping a low profile so it doesn't hurt his brand."

"Speaking of low profiles," said Rachel, ignoring the latter comment. "What can you tell me about Dee Dee Rivers?"

"The extreme selfie girl?" he asked. "As far as I know, she's left the conference. From what I heard, some of the big-name influencers told the BuzzCon organizers to kick her out. She was becoming a royal pain in the ass."

"In what way?"

"Following influencers around and pleading to be let into influencer pods," he said, checking his watch. "I'd better get going. I want to get some sun and have a swim," he said. "The morning seminar starts in an hour. Are you coming?"

"Maybe," said Rachel.

Rachel watched Chad head toward the beach, his towel flung over his shoulder. She got up and dived back into the water, swimming a few more laps to cool down, before floating for a while with her eyes closed. It was pure relaxation.

Returning to her towel, Rachel noticed a series of missed calls on her phone. She hadn't heard the phone ringing because of the bubbling noise from the Jacuzzi. The missed calls were all from Joe.

Joe didn't pick up when she called him back. She scooped up her things and went up to her room, where she showered and changed.

She tried Martinez again as she sat on her balcony looking out at the ocean, which was a swirl of blues and greens under the cloudless sky.

"Joe," Rachel said when he picked up the call.

"Thank God! I've been trying to get hold of you."

"I was swimming. I didn't hear the phone ring. What's going on?"

"Terence Bailey has disappeared. There was a screwup. The prison released him ahead of schedule. We have a team watching the halfway house where he's supposed to stay. So far he hasn't shown up. He also wasn't on the bus, which is the only way he could get to town."

"Unless he got a ride."

"Yeah, a ride," Martinez said. "That's exactly what I'm afraid of."

"You think his accomplice picked him up from prison?"

"I do. And right now we don't have any way of tracking him. He has no phone. Rachel, I know your view on this but it would make me a heck of a lot less worried if you'd fly on home. I have reason to believe that Bailey might be coming for you. It's my fault. I should never have brought you down here to meet with him."

Rachel could tell that her presence was distracting Joe from doing his job. She made a split-second decision. "I'll head to the airport as soon as I'm packed."

"Thank you. I know it goes against the grain." Joe's relief was evident.

"Joe, Grace Milroy said that Terence Bailey's sketch is of Hailey, her daughter. It's possible that Hailey was another of his victims."

"Good work, Rach. We'll follow up on this as soon as we find Bailey," he said. "I have a favor to ask you before you leave."

"What is it, Joe?"

"I was looking back at the video of your meeting with Bailey at the prison. He said a few things that were weirdly cryptic. I can't figure out what he meant by it all. I've emailed you a transcript of your exchange with him. Can you take a look at it and see if any ideas spring to mind. I'm wondering if he accidentally spilled information that might help us get a lock on where he might go."

"Sure."

"Thank you. I appreciate your assistance, Ms. Krall."

In the space of a second his tone had become stiff. Rachel could tell that he was no longer alone.

"There's one other thing, Joe," said Rachel. "I know there's someone with you and you can't talk freely right now but I want you to know something. I don't want you to feel bad that you brought me down here, or that you arranged for me to meet Terence Bailey. I especially don't want you to regret last night. Because I don't. I have no regrets. Not about any of this. And not about you."

Chapter 62

Terence Bailey had been a lanky twenty-one-year-old when he was first imprisoned. He was twenty-seven when he was released, forty pounds heavier, rippling with muscles and covered in handmade prison tattoos.

"His old clothes were too small for him," the prison social worker explained when Joe Martinez tried to get a detailed description so that local police could keep a lookout. "He couldn't zip up his jeans or button his shirt."

The social worker recalled that Bailey had selected a pair of dark jeans and a T-shirt from a charity bin kept at the prison for released prisoners when he'd changed into civilian clothes that morning. He'd worn his old work boots, which had been kept in storage for him.

After Bailey had left the prison, the social worker went out to the bus stop to distribute food and bus vouchers provided by a church charity to the released prisoners. He'd forgotten to hand them out earlier and he knew there was still time, since the bus didn't come for another quarter of an hour. When he reached the bus stop, the other men released that morning were sitting in a row on the bench, their belongings in the dust by their feet. Terence Bailey was not among them.

"What happened to him? Did he walk off?" Martinez asked.

"I would have seen him if he'd walked off. There's only one road into the prison complex," said the social worker. "It's more likely that someone picked him up."

"I assume there are CCTV cameras of the outside of the prison."

"There are. I'll ask the guards to pull the footage so you can take a look," the social worker said.

The prison guards rustled up the CCTV footage for Martinez to view. He did so on a large monitor in the same room where Torreno had watched Rachel Krall's meeting with Bailey a couple of days earlier.

The footage from the first camera showed Bailey walking out of the prison gates carrying a cardboard box. The prison records said the box included a sketchbook, two canvases, and miscellaneous brushes and paint.

He was dressed in the secondhand clothes the social worker had arranged for him. The T-shirt looked gray on the poor-quality CCTV footage, although it might have been white or even blue. Martinez took a screenshot of Bailey outside the prison in his civilian outfit and sent it to Torreno to distribute so the local cops could keep an eye out for him.

Martinez watched Bailey stumble in the dust once he left the prison walls. It looked as if he was overwhelmed by the wide-open space. He held his box of belongings with one hand while shielding his eyes from the sun with the other. Being free was clearly a shock to his system.

The guards had to pull up footage from three different cameras until they found an angle that showed what had happened to Bailey after his release. The third camera angle captured a black car parked along the stretch between the prison gates and the bus stop. As Bailey walked past the car, the driver opened the window slightly. There was a brief conversation and then Bailey climbed into the back seat.

"It's a black Ford, same model as the one that tailed Maddison at the strip mall on the day she went missing," Martinez told Torreno over the phone after watching it again. The angle of the camera made it impossible to read the plate numbers.

When Martinez freeze-framed the video, he noticed a piece of paper propped up by the windshield. It looked like the decals that rideshare drivers kept on their windshields to distinguish the vehicle from ordinary cars.

"Contact all the rideshare companies," he instructed Torreno. "Find out if any of them had a car at the prison this morning."

"I'm on it."

After the call, Martinez followed a guard to a room where Bailey's cellmate had been brought in from laundry duty to be questioned by him. The cellmate was an aging former armed robber who'd been in and out of prison for years. He'd returned to prison five months earlier after being charged with using a fake credit card. The prison guard said that he and Bailey weren't close but it was almost impossible for a prisoner to keep secrets from his cellmate.

"Terry didn't tell me nothin'," said the cellmate.

"Did he say what he planned to do when he got out of here?" Martinez asked.

"He was planning on doing what we all do when we get out: get a roof over his head and a decent job," he said.

"Was anyone supposed to meet him when he got out today?"

"Not likely."

"Why?"

"Because he asked me how much it costs to take a bus to Daytona. I told him that I didn't know because I've never paid. The prison social worker gave me a free bus voucher the last two times I got out of here. Every cent counts when you have nothing."

Martinez's phone vibrated with a call as he wrapped up the conversation.

"Joe, you'd better sit down for this."

"I'm sitting," said Martinez as he walked down a corridor toward the visitors' area.

"The Canadians gave us the name of the owner of the phone that Bailey texted from prison. I can't get my head around it."

"Spit it out. Who did Bailey text?" Martinez asked evenly.

"Maddison Logan," said Torreno. "The phone that Terence Bailey messaged belongs to Maddison Logan."

Chapter 63

Rachel took a moment to enjoy the panoramic view of the ocean from her hotel room balcony before calling the airline and changing her flight. Her flight was via Atlanta, leaving in three hours. She texted Joe to let him know that she'd be heading to the airport shortly. He "liked" the message but didn't respond.

Back in her room, she tossed her mini suitcase on the bed and packed her neatly folded clothes. She also packed up the BuzzCon outfits and the giveaway bag. She'd leave them downstairs with the concierge with instructions to return them to the conference organizers.

Rachel went out to get her swimsuit hanging on the balcony. It was bone-dry. Looking down onto the pool area, she saw an influencer being photographed doing a yoga pose while sitting on a flotation device in the pool. Her photographer was standing waist-deep in water as he photographed her.

She felt ambivalent about her rushed departure. It wasn't her style to cut and run, especially when she and Joe had made so much progress by putting their investigative minds together on the case. They'd come up with a number of solid lines of inquiry. Rachel had been looking forward to following up on them.

And then there was last night. It felt wrong to leave without saying goodbye to Joe. There was as good a chance as any that they would never see each other again. If they did meet up, as Joe had insisted they would, then the spark that had drawn them together last night might have burned out. In Rachel's experience, life had a tendency to get in the way of even the most promising relationships.

Rachel collected her toiletries scattered on the marble counter of the bathroom. The hotel room phone rang just as she'd packed them all away in her suitcase. She lifted up the receiver of the phone next to the bed.

"Ms. Krall, this is hotel reception. Your car is here."

"Car?"

Joe must have gone to the trouble of arranging a ride to the airport. Rachel was touched. "I'll be down in five minutes to settle the bill. I'm almost done packing."

"You can do express checkout on your phone," the reception clerk said.

Rachel asked about the BuzzCon items she wanted to return. The reception clerk said she should leave them in the room. Someone from the concierge's desk would collect them and hand them over to the conference organizers.

Rachel zipped up her suitcase and wheeled it behind her toward the elevator. Terence Bailey had been on her mind ever since Joe Martinez told her that Bailey had disappeared after leaving prison.

In the brief time that she'd known Joe Martinez, she'd learned that he kept his composure despite enormous pressure as the head of a missing persons taskforce. When she'd heard the concern in his voice during their phone conversation earlier at the pool, she'd known that he was genuinely worried that Bailey might come after her.

There were undoubtedly chilling signs that Bailey was nursing an obsession toward her. After all, he had drawn her portrait with the words "Memento mori" written at the bottom. "Remember, your death awaits." Then there were Bailey's remarks when he was led away from Rachel at the prison. "The scariest monster is the one that hides in plain sight."

Rachel didn't believe that Bailey would risk more jail time to act on whatever violent thoughts he entertained toward Rachel. Still, nothing was outside the realm of possibility. If heading home allowed Joe Martinez to concentrate on finding Terence Bailey and saving Maddison, if she was still alive, then it would be well worth it.

As Rachel waited for the elevator to reach her floor, she read over the transcript of her meeting with Bailey that Joe had emailed her. Joe was right. Some of Bailey's comments appeared to have been deliberately chosen. It was possible that he had tried to tell her something by stealth. He'd have known that the prison staff would be listening into the conversation. Under such circumstances it would make sense to communicate with cryptic hints.

According to the transcript, when Rachel complimented him on his paintings, Bailey had responded by saying: "There's a lot more to a painting than what meets the eye. They give me a few boring colors and some canvases that I have to reuse. One painting over the next."

The likely meaning of that phrase occurred to Rachel as the elevators opened on the lobby floor and she stepped out, pulling her suitcase behind her. It was a crazy idea. Still, Joe was at the prison. He could easily check to see if her hunch was right.

Rachel clutched the handle of her suitcase while she walked toward the hotel's main rotating door. Eric and Zoe strolled past hand in hand from the breakfast café. They had eyes only for each other. Whatever relationship trouble they'd had appeared to be over.

Rachel paused in the lobby to call Joe and tell him about her theory. The call went straight to voicemail. She left a quick message summarizing where she thought Bailey might have hidden information as an insurance policy to protect himself while in prison.

"By the way, thanks for arranging the car to the airport," she added as an afterthought. As she wheeled her suitcase through the lobby doors, she began texting Joe in case he didn't check his voicemail frequently.

"Ms. Krall, your car is waiting for you. I'll take your bag."

Rachel followed the doorman to a black car in the taxi queue. Her eyes were mostly on her phone as she typed out the text message. She scrambled into the back seat as she finished writing the last sentence of the long, detailed text to Joe.

"The warden is going to be pissed, Joe. But trust me on this," Rachel wrote.

Rachel plugged her phone into a charger next to her seat, grateful for the extra charge so that she wouldn't run out of battery on the flight home.

"Which terminal do you need?" the driver asked as they drove toward the airport.

"American Airlines."

"That's terminal one," he said, changing lanes as they headed out of town.

Rachel checked the other phone messages and emails that she hadn't had time to look at earlier. She looked up briefly from her phone screen. They passed under an overhanging road sign that indicated they were getting close to the airport. As she returned her attention to her phone, she detected the faintest whiff of an unpleasant odor. It smelled like a garbage truck. Except it couldn't be a garbage truck because when Rachel looked out the windows, she saw that they were the only car driving on a lone stretch of road beyond the airport. They'd missed the turnoff.

Rachel's eyes widened in surprise. The driver caught her gaze in the rearview mirror. He flashed a broad, knowing grin.

"The scariest monster is the one that hides in plain sight." Terence Bailey's comment rang through Rachel's mind just as the driver spun the steering wheel, speeding off the road straight into a row of fir trees.

Chapter 64

Joe Martinez took his phone out of his inside jacket pocket and read Rachel Krall's text message while he waited for the prison clerk to unlock his service weapon from the safe.

"Turns out I have to go back inside," he told the clerk after reading Rachel's message.

Martinez was pleased that he'd sent Rachel the transcript of Bailey's comments. He'd trusted her instincts. Now that he'd read the theory she texted him, he had to concede that there was probably something to it. If anything, he was slightly disappointed in himself that he hadn't seen what he now realized was kind of obvious.

A guard led him into the administration buildings of the prison where he'd taken Rachel on that first day for the initial briefing before she met Bailey. He walked through the same maze of corridors until he reached the staff cafeteria. It was filled with the clatter of cutlery and the hum of chatter as the early shift of prison guards ate lunch.

Martinez helped himself to a knife from the cutlery section before heading to the carpeted conference room alongside the cafeteria.

He could tell which paintings Terence Bailey had painted without looking for his signature. Bailey had powerful brushstrokes and a peculiar eye for detail. By contrast, the other oil paintings on display were dull and uninspiring. Martinez settled on the largest of the paintings that hung in pride of place in the center. It was the portrait of the warden. Rachel was right. The warden would be pissed when he found out.

The portrait sat in an ostentatious gold frame. Martinez lifted the frame off the hook, turned it around, and propped it against the wall. He ran the tip of the cafeteria knife along the edge of the brown paper stretched over the back of the canvas. As the brown paper fell off, he saw the reason why the framer had put it there. It was to cover another painting on the back of the canvas, just as Rachel had suggested in her text message.

Bailey had told Rachel that he'd had little access to art materials and often had to reuse canvases and paper. That's obviously what got her thinking that Bailey had left his secrets on the backs of his canvases.

The painting was of a white stucco farmhouse surrounded by a long timber fence. A metal gate led into a long driveway. Parallel to the driveway, a pathway lined with rosebushes in full bloom led to a front porch. A white car was parked in the driveway in front of a corrugated iron shed. It was only when Martinez took another step back that he noticed the blur of cars on a road in the far corner of the painting. The farmhouse was near a freeway.

Martinez took down all the paintings that Bailey had painted. He put them all on the ground facing the wall and sliced open the brown paper on the backs of each of the canvases.

Among the paintings that Bailey had painted on the back of the canvases of prison guards and prison life was an oil painting of the goth-looking girl with the piercings wearing the Ouroboros necklace on a black satin ribbon like a choker around her neck.

There were other random paintings he'd stopped and started. Portraits of other prisoners and scenes of prison life. The last one was different. It was a menacing portrait of a man with a ruddy beard and a baseball hat pulled low over his head. He had sharp blue eyes and a thin mouth. Martinez took photos of all the paintings.

"They're to be held as possible evidence," he instructed the guard who stayed behind to rehang them.

As he drove away from the prison, Martinez went over the voicemail messages that he hadn't had time to check. The first two were brief messages from his team. The last was from Rachel. It was a repeat of the text message she'd sent suggesting that he check the back of Terence Bailey's oil paintings at the prison, since she believed they might offer clues to his whereabouts.

Even though Martinez already knew the contents of the voicemail, he was enticed by Rachel's voice to listen to her entire message. One of the podcast critics had called it "the sexiest voice on the airways." Joe Martinez concurred.

"By the way, thanks for arranging the car to the airport," Rachel added as an afterthought before hanging up.

Martinez pulled his car over to the side of the road. He played that part of the message again. He hadn't ordered a car for Rachel. Neither had anyone on his team. No one else knew that Rachel Krall was heading home.

Martinez dialed Rachel's phone. It went straight to voicemail. He tried several more times. Each time it went straight to voicemail without ever ringing. After the fourth attempt, Martinez called the hotel and asked to be transferred to Rachel's room.

"I'm sorry, sir. Miss Krall has checked out."

"Do you know when she checked out?"

"She left about forty minutes ago. A car arrived to take her to the airport," said the receptionist. "Actually, we've been trying to get hold of her too. We arranged to do an express checkout and she hasn't yet confirmed it on her phone."

Martinez asked the receptionist to transfer him to the hotel security manager. Without wasting much time, Martinez explained that he was from the FBI and he needed him to pull up footage of the hotel driveway from around forty to fifty minutes earlier.

"Look for an attractive woman with long copper hair. Slim. Medium height," said Martinez.

The phone reception was getting poor as he drove through the Delta Springs State Forest. He called back a few minutes later as he left the forest.

"We have footage of a woman getting into a car. She fits the description that you gave me," said the security manager. "She was picked up by a black Ford. The doorman said the guy was a professional driver.

"I've seen that car before," the hotel security manager told Martinez. "Gimme a minute. I want to check something."

Martinez kept the line open while he sped back to town.

"I just checked with the doorman." The hotel security manager was back. "The same car was at the hotel a couple of times yesterday, dropping off and picking up guests. I took a look at the security camera footage, and the plate number is different from the one today."

"The bastard must have a whole pile of plates," Martinez said out loud once he'd hung up. He called Torreno at the incident room.

"Rachel Krall was picked up from her hotel by a black Ford this morning. It's the same model as the car that picked up Terence Bailey. It happened almost an hour ago. I'm heading back. Make sure we have that short list of cars by the time I get back. You have twenty minutes." He hung up the phone and pressed his foot hard on the gas pedal.

Chapter 65

It was close to midnight by the time that Hailey Milroy and Aysh Philips returned to the car with takeout burgers and fries from a gourmet burger joint on the main strip.

They'd gone for the takeout option because they hadn't wanted to leave the kitten alone for long in her box in the back seat of the car.

During the fifteen or so minutes that they'd been gone, someone had slashed a back tire of Hailey's car.

She was understandably upset. She'd used every cent she had to buy the car. She didn't have extra cash to replace vandalized tires.

They weren't sure what to do. Aysh's mom was asleep. She generally went to bed early because she woke early for work at the hotel. Her brother wasn't answering his phone. He was probably asleep as well. As for Hailey, well, who was she going to call? Grace, her mom? Her mom's boyfriend? She wasn't talking to either of them. As for turning to friends for help, her phone battery was dead and she didn't know their phone numbers by heart.

In the end, Aysh and Hailey ate their burgers leaning on the car hood. Once they were done, they figured they'd split a cab to get home. Hailey would come back the next morning to sort out the car.

Just as they'd finished eating, a car pulled up. On the windshield was a rideshare sign. It seemed like a stroke of good luck.

The driver was nice. Super polite. His voice was laced with concern.

"Is everything all right?"

"I have a flat." Hailey pointed to the rear tire.

He climbed out of the car and dropped down on his haunches to examine the slashed tire. "That's too bad." He rose to his feet. "It's not a flat. Someone cut it. Some people can be real assholes. You'll have to replace it. Let's see if your spare is decent. I'll change it for you if it is."

He opened the trunk and took a look at the spare.

"It's flat. You can't drive with it. I can call a cab for you, if you want."

"Aren't you a cab?" Hailey asked.

"Well, technically I'm a rideshare," he said.

"Can we hire you to take us home?" Hailey asked.

"It has to be done through the rideshare app and I've already shut mine down for the night. I'm heading home. It's been a long day." He looked like he felt bad driving off and leaving them in this predicament. "I'll tell you what, I'll drop you both home on my way. No charge."

They were so taken by his kindness that they agreed. They placed the box with the kitten between them on the back seat and climbed inside.

The kitten, which had been placid when they'd driven earlier, began to mew restlessly in the box as they drove. There were two mini water bottles in the back seat. The driver told them to help themselves to water. It was a hot night.

They each took a bottle and drank. Not long after, they fell asleep. When they woke, they weren't in the city anymore. They were somewhere rural. They could tell by the shadows of trees flitting past as he drove. The driver looked back at them as they sat staring ahead, groggy and confused. He told them he had to stop for gas.

"After that, I'll get you ladies straight home."

He pulled into a sleepy gas station and filled up his car. As he was putting the gas nozzle back, Hailey tapped on the window.

"I need the bathroom. I have to go badly."

"I'll ask if there's a restroom nearby." He was visibly annoyed.

He went into the gas station store to pay, locking them in the car before he left. When he returned, he was holding a key. He drove around to the back of the squat gas station building where a restroom sign was scratched into a blue metal door. Rusted oil cans littered the dirt alongside an untidy hedge that stretched along the boundary of an empty field.

Both girls climbed out of the car, disoriented and confused in the darkness as they waited for him to unlock the single-stall restroom door. Pretending everything was normal seemed safer. They both sensed that all hell would break loose once they let on that they knew they were in trouble.

Hailey went into the restroom cubicle while Aysh stood by the shut door waiting her turn. He'd left the key hanging from the lock.

When he turned around, distracted by a sudden rustle in the bushes bordering the boundary fence, Aysh hurriedly locked the restroom door and removed the key.

"What did you just do? Give it back."

Aysh backed away.

"Give me the key, you bitch."

In answer, Aysh threw the key as far as she could. It landed somewhere in the bushes. As he instinctively went after the key, Aysh sprinted toward the gas station pumps.

He chased her, tackling her to the ground long before she reached the fuel pumps. He punched her in the head and dragged her back into his car. He left Hailey behind, locked in the restroom.

Hailey had left her wallet and purse in the back seat of his car. He knew her identity. He could find her later.

Chapter 66

Thomas McCoy is having a good day. Everything is going better than he could have expected. He has a lucky break. Rachel Krall is in her room when the hotel staff call to tell her that her driver is downstairs.

Thomas looks the epitome of a professional driver. He's taken extra care with his appearance. He's freshly shaved and dressed in his pressed suit and crisp shirt. He's super polite to the doorman when he reels off Rachel Krall's hotel room number and asks him to alert her that he's downstairs waiting. The laminated limousine sign on the windshield only adds to the impression of authenticity. Perception is everything.

Thomas isn't sure his plan will work until he sees a copper-haired woman in jeans and an oversized white shirt being directed by the doorman to his car a few minutes later. She's texting as she walks. That's always a good sign. He likes it when his passengers are distracted.

She pulls a compact suitcase behind her. The suitcase is a giveaway. It immediately tells him that she's going to the airport. That gives him something to work with. Luring unsuspecting passengers into his car is always the trickiest part. Knowing her destination makes this all a whole lot easier.

He gets out and takes her suitcase, pausing to solicitously open the rear passenger door before he puts her luggage in the trunk.

On the back passenger seat, he left a plugged-in phone charger, and a complimentary bottle of water. He is pleased when she plugs the charger into her phone.

"Which terminal do you need?" he asks.

"American Airlines."

She sits in the back texting as the radio plays mellow golden oldies tunes. It never ceases to amaze him how people can lose touch with time and their surroundings when they're on their phones.

She's so immersed in typing a message that she doesn't notice when he skips the airport exit and continues to the old airfield road. After a half mile or so, she glances up from her phone and looks around as if finally sensing that something is wrong. It's then that he hears her sniff. As she does, dawning realization distorts her face with fear. He loves that moment when his victim is jolted by a paroxysm of sheer terror. It never gets old.

His eyes catch hers in the rearview mirror. Just as her eyes widen with horror, he sends a burst of electricity through the charger he's lent her, which is plugged into her phone.

She jolts back as she's hit by the first shock of electricity. He steps on the gas and swerves off the road through the gap between the trees and into a clearing.

She's lying in the back seat, still recovering, when he pulls to a stop. She's too spent to put up a fight when he gags her with a bandage from the first aid kit. He puts zip ties on her wrists and ankles. He flings open the specially modified middle seat and pushes her into the trunk without ever lifting her out of the car. Rachel is curled up in the trunk alongside her mini suitcase as he gets out of the vehicle with a screwdriver and spare license plates.

He changes the current plates to the new set that he brought with him. As a final precaution, he tugs at a flap of plastic stuck to the body of the car. It's a piece of black vinyl shrink wrap. He pulls an enormous shrink wrap panel right off the paintwork of the car and crumples it up. He then pulls off all the other vinyl shrink wrap panels, tossing the vinyl refuse into the trunk as well.

It takes a few minutes but it's worth the effort. When he's done, his car is no longer a black Ford. It's now white.

Chapter 67

Rachel opened her eyes. She might as well have kept them shut for all the good it did. It was so dark that she wondered if this was what death felt like. An eternity of darkness. She knew that she was still alive when she heard the drip of water from a tap that hadn't been turned off properly.

She focused on the things she knew. Her immediate surroundings. She was lying on a hard surface. Her legs were tucked toward her chest in a fetal position. Her ankles were locked together. Her hands were sore from zip ties tied so tightly around her wrists that they dug into her flesh.

A gag was wrapped around her mouth. It smelled medicinal. It tasted like a bandage. Rachel maneuvered her jaw and mouth to pry the bandage down until it hung by her jaw. Her natural inclination was to call for help.

She resisted the urge. There was no point calling out until she knew where she was. Rachel pulled herself into a sitting position. She could feel the presence of another person. The hulking figure of a man took shape as her eyes adjusted to the dim light.

The face that emerged from the black shadows was familiar. Scarily familiar. She looked into his ice-blue eyes observing her with keen interest as he loomed over her.

Rachel stifled a hysterical laugh. Joe Martinez had his whole team looking for Terence Bailey. How ironic that Rachel had found him first.

Chapter 68

Joe Martinez was back in the incident room within fifteen minutes, having broken the speed limit several times over as he raced back. For much of the drive, he was giving out orders to his team to look at traffic camera footage in real time so they could track the movements of the car.

Thanks to the timecode on the hotel CCTV footage, they knew what time Rachel had driven away in the black car. That enabled them to pick up the car via footage from speed cameras.

"They headed toward the airport," Torreno told him as he entered the basement. "Here's the last shot of the car before it disappeared."

Torreno played the footage on a monitor on his desk. It showed a black car turning onto a long straight road running along the farther perimeter of the airfield. On one side of the road was a row of towering fir trees. On the other was a long fence that cordoned off the outer airfield paddocks at the airport.

"The car turned onto this road. It should have passed another traffic camera farther down the road within a minute. But it didn't. Nor did it do a U-turn. It disappeared into thin air."

"That's impossible. Nothing disappears into thin air," said Martinez, reaching for his car keys.

Chapter 69

"Are you going to kill me?" Rachel Krall asked the question offhandedly, like she was asking about the weather. She refused to give Terence Bailey the satisfaction of knowing how terrified she was as she lay near his feet, bound hand and foot, completely at his mercy.

"Why would I kill you?" He sounded baffled by the question.

"Oh, I don't know," Rachel said, gesturing to her wrists, which were crushed together with zip ties. "Let's call it a wild guess."

A clatter of movement somewhere else prompted Rachel to look beyond him into the dark haze. They were not alone. Someone else was in there with them.

"Is she awake?" It was a woman who asked the question.

Rachel instantly recognized the woman's voice. After all, Rachel had listened to it enough times when she'd watched Instagram videos documenting this same woman's adventures crisscrossing the country in a camper van.

"Maddison, is that you?" Rachel asked.

"Be quiet," Bailey hissed. "He's back."

Floorboards creaked upstairs. A hushed silence fell as they listened to the slow, deliberate pound of footsteps in a room above their heads. Rachel used the distraction as an opportunity to wriggle out of the zip ties around her wrists. Instead of breaking through, the plastic cut even deeper into her flesh. She gasped in pain.

"It hurts like hell." Rachel winced. "Can you loosen them?" she asked Bailey, making no effort to lower her voice.

"Be quiet. He'll hear you! I can't loosen them," he whispered. "I'm tied to the pillar. This is the closest I can get to you."

Rachel took a good look at Terence Bailey now that her eyes had adjusted to the dark. This time her interest wasn't fueled by fear but by curiosity. His arms were tied behind his back. Just as he'd said, around his waist and shoulders was a harness tethering him to a pillar. That's when Rachel realized what probably should have been obvious to her from the start: Terence Bailey was a captive. They all were.

Rachel remembered the driver's menacing smile in the rearview mirror before she was shocked by electricity. *"The scariest monster is the one that hides in plain sight."* Her monster wasn't Terence Bailey. It was the seemingly affable driver whose car she had stepped into without a second thought.

Rachel grimaced again at the pain in her wrists. She looked around for a way to cut the zip ties. At the bottom of a wall not far from Rachel was a bent nail. Rachel wiggled over to the wall. When she reached it, she held out her hands and sawed through the zip ties using the bent end of the nail to slowly but surely cut through the plastic. Her hands slipped several times and the nail scratched her, drawing blood. Rachel was too intent to get free to notice the pain.

While Rachel worked to break the zip ties, Terence Bailey told her what had happened that morning when he'd come out of prison. As he'd walked past a car parked on the side of the road, the window slid slightly open. A driver told him that he'd been hired to drive him to Maddison. He'd shown him a note written by Maddison telling Bailey that she'd booked the car to bring him to her.

Bailey, who didn't know that Maddison had gone missing, hadn't suspected that anything was wrong. He'd sat in the back seat and helped himself to a complimentary bottle of water as they'd driven away from the prison. Something in the water had made him groggy. He fell asleep. When he woke, he was tied up and tethered to a basement pillar without any memory of how he got there.

Rachel cut through the final section of the zip tie plastic. They snapped off. Her hands were free. She rubbed her wrists as the circulation returned. Once the pain had subsided, she lifted up her feet and began to cut through the zip ties around her ankles.

"Maddison?" Rachel called out softly to the influencer whose voice she'd heard a moment ago from across the basement. "Are you okay?"

"I've had better days." Despite her joke, Maddison sounded listless.

"Who is he and what does he want?" Rachel asked as she worked to free her ankles.

"He killed Aysh Philips, and he is getting ready to kill us."

Maddison stopped talking as the crunch of earth being shoveled drifted through an air vent into the basement.

"What's he doing?" Rachel whispered.

"He's digging our graves," said Maddison.

Chapter 70

Back at the gas station, Hailey called for help at the top of her lungs. She banged her shoulder against the metal restroom door for what felt like hours. Sometime around dawn, she heard the door click open.

Standing in the open doorway was a bleary-eyed young man. He was unshaven and his hair was a mess. It looked as if he'd just woken up. It's doubtful that anyone felt the need for introductions when he let Hailey out of the restroom, so she probably didn't know at that point that his name was Terence Bailey.

Terence, or Terry as he preferred to be called, worked at the gas station as an attendant and tow truck driver. He'd been working there ever since he was fired from his job as a mechanic after being charged with breaking and entering. He was on bail, awaiting trial while his lawyer wrangled a plea bargain arrangement with the district attorney's office.

Terry had spent the night sleeping on a camping mattress in the gas station store. He had given the driver the restroom key in the middle of the night with instructions to leave it in the door as he was going back to sleep and didn't want to be disturbed.

Her voice hoarse from calling for help for hours, Hailey told Terence Bailey the terrifying details of how she'd been locked in the restroom and how she'd heard Aysh's body being pummeled to the ground when the driver caught up to her friend as she'd tried to run away.

Terry remembered the vehicle. The driver had filled up at the gas station several times before. Piecing together in his mind snippets of conversations he'd had with the driver in the past, Bailey gathered that the driver lived on a farm on the outskirts of Daytona.

With dawn approaching, Terry took the gas station's tow truck, driving Hailey to the area where he thought the driver lived so they could look for Aysh. Hailey recognized the car in the driveway of an isolated white stucco farmhouse. Bailey backed the tow truck away and left it in the dark on the side of the road a block away. They went on foot to look for Aysh.

They jumped the fence, ducking low as they ran across the front lawn toward a garage. They immediately saw something tethered to a pole near the parked car. As they came closer, they saw it was Aysh. She was trussed up with rope like a slaughtered lamb. There were jagged stab wounds to her stomach and her skin was ice-cold. They knew immediately that she was dead. Terry tried to untie the rope so he could take her body with them.

Inside the house, a dog barked.

A porch light turned on as the barking became frenzied. Someone was coming out. They both bolted, jumping the side fence and making their way through the long grass back to the tow truck. They must have spooked the guy because as they watched from a hiding place behind a bush, a car drove out of the property and headed in the opposite direction from where they hid. It drove in the direction of the state forest.

When he'd cleared out, they returned to the farm. Aysh's body was gone. He'd taken it with him.

Hailey Milroy and Terence Bailey weren't sure what to do next. He was on bail, facing a prison term. In his dealings with police, he always came out badly. He believed that if he reported what had happened, the police would find a way to accuse him of being involved in the murder. He was also aware that he'd touched Aysh's body and that his fingerprints could be there, making him look guilty as sin in the eyes of the police who already suspected him of murdering young women. They'd told his former boss that he might be a serial killer, which is why his boss fired him on the spot.

Over the course of her rebellious teenage years, Hailey had also developed a deep mistrust of authority. In high school, she'd been accused of breaking into the school and vandalizing a classroom during her freshman year. Even though she'd had nothing to do with it, she'd been expelled because nobody had believed her claims of innocence. As a result, Hailey had little faith the police would believe her account of what had happened to Aysh. She too was afraid that she'd be accused of murder.

Hailey had more pressing concerns. It was only a matter of time until Aysh's killer found her. Hailey had left her purse with her driver's license in his car when she'd gone to the restroom at the gas station. The killer knew where she lived. He knew her full name. He knew what she looked like. He'd be on the lookout for a baby-faced teen with short black hair who dressed as a goth.

As they drove back to town in the tow truck, Hailey decided to skip town. It was dangerous for her to stay. The killer knew her name and her address. Besides, she had nothing to stay for after the blistering fight with her mom, who was clearly under the spell of yet another abusive boyfriend.

Terence Bailey took her to the shared house where she lived. She ran inside, hastily packed a few essentials in an overnight bag, and returned to his tow truck parked outside. He then drove her back to her broken-down car in the car parking lot, where he changed the slashed tire for her. She filled up the tank with gas and drove west.

During that drive, Hailey decided that if she was going to have a new life, she needed a new name.

She'd always liked the name Maddison. And so Maddison is who she became.

Chapter 71

Joe Martinez drove along the road where the black Ford had disappeared after picking up Rachel Krall. As he'd already seen on the map, there were no turnoffs. On one side was a long straight road lined with fir trees. On the other side was a perimeter fence containing outlying airfields and a red-and-white-striped weather vane.

Martinez drove up and down the stretch of road several times, trying to figure out how the black Ford had inexplicably disappeared. When he still had no obvious explanation, Martinez pulled the car over and continued on foot.

After a couple of hundred yards, he noticed black marks staining a white lane marker. He squatted down to get a closer look. They were tire marks. A car had veered off the road. Martinez followed the trajectory of those marks and found tire-shaped indents in a bed of soggy pine needles and tire tread in a strip of exposed mud.

The tire marks headed straight into the trees lining the road. A gap between two particular trees was just big enough for a regular-sized car to pass through if the driver didn't mind his car's paintwork being scratched by twigs.

Martinez walked through the gap. On the other side of the embankment was a small clearing. It was connected by a dirt path to a rural road.

The driver had taken a shortcut. That was why the car hadn't been picked up by the traffic camera system on the road.

Lying on the ground in the clearing was a crumpled ball of paper. Martinez picked it up. It wasn't paper. It was actually a sheet of extra-thick black vinyl wrap crunched into a ball. It took a moment for Martinez to realize what that crushed ball of vinyl signified. A few months earlier he'd watched his neighbor transform a black SUV into a khaki SUV using auto vinyl wrap. His neighbor said he was doing it because the vinyl wrap protected the paintwork and he was doing a lot of off-roading. In this case, Martinez knew exactly why the car had been covered with black vinyl wrap. He called Torreno.

"You're going to have to come up with a new short list of Fords. The car we're looking for isn't black."

"What color is it?" Torreno asked.

"I wish I knew," said Martinez. "Get me a list of owners of that model Ford within ten miles west of the airport."

Martinez returned to his car. He reversed back and drove between the fir trees into the clearing and then out again onto the rural road until he reached a crossroads. The Ford could have gone in any direction. He was about to randomly choose a direction when Torreno called him again.

"There's a Ford registered three miles from the airport. The owner is a retiree, Arnold McCoy," said Torreno.

"What do you know about Arnold McCoy?" Martinez asked.

"Lemme see," said Torreno. "He's seventy-nine years old. Married fifty-eight years to Karen McCoy. They have a son. His name is Thomas McCoy. Aged fifty-six."

"Profession?"

"It says here that he's a farmer," said Torreno. He paused to read. "He also appears to work as a rideshare driver."

"Look up the address on Google Maps," Martinez instructed. He waited a moment until Torreno had pulled up the satellite view of the area. "Do you see a white stucco farmhouse with a corrugated iron shed and rosebushes lining a pathway in the front?" Martinez asked, looking at the photo he'd taken earlier of Terence Bailey's painting at the prison.

"Joe, that's exactly what I see," said Torreno. "How did you know?"

"Long story. I need a warrant and a tactical unit down there," said Martinez. He looked up the address that Torreno had provided. "It's less than a ten-minute drive away. I'll head over there and try to get close on foot. Call me when you have an ETA for the tactical team's arrival."

Martinez parked his car behind a crop of trees a quarter of a mile away from the house. He took binoculars and headed across an open field on foot, keeping close to the trees as cover. When Martinez reached the front of the property, he lay on his belly and studied the layout with the binoculars.

It looked almost exactly like the farm depicted in Terence Bailey's painting, down to the corrugated iron garage on the far side of the house. A man dressed only in work pants was digging near a grove of citrus trees. Martinez moved the binoculars to get a better look at the surroundings. Lying on the grass near the man was a hunting rifle.

A dog barked angrily. It was tethered to a rope on the front porch. The dog knew that Martinez was there. Pretty soon his owner would know too.

Chapter 72

He lifts the garden pick above his shoulders and slams it into the hard ground near the citrus trees. Cracks appear on the surface of the earth. He raises the pick again above his head and slams it into the ground. The cracks get bigger. Eventually, he's broken the ground enough to start digging. He tosses down the pick and lifts up the shovel, using his foot to push it in deep with a loud crunch of soil.

Sweat pours down his face as he digs. His work is paying off. He soon has a huge pile of earth alongside his feet. The work clothes he put on before he carried Rachel Krall down to the basement are damp from perspiration. He left Rachel on the basement floor well out of reach of the others. He should have tied her up properly and tethered her to a rope like the others, too, but it seemed unnecessary, and anyway he didn't have a spare rope. He'll finish digging before she comes to. And then it won't matter anymore.

His equipment is spread out near him. There's a can of hydrochloric acid that he bought at the hardware store, ostensibly to clean outdoor pavers. He'll pour it over the bodies before he throws on the topsoil from the bags of fresh soil and fertilizer that he bought. When he's buried them and covered them with topsoil, he'll plant fresh lemon and orange trees to disguise the gravesite.

From experience he knows how awkward it can be to have to hastily dig a grave while a fresh body lies alongside it. Preparation is everything, as his father used to say each season before they planted. That's why he's digging the grave first. One grave should suffice for all three.

Chapter 73

The steady crunch of earth being shoveled out of the ground reverberated through the basement. All three of them were well aware that each new explosive crackle of soil toppling onto the ground brought them closer to death.

Rachel frantically tried to free her fellow captives as the digging continued in the garden on the other side of the basement wall. The others were both tethered with thick sailor's rope to separate pillars in different sections of the basement. Maddison was at the far end near a toilet and sink. Terence Bailey was opposite the bottom of the stairs. In addition to the crude rope harness that he wore, his hands were bound behind his back with rope.

Unable to find a knife or implement to cut the rope, Rachel tried to loosen the knots of Maddison's rope with her fingers.

"I almost didn't come to BuzzCon. I was terrified of coming back here," whispered Maddison as Rachel frantically tried to free her. "Afraid that he'd find me. But I really wanted to win the Influencer Awards and I figured that he'd never recognize me. I look completely different from that pale teenage kid with the piercings and grim obsession with the color black. So, I came back. Stupidly. And he found me anyway. Through my own carelessness."

"How did he find you?" Rachel asked, wincing as a nail broke as she tried to ease open a stubborn knot.

"He didn't find me. I found him," said Maddison. "I retraced the route that Terry and I drove that night when we looked for Aysh. I found his farmhouse easily enough. It looked just as I remembered it in my nightmares."

"Why go there at all?" Rachel asked.

"It was stupid," admitted Maddison. "I've always felt so guilty about running away instead of telling the police what I knew about Aysh's murder. I figured I could make up for it by finding out his address and giving it anonymously to the police. He must have seen my van driving past from behind the netting curtain of his front window. Next thing, he's at the beach camping ground trying to find out who I am. He must have written down my plate number when I stopped outside his house."

When Maddison heard from Shaz that a man with a noticeable body odor reminiscent of rotting food had been asking campers questions about the owner of her van, she knew that Aysh's murderer was looking for her. She'd never forgotten the smell of him in the car that night with Aysh as they pulled into the gas station. Realizing that he was on her trail, Maddison left the beach campground and drove her van to a camping area near the prison where she thought she'd be safe. She'd signed up online as an inmate visitor volunteer as it was the only way to see Terence Bailey at short notice.

"I wanted to convince Terry to go with me to the police once he got out. I figured it was the only way I'd ever be safe. Terry flatly refused. He didn't talk much. He indicated the prison was probably recording our conversation. From the little he said, I got the impression he was scared the cops would somehow blame him anyway and he'd have to serve more time. Instead, he wrote a note in pencil on the table telling me to talk to you, Rachel."

"I listened to your podcasts in prison," added Bailey from across the basement. "I believed that if anyone could get to the truth about what happened that night, then it would be you, Rachel. There was no way that we could talk to the cops. They'd frame me in a heartbeat."

As he spoke, the digging stopped. The implication was terrifying. The graves were dug. All that remained was to fill them.

Rachel had to move faster. She gave up on trying to loosen the stubborn knots in Maddison's rope and headed over to Bailey. The ropes tying his hands behind his back weren't as thoroughly tied as Maddison's.

As Rachel tried to pry open the knots, the digging resumed. They all sighed with relief even though the pace was slower. He was digging in fits and bursts. It wasn't clear to them whether that was because he was getting tired or he was almost done.

"How did he know to come after the two of us?" Rachel gestured toward Bailey.

"When he went through my fanny pack, he found copies of the prison visitor forms stating that I was visiting Terry. He looked up Terry on the Internet and recognized his photo from that night at the gas station. He knew there were two of us who came to his house that night to look for Aysh. He realized that Terry must have been the second person, and that I was the goth girl. He kept me alive to lure Terry once he got out of prison. Then he found out about you, Rachel, because your name was on a note in my jeans pocket. He decided that I might have already told you things that you'd use in a podcast to reveal his identity," she added. "He got scared."

"So he decided to get rid of me as well," said Rachel. "The cops were wrong. You really had nothing to do with Aysh's murder," Rachel told Bailey as she eased out the final knot and freed his wrists.

"I've done some dumb things in my time. Breaking into Jessica Hewitt's apartment was about the dumbest, even though I had good reason for that. I can honestly say that I have never killed anyone in my life."

Outside, the digging stopped again. This time the silence dragged on longer than before. Longer than it would take for him to drink water or catch a breather from the digging.

Rachel sensed they'd run out of time. She hadn't been able to free Madison or Terence Bailey, although she'd managed to untie the rope binding Bailey's hands behind his back. Rachel rummaged through a pile of old boxes in the corner to find something to defend themselves with when he came down for them.

The boxes were filled with T-shirts and baseball caps. In one of the boxes, Rachel found aluminum baseball bats. The bats could serve as a useful weapon if she had the advantage of surprise.

Upstairs a door opened and then slammed shut. He was back in the house. Floorboards creaked above their heads. They all stiffened at the thump of his footsteps moving toward the basement door.

Rachel was free. She might be able to save herself. The other two were still tied up. They had no chance.

Rachel slipped off her shoes and silently mounted the rickety timber stairs with the baseball bat in hand. When she reached the top, she noticed a narrow ledge by the doorframe. She figured that if she squeezed into the ledge, then it would put her behind him when he stepped inside.

"Dark corners can be danger points," Joe Martinez had warned her when they'd been at the prison. Rachel could use the dark corner by the basement door to her advantage.

She held the baseball bat firmly in a two-handed grip and took a deep breath to steel herself as keys rattled in the lock of the basement door. He was coming in. The door clicked and then opened with a high-pitched screech of rusty hinges. He walked through and descended down the stairs. He was holding a rifle ahead of him. Their time had run out.

Rachel stepped silently behind him. She swung the baseball bat behind her to get momentum and let loose. She hit him in the skull with a sick crack of metal against bone. He pressed the trigger as he fell, firing a single bullet as he tumbled down the stairs.

Her ears ringing from the gunshot and the ricochet that followed, Rachel stepped over his prone body at the bottom of the stairs to grab the rifle. It had fallen on the concrete floor nearby.

Her ears were still ringing so badly from the stray gunshot that she didn't hear him scramble to his feet. He pounced on her from behind as she bent to pick up the rifle. He picked up Rachel and slammed her against the brick wall. Grabbing her by the throat, he lifted her up so high that her legs dangled in the air as she gasped for breath. Rachel gurgled as he squeezed her neck with his hands. She wasn't aware of anything else until she heard a second gunshot.

Chapter 74

Rachel, can you hear me? Rachel?"

Rachel opened her eyes to see Joe Martinez leaning over her. She thought his dark velvet eyes were the most beautiful things she'd ever seen as she lay on the grass looking up at him, his head set against the light blue canvas of the sky.

She had the vague recollection of being cradled against a warm, familiar chest and carried up the basement stairs. She must have passed out and then woken on the grass. Sirens wailed in the distance. Joe kissed her temple before he rose to his feet and carried her in his arms toward the sirens.

A dog barked in the background as the ambulance pulled in. A paramedic rushed out and opened the rear ambulance doors. Martinez lowered Rachel onto a stretcher. For the first time since she'd woken, Rachel realized that she was shivering.

"I think she's in shock," Martinez told the paramedic. "Take good care of her." He squeezed Rachel's hand before heading toward the cops getting out of a patrol car.

"I've cuffed the perp to the stairway rail. There are two others tied up downstairs. We'll need something that can cut through thick rope to free them."

The paramedic put a blanket over Rachel as she was lifted into the back of the ambulance. Another paramedic cleaned the inside of her arm with an alcohol swab and injected her with a sedative that immediately put her to sleep.

Rachel's throat was still too swollen to talk beyond a whisper when Joe came to see her at the hospital later that afternoon. He had to lean forward to hear her speak.

"The doctors told you to save your voice," he'd reminded her.

"I need to know what happened," she whispered.

"Then I'll talk and you listen," he said.

Joe told her how he'd managed to find the farmhouse. He'd been watching the farm through binoculars while he waited for the tactical unit to arrive. He'd seen a man digging a hole that was too wide and too deep to be a ditch. The man wasn't digging a drainage ditch, he was digging a grave.

When the man picked up a rifle and headed inside, Joe knew what the man was about to do. There wouldn't be enough time to wait until the tactical team arrived.

He heard a gunshot. He ran into the house, his gun drawn. The basement door was open.

"FBI," Martinez had called out as he came down the stairs. He hadn't seen Rachel being strangled against the wall at that point as it was out of his line of vision. All he saw was Terence Bailey holding a rifle. "Drop your weapon," he ordered. Bailey dropped the gun to the ground. "Help her," Bailey said as he put up his hands.

It was then that Martinez saw Rachel being held against the basement wall in the corner, her legs dangling in the air as a man squeezed her throat. Martinez opened fire at the man strangling Rachel.

"Maddison told me afterward what happened the night Aysh Philips was murdered," Martinez told Rachel after he'd gone through everything that had happened once she'd passed out in the basement. "Bailey had nothing to do with it. That partial print found on the unburned section of rope must have been from when he tried to untie Aysh. It was all Thomas McCoy's doing. He was the only one involved."

"Has he admitted it?"

"He's not saying anything. He's lawyered up. He's even threatening to sue for that bullet wound I gave him. But we had a cadaver unit brought in earlier. Those dogs sit in the locations of buried bodies. By the time the canine unit finished sweeping across the farm and the surrounding field, there'd been dogs sitting in eleven separate locations. That's eleven likely bodies," he said. "It will take days to exhume them all."

"Eleven victims."

"That we know of. We believe that his parents are probably among the dead. They're both listed as alive and they receive their Social Security checks. But the neighbors told us that they haven't seen either of them for years."

Rachel reached out her hand and touched his cheek. "I'm sure glad you came to find me, Joe. I do believe you saved my life."

"I also risked your life. I shouldn't have involved you in the first place," he said.

"I don't regret it," said Rachel. "You did the right thing bringing me here. You were trying to find Maddison. I was the only clue," she said. "Anyway, we'd never have met if I hadn't come down here."

"True" he said, rising from the chair next to her hospital bed. "But I almost lost you today and I can't forgive myself for that so easily."

Chapter 75

The red hood of the MG was raised when Rachel Krall and Joe Martinez entered the auto shop where Terence Bailey had worked before his arrest for breaking and entering six years earlier.

"One more turn should do it," said a mechanic standing behind the open hood of the vintage car.

"How's that?" asked a second mechanic on a creeper board under the vehicle.

"Looks good. Come on out. Let's see what the engine has to say."

The mechanic under the car rolled out on the creeper board. Emily jumped to her feet and turned the keys in the ignition.

"Back at work already?" Rachel asked the mechanic standing behind the open hood of the tomato-red vintage car.

Terence Bailey looked as if he was in his element. He was dressed in mechanic's coveralls and had grease stains on his tattooed hands.

"How are you?" Bailey asked as he noticed the thick bandage around Rachel's neck.

"I'm feeling fine. My neck less so," she rasped, her voice still husky from her injuries. "It's black-and-blue and yellow. The doctors say the bruises will get worse before they get better. At least there won't be any lasting damage. I'm relieved that Special Agent Martinez was quick enough on the draw to realize that you weren't the enemy."

"Maddison filled him in once he'd cuffed that bastard McCoy."

"Are you back working for Kyle?" Rachel asked as he and Emily continued tinkering with the car engine.

"I'm helping Em out with this car. I've been offered a job at another auto shop up the road. I start next week. I'll be able to help Em with her vintage cars on my days off."

Martinez took an envelope out of his inside jacket pocket and handed it to Bailey. "I thought you might want a copy."

"What is it?" Bailey asked, tearing open the envelope.

"It's Jessica Hewitt's DNA tests. I accessed her DNA and compared it to yours when I was still trying to figure out the case. She's your biological mother. I assume that's why you broke into her apartment that night."

Bailey took out a piece of paper with the DNA results. "I'd gone in there to find papers that proved she was my mother. I thought that she might have kept my birth certificate. It was bad luck the cops came in. She knew why I was there but she didn't do anything to stop them from charging me."

"Well, you're out now and the local cops know that Thomas McCoy was behind the murders of Aysh Philips, Belinda Roy, and Marissa Hubert, among other victims. Some were prostitutes. Others were runaways. Apparently, McCoy's girlfriend helped him lure some of his victims into his car. Until he killed her, too." McCoy's girlfriend's body had been found under a lime tree the previous afternoon.

Thomas McCoy was facing multiple murder charges and potentially a death sentence. He'd said nothing since his arrest. He was being held in solitary confinement for his own safety due to a peculiar genetic condition that gave him a pungent body odor.

"Why didn't you tell me about Aysh's murder when I came to see you in prison?" Rachel asked Bailey. "The police would have found McCoy much faster if they'd known what was going on."

"I didn't know that Maddison had been abducted," he said. "You never told me."

"No, I didn't," Rachel agreed. They should have both been open with each other.

"Besides, a man gets paranoid on the inside. He loses faith in everyone. When I realized that you didn't know that Maddison's real name was Hailey, I thought that maybe you weren't Rachel Krall, and you were sent undercover to entrap me and prevent my release," he said. "It was stupid, but the cops have had it out for me from the start. I regretted it afterward. I texted Maddison a couple of times at the phone number she gave me. I wanted to meet up with you when I got out of prison. I had no idea that she wasn't getting those messages."

"You drew a very creepy portrait of Rachel in prison. It looked to us like a death threat," Martinez said.

Bailey looked perplexed. "What drawing?"

"This one." Martinez showed Bailey the sketch he'd drawn of Rachel, a copy of which he had on his phone. "The guards photographed it during a cell search."

"It was so hard to get hold of art materials in prison that I had to recycle paper. I drew a portrait of Rachel, but the snake motif and the 'Memento mori' on that sheet were sketches for tattoos. They had nothing to do with Rachel."

"Tattoos like the one on your hand," said Rachel, pointing to the back of his hand, where he'd drawn a snake twisted over itself in a figure eight devouring its tail. "What is the significance of it?"

"Maddison has a small tattoo like that on the inside of her wrist. I saw it when she came to visit me in prison. I asked her about it and she told me it was an eternity symbol to remember Aysh. She told me that she'd lost a necklace with that symbol on the night that Aysh was murdered. Afterward she'd had the symbol tattooed on her hand. I decided to tattoo it on my hand as well to remember Aysh." His voice cracked with emotion. "All these years I blamed myself for not realizing there was something dodgy about him that night when he came to pay for his gas and ask for the restroom keys. His eyes were so cold. They looked right through me." He shuddered. "I'll never forgive myself for going to sleep and letting it happen."

"You weren't to know that he was a monster."

He nodded at Rachel's reassurance. "Is Maddison okay?" He changed the subject. "I heard she was hospitalized for dehydration."

"Only for a few hours," said Martinez. "Last I heard she's fine and back living in her camper van."

"I hope she comes to say goodbye before she leaves," Bailey said.

"What makes you think that she's leaving?" Rachel asked.

"Maddison and I talked to pass the time while we were in the basement. We talked about Aysh and we talked about my time in prison. She told me about what she's done over the past few years since she transformed herself from the scared girl that I helped that night into the woman that she is today. Based on what she told me, I think she's looking for something that she's never going to find here."

Chapter 76

Grace Milroy was sitting on a chair by a camping table outside a camper van cutting up fruit for lunch with a small paring knife. She looked up from the cutting board and smiled when she saw Rachel Krall emerge from the trees. Behind her was the FBI agent who'd reunited her with her daughter the previous day.

Rachel sensed a new serenity in Grace. Maybe it was from being in the back-to-nature atmosphere of the campground, lulled by birds chirping in the trees and waves crashing onto the beach across the road. More likely it was because she had her daughter back.

"She's inside cleaning up the mess," said Grace. "Aside from everything else, the police left fingerprint powder all over and there are footprints tracking in and out." She called out to her daughter that she had company.

Maddison came out of the van, carrying a bucket and mop that she put down on the grass before hugging Rachel.

"I'm so happy you came by," she said. "I wanted to bring you flowers at the hospital but when I called to find out if you were allowed visitors, the nurse told me that you'd already been discharged."

"The hotel offered me my room back," Rachel said. "I decided that relaxing on the balcony of an ocean-view hotel room would be better for my recovery than lying on a bed connected to machines for another day. And I was right. I'm feeling much better. What are your plans, Maddison? Or are you calling yourself Hailey now?"

"Mom wants to keep calling me Hailey. I'm sticking with Maddison for everyone else. I feel much more comfortable in Maddison's skin than I ever felt as Hailey," she said.

Maddison was far more complex than her Instagram persona. She was still full of life, but she was also more mellow and introspective than the thousand-watt personality that she morphed into on her Instagram videos. It was like a switch was turned on every time a camera was pointed at her.

In reality, Maddison's social media feed was a way to generate income by creating the fantasy of a glamorous influencer enjoying life to the fullest, while papering over the day-to-day challenges that life threw at her.

There was no doubt that Maddison had experienced terrible trauma in her life. Aside from her messed-up childhood, she clearly carried a heavy burden of guilt for Aysh's death. Rachel sensed that Maddison understood that nothing that she did as a social media influencer would ever come close to the genuine courage that Aysh had shown, sacrificing her own life to save her friend. Aysh could have escaped, and left Hailey in the clutches of a killer. Instead, she'd saved Hailey by locking her in the restroom stall and throwing the key into the bushes. Those few critical seconds had cost Aysh her chance to escape. Ultimately, it had cost Aysh her life.

"What are your plans now?" Rachel asked.

"I'm taking Mom on a trip to California. She hasn't traveled much. It'll be good for her to go somewhere new. Meet nomads on the van trail. After that, we'll see. I'm not good at planning ahead."

Rachel detected worry in Maddison's eyes. She guessed that Maddison knew what all relatives of addicts knew: her mom was only one hit away from falling off the wagon. Taking Grace away might give her a chance to start afresh. By all accounts, Maddison was making a good income as an influencer. She'd be able to take care of her mom until she was back on her feet.

Maddison had tried to help out her mom even while she was on the run. Rachel had learned that Maddison's reason for going to her mom's condo building a few days before she was abducted was to drop an envelope of cash through her mom's mail chute to help with her living expenses.

"Are you leaving after BuzzCon wraps up?" Rachel asked.

"I'm hoping to leave today," said Maddison. "I'm fed up with the lot of them. Everything is a fad to them. My influencer pod even copied my unique infinity tattoo dedicated to Aysh because they liked the design and thought it was 'cool.' They took away all the significance to start a stupid trend," she said, huffing with frustration. "But the main reason is because I'm disgusted that they're keeping the conference going after what happened to Jonny. I can't believe he's dead. I was half in love with him."

"You and just about every other woman at BuzzCon," said Rachel.

"Except his girlfriend, Reni," said Maddison.

"I thought she was crazy about him?" Rachel was surprised.

"Reni is crazy about fame, and money. Being with Jonny gave her access to both," said Maddison. "But I don't think she's in love with anyone except herself. Besides, Jonny was going to break up with her."

"Why?"

"Jonny confided in me that she'd been stealing money from her investors. Nobody else knew except his lawyer and his accountant. Jonny threatened to go public with what he knew if she didn't pay back all the money she'd siphoned off by the end of the month," said Maddison.

"Would Reni have killed Jonny to stop him going public?" Rachel asked.

"I can't see her getting her hands dirty. I can see her manipulating someone else to do it."

"Like who?" Martinez asked.

"Like Eric," said Rachel. "He was upset that his girlfriend, Zoe, was obsessed with Jonny Macon. In fact, now that I think about it, Eric was deep in conversation with Reni during that afterparty. That's unusual given what everyone says about Reni. Apparently she isn't the type to waste her time on the likes of Eric."

"Not unless she wanted something from him," Martinez suggested.

"Of course she wanted something from him. That's Reni to a T. She uses people," said Maddison. "Jonny deserved better than her. If I hadn't rejected him, maybe he'd still be alive."

"Rejected him?" Rachel was surprised. Everyone had said that Reni and Jonny were a golden couple. They'd accused Maddison of being a home-wrecker.

"He wanted to dump Reni and be with me. I told him I wasn't looking for a relationship." She shook her head. "It's sad. Jonny was messed up, but he was a good person."

On the drive back into town, Martinez put the local detective investigating Jonny Macon's murder on speakerphone. Joe passed on the information that Maddison had given them about Jonny Macon. He suggested that they investigate Reni and Zoe's boyfriend, Eric, as possible suspects.

"If we can show that one of them left the hotel in the direction of the jetty the night Jonny Macon was murdered, then we can try for a warrant to search for a Taser, which is the suspected murder weapon," the detective pondered out loud over the speakerphone.

"There's no point looking for a Taser, Detective," said Rachel.

"Why not?"

"All the influencers at BuzzCon received a Taser. It was in the conference gift bag."

Rachel described the key ring with self-defense equipment including a Taser disguised as a perfume bottle.

"I'll tell you what else the influencers all received," said Rachel. "A very cool fitness watch that tracks their calories, steps, and sleep patterns. It also has geolocation."

Many of the guests had worn their fitness watches throughout the conference. In fact, Rachel specifically remembered seeing Eric check his watch at breakfast the day she'd bumped into him.

"If you can get hold of the data from the fitness watches, you should be able to find out who else was on the jetty with Jonny Macon the night that he died."

Chapter 77

Mary Philips was hosting bridge night when Rachel Krall and Joe Martinez opened the gate of her front garden. Her living room was all lit up. The silhouettes of ladies sitting at a card table could be seen from the front porch as they took the stairs and knocked on her door.

"I'm sorry to intrude," said Joe when Mary opened the door, wearing a pretty lavender dress with a pearl necklace.

"Please come in," she said graciously.

Mary led them along a corridor to a sitting room at the back of the house, where she said they could talk privately. She brushed off their apologies at the disruption to her bridge game.

"We're due for a refreshment break," she said. "I am not a good bridge player. I do it for the company. It's lonely these days with my son at law school."

She insisted on bringing them both glasses of homemade lemonade and sliced cake from the front room.

"Now what can I help you with tonight?" she asked, settling into a chair.

"The man we believe murdered Aysh has been arrested," Joe told her. "I know it's not much consolation, but I have no doubt that he'll spend the rest of his life in prison."

"You are right. It is no consolation," said Mary. "It doesn't bring Aysh back."

"No, it doesn't," said Joe. "There's something else. We found out what happened to Aysh the night that she disappeared."

He told Mary the story that Maddison had recounted of how Aysh had saved her life by locking her in the gas station restroom and throwing away the key so the killer couldn't get to her.

"We believe that Aysh was murdered shortly after that happened," said Joe. "Aysh saved her friend's life. She showed remarkable bravery. I thought you'd want to know."

"I'd expect no less of her," said Mary, tears welling in her eyes. "But I so wish that I had her with me now."

Rachel had tried to convince Maddison to tell the story to Mary herself, but Maddison had said that she couldn't bear to look Aysh's mom in the face. She blamed herself for Aysh's death. She was riddled with guilt that Aysh had selflessly helped her escape while sacrificing herself. Rachel explained this to Mary.

She nodded. "She was the young woman who gave me that envelope of cash the other night," she said. "I just knew it had something to do with Aysh."

Mary picked up a photograph of herself with Aysh and her son, Brian, taken at Aysh's high school graduation a few weeks before her daughter's murder. "What kind of monster takes someone's world from them?"

"She's right," Rachel said to Joe as they walked along Mary's front garden path back to the car. Behind them, Mary closed the front door and turned off the porch light.

As Rachel climbed into the car, she saw the silhouettes in the front living room window of Mary and her friends sitting back at the card table to resume their game.

"He robbed her of her daughter to satisfy his own rage," said Rachel. "We're so desensitized to evil, so obsessed with finding out what makes the likes of Thomas McCoy tick, that we forget about the victims. Not just those they kill, but those they leave behind."

Chapter 78

Rachel was running along the beach in bare feet when she heard her name being called out from somewhere behind her, barely audible over the roar of crashing waves.

"Rachel, Rachel!"

She stopped and turned around. Joe Martinez was running toward her. He wasn't wearing the suit and tie he'd worn that morning when he'd left her hotel room. He was dressed only in shorts with a towel strung over his bare shoulders.

Joe had spent the day at police headquarters finishing paperwork and debriefing his team, who were all heading their separate ways that afternoon. He'd extended his stay by an extra day so he could spend it with Rachel.

"I thought the doctor told you no running," Joe called out as he covered the last few yards to reach her.

"The doctor told me not to do a lot of things," said Rachel, her hands on her hips as she waited for him to catch up. Just before he reached her, she turned and resumed running. They ran alongside each other all the way to the Ferris wheel. When they reached it, Joe asked Rachel if she wanted to go up on it.

"Are you crazy!" Rachel looked at him, aghast. "Why the smile, Joe?" Rachel asked when she saw his expression.

"Because I'm relieved," he said. "I thought there was nothing you're afraid of."

"I'm afraid of plenty of things," said Rachel.

"Like what?"

"Like heights," she said. "Cockroaches. I am not a fan of cockroaches. Or reptiles of any description. Peanut butter. Horror movies." She didn't add the other thing that came to mind: serious relationships. She figured they'd cross that bridge when they came to it.

"Well, you were right," he said later as they walked back to the hotel with his arm around her waist.

"Eric came in for questioning?" Rachel asked.

"He sure did. With his lawyer and his girlfriend."

"Wow, so Zoe came too. I am betting there was high drama."

"That would be the understatement of the century."

"So what happened?"

"Eric claimed that Reni told him Jonny wanted to talk to him at the jetty. He went there at two in the morning. He says that Jonny got violent and he was forced to use the Taser in self-defense. It flung Jonny back. He hit his head and went over the side into the water."

"But that's not what happened?"

"Nope. The detective handling the case did what you suggested. He asked Eric for his fitness watch. Checked the geolocation. Eric wasn't anywhere near the jetty."

"But Zoe was."

"According to her fitness watch, she was right at the jetty at the time that Jonny died. It fits in with CCTV footage of her leaving the hotel on foot via the parking garage and footage on the boardwalk showing a woman with long blond hair heading toward the jetty."

"So why did she do it?"

"Honestly, Rachel? We couldn't get a coherent word out of her."

Joe told Rachel that Eric had told Zoe to plead the fifth, and then demanded that his attorney represent his girlfriend. His attorney said he couldn't represent both her and Eric, so Eric fired the attorney and then rehired him to represent Zoe. All the while, Zoe was in hysterics.

"My hunch is that Zoe came on to Jonny, who turned her down. Maybe he said a few choice words to her. Gave her the telling-off she probably deserved. She lost her temper and zapped him with the Taser she received in the conference gift bag," he said. "Toxicology says Jonny Macon was high on cocaine as well as being pretty drunk. The forensics people say it's possible the combination of the drugs, alcohol, and the Taser was too much for his heart. He'd also been taking anabolic steroids to build up his muscles, so it was the perfect storm."

"So she's looking at extenuating circumstances?" said Rachel.

"If Zoe hires a good enough lawyer, she might even get off with a rap on the knuckles."

"Then she'd better make sure not to hire Terence Bailey's old lawyer."

Rachel stopped at a patch of sand in front of a stretch of ocean that looked perfect for their post-run swim. She stripped down to her swimsuit and dived into the water. Joe joined her.

As they floated in the water, Joe told Rachel that he'd met earlier with the family of Dee Dee Rivers, the young woman who'd drowned in the swamp. Her parents had flown to Florida to collect her body. Martinez had given them the photo files salvaged from her phone, which had been waterlogged with mud. He'd warned them the files included the very distressing video that she'd been filming when she'd been trapped in the mud and began to sink. As Rachel had suspected, Dee Dee had been trying to get the "Alligators" warning sign in the background of the video that she'd been recording when she died.

"I wish Dee Dee had listened. I begged her to stop taking photos in dangerous places. Her life was worth so much more than a bunch of stupid photos," her father had told Martinez when they'd met at the morgue.

Rachel and Joe waded out of the ocean and dried themselves off with the towels they'd left on the sand. Rachel wrapped her towel around her waist and they headed back to the hotel.

Laughter and jazz music could be heard as Rachel and Joe came back through the gate. The final cocktail party of BuzzCon was being held in the lobby bar. It had a Roaring '20s theme. That was also the theme of the final gala dinner in which the winner of the Influencer Awards would be announced.

Rachel and Joe took a back way to the elevators and up to Rachel's room, where she tried to swipe her key card against her door. It was proving to be difficult since her back was pressed up against the door as Joe nuzzled her neck. In the end, Joe took the card and swiped it while still kissing her. He pushed the door open and they disappeared into the room.

Later they ordered room service and ate their meal on the balcony looking out at the midnight ocean. It was their last night together. Joe was heading back home the following afternoon.

Rachel was staying for a few more days. She wanted to do a special episode on Aysh and the other victims of Thomas McCoy, those who'd been identified and those who were yet to be identified. "Killers receive so much oxygen in the media. It's time to give a voice to the victims," Rachel told Joe.

Joe checked his phone for messages when they returned inside. When he unlocked the screen, Rachel noticed that the photo of his wife, Steph, was no longer on the home screen. Rather than please her, it left Rachel more confused than ever about her relationship with Joe. Rachel reached for her own phone and scrolled through her notifications.

A notification from BuzzCon on her @runninggirlRach Instagram feed immediately caught her attention.

"Joe, you won't believe this. Maddison won the Influencer Awards semifinals," Rachel said. "She's going into the finals in New York, where she could win millions of dollars in sponsorship deals and a contract with a major streaming platform. It's a huge break for her."

"Maddison didn't even attend most of the conference!"

"No, she didn't. And she's not here tonight for the announcement either. But her name's gone viral on social now that everyone knows about her abduction. Her social media followers quadrupled, which is what helped her win the award," said Rachel.

Maddison and her mom had left the previous morning in their camper van. By Rachel's reckoning they were traveling somewhere along the Florida Panhandle.

"I wonder if she knows that she's won."

"I doubt it," Rachel said. "Maddison told me before she left that she might not be contactable for a while. She's doing a digital detox."

Acknowledgments

Dark Corners is the second of two books—the first being *Stay Awake*—that I wrote over the pandemic, often while under a twenty-three-hour-a-day government-mandated lockdown at home. It's remarkable that neither book morphed into dystopian tales. That would have been too much: art imitating life!

To my husband and sons, thank you for giving me the time and space to write despite the strains from the lockdowns, and the challenges of home schooling and living on top of each other for so long.

I'm very fortunate to have a wonderful team at St. Martin's Press and Macmillan Audio who put so much creative energy into everything that goes into publishing my novels. I'm especially grateful to Charles Spicer, Jennifer Enderlin, and Sarah Grill for their advice and support as well as to the rest of the team at St. Martin's and Macmillan Audio.

I'd like to extend my thanks to my agents David Gernert and Anna Worrall for their support and particularly their feedback on the early drafts of *Dark Corners*, as well as to the rest of the team at The Gernert Company.

Most of all, I'd like to thank my readers. There are days when writing is like doing battle. Every time I come out of it waving a white flag, a message arrives in my inbox from somewhere in the world asking me to keep writing. So, I do! It means the world to me. Thank you!